A Single Drop of Ink

CARLA RAMSEY WEEKS

ISBN: 1469943042
ISBN 13: 9781469943046

Library of Congress Control Number: 2012901239
CreateSpace, North Charleston, SC

In memory of Jessalyn Davis, my real-life sister whose many wonderful qualities I attributed to the fictional Jessie; my sister Sheri; my brother Don.

Just as a single drop of ink contaminates a whole glass of water, so does a single drop of black blood defile the person in the minds of most pre-Civil War Southerners.

Prologue

Island of St. Domingue—1793

Terror is as unfamiliar to Josephine as the sweat that runs like dirty river water down her legs, between her breasts, into her eyes. The heat and her fear are exacerbated by the weight she clutches to her chest. The child must absorb his mother's anxiety yet he keeps quiet as she carries him through the dark undergrowth. Josephine, unaccustomed to physical exertion, is winded early into her trek. She stops, cocks her ear to the night, and when she hears and sees nothing for some time, she allows herself a rest. Crouching, she places the baby on a patch of ground she clears by cautiously running her right hand along the forest floor. She unwraps the thin covering from around him, and the night's light illuminates the young face, eyes wide but clear. She imagines she can read trust there.

What was I thinking? I have put my child and myself in danger based only on the word of servants, darkies I have known to get worked up over something as trifling as an unseasonable thunderstorm or two chicks hatching from the same egg. They see portent in any diversion from the daily norm. Auguste will be furious with me!

Now she thinks they would have been safe at home. She shudders. It was easy to be brave when she first set out. There had still been sunlight, but when the blazing sun slipped below the horizon, her courage had set with it. She looks over her shoulder and contemplates going back the way she has come, but she realizes she is closer to her destination than she is to home. Regrets are useless. She has committed to this path so she has no choice but to continue.

I will not cry! I will not cry!

The child whimpers in response to his mother's voice. Fearing she may be conveying her own anxiety, she bends close and kisses his soft cheek. The proximity calms her and him.

Oh, to be as oblivious of life's perils, Sweet Love.

He lies on the ground, freed arms and legs waving about like they do on a pallet at home. She kisses one flailing foot before cupping his diaper. She sighs when she finds it sodden. The girls had so alarmed her she had fled the house with no supplies. She removes the pins and tosses the wet garment to the side. She temporarily wraps the thin muslin sheet around her son's pale, naked body to keep the blood-lusting mosquitoes from feasting upon tender skin. She stands, unbuttons her bodice, pulls her own undergarment down off her shoulders, unbelts the waistline, and yanks the sheath from beneath her dress. She wraps the baby in the soft material, pulls the linen blanket from beneath him, folds it into a makeshift diaper and fastens it into place with the pins. She is pleased with the results—this is a task usually performed by Jasmine, the child's Creole nurse. She lifts his swaddled form and takes his place on the ground. It is blessedly cool. She removes her swollen breast from her bodice, glad now that she chose to nurse her child herself unlike many of her friends who left the task to wet nurses.

The babe needs no encouragement. When the right breast has no more to offer, he latches on to the left. It is as if he is storing up for the night ahead. She sits crossed-legged upon the ground. In spite of the circumstances, a peace comes to her. Her son has traded calm for nourishment. He dozes at her breast. She is reluctant to move. Josephine whispers reassurances to the baby and to herself.

There's nothing to fear, My Sweet Émile. Your mère is going to take care of you. Your papa will be so pleased I have taken you to safety. We will be to Grandmère's soon where you can sleep in my own soft bed.

For the first time, Josephine realizes the moon is her ally. Though it hangs full and bright, it comes to her in filigreed bits and pieces rendering the forest below a place of beauty, one she would have found enchanting in different circumstances. She longs to lie down and sleep as her son sleeps, deep and untroubled, but they still have some distance to go. They must move on.

Josephine needs to stay close to the road or she will lose her way. Angling to the left where she knows it to be, it isn't long before she hears loud voices. On the Island, there is a distinct caste system, and it is easy to recognize members of the lowest by their unschooled use of the language. She knows the voices she hears are those of Negro Creole slaves. They sound different tonight, not so much in the words they are using but in the tenor of their voices. Never has she heard darkies sound so forceful, so confident, so uncontrolled. Never has she been so frightened.

The girls must have been right to warn me!

Josephine doesn't allow herself to think of what might happen if the men find her and Émile alone in the woods. She falls as far back from the road as she can without losing her bearing. She wants to run but is afraid an ill-placed foot may trip her up or land her in a hole. Occasionally she crouches in the bushes to listen. The child sleeps and the young mother tries not to jar him. She thinks his silence vital. She swats at mosquitoes, prays for invisibility. She still hears voices, but she can see no one.

Ironic—I have always assumed the light skin of my child would guarantee him advantage and privilege; now it may be the death of him. What has the world come to?

The closer Josephine gets to her mother's house, the more convinced she becomes that she was right to trust her instincts and the advice of the servants. As slaves, they are part of a network that carries news faster than the local post.

They told me we were not safe alone at home. I chose to believe them.

Ahead, the moonlight reveals her home for the first fifteen years of her life. She allows herself a few giddy sobs. Glad to at last leave the protection of the forest, she races into the open, across the dirt cart path, and onto the back stoop of the cottage. She switches the baby to her left hip freeing her right hand to bang on the hard surface of the door with energy fueled by suppressed fear and relief. She waits only a few minutes before banging again. She hears movement inside before the door flies open to reveal her brother standing, feet apart, in the doorway. She lunges forward. He steadies her by grasping her by the shoulders. It is a relief to pass her heavy burden to her mother who steps from behind him.

"My God, Girl, what can you be thinking, out like this by yourself with the babe!"

"Please, try not to wake him, Mère."

Josephine pushes away from her brother. She has not seen his hair this disheveled since she was young and living at home. Her mother's attire indicates she too has come directly from bed. She hastily ties an outer gown over her nightclothes. Seeing that it is Josephine, her young sister comes forward clothed only in a nightdress.

"Deckie, will you please take the baby from Mère and put him to bed?"

When her sister takes the baby and leaves the room, Josephine addresses her mother and Thomas.

"I was afraid. Cleo and Jasmine said I had cause to be afraid! Cleo is in no shape to walk this far, and Jasmine is too close to her time, but they insisted I needed to come here now. I could not ask one of the other darkies to bring me because I was scared to death—of them! You would have been too, the way the girls told it."

"What are you saying, Josephine?" Mère pushes Josephine into a chair and crouches in front of her, her face creased in confusion. "You are not making any sense, Girl."

"Mère, let her be." Thomas, younger than Josephine by two years, pulls his mother to her feet to take her place. "What are you trying to tell us, Josie? Are your servants acting up?"

"Not yet, but the girls say they will be, and they say the baby and I are not safe." Josephine realizes she is repeating herself, but, in her eagerness to make them understand, the words tumble. She wills away the tears.

I will not cry, for Heaven's sake! I am a married woman with a child!

"We were to come here until Auguste gets home. Maybe I panicked, but you know how convincing the darkies can be when they get worked up, and they say there is to be trouble, big trouble, that none of us is safe, not as long as there is an ounce of white blood coursing through our veins. I believed them." She grasps her brother's strong hand. "I still believe them. Have you heard nothing?"

Mère looks at her eldest daughter, feels her fear, knows it to be real, but if she can convince Josephine it is ungrounded, she can believe it herself.

"Good Lord, Child, do you actually believe the help is going to rise up against your husband? Or that any darkie is going to turn against him? They would have to be crazy. He is the best white friend they have on this piece of earth. And what is the man going to say when he gets home and finds you gone and taking his child out in the middle of the night?"

Thomas raises a hand, "I said leave her be, Mère."

Their mother gives way. Thomas is a son, the only man of the household unless you count the three male slaves who are housed in the quarter at the back of the cottage. Thomas assumed the status of head of household when his father died a little over a year ago. "Deck," he calls, "bring Josie some water to clean herself."

Mère sits at the table while Deckie gently runs a cool cloth over Josephine's face, the trails made by perspiration indiscernible from those made by tears. The girl washes her sister's arms, her legs. She removes her shoes and washes her feet. "You have bites on your face and ankles, Josie. We need to put something on them, don't you think?"

The adults in the room seem not to hear her.

"Mère, it is not just what the girls said! I heard the darkies from the woods. I have never heard them that way. They were loud...bold... different..." Her sister's ministrations and her mother's calm mitigate Josephine's certainty. Again, she asks her brother, "Have you heard nothing?"

"There have been rumblings," Thomas admits, "but there have been rumblings for years."

Thomas hopes he sounds more confident than he feels. There has been concern among the gentry that slaves outnumber their owners. Some have even gone so far as to suggest they might be wise in asking the motherland to send a force to ensure the darkies don't get out of hand. But the Islanders value their independence, and they are afraid once French forces arrive, they may want more involvement than the plantation owners want them to have. Thomas, young as he is, has given the problem little thought since their own slaves have caused no problems. With just himself and his mother to run their place, one would think if trouble were brewing, their darkies might be among the first to feel empowered to rebel. True, they only have five slaves, and they have been with the family for as long as Thomas can remember. He has sensed no unrest in any of them, and surely he would have if the whole island were astir.

"How about I have Elb drive us back to your house; we see if Auguste is there; and if he is not, we will leave him a note and come back here?"

Thomas's idea sounds like a good one, and she is reassured by her brother's air of quiet confidence. She allows herself to believe her fear is something of her own making. She tries to shake it off like she would a nightmare. She agrees to leave her son with her family and return to the plantation.

"I started to leave a note, but I was afraid one of the darkies might be able to read. I did not want them to know I was striking out alone. Auguste will surely be home by now, and Mère is right. He will be worried about me and probably more than a little angry that I have acted so rashly."

Josephine's young sister has been standing to the side quietly listening. Suddenly, she steps in front of Josie and clasps both her hands.

"I don't want you to leave, Josie. You do not have to go home tonight. Mère, tell her...we can send Elb over to let Auguste know where she is. You are smart about people, Josie. You have always been good that way. Listen to what your heart is telling you. Auguste cannot be angry at you for looking out for yourself and the baby."

They are all surprised by Deckie's outburst. Mère remains quiet. Josie looks into the troubled eyes of her sister, and had Thomas been unwilling to return with her, Josephine would have spent the night in her old room with her son. She looks to Thomas and is reassured by his calm. It would be one thing for a rowdy band to attack a lone mother and child, but it would be quite another for them to challenge an armed man, his driver, and a woman in a carriage.

"We will go home, and if Auguste wants, we can return for the baby tonight. If not, he has been fed, and it is not long until daylight. He will be fine until then."

She goes to her son, and as she bends to kiss him lightly on the forehead, she notices two mosquito bites on his plump cheek. She feels guilty for having subjected him to the elements needlessly, and as she closes the door softly behind her, she asks Deckie to put balm on the bites. Deckie doesn't acknowledge the request.

Josie embraces her little sister. Though young, Deckie has always been a bright, serious child, and now the girl is reluctant to release her. "I do not feel good about this, Josephine," she whispers. "I am afraid."

Josephine feels a chill, and Mère stares at Deckie. She is no longer certain Josephine should leave.

"Maybe it would be just as well for you to go home in the morning, Josie. Auguste will not be any more put out with you if you wait than he will be now. Maybe he will even have time to calm down a bit. Besides, if he finds you gone, he will surely know where to come. Where else would you be at this time of night?"

Josephine understands her mother's hesitancy. It is not that she really believes her daughter is in danger from the darkies. It is Deckie's fear that drives her own. Mère has never let go of some of the superstitions of the Island—and she has told Josephine that she thinks Deckie has a way of seeing that is not common, especially in a girl so young. Josephine has never shared her mother's beliefs—does not accept that anyone, especially her own young sister, can see what is not there to be seen. Too, here in the light of her mother's kitchen, she feels rather foolish. She does not want her husband to think likewise. Maybe if she hurries, she can get home before he does and prevent him from being alarmed by their absence.

"I will be fine. With Thomas and Elb, I will be fine. Auguste will surely be home by the time we get there."

Deckie is not placated. "Please, Josie, do not do this. It feels wrong. I am afraid—you should be too." The girl looks like she is having trouble breathing.

"Leave her be, Deckie," Thomas scolds, but in spite of his admonition, Josephine has to pry Deckie's arms from around her. When Josie meets her brother's eyes, he can read her concern.

"She is just a child, Josie."

Josephine hates leaving Deckie in tears, but she soon begins to feel better because the carriage ride home is uneventful, much quicker and less frightening than her earlier trek through the woods. The crowds of darkies seem to have dispersed. This ride is like any other ride she has taken through the night other than the hour. She cannot remember ever being out this late. She is relieved to see the light from more than one window in the main house as they approach the dwelling, but, at the same time, she is dismayed because Auguste is obviously looking for them.

Thomas and Josephine leave Elb with the carriage, and she is mentally rehearsing what she will tell her husband as she pushes through the back door to the kitchen. Upon seeing the strangers, she is confused. She stops so abruptly, Thomas walks into her from behind. At least five black men, men that are not their own, are pilfering drawers and tossing the contents into flour sacks or upon the floor. More than the sight before her, the smell of tension and sweat make Josephine try to retreat, but the doorway is blocked by her brother who stands open-mouthed, stunned by the scene before them. She shoves his body in front of her trying to regain the refuge of the carriage, but she is not fast enough. The blow of the machete first meets Thomas' head just inches above her own. Josephine screams into Thomas' handsome face as it separates before her eyes. He makes no sound at all as his blood shoots into her eyes, blinding her to the second blow that practically severs her head from her body and mercifully ends all awareness of the carnage that takes both their lives.

Chapter 1

Every year, right after the pleasantries of spring and before the heat of summer, the elite and the comfortably well off of Savannah pack their bags, or rather have their servants pack their bags, and depart the city. Some go to family-owned homes located somewhere in the southern countryside; others go farther north to resorts they and their friends enjoy together, often healthful springs in the cooler elevations of the mountains. Savannah has long had the reputation of being the unhealthiest city on the Atlantic coast, and even though the city government has tried to keep the number of deaths each summer from becoming general knowledge, they cannot prevent the locals from knowing the truth. April and May bring a mass exodus. Whatever the chosen location for removal, it is requisite that it be safely out of the reach of the unnatural influences indigenous to Savannah, New Orleans, and other water-surrounded habitations. Many believe that the deadly yellow fever and other plague-like diseases are connected to the presence of stagnant water, but instead of recognizing mosquitoes as the culprit, they blame epidemics on miasmas emitted by pooled water and waste—vegetable, human, and animal—left in the streets and connected to ever-growing local cemeteries. In the past, the city government undertook what they called a dry-culture program in which they spent large sums of money draining the low-lying water and marshes around the city. They subsidized farmers who were willing to convert their crops to those that require dry conditions, unlike the rice plantations that are flooded throughout growing seasons. The project failed, and in 1820, the most devastating fire in the city's history left cavities from burned buildings that filled quickly during spring and summer rains, and the warm puddles became breeding grounds for the *Aedes aegypti*, the yellow fever carrying mosquito. Thousands perished.

Seven years have passed and a rebuilt Savannah is experiencing an economic boom, but not enough time has passed for the locals to forget the horrific deaths of loved ones and friends. The truly wealthy of Savannah, of whom there are many due to the produce of rice, cotton, and indigo, make their annual cumulative exit, choosing summer residences based on personal preference, fashionable opinion, and proximity to extended family members and social equals. Those of less but some means are wont to depend on the hospitality of relations or friends in healthier locales. There they stay until the first frost of fall, a time when the threat of contagion is greatly diminished, or so they hope.

By mid November the season of sickness of 1827 is behind them. Most people of quality have returned to the city and reestablished their households. Those of a social bent, especially the ladies, are looking forward to cool months ahead filled with making calls and being called upon, leisurely afternoon strolls upon the greens, late nights spent attending socials and hosting galas.

Autumnal Savannah is a grand place to be for those of means, and because of Frederick Barret's drive and his wife Luella's connections, the young couple have become a member of that set quickly. No one is happier to see the summer end than Luella Curtis Middleton Barret. Unlike most of her friends, she has resided in Savannah throughout the summer for the first time in her life owing to the fact that her youngest child was inconveniently due in July, and she failed to head north early enough to safely do so before her confinement. She promises herself she will not make this mistake again. In the future, if Providence allows, she will do as she did with her first two children. She will leave well in advance to go to her mother's place in Greenwich, Virginia. Not only has she been stranded in Savannah this summer, she has had to depend on the help of servants throughout her ordeal, and she has sorely missed the comfort of her mother and sisters.

Today, Luella like most of her class and sex, is preparing for the first event of the season, the return of Charles Gilfert's Charleston Theater Company that is performing Shakespeare's *Midsummer's Night's Dream*. Luella has been looking forward to this evening since Frederick came home with the tickets two weeks past. Happy as she is to begin the social season, Luella feels she is operating under a couple of disadvantages. Due to the birth of Frederick, Jr., her waistline is not quite as small as

CHAPTER 1

she would like it to be, and her swollen bosom is too full for a married woman to comfortably and stylishly conceal. Worse than both of these things, she is now without Minda, her house girl of several years, an inconvenience for which she has only herself to blame.

Minda had been a good enough servant, and she, along with the Barrets' other three slaves, were part of Luella's marriage dowry, so she had tried to ignore her growing unease. Luella had gradually become uncomfortable with the girl's pretty face and youthful bearing, her apprehension intensifying over this last period of confinement. During the months before little Fred's birth, her girth had surpassed that of either of her previous confinements, and after his arrival, due to the extreme heat of the low country days and the need to convalesce, she had not regained her girlish figure as quickly as she had hoped. She feared that at just twenty-three she was in danger of becoming prematurely matronly as so many mothers were prone to do. Her efforts to keep Frederick's eyes from falling upon the servant had grown tedious, and had Minda chosen a local boy from one of the other houses and had a child or two of her own, she would have been happy to keep her. As things were, Minda had become a thorn in her side, and even though she knew there were surely no grounds, she had grown more and more uneasy when in the company of the two of them. She had wondered if Frederick's eyes lingered a little too long on the girl as she helped serve dinner, if the lengthy time he spent upstairs with the children was entirely out of fatherly devotion. She had decided not to take chances. Too many of her acquaintances had to pretend they did not notice the light-skinned additions to their households. The thought of her noble Frederick participating in such a base act with another woman, especially one of color, made Luella sick to her stomach. Though she would never admit it even to herself, she feared being betrayed within the very confines of her own household.

Minda has been gone for some time, yet Luella still feels guilty about leading Frederick to believe her an inadequate nurse for the children. Knowing that her friend Bette Stiles was in need of a house girl, Luella convinced herself she would be doing Minda no disservice by selling her to them. She could think of no plausible reason for selling a servant she had brought with her from Virginia, one whose own mother and two siblings belonged to them as well, so Luella had brought forth several instances of petty grievances, just enough to cause concern but not grievous enough to warrant harsh punishment.

3

"Minda is too easily distracted while watching the children at play on the green."

"Minda was not in the nursery when I went up to check on the children this morning."

"Fredie's bottom has a rash that would not be there if Minda was changing him as often as she should."

"Minda seems more concerned with her own appearance than she does that of Matilda and Robart."

After a month of these complaints, Luella finally told Frederick she thought it best to sell her while they had both a buyer and a good home for Minda. She suspected he knew the real reason she wanted to be rid of the girl, and the ease with which he agreed to sell her to the Stiles assured Luella that her worries had been ungrounded.

More surprising than Frederick's reaction, however, was Minda's, or rather her lack of reaction. She had thought Minda truly devoted to the children, motherly almost toward them, so she was quite put out when the girl merely replied "Yes, Massa" when Frederick had given her the news. She had not met Luella's eyes before leaving the room nor had she said goodbye on the day Frederick took her to the Stiles. Frederick had taken care of the whole transaction, the timing of which proved advantageous for Bette who surely rejoiced in having her help with the children for what always proved an arduous task of relocating for the summer. Though Luella had missed her assistance greatly, at least she had not had to encounter Minda while visiting Bette. It makes her a bit uncomfortable to think that reprieve is at an end now that it is just a matter of time until she will run into her previous servant and, she acknowledges grudgingly to herself, her one time childhood playmate. She feels a pang of guilt, this time not for lying to her husband, but for selling a family slave for no good reason. She has yet to explain her reasons to her mother, purposely ignoring her written inquiries on the subject.

Luella scolds herself for once again worrying about the whole Minda issue. Instead, she must prepare her own toilet while Dovie helps Mammy. The two of them are responsible for preparing meals, keeping the house clean, and tending the children, so she knows she can expect little assistance from either. Knowing that it will take her much longer by herself, Luella begins her preparation for the evening right after midday dinner.

Luella steps into the waist high tub, sits, and awkwardly pours the first pitcher of water over her own neck, her back, her upper torso.

Goosebumps immediately rise upon her pale skin, and Luella savors the relief from the heat. She lathers her skin with the lavender soap she saves for special occasions. She quickly sponges her midriff while diverting her eyes from the soft, rippling flesh that had once been smooth and taut, a point of vanity for her. *Thank God for corsets*, she thinks before quickly asking for forgiveness for her irreverence. She will have to call Dovie or Mammy to help her because there is no way she can lace herself as tightly as she will need in order to wear her new dress.

Luella rinses the suds from her upper body with a second pitcher of water and is irritated when she involuntarily shudders so hard she almost drops the vessel. The water is not sufficiently heated and she determines to scold Dovie about taking shortcuts. She hurries through the rest of her bath, disappointed that it has not been the luxuriating experience she anticipated. After drying quickly, she pulls on an under sheath, and when that does not warm her, she crawls beneath the linens of her bed. Dovie will just have to remake it—a fitting consequence for cold bath water. But even the covers do not abate the shivering, so she stays huddled there for at least an hour before she calls for Dovie to bring her pen and paper. By thirty minutes after two, she has Dovie summon Lewis to take a note to his master at the office of Barret and Co.

Frederick is not alarmed to see Lewis at his door with a note from his wife. She often sends him little missives, most of them requesting small favors like bringing something home from the mercantile or stopping to pick up a medication from the apothecary. He opens the folded paper and reads,

My Dearest Husband,

It is with deepest regret I relay to you the need to alter our plans for the evening. I seem to have picked up a chill, and though I am sure it will pass quickly, I am quite too indisposed at this time to attend. Please, I beg you, feel free to go alone or send word as soon as possible that we will be unable to be a part of their number. If you choose not to attend, perhaps there is someone you know who can take our seats. I am sadly disappointed as I know you will be. I am, as always, your devoted wife,

Luella

As Luella anticipated, Frederick is more than a little disappointed. Both he and Luella love society, and they have been looking forward to reuniting with friends they have been separated from all summer. Acquiring the tickets had been no small task, and he had personally purchased a beautiful rose-colored satin for Luella's new dress with which she had been delighted. What a shame she will have to delay wearing it. Too, Frederick knows the importance in Savannah of mingling with those of longstanding position in the community. They have worked hard at making contacts and fitting in. Savannah is known for its tight societal web to which one is either born or admitted only through familial connection, individual advancement, or virtue exceeding the norm. It exasperates Frederick to miss an opportunity to promote themselves to those who matter.

Because Luella has been blessed with good health, has seldom been ill and never seriously, Frederick decides to return with Lewis to see if the evening might still be salvaged. Upon entering their chamber, he is pleased to find her sitting up with a healthy color in her cheeks. In fact, she looks radiant.

"My dear Frederick, solicitous as always," Luella smiles from her pillow.

Frederick removes his hat and jacket. He unbuttons his shirtsleeves and begins to roll them, relieved to feel some reprieve from the heat of the day. "Of course, I came to check on you, My Dear Wife, to see if there is anything I can do to ease your discomfort. It is so unlike you to be indisposed."

"I know, Frederick, and I am sorry to have taken you from business, and as you can see, I am fine. But I do think you will have to become a bachelor again for the evening. Just promise me you will not enjoy the experience so much you will want to repeat it often."

"You may want to reconsider exposing this season's belles to the wiles of one so experienced in the art of seduction and charm," he begins in kind, but upon taking her hand, his smile fades.

"Good God, Luella, you are burning up! Dovie," he yells, "bring me a pan of cool water and send Lewis for Dr. Waring."

"Please, Frederick, you must not excite yourself nor should you take the Lord's name in vain." Luella pulls her hand from his. "And you should not have come home from work. I will be fine. I am just a little achy and my head hurts something frightful, but we can wait until morning to call for the doctor. I am sure there will be no need by then. If you want to make yourself helpful, you can send for Patience to nurse Fredie until I am better, and please ask Dovie to put Mattie and Robart to bed without their night kisses. Rob is teething as it is; he certainly does not need to catch a cold right now."

"But you are really flushed, My Dear. There have been several cases of typhoid this summer over in Yamacraw, and I..."

"Frederick, I have rarely left the house this summer, and I assure you I have not been promenading through Yamacraw! Why ever would I be in the colored part of town? You are worrying needlessly. It is very dear of you," she places a warm hand on his cheek, "and if you must hover, will you please ask Mammy for a glass of something cool to drink? I must indeed have some fever for my throat is parched." She slides farther beneath the sheets and closes her eyes. "A cool drink, a moist cloth on my head, a few hours sleep, and I will be fine."

By afternoon, Frederick concedes that Luella must have been right. Other than some back and leg pain, she is resting comfortably. He thinks seriously about attending the theater alone, but he decides the advantages that might be attained through discourse with those of importance could be negated by an impression that he is one to choose gaiety over his wife's needs. Instead, he decides to return to the office to finish up some tasks he neglected earlier. He sends the theatre tickets to his cousin Brigitte Maxwell who is in town for the week. He knows her husband Alexis tried to purchase tickets after their arrival, but there were none to be had. It pleases him to provide cause for Brigitte's happiness. It seems that has often been his objective since first meeting her upon his arrival in the States.

Returning home late, Frederick does not kiss Luella as he usually does fearing he may wake her. He lies on his side of the bed, sleep evading him for some time as his mind wanders. He thinks of all he accomplished at work, and he anticipates Sunday's church service, the meal afterward with his own small family and their friends the Maxwells. He smiles as he imagines Brigitte's appreciation for the tickets. Finally, he sleeps deeply and it takes him a moment to orient himself when he is awakened by Dovie's shriek. He bolts upright and stares into the girl's wide eyes.

"Sweet Jesus, Massa, Mizz Lella, she yella as cornmeal!"

Dovie has come in to check on Luella when neither of them came down for breakfast, and it takes Frederick only seconds to realize the servant is right—his wife is a ghastly ocherish hue. One look at her and he springs from the bed in his nightshirt.

"Send Lewis for Dr. Waring, Dovie."

Dovie does not move. She stands by the bed and stares at her mistress who by this time has awakened, shaken by the clamber around her, but otherwise alert and seemingly free of pain.

"Dovie! I said send Lewis for Dr. Waring!"

"Frederick, there is no need to yell at the girl. I am feeling much improved."

Luella's eyes follow the path of her husband's, and she lifts first one hand then the other, turning them before her face. Gasping, she pushes back the bedding and pulls up her nightdress. The eyes that meet her husband's are full of raw fear, and in anguish he realizes how young his wife really is. She is not much more than a girl. He struggles to control his own terror, for he has seen this color before and knows what it entails. He opens his mouth to comfort her, but no words come.

"Frederick, what does this mean? Tell me it is not what I think it is; it cannot be! I have been nowhere to contract such a disease! Surely..."

Frederick lies beside her and takes her in his arms. "We have no way of knowing what it is, but Dr. Waring will be here soon, and he can start treating you, Dear. Let us not borrow trouble. Worry makes anything worse and nothing better."

Frederick's fear is a palpable thing, and Luella feels it. She lies still for a minute, then sitting upright she pushes him from her. "You mustn't hold me, in case it is contagious. You must leave this room and tell the servants to stay away and keep the children away. Only Dovie may attend me. Please go."

Tears shine in her eyes. Frederick shakes his head and tries to console her. "Luella, if you have some contagion, I assure you my upbringing on the Island has provided immunity to just about any ailment of a serious nature known to man."

She falls back against her pillows. They lie there together until the doctor arrives. He stops just inside the doorway.

"It's true then. You have yellow fever."

"You cannot know that, Man!" Frederick protests, though the doctor is only confirming what he already thinks. "You have not even examined her!"

"I am afraid I do not have to, Mr. Barret, and I am sorry."

"But it is November! There is rarely a case of yellow fever this late in the year!"

The doctor's voice gentles. "Please do not hate the messenger. This November has been unusually hot and humid, and Mrs. Barret's makes the fourth case of yellow fever I have seen this week. There is nothing else I know that comes on so fast and turns the skin that color. It has affected the liver. Now let us do what we can."

Frederick knows if anyone knows what yellow fever looks like, it is Dr. William Waring. He tended the town's sick in the yellow fever epidemic of '20, and he is considered to know as much about the disease as anyone in the country.

Frederick sinks once again to the bed and holds Luella's hand. She cries quietly while the doctor explains what is to come and what they must do to try to preserve her life. Frederick is numb. His mind will not allow him to think about what lies ahead for his wife, the mother of his children. And what of his children? What of the threat to them? For once in his life, he is happy for the blood that runs through his veins, the heritage that may save the lives of his young children. He silently prays that Providence has indeed passed his immunity to them. He must be calm. He wills himself to be—he knows he will need an alert presence of mind to deal with the storm to come.

The doctor bleeds Luella. She averts her face and closes her eyes as he places the slimy parasites on her skin. That task accomplished, Dr. Waring prescribes salivants and cathartics. He then leaves, designating the happy home of yesterday a house of death on his way out by placing upon their door a bold, black X.

Frederick chastises himself. How careless to have been lulled into this false sense of happiness, to think all could continue right in his world when it has been marked from the day of his birth by trouble. Maybe he has not taken the danger of sickness seriously enough. Since he was unscathed by the 1820 epidemic, maybe he has thought not just himself invincible, but his family as well. *But it is November—the time for real worry should be behind us.*

He tries to calm himself. The last epidemic had been the worst in history, and people had beaten it—there were survivors—and Luella has been remarkably fit all her life.

Morning brings the harsh reality that his dear wife will not escape easily. What ensues over the next several days should be reserved for the realms of deepest hell, in Frederick's opinion. His own stomach heaves as Luella spits mouthfuls of black blood into the basin Dovie holds. Had he stayed in the room, Dovie would have been carrying twice the number of basins. He is amazed at the servant's strong stomach and gentle manner. He himself feels unmanned by the viciousness with which his wife is being taken from him. He tries to pray, but his mind wanders from the task. He finds himself asking over and over, "God, please do not take my wife…please do not take her…please do not take the mother of my children…"

He thinks of rummaging for his rosary, the one he discarded when he married Luella. He had traded in the church of his youth when he joined the local Independent Presbyterian Church. He now seeks the solace of the repetition and the beads that would give his hands something to do while his mind races with anxious scenarios. He catches himself mentally listing the things that will have to be done, then scolds himself for his lack of faith. God surely will not answer the prayers of a man who does not believe in the outcome for which he prays.

The hours produce a macabre routine, Frederick's role comprised mostly of watchman outside his bedroom door, entering only when an increasingly exhausted Dovie exits with the latest bowl of stench to tell him it is safe, at least for the time being, to go back in. He sits by her side, trying each time to remember it is Luella beneath the awfulness. Finally, when he reenters the room, it appears that the onslaught has ended. Luella lies beneath the covers a maize-colored waif. So corpse-like does she already appear, he is startled when she opens her eyes.

"Please do not be sad, Frederick," she pleads. "There are things we must discuss while I have the strength to talk. We must make the most of the time there is."

They lie together throughout the night, talking when Luella finds strength. At times, so shallow is her breathing that Frederick thinks the end has come, but she again speaks, instructing him on what must be done for the sake of their children. She conveys what she knows of each child's nature, things she has noticed that she thinks he may have overlooked. She tells him to contact the Stiles and ask that Minda be returned until Luella's mother and sisters can arrive. She wants him to send for them immediately. She says the children must go with her family to Virginia or one of her sisters must stay with him in Savannah, that he cannot handle the household on his own. She gives him messages for her mother and for her sisters and brother. Her last concern is for him.

"I have been happy, Frederick."

She unburdens herself of petty sins. She asks him to forgive her for suspecting him wrongly and for sending Minda away. She prays aloud for God to be merciful and forgiving. So lucid is she that at times Frederick dares to hope she may still recover. Morning brings an end to his hopes. She opens her eyes one last time. He has to lean inches from her to hear her words.

"Is Patience here…to nurse the baby?"

Reassured that she is, Luella closes her eyes. She passes peacefully, her soul ebbing slowly instead of departing in haste, her body looking no different in death than it has for the last two days of her life.

Frederick does what needs to be done. He sends word to Mrs. Middleton letting her know that because of the nature of Luella's death, a funeral cannot wait and the body must be interred as soon as possible. He conveys Luella's wishes in regard to the children and asks that she come as soon as possible. He also pens Luella's last words for each of them. He describes the last days of Luella's life in as much detail as he can recall because he knows they will want to know the particulars. Dovie prepares the body. Frederick has her dressed in the rose satin intended for the theater, and she is buried in the Laurel Grove Cemetery on a plot he hastily purchases. He stands on the bare expanse of ground and listens to the words of the minister. It is just the two of them: he the lone member of his family, the pastor the only member from the church. He has told no one of the service, but he knows if they had truly wanted to attend, they could have learned the time from the pastor. Though Frederick would have loved to have company in his sorrow, he does not resent their absence. He does not want to risk the lives of his own family, so he certainly expects no one to risk theirs. He feels the weight of each full shovel of dirt as if it falls upon his soul. Neither he nor the minister stays to watch Lewis complete the filling of the grave.

Frederick returns alone to his townhouse. He goes directly upstairs and gathers his daughter and eldest son in his arms. He holds them on his lap and they sit beside the cradle of the baby. They stay that way until the children's restless squirming makes him release them to Mammy who is waiting outside the door. He will remember all that Luella told him of his children in her last hours on Earth. He will meticulously follow her instructions except for one: he will not send word for Minda to return.

Chapter 2

Baltimore, Maryland

I open the back door to the Maxwell's rented town home as quietly as possible. My feet throb inside the tight lacings of my boots, and I long to release them from their bondage. I put my basket down on the kitchen worktable and make my way along the hallway to the stairway that runs perpendicular to the front parlor. I know if I can make the stairs, I may actually gain the refuge of my room without Brigitte knowing I have arrived.

"Jessalyn, is that you?"

Damn!

"Yes, Mrs. Maxwell."

It had better be! If it is not, you should be running into the street to sound the alarm.

If Brigitte knew what the people of the world are capable of, she would not leave her doors unbarred to sit alone in her parlor waiting for any and all to walk right in. I will not share this with her, of course, because she is already too dependent on me. If she thinks there is cause for worry, I will never again be able to leave her sight when Alexis is away.

I take the hat from my head and perch it on the newel post at the foot of the stairs. I cast a wistful look up into the darkness above, place a smile on my face, and enter the parlor where I find Brigitte Maxwell doing exactly what I knew she would be doing. She is sitting in her favorite fireside chair with a half-empty glass in her hand. On the table by her side is the decanter that is never far from her by this time in the evening.

"There you are at last, Jessalyn! I thought you would never get home. Sometimes I wonder if you remember which is your real job and which is your hobby!"

By hobby, she is referring to my sewing and millinery business. The fact that she thinks someone of my station has the luxury of a hobby shows how little she understands the lives of those in service to women like her.

"Have you needed something while I was gone?" I ask.

"It is just that the house is so empty with Alexis gone," she whines. "I sent the boys up over an hour ago, so I have had nothing to do other than sit here alone. You know how I hate being alone!"

I cannot help but know as she tells me every time she finds herself in that condition. I want to list the many ways she could make herself useful, but I will not, for it is true that her employment is listed as my real job and her husband, naval officer Alexis Maxwell, my patron. Without that patronage, I would be unable to make the clothing and the hats for the fine ladies of Baltimore, nor would I have lodging in a safe part of town. The Maxwells provide me with room and board and a small salary in exchange for my services. In theory, I am their cook. They have a lady who comes in twice a week to clean the apartment, but it has fallen on me to keep the place presentable the rest of the time. When Alexis is in port, I have no difficulty keeping up with the cooking and the cleaning. I usually have my nights free to do the sewing that provides the money I am hoarding in hopes that I may someday have the opportunity to actually own something of my own. Life only becomes difficult when Alexis is at sea.

"Will you sit with me while I have a glass of wine to relax myself before bed?"

If Brigitte gets much more relaxed, I will have a hard time getting her up the stairs to her room.

"Of course," I say and sit in the chair opposite her. "Have the boys done their lessons for tomorrow?"

"Neither said anything to indicate otherwise," Brigitte tells me, "but you may want to ask them when you see them at breakfast in the morning."

"I will," I promise, and I make a mental note to rise a little early in case one of them needs help.

"Tell me what the Klein woman commissioned. Is she preparing for something special that might be of interest to me?"

From past experience I know Brigitte is especially interested in knowing if the women I work for are planning house parties, trips abroad, weddings, or additions to their families that would require the letting out of clothing or the making of confinement dresses.

"Nothing exciting," I tell her. "Mrs. Klein commissioned a hat for herself, a summer day dress each for her daughters, a vest for Mr. Klein, and some undergarments for all of them."

I am relieved I can answer truthfully without divulging confidences, but I can tell Brigitte is disappointed. I can only imagine the look on her face were I to tell her what I actually know about the Kleins—that their oldest will never wear the summer dress I am to make for her. I intend to make that garment last. If the girl's life force is as weak as I sensed it to be when I took her measurements, it will not be long before they cancel the order entirely in favor of mourning clothes for the rest of the family.

"I am afraid I have nothing interesting to share tonight," I continue, hoping she will release me.

"It doesn't matter," she assures me. "It is enough to just listen to you talk. Have I told you how much your speech reminds me of my dear, departed mother? I take comfort in just hearing your voice."

I have to make an effort to repress the sigh I feel building in my chest, for this is something else I hear almost nightly when Alexis is away. I am sure her mother did speak with the same intonations and accent that I do seeing as she was born on the Island, and, because my father was white and my mother of mixed race, I grew up in a household not so different from her own. Even Brigitte retains a hint of her mother's French ancestry in her speech. I look into her large, slightly unfocused hazel eyes, and my heart softens toward her. She is a beautiful woman. Dark upswept hair frames a soft oval face, one that still looks remarkably young considering the amount of alcohol she consumes.

"I am sure the similarities are superficial, Mrs. Maxwell, as your mother was educated in France. Though my tutors were French, surely Island influences have rendered my speech less genteel."

Though Mrs. Maxwell often waxes sentimental when it is just the two of us, the comparison between her mother and me is only one she makes when we are alone. I cannot imagine her making such a comment among the ladies she has in for tea, and I am wise in constantly acknowledging the difference in our stations.

Brigitte claims to like to hear me speak, but in truth, I say very little when we are together. Sometimes I wonder why she needs me here at all as little attention as she pays to my presence. When the night is this far gone and the decanter is this near empty, I become just a body in the room, one that dare not judge or repeat what she hears. Though I have been in the Maxwells' employment only a little over a year, I could tell each of the stories with as much detail as she tells them to me tonight, so often have I heard them. They revolve mainly around her early womanhood as a femme fatale living with her mother in the boarding house she established to support the two of them after coming to the United States. The high point of those years seems to be the rivalry for her affections between her husband and her cousin, a younger, dashing man, one who had gone on to become quite the successful businessman in Savannah, Georgia. I have come to wonder if she might have chosen differently if she had foreseen the younger rival's success. She has commented on more than one occasion that she bets his wife does not wait alone for her husband to return from business.

Tonight I sit for at least an hour before Brigitte at last begins to nod off. I rise, take the glass from her hand, and help her out of the chair. I maneuver her up the stairs in front of me, keeping an arm below her on the banister in case she should tumble backward. She is a petite woman and I have no fear of being unable to catch her should she fall. There are times I leave her fully dressed on the bed, but tonight is not to be one of them.

"Jessalyn," she slurs, "surely you would not leave without helping me undress."

I turn back, unbutton, unlace, and tuck her beneath the covers. I fold her clothes and leave them on a chair to deal with tomorrow. At least she has not asked me to brush out her hair—that will probably come tomorrow when she awakes to find it a tangled mess. I blow out her candle and continue up the stairs with my own, at last free to take off my shoes and rest the few hours until dawn.

Chapter 3

Savannah, Georgia

Frederick Barret is somewhat angry. The sermon he has just heard has not brought him peace, and he makes his way directly from the morning service to sit by the still heaped earth of his wife's grave, a lone scar on the surface of the unmarked plot of land. He misses his wife; he misses his children; he misses the life that he has worked so hard to attain. He is still convinced that Providence has lulled him into an optimism not normally of his constitution, only to rip that which was most precious to him from his arms in a foul and despicable manner.

The last eight years of uninterrupted happiness had gone far in mitigating if not erasing the horrors of the first nineteen years of a remarkably miserable life. Had he grown complacent in his prosperity? Did he not value enough the gifts of a blessed life: two healthy sons to carry on the distinguished if not always honorable name of Barret, a beautiful daughter to bring warmth to a man's heart in a way that even the best of sons cannot? And what of Luella? Had he not cherished her sufficiently to appease the Giver of life's most precious gifts? If he had wavered at times in his total devotion to her alone, was that not the course of most mortal men, and in doing so, had he loved her less? God must have found fault with his thoughts and actions, for His judgment was evidenced in the gruesome way He had taken Luella after six short years of marriage...young, pious Luella who had been all one could expect in a wife. Luella's death must be evidence of God's displeasure with him.

Though three months have passed since Luella last drew breath, he still awakes to the image of her yellowed countenance, a lingering heavy, malignant odor in his nostrils. He recognizes the smell as that of blood combined with human waste that dominated the bedroom, seeped into the hallway, and wafted down even into the living areas of his home while Luella fought hard to keep the Reaper from their door. The house had smelled of it for days afterward. He had smelled it even after the children had gone. And now, though he can keep the memories of his wife's awful death at bay during the day, he must sleep, and the nightmares take advantage of that weakness by hanging on into waking to remind him they are still there. Again, he wonders if these nightmares are punishment for ingratitude. Maybe he had become distracted with worldly things like prestige, making money, acquiring possessions. And he had arrogantly supposed his own exposure to yellow fever from the inception of his ill-fated life in Saint Domingue would protect the lives of those whom he loved most. He should have sent Luella and the children to Virginia before it was too late. He should have made them stay there until the first truly cold spell of the season. He had wanted to keep his family near him, and this selfishness probably cost him his wife, his children their mother.

Frederick's anger leaves him. In its place is an uncomfortable contrition. It is not Frederick's way to languish in self-pity and doubt. If so, he would never have survived almost two decades deprived of both mother and father on a heathenish island far from his French forbearers. But neither does he consider himself one to ignore his own mistakes. He prides himself on learning from them. He now determines to gather himself and his considerable resources and carry on. He must look to the future of the remaining family God has graciously spared. He rises to his knees, and there, by Luella's grave, he thanks God for his dependent children and promises to prove a more loving and devoted father than the one who gave him life but not sustenance.

Children need a mother, and men of quality need wives. Therefore, he must set about procuring a gentle, noble woman who will prove a model for his children and a helpmate to himself. He cannot imagine anyone pleasing him as much as Luella, but he knows it will be best for all concerned if he does not stay single long.

"God," Frederick promises as he kneels in the dirt, "if you will allow me a second chance at happiness, I will be a better husband, a better father, a better person. I will put you first, God, and my family second. Though I will try always to put to use the innate gifts you have given me, I will not get caught up in the trappings of this world but will use my gifts to exalt you. Within my means, I will care for the needy, those of my own acquaintance and those who come to my attention. I will further your church and endeavor to keep your commandments..."

Having promised all he thinks God might expect of him, Frederick sits back, uncharacteristically mindless of the state the dirt will render his best trousers. He looks around to assure himself of solitude before addressing Luella.

"My Darling, I know you cannot possibly comprehend the devastation your loss has rendered in me, for if you were to catch but a glimpse of it, you would be unable to experience the joy of Heaven. Nonetheless, I need to talk to you as I did when you were living and privy to my thoughts. Odd that I appreciate your council so much more now that I no longer have access to it."

Frederick loses himself in the one-sided conversation. As he tells Luella how much he misses her and their children, it comes to him that though he can do nothing about missing her, he can do something about the latter.

Luella's family—her mother Matilda, her two sisters Abigail and Sophia, and her brother George had come to Savannah immediately after her death staying just long enough to pack up the children, and then he had escorted them back to Virginia as quickly as possible to prevent exposure to a similar fate. He has visited them twice since Luella's death, each time for over a week, but he wants his children home. He resolves to visit them immediately, and while there, he must set his mind to the problem at hand.

"I will not marry hurriedly," he promises Luella, "but I will begin to look for a suitable mother for our children so when a proper time of mourning has passed, I will be in a position to act wisely. As you know, Luella, I try never to make decisions in haste."

The closest Frederick has come to acting hastily in love, he reflects, was in regard to his own cousin Brigitte when he was little more than a boy. He would have married her for love alone had she been willing to have him, though it would have done nothing to secure a better life for him or their children. It had been the older Brigitte who had been ruled by her head and not her heart. She had chosen the naval officer Alexis Maxwell over him. At the time he had been crushed, but he had learned from her.

Conversely, Frederick's pursuit of Luella had been well thought out and deemed judicious long before he courted her. He had chosen wisely. As he sits by her grave and reflects upon his wife's virtues, an inspiration comes to him, perhaps, he determines, more than an

A SINGLE DROP OF INK

inspiration. *Could Luella be instructing him from beyond?* Her last wishes had been that he turn to her family for help. Had she been trying to tell him more than he was capable of hearing at the time? She had said he could not run a household without their support. Maybe she had been trying to tell him she wanted him to consider one of her sisters as a mother for her children. Though many people, especially Northerners, frown on marrying within a deceased spouse's close family, the practice is quite common in the South, and it certainly will not hurt his standing in Savannah if he takes one of his dear wife's sisters as her replacement. It is not unusual for dying women to actually ask the husband to marry a sister, and maybe that was what Luella was trying to do, as gently as possible, on her deathbed. He can see as wise now what he would have deemed barbaric just three months ago. He had thought long and hard before pursuing Luella—why not consider likewise a second time?

Luella's uncle, her mother's brother was George William Robart, the man whom Frederick admired most in the world. A Virginia sugar and cotton factor, he had seen potential in the young Frederick and employed him as a clerk in his St. Domingue office. It was William, as he was called, who had been responsible for bringing Frederick to the United States and setting him up in business. In many ways, William had saved his life, and all he had attained in Savannah he likewise owed to him because William had given him a start and quickly made him partner. William had believed in him. Frederick loved William as he assumed one would a father. In honor, he had named his first son after him. Frederick valued the connection to the Robart family and the intimate relationship it provided with William almost as much as he had valued the relationship with Luella. From the beginning he knew there would have been no introduction to his wife Luella had there been no William willing to take a chance on a young, uneducated foreigner with no intact family to commend him. Therefore, he is loath to sever that intimate bond with the Robart family.

Frederick is a pragmatist, and now he realizes there can be no more logical source for a woman of virtue than the family of his dear, dead wife who still has remaining in the bosom of their Virginia home two unmarried sisters, nieces to William and devoted aunts to his own three children. Both women loved their sister dearly and surely hold a special place in their hearts for her partially orphaned offspring and, hopefully, the man they have so warmly accepted as brother. Again, he remembers that Luella herself has instructed him to turn to her sisters for help. Surely that means she would have been pleased for him to choose one of them to mother her children over someone she did not know. There at Luella's grave, it comes to him, a feeling of peace, possibly even a benediction for the plan. Surely Luella is letting him know she agrees with his thoughts.

Frederick makes a decision. He will go to visit his children often, and if Providence in Its mercy allows, he will begin to rebuild the life that was so pleasing while it lasted.

Chapter 4

My first view of Savannah is one of which I will want to remember every detail, but I know my memory will more than likely fail me. Though it is beautiful to behold, I cannot fully focus my attention on it so numerous are the sights, sounds, and thoughts vying for attention. I stand at the rail, unbothered by the way the breeze is creating havoc with my hair, and try to concentrate on the sight before me. What I would really love to do is unbutton the bodice of my high-necked gown and let the cool air reach places that could do with a good airing. I smile as I imagine the reactions of the other tightly laced ladies lined up with their men at the rail like horses at a feeding trough. I visualize their expressions if I were to start hurling my heavy outer garments piece by piece over the side of the steamer into the Savannah River. Then again, I cannot imagine my husband or the other men on board standing idly by until I stand clothed only in a thin lawn sheath.

My husband. How odd to be calling anyone husband, let alone Frederick, my brother-in-law of the last several years. Odd indeed, but not as odd as the path my thoughts are taking on this most momentous occasion—my first sight of my new home and the beginning of life as a wife and mother. I can almost hear my own mother scolding, "How can you possibly be letting your mind dwell on wild, silly thoughts at a time when you should be focusing on what is important!"

And she would be right. This moment is a turning point in my life, the biggest change I have experienced in life to date, so I will endeavor to give it due attention.

I look out over the buildings lined up behind the Savannah port, and I realize that both Savannah and my husband are quite different from what I thought they would be. My one visit to Savannah might as well have been a visit to the moon for all I noticed about the place. My mother, my sister Sophia, my brother George and I had come overland because Mother thought it would be faster than by ship. If we had known how rugged the trip by coach would be, we surely would not have undertaken it. I remember little of the journey other than discomfort and grief. I spent most of the time bouncing along at breakneck pace weeping or trying to keep Mother or Sophia from weeping. It truly was a trek of tears. So desolate had been our company that George chose to ride outside with the driver. We stopped only when necessary, eating the contents of the basket the servants had prepared and actually relieving ourselves at various out-of-sight places to which George directed our driver Justice. All in all, the trip had been a miserable journey at the end of which awaited more misery.

Our return to Virginia with Frederick and the children had been more comfortable than our mad dash to Savannah, but it was even sadder because we were witnessing first hand the children's loss and confusion and Frederick's inability to console them or himself. My, how circumstances have changed since that journey. The Frederick standing beside me bears little resemblance to the one who escorted us home. In my wildest imaginings—and I have many—never would I have envisioned this day, this scene. Neither, I am sure, would Frederick have dreamed of returning to Savannah with me as his wife.

I glance sideways and up a bit. He stands inches from me but a little closer to the rail, so I think he will not notice me observing him. My heart flutters in my chest at the sight of him. He is such a handsome man! I like everything about his looks though I do not recall thinking him so very handsome when he came calling on Luella. For the life of me I do not know how I failed to be attracted to him even then. Maybe it was my youth and the fact that I knew he had eyes only for Luella. Perhaps I just hadn't looked closely. Perhaps he has become more handsome with age. Regardless, I am attracted to Frederick in a way I would not have dreamed possible a few months ago. I love the way his dark hair curls around his ears and brushes the collar of his jacket. I love the straight line of his nose, the way his soft, full lips seem out of character with the strength of his jaw. He seems so solid, so strong, though he is but a few inches taller than I.

It is hard, now, to believe I was repulsed when I first realized Frederick had set his mind on me. I know that many men take as second wives cousins and even sisters of their first wives who *up and die* on them for various reasons. It is Biblical, after all. Mother approved of Frederick's interest in me, so I knew it had to be alright with God. I cannot imagine a more Godly woman than my mother.

Frederick has been in correspondence with Mother for years. He wisely sought her blessing before first courting Luella and again when he set his mind on me. I assume he knew how important her approval would be considering we had no father to look out for us.

I remember little of my father. He moves through the few memories I have of him as a shadow figure, sort of a faceless daguerreotype with gentle hands and a deep voice. I have never seen an actual likeness of Cedric Middleton, but Mother spoke of him with almost as much reverence as she did God. I remember her telling Luella that Frederick reminded her of our father. I can think of no higher praise short of proclaiming him a saint.

But regardless of Mother's approval, the concept of sisters marrying the same man bothers me. I have always been horrified at the predicament in which Leah and Rachel found themselves. True, they were married to the same man at the same time, but it caused enmity between them. I loved Luella dearly. I want nothing to cause discord between us, if it be possible to displease a sister after she is dead. We were only a little over a year apart in age, and I thought Luella all any female could hope to be. The truth is, I would have gladly been Luella, but I would never want to replace her. It would have been unthinkable to compete with the living, breathing, fallible Luella; I would hate to be compared to the one who *up and died* leaving in everyone's memory a perfected version of an already saintly personage. After all, I knew why Frederick chose Luella over me in the first place. The way I looked at it, I was going to be Leah in the marriage equation, and I certainly did not want to be a part of any scheme in which Frederick, or any man for that matter, woke up one morning to realize he had been duped.

But time had changed things—time with the help of Uncle William and Mother. Heaven knows my uncle would approve of keeping his adopted in-all-ways-but-legal son in the family. Uncle William has known Frederick since he was little more than a child, and Frederick is as noble in his estimation as Luella is in mine. Then there are the children, the only remnants of Luella left on this earth, and I love them simply for the fact that they are part of Luella. For two years now I have helped Mother care for them, and I have grown to love the little urchins for themselves, even more than I love my older sister Anne's children. Mattie, Robart, and little Fredie need me more than do Anne's daughters. The Barret children seem to love me in return. Mattie is the only one of Luella's three who can remember their mother, so at least there will be little comparison in their young heads.

The united efforts of my mother, my uncle, the children, and the whole state of Virginia would not have been enough to persuade me to take my sister's husband as my own if Frederick himself had not set out to convince me that I, and I alone, can complete his happiness. Frederick was smart in his approach. In the first visits to see his children, he treated me no differently than he did the married Anne or our younger sister Sophia. I suspect he chose me over Sophia because he could not help but notice the children are more drawn to me. Though Sophia is younger than I, I do not think age was a factor in his choice. Frederick proved by his first marriage that he had no aversion to taking a young bride. Luella had been only seventeen, not even legal in the state of Virginia, so Frederick whisked her off to Washington City to marry. Sophia was older than seventeen when Luella died, so I know he could just as easily have courted her if he had felt inclined in that direction.

I think Sophia and Anne were as surprised as I was by Frederick's pursuit. Initially unsuspecting, we had all treated him much the way we had when Luella was alive. Anne was not around the house as much as Sophia and I during his visits, so we, along with Mother, entertained him much as we would have Uncle William or Anne's husband Edward. Sophia and I had been our normal, unpredictable selves in discourse with our brother-in-law, but with time, Sophia was drawn away by other interests while I found myself looking forward to his visits. My pleasure with Frederick's companionship was unexpected because he had always seemed so *appropriate*. I was surprised that he seemed entertained by my own waywardness, not at all offended by my irreverent comments or with what I myself consider my unconventional way of looking at things. It was not long before I considered myself his close friend, so I thought little of the occasional touch or slightly intimate gesture. I have been exposed to my share of male attention, so it was the prolonged holding of my eyes with his that first gave me an indication that Frederick's intentions might be traveling an un-platonic path. The first time I noticed, I was so taken aback that I left the room and avoided him almost completely on his next visit. But Frederick is a determined man, and he is persistent if nothing else. Gradually, swayed by the desires of my family and my affection for his children, I allowed myself to be lulled into a relationship in which I awoke one day and found myself betrothed to my sister's husband.

Now, standing at the railing of the *Enterprise* beside my spouse of a week, I smile as we steam into Savannah Harbor. I am enthralled with the picture River Street makes in the hour before dark. The other ships vying with ours for position on the dock create a picturesque scene. The jutting masts and irregular sails of the older vessels form a lovely skyline against the backdrop of the night sky. Having lived in the middle of Virginia all my life, this coastal scene is both novel and captivating. Of course, it is all made more so by the aura of romance associated with my newly married state.

The last week has been one of rather pleasant surprises. The journey has been decidedly more enjoyable than my first and last to Savannah, and marriage is turning out to be a more promising situation than I had anticipated. Even the intimacies of marriage are far from the ordeal Mother has hinted at, and I find myself looking forward to the evenings almost as much as Frederick apparently does. When he focuses those intense brown eyes and his undivided attention on me and me alone, I quite lose myself and become someone I am embarrassed to recall come morning. It took me until the midday meal to merely meet his eyes after our first night together as man and wife.

Once again, I let my gaze slide sideways to my mate in life. The wind blows his hair back from his face so I may better admire the strong jaw line. I imagine him to look like the French aristocrats from which he descends. It took just one night as a wife to completely dispel any brotherly impressions I might have retained of Frederick. I have a brother, and Frederick ignites feelings I cannot imagine feeling for George. I pinken even at the thought!

Though I still have not been able to completely rid myself of the notion I acquired a husband much as I acquired most of my clothes—as my sister Luella's hand-me-downs—I am not at all unhappy with the current state of affairs. It is all a little bizarre, and when I let my mind settle on the fact that she and Frederick must have done with their nights what he and I have done with ours for the last week, I get a queer little flip-flopping in the pit of my stomach. Frederick and Luella shared that intense intimacy for years, and Abigail, Robart, and Fredie are and will always be reminders that Luella experienced first everything I am experiencing now.

I push back from the railing and exhale more loudly than I intend, drawing Frederick's attention.

"Care to tell me what you are thinking, My Dear?"

I almost laugh out loud. God, if he only knew! But I have lots of experience masking what I really think. I have been doing it ever since I realized the truth is not something to be given lightly or completely. It is not even something people really want. So I do what I often do. I offer partial truth. It keeps me from lying and thus displeasing God, and it keeps the listener happy.

"I am thinking how much more pleasant this trip to Savannah is than the last one."

Even this much truth is too much for Frederick.

"I was afraid you would be taken back to that time, and I do not want you to be." Frederick picks up my hand and brings it to his lips, his brown eyes almost black with passion. "Tonight is about new beginnings, about us, not about what has gone before."

I smile and place a look of delight upon my face to mask the sadness at the thought of Luella as *something that has gone before.*

To smooth the worry lines on Frederick's face, I smile more broadly. "That is what tonight is about," I agree, but in my mind I add, *and I am sorry for that, Luella.* I would not be recently married and sailing into Savannah or talking about new beginnings if she had not had the misfortune to suddenly *up and die.* I briefly enjoy the words *up and die,* a small act of rebellion against my mother who forbade me as a child from using the expression and others like it.

"You sound like a young darkie or common cracker when you speak that way, Abigail Marie, and I will not have it."

I have not used the expression aloud again, but it is one I use often in my head because it, like many other colored or common sayings, is such a better description of what Luella and my father did than the socially acceptable *passed away* or *expired.* I wonder now, on my first night in Savannah, how much more up and dying there will be in the midst of a lot of up and down living before I myself go the way of Luella.

"New beginnings—that is what tonight will be about."

I, Abigail Marie Middleton Barret, take the hand of my husband to disembark into the city of Savannah to live my life where my sister has died and made a place for me.

Chapter 5

It was late and I was so tired when we finally made it home last night, I fell into bed beside my husband and slept the night away without waking once. Now, my eyes open to strange surroundings. I am gripped by panic before I realize where I am. Reclining against the pillows, I take inventory of the room: high ceiling, flowered walls, mahogany clothes press with matching bureau, basin stand, and necessary chair. Just inside the door rests two traveling trunks, Frederick's and mine. The breeze stirs the parted curtains at the windows across the room. I wonder how Frederick has managed to get out of bed, dress, and leave the room without waking me. I must have been sleeping like the dead not to hear him or the street noise that now makes its way clearly into the room. I push the coverlet aside noting its thinness. Cool nights at home in Virginia required two blankets, and here, I can sleep comfortably with no covering at all.

I am excited—anxious to investigate my new surroundings. I make my way across the room to look down on the bustling enterprise of the street below. Drayton Street—that is what Frederick told me it is called. This is a strange sight. I have lived my whole life on the plantation, and though I am accustomed to waking to the activity of the household and grounds, the street below is an entirely different vista. The sandy street is wide enough to accommodate individual men on horseback, several four-wheeled conveyance wagons, and at the present, I can count four two-wheeled carriages. As I watch, one of the horses lifts its tail to relieve itself right there in the middle of the street. Though I am in my bedroom, I am so close I can here the plopping noise the excrement makes as it hits the sand. No one seems to notice. There is movement everywhere—and color and bright light. I squint to take it all in. So this was Luella's world, the one she wrote of so enthusiastically. It is a backdrop every bit as exciting and dramatic as I imagined, maybe even more so. And this is to be my home now!

Before I can determine how I feel about this, a woman on the sidewalk below, dressed as if she is attending a gala instead of walking down a dirty street in broad daylight, glances up and waves at me as if I am a neighbor. Appalled, I step back from the window. I have been standing exposed in only the under shift I hastily went to bed in last night. I must remember I am not in Virginia any more.

Someone has brought me water. I fill the basin and freshen up the best I can without unpacking my belongings. I am in a hurry, so I dress in the same clothes in which I arrived. There has been no time for brushing them, but I plan to change into a housedress as soon as I explore a little, so Dovie can clean the dress before she puts it in the press. I follow the only sound I hear and end up at the back of the house in the kitchen where I find Mammy. I have known Mammy my whole life, she and Dovie. Both came to Savannah with Luella when she married. So had Minda and Lewis, but Minda had proven unsatisfactory and been sold. It had made us sad when we received word of it because Minda and Dovie were our playmates when we were young. They had tended us, as well. Mama had said the grievance must have been grave for Luella to let her go, but no explanation for it was ever given, at least not to me. I intended to ask Luella about it, but she up and died before I had a chance.

"Guh monin, Mizz Abby. You done slep haf da day way,"

Mammy's smile greets me, and seeing her makes me feel less of a stranger to this house. Without asking she starts putting the makings of a breakfast on a plate for me. Mammy's appearance does not really match her name. She probably is no more than forty-five, but she was our nurse, and Mammy was what we called her then and what Frederick's three call her now, even though Dovie is actually the Barret children's nurse. Mammy is the cook and housekeeper. Both Dovie and Minda are her daughters and Lewis her son, but Mammy still looks young. I have never been able to ascertain the ages of the adult darkies. I guess her at about forty-five because I know Lewis is about the age of my sister Anne, Minda the age of Luella, and Dovie a year or so younger than myself. Mama tries never to split a family, so she sent all of them together with Luella. I cannot remember now who their daddy is. I am not sure I ever knew.

"I guess I was more tired than I knew, Mammy. Where is everyone?"

"It be nigh on dinna time, Mizz Abby. Yo husbun done gone ta wuk, and da chilrun on da green wid Dubie. Yo bes go haid an eat sumpin an be bou makin yosef quain wid da house fo da chilrun be back takin yo time."

I do as I am told, glad that Mammy is at least one constant in my otherwise shifting world. I eat the meal right there at the rough wooden table, not wanting to take the time to go back to the dining room. I wonder what Frederick would think of this. I know Mother would not like it. We were never allowed to eat in the kitchen with the darkies at home. I am in a hurry now, so it seems silly to make Mammy carry it to me. The food tastes as if it came out of the kitchen at home. I leave the dirty dishes and Mammy and set about getting to know my new home.

One of the few things I noticed the only time I was in Savannah was how narrow many of the homes are, including that of Luella and Frederick. Theirs, that is now mine, is a three-story brick townhouse like many others on the street. The bottom floor is two larger rooms set in front of two smaller ones. The rooms are divided by a hallway into which the front door opens. The building has no front porch—the steps lead directly to the doorway with the top one being wide enough for a couple to stand abreast. I think this is a rather abrupt entry into the house compared to the wide verandas of home. I guess families do not while away the evenings on the front porch here in Savannah.

The hallway serves as a greeting area and access to the staircase that runs up the right side of the passageway. I enter the doorway to the left and find a rather formal parlor filled with furnishings Frederick has told me are rented. They are in good condition, probably because the room is rarely used by the children. Directly behind that room through pocket doors that can be drawn to make the two rooms into a large one is the smaller family parlor. The furniture here shows some sign of wear though it is still in good enough condition for family, especially since the children will be hard on anything they use on a daily basis. I sit on the burgundy horsehair sofa. I prefer this room to the more formal one. I wonder if Mattie or Robart is responsible for the loose spring I can feel beneath me. I think Robart the more likely of the two to have jumped up and down on it.

Across a back entryway is the kitchen and directly in front of that, the dining room. It is unusual for the kitchens to be inside homes in Virginia, so I do not know if this layout is the norm or unique to this townhouse. Exiting through the back door, I decide it is probably common here due to the small lots upon which these particular houses are built. I remember Frederick telling me that our home actually sits on a half-lot, and there is only room for a small carriage house with the

31

slave quarters above it and a small patch of land used for a vegetable garden. I walk to the edge of the carriage house, and looking around, I spy the ever-necessary privy. I suppose Mammy and Lewis live above the carriage house. I know Dovie sleeps inside the main house in the room with Mattie right next door to Rob and Baby Fredie. I see no well, and I vaguely remember Luella commenting on the community wells, one I think on each square. I am looking forward to seeing more of the squares. Frederick tells me the city takes great pride in their beauty. The town is laid out around several of them and they serve multiple purposes. As well as being the location for public wells, privies, and ovens for those who need them, they are also community greens in which families from adjoining streets congregate to socialize.

I reenter the house through an opening set a few feet from the kitchen door centered on the back wall. I am once again in the dark rear entryway. The configuration is impractical in that it doesn't allow for airflow from the front to the back of the house, and it is somewhat claustrophobic in spite of the high ceilings. I wonder if all town homes in Savannah will prove this close. I am relieved to open the connecting doorway into the front hallway.

Upstairs again, I go right off the hallway into what I know must be Mattie's room. Dovie's mattress is stored beneath the girl's bed for convenience, and the room looks spacious and neat even though it is apparent a child spends time here. Off the same hallway another door takes me to a smaller room crowded with Rob's bed and Fredie's crib. I notice we need to change Fredie's crib out for a bed like his brother's soon.

At the far end of the hallway is a ladder. Apparently the third floor of the house is an attic used for storage.

The tour brings me back to the room I am to share with my husband. It is spacious with the same amount of room used for both children's rooms. It is long and narrow with the four-poster bed positioned at the far end to capture the breeze from the open windows.

I light upon the bed, and though I know I need to resist, I give myself up to the mood that has finally won out and dispelled my earlier good spirits. I feel terribly sad. It is impossible for one with no leanings toward despondency to understand how quickly one with my proclivity can slide from near elation into an abyss the walls of which appear almost impossible to scale. Just this morning I had awakened ready to take on the world, and now, just in the time it has taken me to walk through the rather small house I am to call home, I find myself bereft, wanting nothing more than to climb back into the bed upon which I sit, to pull the covers over my head, to sleep the day away. Each room I entered has made me more aware of Luella. I do not literally feel her presence. I just see her touch upon the furnishings, her taste in the dishes. I imagine her flitting about each room, laughing aloud. I hear her conversing with Frederick at the dining table. I see her playing with the children, listening to their prayers. And now, as I sit upon this unmade bed, I realize I have just slept the night away in the bed, most certainly, in which Luella died.

Dear God! I clutch the bedpost closest to me. This is the bed of my beautiful, vivacious sister, the same sister I ran and played with, slept with, shared secrets with, even giggled with over the men we would both eventually marry. Luella died right here!

I pull my feet up beneath me and curl up on the foot of the bed. Not only did Luella die here, she lived here, and not alone, but with Frederick, my husband—Luella's husband first. I try to block the image of Luella and Frederick from my mind, but it will not be banished. I see them here. I see Luella with her pale skin naked upon the bed, her dark hair splayed out on the pillow, Frederick positioned above her. I close my eyes to stop the progression of my thoughts, for I do not want to even imagine the two of them carrying out the unspeakably intimate act that has had to take place right here on this bed. How many times have Luella and Frederick made love here? Fifty times, a hundred? Frederick and Luella, doing that...

I push myself from the bed, dragging the covers with me. I will not lie in the same bed in which Frederick lay with Luella. I do not know where I will be sleeping, but it will not be here. It is simply too much to ask of me. *I will not do it!*

I cross to the clothes press and jerk it open. It is empty. Thank God! I could not have borne the sight of Luella's clothes. Turning to the bureau, I pick up the silver-plated brush and comb that lie there. I wrap them in the linens and place them on top of the bare mattress. I turn my back on the bed and walk from the room.

Chapter 6

Frederick Barret cannot wait to go home for his afternoon meal, so he leaves his office earlier than usual even though he has much to do to catch up from his time away. It will be his first meal at home with his new wife and children. How he has longed to have them all back under his own roof!

Frederick arrives to find Dovie and the children in the family parlor. She holds Fredie while Mattie and Robart play a game on the floor. He is disappointed that his wife is not there with them.

"Where is Abigail?" he asks Dovie.

"Mizz Abby mus be ailin, Massa," Dovie tells him. "She be layin on Maddie's bed ebber since we come back from da green. Dat be a spell."

Confused, Frederick hurries upstairs to check on his wife. He finds her lying on the small bed, back to the door, in the same clothes she wore yesterday. He sits beside her and leans across her still body to see if she is awake. Her eyes are open, but she makes no move to greet him. Alarmed, he places his hands on her shoulder and gently turns her to face him.

"Whatever is the matter, Abby?" He feels her head and is relieved to find it cool. "Are you sick? Has something happened?"

Abby meets his questioning gaze with eyes that are strange to Frederick. Though she looks at him, it is as if she does not see him.

"I just decided to take a nap, Frederick. It appears the excitement of the week and the journey has worn me completely out. I am sorry. I will get up immediately."

She attempts to rise, but Frederick's body pinning her own makes it impossible to swing her legs to the floor.

"Why are you in here, Abby, instead of in our own bed? Do you find it uncomfortable?"

Abby blushes and, to avoid his eyes, she straightens the front of her dress and smoothes her skirts. "I do find it uncomfortable, Frederick," she lies. "Would it be greatly inconvenient to change it?"

"Of course not, Dear," he acquiesces, but he is confused. "I would have taken care of it today had I known, but when I left you this morning, you were sleeping so peacefully, I would never have thought you passed a restless night."

Abby flushes pinker. "I guess I was so tired from the restless night that I finally just fell asleep from exhaustion."

Frederick pulls Abby to her feet, and they join the others downstairs. Both are reserved throughout the meal, Frederick because he is bewildered, Abby because she is trying to think of a way to tell Frederick she will not be sleeping with him tonight. When they are finished eating, Abby simply sits there, so Frederick finally rises and calls Dovie to collect the children. The room becomes uncomfortably quiet when the two of them are alone.

"Dear, are you sure you are well? Did something happen today to upset you?"

"I guess I am just a little saddened to be among Luella's things. I had not anticipated how much it would remind me of her, how much I would miss her."

So that is it! Frederick feels foolish. *Why didn't I think of this possibility?*

He has become accustomed to being in the house without Luella, but he should have known this would be a hard day for Abby. She and her family had only been inside the house for a short time, long enough to collect the children and their things after Luella died. They had spent only one night at the City Hotel before returning to Virginia.

"I will be fine in a day or two when I become used to my new surroundings. But if it is acceptable to you, I would like to sleep alone tonight, maybe in Rob's bed if you do not mind sharing yours with him. Maybe I will sleep better there than on the uncomfortable bed in your room, and tomorrow I will be fresh to start a new day."

Abby wills herself to meet Frederick's eyes, and she sees dismay there.

"You do not wish to sleep with me tonight?" Frederick asks.

Abigail rises, crosses to his chair, sits at his feet, and places her head in his lap. "Of course I want to sleep with you. But I do not think the two of us will fit on Rob's small bed, do you?"

At last Frederick understands. Abby does not want to sleep in the bed he shared with Luella.

What an idiot I have been!

He pulls her up into his lap, takes her face in his hands. "Look at me, Abby," he implores. "That will be fine. And I will have a new bed delivered tomorrow. Please forgive me for my insensitivity, Darling."

It crosses his mind that finding a bed on short notice may be easier said than done, but he keeps the thought to himself. Instead, he kisses the lips of his new wife. She sits there for a moment longer before getting to her feet.

"You need to get back to work. I will have Dovie put Rob in your bed tonight, and thank you for being so considerate."

Considerate. He has been far from considerate. But inconsiderate or not, he is not willing to begin his new married life in separate beds. That is not a precedent he wants to set.

When night falls and it is time for the children to be put to bed, Frederick waits long enough for Dovie to move Rob and Abby to retire. He then makes his way upstairs and prepares for bed himself. Instead of crawling into the large bed with his sleeping son, he goes to the room where Abby sleeps with Fredie. He quietly closes the door to the adjoining room in which Mattie and Dovie sleep and crawls into bed beside his wife. She makes room for him but says nothing. He gently pulls her nightdress up over her hips and places his hand over a small breast. She shivers and so does he, but for different reasons. She is still so new to him—he cannot get enough of her. He had actually thought of trying to do this today when he was home for dinner, but he had been unable to think of a way to get her alone without the whole household knowing. Now, he turns her toward him and kisses down her face until he finds her lips. He pulls the gown over her head, and positioning himself halfway across her body, he begins to kiss his way down her neck. He is disappointed in her lack of response, but his body reacts nonetheless. Afterward, he remembers Fredie sleeping in the crib nearby and fears his groans may have awakened him. He lies quietly on top of his wife listening to the silence. He rolls to the side, turning his wife so that he cups himself around her. He falls asleep immediately.

Abby tries to disentangle herself from his embrace, but the narrow width of the child's bed encumbers her efforts. Eventually she gives up. She thinks of getting out of bed to wash away the uncomfortable stickiness. "This is what I deserve for lying," she thinks. "Ironic, too. Because of my dissembling, I will lie awake sleepless as I claimed to last night."

Abby is wrong, however. She sleeps, and when she does, she dreams of Luella for the first time since her death. They are back in their room in Virginia in their bed together. Luella's back is to her, but Abby can hear her giggling.

"What is so funny, Luella?" Abby asks, putting her hand on Luella's shoulder.

"Odd," Abby thinks. Luella's shoulder is bare. Never do they go to bed without clothing.

"Where is your nightdress, Luella?" she asks.

"Oh, you silly child," Luella laughs, and she turns to her, her face flushed and happy. Abby should be surprised when Frederick's face rises above Luella's shoulder as he props himself on his elbow to look at her, but she is not surprised at all. It is as if his presence there is expected— as if he belongs there. She immediately recognizes the sated look on his face—the one she has seen after their own passion is spent. She is heartbroken.

Abby awakens with a jerk. Frederick barely stirs. She lies there for some time, wide-awake, her pulse finally easing back to normal. Her heart hurts, for herself and for Luella. For Luella because she is gone and will never experience earthly love again. For herself because she feels betrayed, even though she knows it is silly. At the same time, she feels herself the betrayer. A wave of incredible sadness envelops her. She flips the feather pillow beneath her head to avoid the wet spot her tears make.

"I am sorry, Luella," she whispers.

Frederick's heavy arm pins her to the mattress.

Chapter 7

"Dear, what are your plans for today?"

Frederick speaks to his wife from the end of the table. He asks more out of courtesy than interest, his real attention drawn by Matilda and Robart on the left and Fredie and Dovie on the right. Frederick is aware that it is unorthodox to have young children and a servant dining at the table with adults, but he defies convention in this practice. Abby had not objected, and he was touched when she said she knew how much pleasure it gives him to be with his children. Long days at the office leave little time in the evening at home, so what time Frederick has he likes to spend with his family. It has become their practice to eat dinner and supper with the children unless evening engagements include dining out. Abigail assumes the long separation from the children due to their mother's death is the cause for much of his need. What Frederick has not told her is this convention is one of the few concessions he allows himself in adherence to the way he was reared. In his life on the Island, he had eaten all his meals at the table with adults, and he considers the custom superior to that of Americans. He knows that his children will draw comfort from the association with their parents. While he is enjoying their presence, he believes his children will be gleaning knowledge and understanding from the conversations of their parents and security from their mere proximity. He leaves it up to Dovie to instruct them in the proper behavior of children. Rarely does he or Abigail have to remind Matilda and Robart to speak only when spoken to, and he is sure Fredie will learn that in due order.

"Today is laundry day, as is every Tuesday, but we need to get started early because I want to pull the children's summer clothing from the attic and see what can be salvaged for Fred from Robart's wardrobe. I doubt seriously that Matilda can wear anything from last summer since she has acquired at least two inches and several pounds. I'd like to have Mrs. Dyer in to take both her and Robart's measurements by the end of the week. I am running out of time to get their things made if we are to leave for Mother's by the end of May."

The reminder of their summer away from him casts a pall on his mood. He tries to make light of his feelings.

"It is a cruel thing to be separated from one's bride so early into the honeymoon, especially when the couple has been enjoying getting to know each other so completely."

Abigail glances at Dovie who pays no attention to the comment or chooses to act as if she does.

"Have you forgotten, Mr. Barret, that you will be joining us shortly?" Slightly arching her right brow, Abigail adds, "And if it be true that absence makes the heart grow fonder, you will appreciate all that you have that much more for the temporary lack of it."

Frederick laughs. He still has not gotten used to the flirtatious side of Abigail. In fact, there is much about Abigail that still surprises him. He expected her to bring order back to his life, something he had sorely missed in two years as a widower. With order he had expected the return of control. Having known chaos, Frederick never underestimates the power of order. But, Abigail has brought much more. Bearing a physical resemblance to his first wife, he had expected her to be much like her in thought and action, but he could not have been more wrong, or pleased, for that matter.

Though it would be hard for Abigail to believe, Frederick feels none of her guilt about Luella. Practical as he is, he now feels that Luella's death was a part of life, and one over which he had no control. Too, having no memories of his own siblings and thus no attachments regarding them, he would be surprised to learn that Abigail thinks of herself as her sister's usurper, and it never occurs to him to try to reassure her or make her think otherwise. Though he mentally makes comparisons, he does so in much the same way he does with his children. He loves them all, but just as Matilda's personality is more pleasing than that of her younger brothers right now, Abigail has characteristics that Luella lacked. Having not known them in a wife, he had not missed them. He thinks it true that a luxury once experienced becomes a necessity, and he knows already that Abigail's absence will cause him more distress than did her sister's.

Luella was a good wife and mother. She had been a stable, calming influence upon the children, the servants, and him. Abigail is anything but calming. Abigail creates energy wherever she goes, and then it is as if she sucks the air from the room. It is as if she is fueled by an intensity that Luella never had or wanted to have. Luella never questioned life or her place in it. It is as if Abigail is in constant contemplation, and often he is left guessing as to what her thoughts are or what she may do next. Luella provided a comfortable, predictable existence, and when he married her, he thought he needed nothing more. Abigail provides excitement and challenge. She makes him feel young again, but she also keeps him slightly off center. Most of the time she exudes an air of expectancy that is contagious. Occasionally he comes home to a much more contemplative woman than the one he left at breakfast. Though she has not repeated the withdrawal he witnessed the first day in her new home, he knows it is a possibility with her, one that he wants to avoid at all costs. Frederick is almost uneasy when he is away from her, and he finds himself rushing his work and cutting short business trips in his desire to gain assurance that he never really felt in the first place. He is not sure if he prefers his feelings for Abigail over those he experienced for Luella, but he knows, having now loved them both, that Abigail draws and will hold him as Luella had not. He feels no disloyalty whatsoever for acknowledging his choice in his mind. It is what it is, not something of his making.

"I assure you I would love to be with you the whole time, and things are going well at the office, but one never knows what the summer months may bring. I have assured William I would stay here at least until the threat of pervasive illness is past. I thought I would tell him today that I will leave the last week in October. I can enjoy a month with you and the family, and then we can get back in time for me to prepare for the busy month of December."

"Frederick, you must not rush, as much as I would like to have you with me. I really would not mind staying until the beginning of December. You know that now that Sophia is married, Mother would be pleased to have us stay with her. George is there, of course, but Mother without one of her daughters is lost. Besides, Savannah is sure to be healthier in December than in November, and with three young ones, we must not take chances. You, of all people, should realize that."

Frederick has been expecting this. Even though they have only been married a few months, Abigail is obviously looking forward to returning to Virginia for the summer. He wants her to do so. He will not quickly forget what yellow fever can do to one's life, but he has been dreading her departure. He is more than a little hurt that she seems unbothered by the impending separation. Now, he is not pleased to learn that she plans to stay beyond the first frost.

"Abigail, your mother cannot expect one of her daughters to be with her at all times."

Frederick recalls Luella telling him years before that she thought Abigail too attached to their mother. Though Frederick has noticed nothing unusual in their behavior while together, he has noticed that Abigail writes her mother daily whereas once a week had been often enough for Luella, and Abigail seems more distressed by lengthy absences from Mrs. Middleton. He is beginning to think there may be some validity to Luella's concerns.

"Besides, both Ann and Sophia are within a few hours ride of her, and they can be there in no time if she should need them."

Abby finally catches Dovie's eye, no easy task since Dovie wants nothing more than to hear the rest of the conversation. The servant cannot ignore her mistress's raised eyebrows when at last she casts a glance her way, so she takes the baby from his chair and calls to the other two, "Come now, lil uns, le Dubie clean dem faces an git on wid da day." She turns back at the doorway, "An gib yo papa a big kiss fo he leebs fo wuk."

Abigail continues to eat while Frederick kisses Robart and Fredie. He lifts Mattie over his head, her two small booted feet protruding from the white billows of her petticoats. Abigail is relieved to see her husband's face soften at his daughter's giggles.

Abigail wipes her mouth with her napkin.

"Dear, you know I will do just what you would have me do, but would it not be wise to see what the early part of the season brings? Only Providence knows if any or all of us will be living by that time."

"Do not speak that way, Abigail! We have had enough calamity without inviting it. If you deem it best to stay longer, of course that is what I would have you do. But I know how attached you are to your mother, and I feel like you still think of Hickory Grove as your home. I want your home to be here with me and our children and our future children."

He rises when he notices the wrinkled mess Abigail has made of her napkin. He puts his arms around her.

"Dear, I know Luella died in November, but it does not mean November is unsafe in Savannah. She had been here all summer; there is no telling when she contracted the disease."

Abigail leans her head into his hip, then pushes back, stands, and addresses Mammy who has entered to clear the dishes, probably, Abby thinks, because Dovie sent her mother to hear the rest of the conversation. "Mammy, please tell Dovie we need to start the laundry as soon as possible. We are going to get the children's clothing in order today so we can determine what we need to have made for them."

She puts her arms around Frederick's neck and lays her head against his chest. After Mammy leaves the room, she rises on tiptoe and presses her lips hard against her husband's. "You know my home and my heart are here with you. Everything will be fine, Dear. You have a wonderful day at the office, and I will be looking forward to tonight." She lets her hand slide to rest right above the fly of his britches. She smiles archly up at him before following Mammy from the room.

Frederick finds himself smiling after her, but the smile fades when he realizes he has no idea what to tell William regarding his plans for the fall. He decides he will address it again at dinner, or better yet, tomorrow morning at breakfast. He will not risk distressing Abigail right before bedtime.

Chapter 8

Greenwich, Virginia

I awake in my bed in my room at my home at Hickory Grove, and that is the way I still think of all three: *my bed, my room, my home.* I am more rested and at peace than I have been since leaving *my bed, my room, my home,* my mother's place in Virginia last summer. I miss my husband, but I do not miss *my sister's bed, my sister's room, my sister's home* in Savannah, for that's the way I think of them. Resting propped upon pillows facing the window that looks out upon the clump of trees for which our place is named, I resolve to do something about Savannah. I am twenty-four years old, and it bodes ill for my future to continue to think of my mother's home as my own. Since I cannot remain here, I know I must make a home in Savannah that will be my own, not my sister's. To that goal, I rise from bed, take pen and ink from the desk beneath the window, and sit to convey my thoughts to Frederick. I hate confrontation, and though it may be cowardly of me, it will be easier to express myself by a method that prevents discourse or interruption. This way, I can relay my thoughts without worrying about Frederick's. Without his will to alter my course, I can make the journey from beginning to end on a path of my choosing. I write hurriedly, marking out, beginning again. Finally I have what I want to say upon paper. I copy it neatly, then read it aloud to see how it sounds.

Hickory Grove, 9 June, 1830

My Dearest Frederick,

Though we've been apart a short time, I know you will be eager to hear of the safe arrival of your wife and children at their desired destination. I am happy to relate a relatively pleasant trip other than the expected travails associated with traveling with young children. Though Matilda awoke the second morning with slight fever, it departed by evening after keeping her quiet and as cool as the situation allowed. There appears to be no ill effects whatsoever with any of them, as this morning I can see them as I write. They are playing on the front lawn with Anne's Luella and Caroline attended by her Rose. Though I love motherhood, it is a relief to allow the vigilant eye some rest as I know there are others to attend them with the same love and devotion that any mother herself would exhibit.

I take this opportunity to reveal my heart to you, My Beloved, in a way I find myself unable to do when in your most desirable company. When I am with you, so eager am I never to cause you a moment's worry or dissatisfaction, I, due to no fault of your own, tell you what I think you want to hear as opposed to what I truly feel or want to say. I know this is a most grievous fault in myself and one for which I must ask you and our divine Savior to forgive me. Daily I pray for the ability to be honest above all else because I know God hates a dissembler.

Please take a deep breath, my sweet Frederick, for though I have not known you intimately long, I know you well enough to expect you to be in a high state of anxiety by the few words I have imparted, so know now that the children are well, I am fine, and my love for you is strong and unwavering. My unhappiness lies in a situation that you could know nothing of for I have been too weak and poor in character to tell you because I know it springs from the silliness of a female heart, the workings of which one of your masculine strength could never fathom. It is simply this: I would like to begin the second year of our marriage in a new home. Before I bear children (who I cannot possibly love more than those you brought to me), I would like a fresh start in a dwelling that will not evoke memories of my dear, beloved Luella at every turn. You have provided for me so lovingly that I hate myself for asking this of you, but I have given much thought to your worry that I may be unnaturally drawn to my childhood home, and I want above all else to set aside such childishness and think of only the place that shelters you and our children as my home. Home should truly be where the heart is, and my heart is first and foremost with you, as is only right in our heavenly Father's eyes.

Know that our present house is more than adequate, and I am willing to have even less in size and furnishings if that will make a move less of an encumbrance to you, my most thoughtful and generous husband. I ask that you indulge my inferior sensitivities and judge me less harshly than I deserve. I ask that you destroy this note as I would be most embarrassed for anyone but your dear self to know of your wife's foolishness.

Fredie wants me to tell his father that he is a year older than when he left you. He loved the special attention he received from Grandmother, Aunts, Uncle, Mother, Sister and Brother on his birthday. I am sure you were all he lacked to complete his total happiness. When you come, you must remember to tell him how much older he looks now that he is a young man of three.

Mother, Sisters, and Babies all send their love as does Dovie. Give Mammy our hellos. I worry not at all about you knowing you have her to depend upon for your every need. Please write me by return mail to relieve my anxious heart about the matter of which I write, and know me to be, as always, your faithful if troublesome wife,

Abigail

Mother asks me to please tell you she looks forward to your visit and to give Mammy and Lewis her remembrances, as well.

There, the deed is done. I am anxious, because it is true I do not wish to worry my husband or cause him distress. Nonetheless, I am relieved to have spoken at last on the subject, though I was not brave enough to do it in person. I am also more than a little pleased with how eloquently I have presented my case. In re-reading it, however, I find it sounds unlike me. I wonder if Frederick will think the same. I decide it is best to leave it the way it is because, if I put to paper the thoughts that run through my head in the manner they come to me, he would more than likely think me odd. Now, the waiting for a reply begins.

I spend the rest of my day in the company of Anne, Sophia, my mother, and the children. Their company distracts me, but beneath what I hope is a calm demeanor, a nagging disquiet plagues me. I am relieved when the children are in bed, and I retire to my room early in an effort to avoid an in depth conversation with Sophia who is sharing my room. I seek solitude, but that is not to be. I only have time to undress and get in bed before Mother knocks gently before entering. I feel guilty that I am not pleased to see her. Mother has a hyper diligence where I am concerned, and though I love her dearly, her delving sometimes drives me to distraction. To compensate for my errant thoughts, I smile warmly at her.

"It is so good to have you home, Dear. I have missed you more than you can imagine."

I am surprised. Mother rarely thinks it necessary to put into words what she thinks should be a given. She is my mother; she would think it unnecessary to state the obvious. We children know her to be honest, Godly, and always mindful of her role as sole parent and provider, and though we all know she loves us, it is not because she feels compelled to tell us so. Neither is she demonstrative. I can count on one hand the times she has hugged me.

The time away from her has caused me to look at her with a new perspective. Anne will look like her when she grows older. Both Sophia and I are smaller in frame, and we lack her strong facial features. The years have added pounds to my mother's angular frame and there are wrinkles I did not notice before I left. Tonight she seems softer, less intimidating. I wonder if this is due to a change in her or one in myself. Regardless, my mother seems more approachable.

"Abigail, is there something on your mind that it would help to disclose?" She hitches her dress to sit, so I make room for her beside me on the bed.

I sigh. I purposely avoid my mother's eyes because I know the question is more or less rhetorical. I have grown unaccustomed to shielding my thoughts from her intense gaze because I have forgotten how perceptive she is. I know she will not believe me if I say nothing is wrong.

"I miss Frederick," I say truthfully. "I love being with you, but I feel somewhat guilty about leaving my husband alone. I am sure he is missing the children—he has been reunited with them but a few months."

"Are you sure that is all that is bothering you?"

I wonder why she bothers to ask if she is not going to believe what she hears.

"How have you been in spirit over the last year? Your letters tell me much of the children and of Frederick and of Savannah, but they tell me little of you. I find that revealing."

I am irritated. I realize I have enjoyed not having to explain my every sigh, facial expression, offhand remark.

"Mother, you read too much between the lines in this case, I fear. Marriage is much more satisfactory than I had anticipated. In fact, if I had known it would turn out so pleasant, I might have been more eager to enter the state. And what should a wife talk of but her family and friends? Have you not taught me all my life to think of others first? You would surely have been disappointed had I sent you letters full of myself and my petty goings and comings."

"It is not your comings and goings I am interested in, Daughter, and you know it. It is your state of mind. When you left, you promised me you would keep me informed as to what you were feeling and thinking? You know you have always been able to confide in me."

"Well, Mother, perhaps I have come to realize that it is my duty as a wife to confide in my husband that which I would have once confided in you. You wanted me to marry; do you not also want me to behave as a wife should? Did Luella confide, and do Anne and Sophia share their every trivial thought?"

Mother is clearly displeased with my response. "You are not your sisters, Abigail. You know your propensity for despair, and I just want to make sure you are not giving in to the Devil's vice of despondency. Your nature is a cross you must bear, but it is not one you can let overcome you and rob you of your gift of eternal life."

"Alright, Mother, if you want truth and access to my inner thoughts, be prepared for what you hear, because of late, I am having a hard time understanding how a loving, gracious God can create me with a "propensity," as you say, for despair, then desire a perfect creation. Would an earthly father thrust a brick in his daughter's pocket and throw her into a well?"

Mother gasps. "Stop it, Abigail. That is pure blasphemy and you know it! You have been brought up in the Word, and you know it was not God who created sin or allowed it into what was a perfect plan. It was his tolerance for free will that became the stumbling block for humans, for that which is a gift can also be a curse. You must decide, as must we all, which we will make of it."

I allow myself to sigh, but I know I am only creating trouble for myself. I have gone too far. Falling back into the habits of the past, I turn to placation for escape.

"Yes, Mother, forgive me. You are right. I can overcome my faults just as others overcome theirs. I will pray more resolutely to do so. There is, however, no great burden in my life that I am hiding from you. Perhaps I am just growing up at last."

Apparently mother believes my contrition because she hugs me tightly. This is so out of character for her, I know she must have truly been worried about me.

"You know that my desire and daily prayer for you is that you will lead a happy and productive life pleasing to our Maker. And I am glad you are drawing closer to your husband. That is what Luella would have wanted you to do."

Her words immediately dispel the tenderness I am feeling toward her. I push her from me a little more roughly than I intend, and the frown she directs toward me is fierce enough to make me scramble to make amends..

"I am simply tired, Mother. Now please let me have time to pray before I fall asleep in mid thought."

"As you wish," Mother rises. Her lips are pressed into a straight line of disapproval. "But while praying you should dwell upon honoring your father and your mother, and as far as I know, I have been both and therefore deserve a double portion of respect."

She leaves the room. I immediately feel contrite. I have let my worry over Frederick's response to my letter affect my behavior and tarnish my homecoming. I slide from the bed to kneel before God. I ask him, as I do every night, to help me be the person He would have me be because for the life of me, I cannot seem to get the job done on my own.

It is hours before Sophia comes to bed. I pretend to be asleep for I am weary and disheartened and do not want to talk. I remind myself that tomorrow is another day and there is really nothing to worry about. Even if Frederick is irritated by my request, he will get over it. After all, if we are to stay married for the rest of our lives, there are bound to be obstacles we must overcome.

Chapter 9

Savannah, Georgia

On the day that his family left Savannah for the summer, Frederick asked Lewis to bring any correspondence to him that appeared to be in Abigail's hand, and he gave the servant a paper in her writing to which to compare it as Lewis does not read or write. Frederick did not expect to hear from them for at least a fortnight, so he is delighted to receive a letter within a week of their departure. He closes his office door immediately so he can enjoy the letter in privacy. Quickly scanning the first paragraph to insure the well being of his loved ones, he is brought up short upon beginning the second. Just as Abigail anticipated, her words bring on heart palpitations that are diminished little by her admonition not to worry, so it is with relief that he finally finds his way to the point of the letter.

He has to sit back to take in exactly what it is his wife is telling him. His first reaction is confusion. His wife doesn't like their house? Maybe it is a bit small, but it is in a good location. He had felt lucky to obtain it at a price he could afford when he and Luella were first married. But no, it is not the house; she says she will be happy to have less in size and furnishings. She wants a home in which to "start fresh."

Frederick's second emotion is remorse. How could he have been so stupid? What wife doesn't want her own home, one that she herself has set up for housekeeping! Abigail has acquired not just a ready-made family; she has inherited a houseful of someone else's belongings, and she has done so without complaint. Or has she? Vaguely he recalls her displeasure with

51

the bed. He had replaced it immediately, but in retrospect, he sees himself as an insensitive cad to have brought his wife home to the bed in which her dear sister died. After a time of reflection, he perceives himself as so thoughtless that he has done everything wrong short of prying Luella's ring from her hand to force upon that of her replacement. Already sentimental by separation from his family, Frederick draws forth his own pen and paper to try to undo the injustice he has done his young bride.

Savannah, 15 June, 1830

My Sweet, Sweet Abigail,

I hate to begin my first response to you since we parted with an objection, but I fear I must. In your remembrance of 9 June, you bare your heart of a concern you claim is of "no fault on your part," when in truth, it is a situation all of my making. It is hard for me to think now that I was so insensitive to your feelings. My only defense, Dear One, is that I am a man, and one so jaded by years that I have lost sight of what it is like to be fresh and young and noble. How sacrificing you were to endure a situation not of your liking for a year out of fear of displeasing your callous husband. And here I must scold you gently, Dear, for not believing absolutely in my desire to make you happy at all costs. What you ask is a minor thing in relation to the lengths to which I would go to make you happy.

As it was easier for you to be completely candid on paper, so, too, will I take this opportunity. I have been remiss in making you understand the depth of my devotion to you. I hate I came to you not as unsullied as you came to me, though I know you understand I could not but value the previous association with your family and that which brought me the blessing of my wonderful children. But know this! You are my one and only wife and the desire of my heart. Know that no other image but your own comes to mind when I hear or think the word "wife." There, it is so much easier written than said aloud, but I pledge to say it often.

Consider the simple request you ask of me as done. Would you prefer that I find a house on my own, or would you like for me to await your return so that we might make that decision together? And what would you like me to do as to furnishings? Pecuniary matters are not to be of concern to you! The company is doing even better than expected, so we are quite capable of making whatever changes you desire without putting a burden on our means. If you have no preference as to how we go about acquiring a new place, I would have us wait until your return so I will be in no doubt as to your wishes in the matter.

Having unburdened myself on that topic and yourself as well, I hope, there is much I would like to know. Has Fredie any more teeth? Has Matilda had any return of fever at all? Is Robart behaving himself with his cousins? It cannot but be my hope that they, but more importantly you, miss me perhaps some, as I miss my family more than words can express. But I am glad you are there. There have been some reports of typhoid and broken bone fever, but none that I have heard as yet of yellow fever. As much as I long for all of you, I rest well at night knowing that you are breathing the healthful mountain air of Virginia. Let me know, too, when you decide to return so that I may make plans to spend a month with you all before we return. I am in no way trying to rush you because I know your situation there with those you love dearly is so beneficial to you.

It does my heart good to know your heart pertaining to your desires to please God as a wife. It is also my desire to please God though I have no claim to your piety. Hopefully, I will become progressively more diligent in my pursuit of Him who has given and taken so much in my life through that desire and my association with one as upright as you. I have experienced the chastening hand of God, and I want to do all possible to stay in his divine favor.

Though there is much more I would like to write, I must hurry to get this in the mail. Know that I would say all that my limited ability prevents to make you know how truly devoted I am to you. Please write me disclosing your desires regarding the house, and I will be your servant in all things. Give my love to Mrs. Middleton and your sisters, and kiss our babies (tell Fredie I hope I recognize such an older man when I see him), but reserve the greatest portion of love for yourself. I try not to think of sending you kisses because I know it will be some time before I can actually receive your much desired own.

I will destroy your letter when I have committed it to heart. I long for another to take its place. Give greetings to the servants and a special one for Dovie. Think of me always as your devoted and loving husband,

Frederick

Chapter 10

Hickory Grove

The morning brings rain, and the children are all inside. Abigail is glad when her older sister Anne asks Rose and Dovie to take them upstairs, leaving the women of the household gathered in the family parlor. Sophia sits beside the window writing her new husband; Anne, Mrs. Middleton, and Abigail busy themselves with needlework. After pricking herself for the third time, Abigail puts down the flannel she is working on for Fredie and crosses to the window.

"Abby, you are as nervous as a backslider in church this morning? Does the rain make you feel confined?" Anne asks.

"Anne!" Mrs. Middleton scolds, "What an expression!"

"Please forgive the vulgarity, Mother," Anne quickly offers, but the wink she gives Abby makes her smile. "I fear I have picked up one of Edward's sayings."

"What is acceptable in a man, My Dear, is often unbecoming in a lady."

"I promise to be more diligent in guarding my tongue..."

"I am fine really, Anne, just a little restless," Abby interrupts. "I am hoping for a letter from Frederick, and I was wondering what is keeping Justice with the mail."

"Oh, Darling, the mail has been here for over an hour. I had Justice put it on the table in the entryway."

"Mother," Sophia squeals, "you know I have been dying to hear from James!" She jumps up and heads for the foyer.

"I am sorry, Girls, I would have told you had I known you were so anxious, but I assure you any news will not have changed within the hour. And, Sophia, it is vulgar to say you are *dying* for so frivolous a reason! You young women and your language. One would think you were reared by heathens!"

"I apologize, Mother," Sophia calls from the hallway, but she does not sound the least bit repentant as she happily announces, "There is a letter from James—and Abby, there is one for you, too!"

Abigail excuses herself to retire to their room while Sophia heads for her favorite spot, the wide steps on the side porch. Each wants to read her letter in private.

"Anne, do you think your sister is doing well?" Mrs. Middleton asks.

"By sister, I assume you mean Abigail."

"Yes, of course I do. Sophia is always fine. You know what she is thinking the minute she does. But you know Abigail. I cannot help but worry about her."

"Mother, Abby has always been reflective, but she seems to be doing wonderfully otherwise. She looks healthy, and she behaves as if she has been a mother for years. The children seem to be quite taken with her."

"She is very good with them, but do you think her rather pensive?"

"I had hoped you would stop worrying about Abigail once she married, Mother. She may be a little more reserved than usual, but I probably was not completely myself either the first year or two I summered here alone without Edward."

"I admit I tend to worry more about Abigail than I do the rest of you. You have always been so sensible, Luella likewise, and Sophia does not take life seriously enough, for my liking. But Abigail, she has battled melancholia since she was fourteen or fifteen, and I would hate to see her give in to it in womanhood."

"As I recall, Abby was more vivacious than either Luella or myself. I am sure she was moody when she was just entering womanhood, but what young girl is not?"

"You have been away from home for a while, Anne, and though there certainly has been nothing serious, I think Abigail bears watching. And I think she has just gotten better at hiding her feelings as she has grown older."

Anne wonders if her mother will ever completely let Abigail be Abigail. She knows some of what she says is true, but Anne has long thought their mother hovers over Abigail too much for either of their own good. She feels sorry for Abigail at times, for she knows she would not relish being constantly under her mother's vigilant eye.

"I think she seems happier than she has been in a long time, Mother. I am so glad she has a family of her own to love, and you know Frederick will do all in his power to make her happy."

She wants to remind their mother not to borrow trouble as she has told them all on numerous occasions, but she thinks better of it. Unlike her mother's relationship with Abby, theirs has never been one that invited intimacy. She knows her mother does not receive admonition easily from anyone, and especially not from one of her children.

Mrs. Middleton gives her attention to the shirt she is finishing for George. They work in silence to the rhythm of rain against the windows.

Chapter 11

Baltimore, Maryland—December 1830

I, Jessalyn Devereux, am about to embark on a new chapter in my life, and I am excited. Brigitte Maxwell has just told me the Barrets can use my services in Savannah, and though I may live to regret it, I have decided to pack up my few belongings and head south again. After all, why should I stay here? I came to Baltimore to help the Maxwells, and now they are leaving, there is nothing to hold me. I hope I do not offend Brigitte with my eagerness to be off. The Maxwells have been good to me, but here in Baltimore, my life has been one of total service to another woman's family. I am still young enough and unjaded enough to hope that a family of my own is still within reach. I take the stairs to my room in the attic in such a hurry that one might think such an eventuality is a certainty instead of the far-fetched dream I know it to be for a woman like me.

A woman like me. I take a moment to look into the glass that hangs on the wall above the trunk I am about to pack. The mirror needs silvering, so the reflection that looks back at me is no clearer than my future, no more defined than my own understanding of who I am.

Just who are you, Jessalyn Devereux, and what is it that you think you can still make of this life of yours?

In truth, I guess I think of myself as not quite anything in a world that requires one to be completely something or run the risk of being less than nothing. If all that mattered in this world was how all the outside parts of a person fit together, I would be fortunate indeed, for I am a pretty superior specimen in that respect. Maybe God, to compensate for all the *not quite rightness* of me decided to make the gifts he endowed me with quite special. I know my long, slender appendages hang well on this slim torso of mine, my upper half proportionally balanced with the bottom. My eyes are set pleasingly apart above a slender nose, and full lips conceal what I am told is a lovely white smile. I know many people consider me beautiful and certainly too many men find me desirable, but, so far, my good looks have proven to be more of a problem than an asset. Skin not light enough to be white nor dark enough to be black makes many people uneasy, especially women. My not quite black hair hangs in loose curls on the rare occasions I free it from its characteristic bun at the nape of my neck, and it along with my green-flecked brown eyes declare miscegenation as surely as if a big "M" for mulatto were carved into my forehead. In America where race is everything, I am a visual reminder to anyone who looks at me that someone, probably a man or I would not have been allowed to live, has crossed a line he should not have crossed.

I am also what many people consider not *quite right* in other ways. It is not that I am not bright enough or capable of understanding, it is the opposite. Immodest as it may be, I acknowledge I am more than ordinarily intelligent and I understand, or more accurately, I *know* what is not quite normal for mortals to know. Since childhood I have been seeing what others apparently do not see, and it took me but a couple of years of seeing to realize my visions—I call them that for want of a better description—are often best kept to myself. I can do only so much about my outward, visible differences, but I can control what others know about what I think and feel. Thank God I at least have that.

I am labeled a free woman of color, a description I find ludicrous. I would have to be a halfwit to believe myself free or of any particular color. In the eyes of everyone who is white or can pass for white, I am no better than a slave. Though I have run across several other free people of color, I know myself to be different even from them because of my *knowing.* Consequently, I am and have always been more different than anyone I know, have ever known, or have reason to believe I may encounter.

I could be bitter about my lot in life, but I am not quite that either. I, like Frederick Barret, am a pragmatist, so when Brigitte Maxwell suggested she might contact him about a position as a cook or a seamstress, I mentally checked off the pros and cons of such a move, and now, after receiving the news that he can use me, I will board a steamer for Savannah. Though Brigitte would have had me wait until they leave, I want to be on my way as soon as possible. It will not hurt the woman to fend for herself for a week or two. I plan to leave tomorrow.

I wish, not for the first time, that I might see what lies ahead for myself, but that has never happened and I know I will just have to pray and hope for the best. Having made the decision to go, I will not look back. I will not miss Baltimore any more than I missed the Island or New Orleans. Sometimes I miss people, but I never miss places. I do not feel at home in my body most days, so I have never connected a place with the concept of home. When there was no longer family on the Island, it was simply a place to be, and not a pleasant one at that, so I had taken the first chance offered to leave. I had still been naïve then, thinking it would be impossible for people to judge me more for my color than did the Negroes on the Island. There, since the Revolution, I had not been black enough, and, unknowingly, I had sailed for a land in which what little blackness I had would call into question even my basic humanity.

Savannah. I know almost nothing of it, but I choose to go anyway. The Maxwells and their two young sons are the only people in Baltimore I can really say I care about, and they are leaving. Alexis has been assigned to overseas duty, and Brigitte is determined to be where he is. I do not blame Brigitte. She needs to be with Alexis—he keeps her anchored. Besides, I understand the longing to be with family, any family. Though I hesitate to admit it even to myself, I still hope for a better life with friends and a family of my own. Though Savannah means moving farther south when common sense tells me I would be wise to move north, I want to think that it can be a place where I can belong, a place where I can be *right* enough, if not *quite*.

Enough reflection. I pack a trunk containing one of my two best dresses and two I know will be suitable for my new role in life. I made all of them as well as the undergarments and night dresses that go into the trunk. A seamstress as well as a cook, I have supported myself thus far with my skills, and I plan to supplement my income in Savannah by hiring out my seamstress and millinery services to the Barrets, or if they are not interested, to others in the community. I tuck the sketched likeness of my mother and my three favorite books along with a journal in the bottom of the trunk beneath the undergarments. The trunk contains all my worldly possessions except for two items. I sew the felt packet containing my life savings of three hundred and sixty eight dollars into the inside pocket of my dress. Tomorrow I will tuck the remaining item, a deceptively delicate four-inch blade sheathed in soft leather, between my breasts. Come dawn, I will begin my journey to Savannah where I will start a new life with a new name. I have discovered here in the States, many white people find the name Jessalyn Devereaux uppity, so I will leave it behind with the Maxwells and Baltimore. Tomorrow I will become Jessie Davis, and I will strike out for what I fear may be my last chance for a happy life.

Chapter 12

Hickory Grove

I have thoroughly enjoyed the last two weeks, and even Mother has found no reason to try to draw me out so ebullient is my mood. The weather has been pleasantly mild, and the children and I have been out of doors most days. I find myself daily amused or gladdened by something one of the children says or does. The stay in Virginia has been good for them. Mattie and Robart have easily fallen into a routine that was familiar to them, and little Fredie is happy as long as Dovie and I are close by. The children talk of their father often, and today I will help them write a letter home to him. Since receiving Frederick's letter, I feel as if a weight has been lifted. I immediately wrote and told him whatever place he chose for us would be fine as would his choice of furnishings. I have been positively gay since learning Frederick is not upset with me nor does he think me foolish.

After an early walk with the children and Anne, I return to the house to find yet another pleasing letter from my husband. Frederick writes that he has decided to rent a house for another few years, and then, he promises, he will build me a dream home that will rival the two built by architect William Jay for the Richardsons and the Scarboroughs. I laugh aloud when I read this because, though I think Frederick quite capable of providing wonderfully for his family, the two mansions are the talk of Savannah. I will write to him that we must certainly have more children if he plans to need a house the size of those.

Through the help of his friend John Andrews, the president of Planter's Bank where Frederick is a member of the Board of Directors, Frederick has found a house just two blocks from the Independent

Presbyterian Church. I can tell that he is pleased with himself for having found it, and equally pleased that it comes fully furnished. I agree it is a good idea to postpone investing in expensive furniture until we furnish a home of our own. As usual, Frederick has been practical. I am relieved I will not yet be called upon to make decisions about household purchases. Though I would not tell Frederick, I still feel inadequate in my role as mistress of the house. So far, he has not seemed to notice, and I think the reason he has not is he likes making many of the decisions himself. Frederick is a very capable man, and I have discovered he is interested in even the minutia of running a household. Perhaps this is common in men. George is the only man I have had any experience with, and he has always seemed far more interested in crops, animals, hunting, local politics and business than he has in household matters. I smile to think of George telling Mother what she needs to do with the servants or the running of the house. I am sure Frederick will become less involved, as well, once I become more efficient.

The last paragraph of Frederick's letter comes as a total surprise to me since there has been no discussion over the last year about increasing the number of our servants. I read the passage several times.

My cousin Brigitte has written me inquiring as to whether or not we might be in need of a good cook as she and Alexis are leaving Baltimore and want to place theirs in a good home. I hope you will not be displeased that I have agreed to take her without first consulting you, but time was of the essence, and Brigitte had to make other arrangements if we were not interested. I thought to relieve Mammy of her cooking duties to allow her more time with the children, and as it is my prayer, My Dear Wife, that our family will soon be growing, her time will become more and more needed as a nurse. Brigitte assures me this woman has been with them for several years and is both an excellent cook and a seamstress of some local repute. I have hired her primarily as a cook, but if you are pleased with her, you may want to utilize her services as a seamstress, as well. I know this is a departure from our practice of purchasing our servants, but as Jessie (that's what Brigitte calls her) is a free person of color, she is not for sale. I think the arrangement may work to our advantage as she will rent her own lodgings therefore requiring less room for her upkeep in ours. If you are displeased with this arrangement, I can always find her employment elsewhere in Savannah when she arrives. Brigitte tells me the cook plans to be with us before the end of the year.

Frederick ends his letter with his usual love and regard for the children and family members as well as remembrances to Dovie.

I sit for a while reflecting on Frederick's addition to our household, if that is what one calls hired help. I have never met Brigitte Maxwell, but I know from Luella that both she and Frederick held her and her husband in high regard, and the four of them had enjoyed each other's company. I try to imagine what kind of cook the Maxwells may have hired.

In truth, I often feel inadequate dealing with the servants we own, maybe because Mammy practically raised us and I grew up playing with Dovie. Likewise, Lewis grew up with me here at Hickory Grove. Maybe it will be easier to work with someone new who depends on wages. I have no experience whatsoever with hired help. Mother has hired her people out when they were not needed at home, but, to my knowledge, we have never employed laborers. And I have never personally known a free person of color. Regardless, I have nothing but respect for Frederick's business sense, and if he thinks it is a good idea, I am more than happy to have extra help to relieve Mammy. I am gladdened that Frederick, too, wants more children soon. I admit giving birth scares me because there is great risk involved, but I want to give Frederick a child. I cannot imagine loving one more than the three we have, but still I want to know what it feels like to have a life growing within me, one that is an entity in itself but, nonetheless, connected to me in a way that is wondrous.

I take my letter with me when I go in pursuit of Mother and my sisters. I am eager to tell them that I am to return to a new home with additional help. For the first time since coming to Virginia, I am impatient to return to Savannah and a home I can now consider my own.

Chapter 13

I have traveled by steamboat before, so I know what to expect. When I arrive at the dock in a hack, the attendant rushes to unload my trunk. He has it directed before he gets his first good look at my face. Even then, he hesitates. It is not until I present my pass that he is able to determine the correct demeanor for the occasion. His countenance immediately changes and I am shuffled to the midst of my kind, or as close to my kind as he can ascertain. I look coolly into his eyes until he looks away—the small victory gives me courage.

I wait patiently to be directed to our place among the baggage. I and the few other Negro passengers form a small group. There are other Negro servants on board, but they are allowed to stay with their owners for now. I look around me. I wonder what are the stories of the four others, two women and two men. The men do not appear to know the women, but each is with a traveling companion of the same sex. Are they, like me, going to new homes? Are they being sent ahead or are they following their owners? I catch myself. What makes me think they are slaves? True, they are all darker than I, but might they not be free people of color like myself?

I stand erect. There is no place for me to sit unless I sit on some of the baggage that waits with us. I try to examine my traveling companions without them knowing. I am dressed much better than they. That fact plus the lightness of my skin makes me unapproachable, I suppose, for though the other four talk among themselves, no one has even looked into my face, let alone initiated a conversation. It is just as well. If I open my mouth, I will be considered even more separate, for my English, not my first language, might as well be another language altogether from theirs. Unlike the black Creole of my homeland, this is a mixture of I know not what. Having done the marketing for the Maxwells and in New Orleans where I previously lived, I am at least able to make out what is being said. It would be better if I could not. The men stand fairly close to me, but still they raise their voices to make sure I can hear them.

"An den day dem niggas dat tink day bedda dan de res ub us," the taller of the two says.

"Dat be true, but dat jus be da debil settin em up fo a fall, cause a nigga be a nigga ta da wite man, no madda if day done ub in ribbon an bows an suv up on a silba plate."

"Dat true nuff. Jus cuz da massa be wid a bidy's mammy, it doan make no nebber mine ta dat massa. Dat bidy be jus annuda nigga fo da block, migh eben fetch a bedder price cuz a da diffrenz, an aw."

I listen for some time, my mood vacillating between amusement and irritation. Finally, when the two women move closer and join in, I decide to put an end to it. I walk up to the little group, place a pleasant smile on my face, and address the man who seems to be the ringleader.

"Gardez s'il vous plaît bouche cousue avant que je décide de découper vos langues et les coller en haut vos nez."

The men gawk, probably more caught off guard by what I hope is an endearing smile than by the threat to cut out their tongues and stuff them up their noses. None have any idea as to what I am saying, but they recognize the tone, and experience has taught them it is best to sit up and take notice. The men nod, both dropping their gazes out of habit, one going as far as to mumble, "Yessem, Missus."

They, along with the women, move as far away from me as our circumstances allow. I stand alone, the centerpiece of trunks and carpetbags. My isolation does not bother me. I am used to it.

Finally, all seem to be aboard and in place. The baggage is moved and we are allowed to move about the deck. I make my way along the rail as far away from the white passengers as I can get. This puts me at the end away from the harbor, and I face outward into the ocean. The steamer begins to move, and I turn for one last look at Baltimore. I see the white passengers waving and calling out their goodbyes. I cannot see the people on the dock, but it is just as well. There is no one there to see me off. It is early, and there was no need for the Maxwells to bring me to the harbor. Not that they offered. I think Brigitte is put out with me for leaving before they did. I am not sure Alexis even knew this was the morning I was to depart. I said goodbye to the boys last night, so even if there were room for me among the crowd at the other end of the ship,

I would choose to be where I am—facing outward toward the ocean, looking, I fancy, toward Savannah and a fresh start.

I stand at the railing until my legs grow tired. I wonder around until I find a bench to myself. I would like to read from one of my books or even a newspaper, but I know better than to do that. Slave laws prohibit reading and no one, including the unfortunates on board, will appreciate me distinguishing myself as literate. Instead, I try to occupy my time with pleasant thoughts of the future. It doesn't take me long to realize this isn't going to work. I am just too uncomfortable. I concentrate on relaxing my body as much as I can on the hard bench. I start with the muscles in my legs and move upward. I let myself fall into the rhythm of the ship, and before I know it, I have actually dozed. I awake and walk about. I sit. I sew. I doze. I awake and walk about. I am restless, but I know impatience will do me no good. I try to keep my mind from thinking about my need to urinate.

When we dock in Charleston, I wait with my colored companions for our betters to disembark before searching for a place to empty my now throbbing bladder. Finally, I ask a Negro porter where the facilities are, and he directs me past the ticket office and behind the row of loading docks that line the harbor. At last I find a small, one-hole privy that looks like it could be pushed over by a strong breeze. On the door there is a piece of board with the single word *Nigger* scrawled in what looks like charcoal. There are cracks large enough to see through in the rickety structure, so I look around to make sure I am alone. One of the two hecklers from the ship is approaching. Now I can either wait for him to go ahead of me or I can use the facility knowing he may very well be able to see me through the cracks. The man notices me looking at him, and I am relieved when he stops some twenty feet from where I am standing. He turns his back and crosses his arms. I feel a rush of gratitude. As quickly as I can, I bunch my skirts around my knees, open the door and step into a space too small for my skirts to hang freely. The stench makes me want to gasp for air, but I know better. I try to hold my breath while I do what I have to do. I use one of the two handkerchiefs I have in my pocket to clean myself before tossing it into the hole. The floor of the privy is so filthy that I would not completely drop my skirts if there were room for them. I rush from the privy with my skirts still clutched in my hands. I am relieved to see my traveling companion still has his back to me. As I walk by, I say "Thank you, Kind Sir." The man does not look up to meet my eyes, but he dips his head to let me know he has heard.

This leg of my journey gets worse before it gets better. While waiting to re-board, I lean up against a wall a good distance from the other travelers. I see a white gentleman approaching me. At first I think him to be quite old, but as he gets closer, I realize the shock of white hair hanging below his hat is probably premature. The face beneath it is relatively unlined and his carriage is erect. He is probably no more than sixty, and I can tell by looking at him he thinks himself attractive. The edge to his eye and the slant of his mouth let me know he is not interested in passing time in idle discourse. I have much experience with his kind. I acknowledge his greeting with a nod only and turn a little to my left hoping this interlude will prove innocuous. Undeterred by my efforts, the gentleman moves to stand directly in front of me.

"So, what might a young beauty like yourself be doing traveling alone upon the sea?" he asks.

"Je suis désolé, mais je ne parle pas d'anglais," I reply, striving for a civil but decidedly cool tone.

Unfortunately, the man speaks French, and he is thrilled with the opportunity to reply in kind.

"I'm sure a mulatto like yourself, lovely as you may be, might welcome the opportunity to do better by yourself. I, being alone and having a day or two to while away here in Charleston, would love to entertain you while allowing myself to be entertained." The man's smile reveals small uneven teeth stained by tobacco. "All at considerable compensation to you for your valuable time, of course."

I, who am shocked by little, am surprised with the boldness of this man. I have endured many an insult, but no one has ever straight forwardly asked me to sell my favors. My fingers tingle with the desire to slap his face, but I know I am in no position to indulge this impulse no matter how much the man deserves it. I decide to play the part of the innocent.

"Thank you for your kind offer, Sir," I begin. "Being new to your country, I would love to have someone show me around, but this is not my destination."

"But could we not make it so?" the man interrupts, moving a step closer. I fear my civility has encouraged him. Grasping for the first name I can think of that might carry some weight, I improvise.

"Monsieur, my father, James Wayne, is waiting for me in Savannah. I must not delay, you understand, no matter how enjoyable the distraction might be."

His eyes immediately lose their lecherous edge, and I know I have struck gold.

"Are you referring to the Honorable James Moore Wayne?"

"Yes, indeed. Do you know of him?"

I have heard the Maxwells speak of the congressman as an acquaintance of Frederick Barret. Apparently this man is impressed by my alleged connections.

"So you are the daughter of the Honorable James Moore Wayne, that sly devil! I would never have pegged him for a delver beneath musky sheets!" His laugh tells me he is delighted with the information. "But I guess you are living proof!"

I stand eye-level before him, determined to keep my own gaze wide-eyed and unsuspecting. His eyes narrow once again, and his mouth pulls to one side.

"It appears your father and I have more in common than I knew."

I continue to stand there, my head cocked to one side as if I am having a hard time understanding his flawed French, and I guess he weighs his options and decides it would be unwise to run the risk of offending the Honorable Mr. Wayne.

"Please give him my regards, and I will be sure to let him know of our meeting the next time I see him."

I notice he does not give me his name, but I cannot help but be pleased with myself when he tips his hat and goes his way. I am nonetheless glad to board the steamer before he has time to give real thought to my claims. What reputable statesman, powerful or not, would bring an illegitimate daughter of color from France to mingle with his southern family and friends? Once again facing out toward the ocean, I smile. I sincerely wish I could witness the next meeting between the Honorable Mr. Wayne and the obviously dishonorable lecher from the station. I hope I someday get to lay eyes on the former, for it would be interesting to see how old a man he is for me to pass myself off as his daughter. People often assume I am younger than my age, and in this case, that seems to have been to my advantage.

The rest of the trip is uneventful but exhausting. I am worn out from hard benches, unaccustomed idleness, and sleeping on the floor of the deck. It is near dusk the day we steam into Savannah Harbor, and I am relieved to find Frederick Barret waiting for me. He has also kindly taken it upon himself to acquire lodgings for me in an area of Savannah he refers to as Yamacraw. It turns out to be a single room in a boarding house owned by a free man of color. Though certainly not up to the standard to which I have become accustomed, it is clean and appears to be safe. Frederick leaves me there with a promise that he will return for me tomorrow.

As I lie in the narrow bed, I think I am too tired to sleep, but I am hopeful. The climate here reminds me of the Island, and the parts of Savannah through which I passed in route to Yamacraw are beautiful. I had the impression of lush plants and neat houses laid out in an orderly fashion. Yamacraw itself is a totally different matter. Though I have not seen the entirety of the neighborhood, it appears to be a hodgepodge of small clapboard structures, shanties, makeshift tent-like dwellings and shacks with an occasional respectable building like the one in which I am staying thrown into the mix. I could be discouraged by what I have seen in this part of town, but I am in an optimistic mood. I assure myself that I will find a decent place to live in Savannah, even in this impoverished section they call Yamacraw. I will stay in this boarding house long enough to get acquainted with the Barret household; I will then go about finding a place of my own.

I roll my flannel of money into my softest shawl, place it under my head for a pillow. I am eager to sleep so I can get up in the morning and start my new life. I allow myself to dream of a fresh start that will include family and friends because I have learned that fear and worry will not prevent bad things from happening. I have decided I will take pleasure when and where I can. Surprisingly, I sleep well the first night in my newly adopted city of Savannah.

Chapter 14

I am glad to be back in Savannah. Though the trip has been more or less uneventful, traveling with children is exhausting under the best of conditions. The baby has been restless most of the trip and has taken all of Dovie's attention, so that left me to deal with Mattie and Rob. One can't ask for a better child than Mattie—she acts as if she is fifteen rather than seven, but Rob is a different story altogether. He has tremendous energy, and his restlessness kept me on my feet most of the day. The departure held his interest as long as we were in harbor, but as soon as we were out of sight of land, he became bored with nothing to hold his attention but the passing water. I began to question the wisdom of returning by steamboat, but when I considered the alternative, being trapped in a carriage with all three children and Dovie, I decided this had been the best possible plan. It is just that I am unused to having sole responsibility for the children.

About half way through the trip, I sorely regretted that Frederick was unable to come to Greenwich and return with us as we had originally planned. The hiring of the cook and unexpected business matters had kept him in Savannah.

Mattie spots her father before I see him, and tired as I am, I cannot help but be elated by the happiness I see on his face and the enthusiasm with which Mattie and Rob throw themselves at him. Frederick acts as if he isn't quite sure Fredie is the same son who left him several months back, so much older does he look. He is such a good father! Though I can't judge from experience, everyone comments on his devotion to his children, and I cannot imagine one being more attentive than Frederick.

Conscientious of propriety as usual, he chastely kisses me on the cheek. The intensity of his gaze lets me know that it isn't just the children he is glad to see. He has apparently made an effort to look his best, and my chest tightens with emotion. My husband is indeed a dapper man!

Frederick has brought Lewis along with a cart for our luggage, and he sends Dovie along to help him. Mattie lets go of her father's hand just long enough for him to take Fredie from Dovie, then she recaptures it, dancing along beside him filling him full of news from our voyage. I hold Rob's hand and he pulls me along beside the trio, trying his best to get a word in edgewise. We all pile into the carriage, and we arrive at our new house without Frederick and me getting to say more than ten words to each other.

I am pleased when we pull up behind a three-story building located on the corner of Broughton and Drayton. I notice the house is not far from our original home, and its garden practically backs up to Wright Square. I remember there is another square just a block or two in front of the dwelling as well, but I cannot remember the name of it at the moment. The back garden itself is rather small, but the close proximity to both squares will give us plenty of space for outings and social gatherings. I am pleased for the servants' sakes that they will not have far to go to gather water. I am even more relieved to see there is a small privy to the side of the carriage house. Not all homes in town have these, and I would find it most distasteful for my own family to have to depend on proximity to the squares for that, the basest of necessities.

"How perfect, Frederick!" I exclaim. "The children will have wonderful places to play!"

I can tell Frederick is relieved by my enthusiasm. "I hope you like the interior and furnishings as well," he tells me. "It is quite a good deal, and we are still within walking distance to church and to my office on River Street."

Dovie appears to take Fredie, and I know she must be as eager as the children to explore our new home.

"Dovie, please take the children ahead and get them settled while I take Mrs. Barret on a tour of our new home."

They disappear through the rear entrance, and Frederick and I are finally alone.

"Let's enter through the front, Dear. I need to talk to you about the layout of the house and explain my plans." He takes my hands and smiles warmly into my eyes. "I hope they will be agreeable with you." Looking around to make sure we are unobserved, he presses his lips hard against mine. "I've missed you so much," he whispers. "I feel like we are newlyweds all over again."

I stand on tiptoe to kiss him a second time. I think about doing more, but I know my husband worries much about convention, so I settle for linking my arm in his as we walk to the front of the building. I stop when I get a good look at the entrance. I am taken aback to see that the front of the building looks more like a storefront than a home. Frederick notices my reaction and rushes to explain. "It was a small mercantile, but the owner was undercapitalized and it failed. It has wonderful potential if it is managed properly!"

"But I thought this was where we were going to live."

"It is, Dear; it is! But it can be both our home and our store! There is plenty of room on the top two levels for our rooms." Frederick is talking rapidly and he is waving his hands about in his excitement. He realizes this and stops to start again.

"I am getting ahead of myself." He pulls me through the door into a large room fronted by the door with large, display type windows on each side. Holding my hand with his left, he uses his right to encompass the expanse of the room. "This will make a great store, Abby! And we will not have to use a middleman. I have been corresponding with William, and he knows I am ready to branch off on my own. Since he married, he is trying to simplify his business—travel less, have more time for family, so me wanting to branch off on my own is fine with him."

"I am not following you, Frederick. Are you planning to give up the factoring business and run a store?"

"No, not at all. There is no way I would make enough money with just the store. I am talking about doing both. I will buy out William's interest in the business, and I will supply the store directly. I will hire someone to run the store, and we will profit from both the business and the store. In fact," here he appears a little nervous, "I have taken the liberty to put it all in motion. That is why I could not join you in Savannah. I wanted to surprise you."

"Can we afford to do all this, Frederick?"

I have never been interested in knowing the specifics of our finances, but this sounds like a big move, one I am surprised he has made without at least discussing it with me.

"Yes, Dear, I assure you we can. If we could not, I would never take the risk." I know Frederick means what he says. Never would he chance destitution. He suffered for years in that state, and I know he will do all possible to never experience penury again.

"There is little risk involved, don't you see? We are renting this house to live in anyway, so there is no extra expense incurred there. The only costs will be stocking it and manning it. We already import much of what we will sell—from the Indies—now I will just sell directly to the public. If the store fails—though I cannot imagine it doing so—I will just go back to doing what I've always done."

Frederick's excitement is contagious. Though I cannot imagine living above a store, I certainly do not want to dampen his spirits.

"I am assuming there is access to the upper floors without coming through here?" I ask tentatively.

"Of course, of course! Through the kitchen now, but I plan to make a stairway from the hallway window upstairs to the back garden. We will turn the wagon shed in the back into a carriage house with space for the servants above it, and we will have plenty of room. The landlord has even agreed to reimburse me for the materials for the improvements. Here, let me show you the rest of the house."

Frederick pulls me to the back of the house and through a doorway into a hallway with a door to the left to what I suppose is the kitchen. Running up the right side of the hallway is a rather steep stairway to the second floor. Frederick chooses to bypass the kitchen for the time being, and up the stairway I go pulled along behind him. My skirts brush the wall to the right as I hold tightly to his hand.

The stairway ends in a landing off of which leads another staircase to the third floor. The rooms off of each side of the landing are nicely furnished, and I am relieved to see the structure has been built to house a family. There are high ceilings with nice crown moldings and the walls on this floor are covered in a muted floral wallpaper. The room to the left is apparently a dining room. In the center of it is a large mahogany table with six chairs encircling it. On each side of a coal-burning fireplace is another matching armchair that can be used at the table as well. The mantle is topped by a rather ornate gold-framed mirror that arches directly under the picture rail that runs around the circumference of the room several inches below the ceiling. To the right of the entry door stands a mahogany sideboard. All together it is a pretty room. The furniture and carpet, though not new, are in good condition, and there is plenty of light through the two windows at the front of the room. They are open now, and I can see a fine layer of dust that no doubt has made its way in from the street. I can clearly hear the street noise, but I guess that cannot be avoided. I still haven't gotten used to the daily noise in Savannah, and it seems particularly loud now after the quiet summer I have spent in Virginia.

Frederick pushes two solid wood doors inward at the back of the room to reveal a small bedroom behind them. I was expecting a smaller family dining room or an informal parlor. I am also surprised to see a servant's pallet beneath the bed.

"The previous family used this as a bedroom. Mammy is sleeping in here until we finish the quarters out back. After that's completed, I think we may make this into a more intimate dining area for the family. What do you think of that idea?"

"I think it is a splendid idea. A sleeping chamber this close to the dining room would be inconvenient."

Walking through the bedroom and out a door on the inside wall, I find myself back on the landing. Two doorways off the opposite side of the landing open into the expected parlors, one larger in the front with a smaller in the back connected with glass doors. They are not pocket doors, but at least they are wide enough to form a fairly large passageway from one room to the other in the event we have a gathering of more than six or seven people. These rooms, too, are furnished modestly but nicely with the front parlor crowned with wider molding than the back. The fireplace in the formal room matches the one across the landing in the dining room. The mirror above it appears to be identical to the one in the dining room.

As we pass through each room, I am lavish in my approval, finding something in each room to specifically point out as pleasing or useful. By the time we make it to the third floor, Frederick has relaxed and is thoroughly enjoying his role as guide. The top floor consists of three rooms, all set up as bedrooms. The front two are equal in size. They open each way off the landing, both lit by two windows on the front and one on each outside wall. They, too, are papered, but the patterns in the two front bedrooms are more feminine than that of the living areas downstairs. Both are quite lovely, and I reassure Frederick that he has done a wonderful job in choosing one for us and the other for Mattie and Dovie. At the back of the landing is the final door, and there we find Dovie and the children. Mattie is sitting on one of the boy's beds while Dovie unpacks the children's clothing. The boys play on the floor, glad to be reunited with their toys after a summer away from them. This room runs the length of the building but is narrow in width, a fact made more noticeable by the sloping back ceiling. Its walls are whitewashed horizontal boards. It lacks the finished look of the other two rooms and it seems rather close, but I reassure my husband that it will be fine for the boys.

"At least the windows along the back will allow for a breeze if we leave the door into the hallway open. The window there will provide a nice cross breeze."

The tour of the upper floors completed, we return to the bedroom we will share. "Thank you." I wrap my arms around Frederick's neck. "You quite amaze me. I swear you have done a much better job of arranging everything and everyone than I would have! Is there anything you cannot do, Mr. Barret?"

"I cannot live without my family," he answers smoothly, "especially my desirable wife."

I laugh and pull him down on the bed where I let my hand roam from the inside of his knee upward.

"We have yet to see the kitchen, Darling, and Lewis will be up momentarily with your trunk. Besides, I will need more time than we have now to show you how much I have missed you, Mrs. Barret, so let us finish the tour, have an early meal, and get the children to bed. I know they must be exhausted. In fact, I think it would be best if we all made an early night of it."

Frederick laughs and kisses me. Sometimes I wish he were a little less circumspect. He once told me Luella had never initiated their lovemaking, that she had always been compliant, but never the active participant I am. I assume it is abnormal for a woman to talk of such things or to actually go as far as to invite the act. This is one of the things Frederick says he loves about me. One would assume it would be one of the things he has missed while I was gone. I can tell he is reluctant to release me, and the fact that he does indicates how eager he is to continue the tour. We make our way back down the two flights of stairs to check out the kitchen.

When we enter the room, my first thought is that we have company. A tall woman with regal bearing is standing with her back to us at the counter in front of the only window. Mammy is peeling potatoes at the table, and the second thought that registers with me is that Mammy is not happy. Never one to hide her displeasure, Mammy looks up to greet me with the expected, "Wekum home, Mizz Abby," but there is no smile on her face, and she doesn't address Frederick at all. Before I can give the situation much thought, the woman at the window turns and any concern I might have had for Mammy's unusual behavior flees my mind.

The woman is nothing short of beautiful. Dressed simply in a dove gray dress, high-necked and belted at the waist, she wipes her hands on a cloth, lays it on the workspace, and walks across the room toward us. The woman moves gracefully, back ramrod straight, head held high.

"Abigail, this is Jessie, our new cook," Frederick says.

Mammy rises, slaps the paring knife she has been using on the table, and huffs out of the room. I can hear her muttering under her breath as her skirt brushes mine on her way out.

The poised Jessie seems not to notice. She extends me her hand, tilts her head forward in what may be an acknowledgement of respect, and raises it to smile warmly. "Madame Barret, it is a pleasure to finally meet you."

I realize my mouth is probably gaping open. This is our new servant! I automatically take the lady's hand, and I find myself tilting my head forward in much the same gesture Jessie used.

"My, Jessie, you are not quite what I expected!" I blurt.

Jessie responds with a deep, throaty laugh. She speaks with a slight French accent I recognize as West Indian like Frederick's. "I assure you I am more competent than I look."

I flush. I am still not at ease with the position of lady of the house, and now I am expected to oversee this woman? I am intimidated, to say the least. Jessie is at least four or five inches taller than I and obviously much more self-assured, not to mention the fact that I am hard pressed to recall ever meeting anyone as striking. Though I know Jessie is a woman of color, she is only slightly darker skinned than many of our white friends, including part of our own family. Her lips are full, her nose straight, and I am close enough to tell her eyes are more hazel than brown. What in the name of the Good Lord must Frederick be thinking!

Apparently reading my mind, Frederick takes the opportunity to intercede. "Abigail, Dear, Jessie is already proving to be quite an asset. Brigitte certainly did not exaggerate when she said she had the best cook in all of Baltimore. In the short time she has been here, I have eaten like royalty. We must be careful as to who we have to dinner or they will be trying to hire her away from us!"

It is so uncharacteristic for Frederick to even comment on a servant unless it is to imply a need for improvement that my gaze is at last torn from the woman in front of me to rest upon my rather flustered husband. He is nervous, I realize. He must have known I would be surprised by this new household member, but he, too, must have been shocked. It is not as if he had the chance to meet the lady before she came. Now, I realize, he is almost apologetically asking me to accept her.

"I cannot wait to experience her gift," I manage to get out.

Jessie, apparently unfazed by the awkwardness of the moment, continues to smile at me as if Frederick has not spoken at all. "You must promise me that you will let me know if you find my dishes too foreign, for I trained in New Orleans, and I tend to lean toward French cuisine as that is what I learned there and what we mostly ate on the Island. Since you were not here, I have been preparing whatever came to mind, but now that you and the children have returned, I hope you will tell me if my choices are unsatisfactory. The Maxwells are the only family I have cooked for, and Mrs. Maxwell's mother, like your husband, grew up in the Islands, so the food I cook is not so alien to them. It may take me a while to adapt to local recipes, but I assure you I am both willing and capable."

Though I have no experience whatsoever with dealing with hired help, I am quite sure most do not speak, look, or act like this lady. However, Jessie seems eager to please and as respectful as anyone could ask, so maybe her addition to the household will not be the calamity I first feared. Too, after having met Jessie, I am especially glad the woman will not be living under our roof.

"Frederick wrote me, Jessie, that you have taken a room in Yamacraw. Have you found your accommodations satisfactory?"

I feel as if I am addressing a visitor rather than a servant.

"Yes, the room was fine, and I so appreciated Monsieur Barret for obtaining it for me. The man who owned the boarding house was quite kind, as well. In fact, he has been gracious enough to help me find a small home of my own. It needs work, but I think I can make a pleasant home of the place with some time and effort."

"You mean you've bought a home of your own!" I could be no more astonished if she had just told me she descends from royalty.

"Yes. I had saved a little money over the years, and with Monsieur Barret acting as my patron, I was allowed to purchase a small place a couple of streets over from the boarding house he found for me. I am thrilled, as you can imagine. This is the first home I have owned."

Suddenly eager to get Frederick alone, I take him by the hand and begin what I hope is not an obvious retreat. "Jessie, I hope you will be happy in Savannah, and I am delighted to let you continue preparing whatever you have been preparing for the Maxwells and Frederick. I promise you I will let you know if any changes need to be made."

At least I will not have to worry about providing a menu. The food will have to be unpalatable for me to want to assume that duty.

In the hallway, Mammy is half-heartedly dusting a lamp on a stand by the doorway. It is obvious she has been eavesdropping, and it is equally obvious she has not liked what she has heard.

"Mammy, now that Abigail is back, she will be able to explain your new role with the children."

Mammy does not look up or respond. Sympathy for my childhood nurse makes my voice soft when I address her.

"Mammy, I am so relieved to finally free you up to take charge of the children. Dovie is wonderful, but I so want our children to grow up with the same care I had. And, though we do not want it to be known yet, if Providence is willing, we will have more children than poor Dovie can handle on her own."

Somewhat mollified by the praise and the shared confidence, Mammy's demeanor lightens. "You sayin you be wid chile, Mizz Abby?"

"No, Mammy, not yet, but we both hope to be enlarging our family, and now that you have been freed from the burden of cooking for us, we will not have to worry about the children getting the care they need."

"You know Mammy lub dose chilrun, Mizz Abby, bu Mammy da cook fo dis fambly sin Mizz Lella come hyur wid da Massa, an I ain haid no plains ebber, so sho wuz a sprize wen dat wite gul show up in Mammy's kitchen an go ta bossin er roun lack she own da place."

I want to smile, but Frederick is not amused.

"Mammy, you best remember your place. I made the decision to hire Jessie, and the last I heard, I was still making the decisions around here."

"Yes, Massa, thet sho nuff be da truff." On the surface, Mammy looks repentant, but I have known her all my life, and I can see the displeasure in the set of her lips. Though I know Frederick won't like it, I address her again.

"Mammy, it is unfortunate that I was not home to tell you of the changes. You have been a wonderful cook, but I think taking care of the children is more important than putting food on the table. I will sleep better knowing that Dovie will have the help she needs—that our children will have you to rock them, to tell them the same stories you told us, and to nurse them when they are sick. Now you go on up and help Dovie, and we'll talk more tomorrow about how we will change things."

"Mammy know she jus a nigga, Mizz Abby." Mammy is still hurt. "An she do wat she tol ta do." She turns to me one last time before heading up the stairs. "Do dat mean I be sleepin wid Mattie sted a ow back wen da quawtas finish?"

"No," I say, and though I have not given it any thought until now, I am sure Mammy has been looking forward to having a room separate from the house. "I think it will be best for Dovie to sleep on the floor in Mattie's room. We will make sure you have your own bed in the quarters you will share with Lewis."

"Dat be good, Mizz Abby." Mammy still doesn't smile, but at least she says good night before she continues up the stairs.

As I expected, Frederick is irritated with me. "Abby, I have told you before, you are too easy on them. If you are not careful, they will run right over you."

Frederick's patronizing tone makes my skin prickle. "Mammy has been with my family since the day I was born. She has never failed to do what I have asked her to do since I have been old enough to ask her, so it would please me if you would allow me to continue to handle Mammy in the way I see best."

Frederick's tone of voice turns soothing. "I know she belonged to your family, and you are right. She is your responsibility, and I apologize for interfering. Besides, I certainly do not want to spend your first night home discussing the servants."

I bet you do not, I think, but that does not mean I am going to wait until later to discuss our new cook. "I agree, Darling, but let us sit in the parlor and talk about Jessie before we completely drop the subject of servants. There is so much I want to know."

Frederick quietly follows me into our new parlor where we sit facing each other on the settee.

"Frederick," I go directly to the point, "who is this woman, and what were you thinking?"

Frederick takes my hands and holds my eyes with his own. The only indication that he is nervous is his heightened color, but apparently he has expected my reaction to Jessie, and he speaks with confidence.

"This woman, as I told you in my letter, was the cook of Alexis and Brigitte for some years, it seems. She comes highly recommended."

"But Frederick, look at her! She looks like she herself could own the house. In fact, she does own a house! Whose servant owns their own home?"

"Now, Abby, you are used to the way things are done in the country. It is not uncommon for servants in Savannah to live away from their families…"

"She does not just live away from us, Frederick! She owns her own home—and with your patronage!"

"That, too, is becoming more common, Abby. She has the money to buy her own home, and what could it hurt for me to sign for her! It just makes it more unlikely for her to leave our employment for someone else's."

"And it means so much to you already that she does not?" Frederick's explanation is having the opposite effect from the one he intends.

"Of course I do not want her going to someone else's house! Do you realize how prestigious it is to have someone of her caliber in our employ? You have not yet sampled her cooking, but when you do, you will realize that we will be the envy of Savannah! And that is just her cooking. You will have at your disposal an accomplished seamstress as well!"

My drawn eyebrows must indicate I am not swayed by his enthusiasm. "Brigitte wrote me that Jessie made all of her clothes, and there was a waiting list of friends wanting her services. The Maxwells hated letting her go, but they had no choice. Do you not see, Abby? Their loss is our gain!"

I do not like confrontation, but I cannot let this subject go.

"Frederick, the woman seems as genteel as you or I. How in the world did a servant become so accomplished, so refined?"

"Before the Revolution, it was not unusual for people of color on the Island to enjoy many of the privileges white Americans do. According to Brigitte, Jessie was born into a family of such privilege. Her father was white, as you can tell by her complexion, and her mother was mixed. She grew up on a small plantation, but her father died, and her mother lost their holding in the Revolution. When the niggers took control of the Island, Jessie and her mother made do living here and there, but Jessie was the last of her immediate family when her mother died, so she hired herself out. Brigitte tells me there was some previous business connection to her own mother, and hearing of Jessie's plight, Brigitte offered to take her in. That is how, it is my understanding, she ended up in America."

I am softened by the story of the woman's past. I would never have guessed by looking at her that she had struggled a day in her life.

"But how am I to manage a woman like that, Frederick? I feel inadequate already. I cannot imagine her taking orders from anyone, especially me."

Frederick knows the danger has passed. He relaxes and smiles at me. "I think you will be pleasantly surprised, My Dear. And if you are not, she will answer directly to me. I cannot wait to see the expressions on our friends' faces when they dine at our table. We will be the envy of everyone in town!"

I sometimes think Frederick cares too much for the opinion of others, but I assume it is important to make a good impression if one is to succeed in a place like Savannah. Luella used to write me of the challenges of fitting into local society, and I have witnessed the cliquishness of the town firsthand. Here, what one has and who one knows seems to be quite important.

"Just give her a chance—that is all I ask," Frederick cajoles, "and if you are not convinced she is an asset in the next few months, we will find her employment elsewhere."

"Alright, Frederick," I concede, as he probably knew I would all along. We make our way upstairs. I assume Jessie will lock up and walk the sandy streets to Yamacraw into a world far different from the one here on Broughton Street. I wonder what her life will be like there and what it was like on the Island. Was it as hellish as Frederick claims his was? I feel sympathy for the woman who looks so regal and competent, but I once again doubt I am up to the task of managing her.

Frederick and I enter our new bedroom together, and I think no more that night of the cook we call Jessie.

Chapter 15

I can tell Madame Barret has misgivings but I have none as I walk through the streets to what I already think of as home. I know, as I know many things, that she and I will get along wonderfully. I knew the minute I touched her hand, brief though the touch was. I felt the warmth and sincerity of a decent human being. I could also feel my young mistress' resistance, but that sensation was overpowered by the many positive ones I felt through the brief contact. Frederick Barret has done well in marrying Abigail. I wonder if he knows how fortunate he is.

I make my way through first the lighted streets, then the dark ones, where what light there is, is put off by candles or lamps in the rough, mostly thrown-together structures along the street. Though the doors and windows are open, the light does not make its way to the path I walk, but the sand is light and I have no trouble finding my way. I pay little attention to the odors I found hard to endure when I first arrived here. Now, as I leave the sidewalks of the town proper and enter the sandy paths of Yamacraw, I simply pull my dress up high enough to avoid the waste and refuse. The city has waste men, scavengers they are called, who patrol the squares and the better streets to haul off any matter that may be offensive or unhealthy to the genteel, but their jobs do not require them to bother with the areas inhabited by poor whites, slaves, and that minority like myself, a group called, paradoxically, free blacks. The scavengers themselves may live here. Though I am used to stepping over offal and debris, I still avert my eyes from the animal carcasses that lie where they died, were thrown by owners, or dragged by nonhuman scavengers. They remind me too vividly of the refuse of the Island, once human in nature left lying broken and dead in the streets, dispatched with no more concern than if they had been the dogs, cats, or other creatures now rotting in the pathways and scratch gardens of Yamacraw.

My spirits lift when I am able to make out the outline of my own small house. It is set about twenty feet back from the street. I feel something like happiness when I see the dual flames of Moses Tucker's lanterns and hear the thud of his hammer. I hope someday to have a sidewalk running from the stoop Moses is building for me to the road. I also want to plant flowers and create a front garden of sorts, something like my family had when I was a child. Of course, the yard will be much smaller, and the house will never be as grand, but I know I can make the property look welcoming and homey. I still cannot believe this little place, modest as it is, belongs to me. It is the only thing of any real worth I have ever owned.

"Moses, you are coming right along! I did not expect you to get so much done today."

"Yes, Mizz Jessie, by tamarra I be gettin da roof on, an den you haf a place ta wipe yo feet and be in odda da rain."

Moses is a big man, a kind one. I liked him and felt a kinship to him from the moment I met him at his boarding house. We share the common bond of being members of a minority within a minority in Savannah. Unlike me, however, Moses has been a slave. At dinner one evening at the boarding house, he sat uninvited across the table from me and proceeded to tell me his life story. I was a little taken aback at first, but the longer he talked, the more impressed I became with him and his resourcefulness. It turns out he is quite the storyteller. I sat there for a good two hours listening to him tell me about his life and that of his sister Lavinie.

Moses was fortunate enough to belong to a North Georgia small plantation owner named Beech Tucker who had an only son named Beckham who lived in Washington City for many years after leaving his father's household. In Washington City, this Beckham had become friends with a lady who had organized a group of women, women considered quite radical, I am sure, who dedicated their lives to campaigning against what they called "trafficking in human flesh." Though the son had stopped short of becoming a full-fledged member of the group, their influence had rendered him uncomfortable with slave ownership. Too, Moses explained he was a man who appreciated simplicity and disliked change. He had become content with his city lifestyle and saw no reason to complicate matters with the encumbrance of the five slaves his father deeded to him. Moses and his sister Lavinie were two of the five the young heir emancipated. Moses' sister had married while she was still a slave, but the marriage appeared to be doomed because the husband had been sold off to a man in North Carolina. As soon as the sister Lavinie was freed, she set out for North Carolina to be close to her husband. In Moses' mind, God has indeed been good to him and his sister, and gratitude for his deliverance makes him determined to do well in life. He said he wants to show the white man that Negroes are capable of being good, law-abiding members of society capable of caring for themselves and their own. To this end, Moses moved southeast to Savannah where rumor had it that black men, even slaves, had more freedom than on plantations and small towns elsewhere. In his five years of freedom, Moses has managed to acquire enough resources to buy the small plot of land in Yamacraw on which he built his five-room boardinghouse. His next goal is to save enough money to send to Lavinie in North Carolina so she can attempt to purchase her husband.

Since leaving the boarding house, I have only seen Moses one time, and that was when I went by to ask him to build me a porch. I am sure Frederick Barret could have found me someone to do the work, but I feel drawn to this large, friendly man. I was pleased to have a reason to talk with him again—and to see him. I must admit I find him nice to look at. It is rare for me to have to look up to speak to anyone, even men, but standing on my newly boarded floor of the small porch he is building, I am eye to eye with him even though he is standing on the ground. He is probably as tall as anyone I have ever met, and the muscles of his bare upper torso are easy to make out even in the dim lantern light.

"You have done enough for one day, Moses," I tell him as I deliberately place a hand on his shoulder. His skin is smooth and surprisingly cool considering the heat of the day. He jerks reflexively, and I know I have surprised him with my touch. I read confusion in his dark eyes and feel a little guilty for his discomfort, but I do not remove my hand. I can usually tell much about a person by simply making physical contact, but all I can sense from Moses is an overall impression of goodness. I am disappointed. Trying to read more, I leave my hand there longer than he can possibly consider casual, but Moses simply stands there looking at me as if he, too, is trying to draw understanding from the touch. Finally, I pull my hand from his shoulder and take a step back. Not knowing how to explain myself, I don't try. I simply smile at the man, and his own smile reassures me that he is neither offended nor ill at ease. I like this about Moses. Though he seems interested in me and as polite as any man, he does not appear to be intimidated by my light skin or my looks. Rare is the man who is unaffected by one or the other.

"How old are you, Moses?" The question is out before I know I am going to ask it.

"Doan righly know, Mizz Jessie. Da massa, he din pay no mine ta dat kine da ting wen I wuz a chile, but I rekun I haf ta be fotty, mabe a year a two mo. I know I ain no chile fo a long time now, bu neeber do I sidda masef an ol man. Wy you ax, Mizz Jessie?"

The smile has left Moses face, and it is I who become uncomfortable. "No reason, Moses." I lower my eyes and turn toward the door.

"Mizz Jessie," he reaches out and places his hand on my arm, "doan yo worry none," he says, still standing with one foot on the ground and the other on the partially framed step of the porch, his head cocked to one side, his expression uncharacteristically solemn. "I be ol nuf ta complish anyting you migh wan done, wat ebber it be."

I turn completely and take a step to close the short distance between us, my face a mere foot from his. His kind, serious face moves me. "I am sure you are, Moses. I am sure you are."

I feel a smile spread across my face, and Moses answers it with one of his own.

"I have some leftover beans and rice I will share with you, if you are hungry, Moses Tucker."

"Doan mine if I do. I awways hongry, Mizz Jessie," Moses chuckles. He follows me into the house and closes the door behind himself.

Chapter 16

I am awakened by the muted tinkling of the bell that hangs on the front door of the store downstairs. It must be eight o'clock, opening time for Barret's Mercantile. Instead of being annoyed by the commerce that goes on each day right beneath my feet, I find it gives me a sense of security. It makes me feel connected to the city and life in general. Every day brings customers from different walks of Savannah through our front door. In my spare time, I like to sit at the front parlor window, shielded from public view by a lace curtain, and watch the traffic of the street. On those days I know before Frederick tells me in the evening how the store has done— what interesting customers have been there. I can even guess at the revenue brought in by the size of the parcels leaving through the front door. Mostly the customers are men and servants, but occasionally escorted women come to check out the latest arrivals of notions or bolts of fabric. Though we have only been in business a few months, I have recognized some of the fabric made up into dresses and bonnets worn by women at church, and even once by two women, Joyce Maddox and Sarah Couper, at our weekly Ladies Beneficence meeting. I know better than to comment on the connection, but I feel Frederick has made a place for us in the community.

Frederick is thrilled with his new business venture, and since our return from Virginia, he acts as if he is on top of the world. He, much more than I, craves prosperity and acceptance. Though I know little of his life before America because he changes the subject each time I try to probe, I know it involved heartache and deprivation. I believe his ambition may be fueled by his past, and though I cannot comprehend what it must have been like for him, I am proud he will never have to live that way again. My Frederick is a very capable, industrious man, and I know I am lucky to be so well provided for. Too, I envy his ability to let go of the past and live in the moment. He has far more reason to despair than I, yet he exhibits no indication he is subject to the moods that have plagued me most of my life.

I throw the covers back and get out of bed, and there at the foot of the bed are the dark green taffeta and petticoats I tossed on the chair when we came to bed late. Dovie has not disturbed me to put them away, and instead of leaving them for her to deal with, I brush the dress down myself and put it in the clothes press. I fold the petticoats as best I can and thrust them into the chest that holds my undergarments. I don't want to look at them because they evoke the memory of last night's party and thus darken my mood. I sit where they have lain and make myself work backward in my mind to discover what it is that is bothering me. This is an exercise I learned years ago to help overcome despondency. Often my mood begins with just an uneasy feeling, but if I leave it unaddressed, the feeling can swell into something more threatening. I have learned that if I work back through my memory to discover the origin of my unease, I can sometimes look it in the face and move on.

Last night's event was an affair at the Telfairs. I hadn't wanted to go, but that was not unusual. I never want to attend large gatherings. Frederick has no idea how much I dread such outings, and I am not about to tell him. Unlike me Frederick loves such occasions. Not only does he see them as a way to further his business goals, he genuinely likes everything about parties. He loves the interaction with other men— the drinks they share around game tables clouded by cigar smoke, the camaraderie, the good food. And in truth, he is a bit of a dandy. He loves nice clothes, for himself as well as for his family, and he takes pride in being asked to dine, dance, or ride with those he considers to be among the best and oldest families in Savannah. He openly admits to me that it is his goal to match them in wealth and influence. I, on the other hand, think little of wealth and influence, and if more of either means increased exposure to the frenetic pace and forced gaiety of Savannah night life, I would be quite happy to continue to live modestly with our small family above the store on Broughton Street. This, too, is a sentiment I will never share with Frederick. I know he would view such lack of ambition a grave character flaw. I work hard to appear cheerful and outgoing when in public. It is strange that I can be so vivacious at home and in the company of close friends, then want to withdraw into the background in large gatherings. I secretly think one of the things that attracted Frederick to Luella over me in the first place was Luella's love for all things social. My sister and my husband were much more equally yoked in that area.

I remind myself that I need to address what exactly it is that is making me feel melancholy today. Do I fear I didn't measure up last night? I start at the beginning of the evening and work my way forward. Frederick had been pleased with the way I looked in the green taffeta. He'd commented on my creamy skin, my tiny waist, my upswept hair. All had been to his liking. And I'd done wonderfully at making conversation and laughing as gaily as the others while he and the other men were with us. I had even actually enjoyed the dancing. It gave me contact with Frederick and a respite, of sorts, from the fray. Frederick had appeared to be delighted with the evening, so why do I feel inadequate this morning?

With the rest of the evening reviewed, I am forced to turn my mind to the time spent away from Frederick in the company of the other women. I let my mind dance around the edges of the parlor as I recollect the evening as if I am an observer instead of a participant. From above the room, I see myself perched on the edge of a settee, a position I now fear looks as if I am ready for flight. In fact, I remind myself of a small green bird, my plumage almost too heavy for my frail bird frame. I seem dwarfed by the women around me, both in stature and substance. They talk of many things, of many people. Though I participate in some of the same charities and attend church with four of five of the women, I feel apart. They speak of events from several years past, of shared relatives and acquaintances, of places they've vacationed together, of summer plans they share. Looking back at myself on the small divan, I see myself as uncomfortable and fidgety. I remember the tight clutching in my chest, the desire to flee the room. But of course I don't flee. Instead, I sit there dumbly with the rigor of a smile pasted upon my white face. I regret declining a drink for the glass would have given me something to do with my hands, and the wine might have loosened my tongue. I let my mind wander and am caught unaware when Mrs. Telfair addresses me directly. I pretend I haven't heard clearly so she will repeat herself, and then my response is all too honest. Mrs. Telfair has asked what it is like to live above a place of commerce, and taking the question at face value, I find myself rambling on about enjoying the comings and goings below, and too late I realize I have actually admitted to sitting idly by the window watching the city flow around me. What a pathetic voyeur I must seem! And then it occurs to me that Mrs. Telfair's question might be a way to point out the inferiority of our lodging.

Now that I have isolated the point of my despair, I determine to do what I've learned to do to avoid the darkness that falls too easily upon me. I go through what I call my *so what, what if* routine.

So what if the ladies know I spend part of my day sitting by the window? Is that such a grievous flaw in my character?

So what if I live above a store? Frederick is not ashamed of it—why should I be?

What if Mrs. Telfair is actually interested and wants to know the truth? How bad can telling the truth and being unpretentious be?

And finally, *So what if Mrs. Telfair and every woman there thinks I am birdlike and inane?* Here, *Because your husband cares what their husbands think!* comes to mind, so I quickly move on to what I realize I truly feel. My worth is not dependent on what the old guard of Savannah thinks of me or my husband. I am a Virginian by birth, of good name and character, and I do not have to answer to anyone, even my husband, I think defiantly. After all, he is the one who begged me to marry him and move to Savannah. I was perfectly happy where I was! And Frederick will just have to accept me for who I am—he is my husband. What choice does he have?

I am proud of myself. I have kept the darkness at bay. Maybe I am leaving my moodiness behind. After all, since moving into our new home, I have been more or less content. Luella, too, seems to be resting in peace at last. I have not dreamed of my sister or felt her presence in the new house on Broughton. It is not that I don't like to think of Luella. I do, but I prefer those memories to be set in the past at Hickory Grove where we grew up—unconnected to my present life with Frederick. Less and less I think of the children as Luella's. They have become Frederick's and mine. Rob and Fredie don't remember Luella at all, and if Mattie does, she never mentions her. I am their mother, and I love that role. I go soft inside each time one of them calls me Mama.

I can hear Mammy urging the children to breakfast, and I am already dressed and heading down the stairs when I meet Dovie heading up to see if I need assistance. The smell from the kitchen makes my stomach rumble.

I join the children at the kitchen table. This has become our habit since the move. Never would I have dreamed of such a practice in Virginia, but Frederick enjoys eating with all the children, and I've discovered I do as well. Only on weekends when Frederick eats with us do we have breakfast in the dining room upstairs. Mammy had begun to serve the children at the kitchen table out of convenience, and it had seemed only natural that I would join them there rather than ask them to all move to the dining room or for me to dine there alone. Besides, Jessie has transformed the kitchen into a colorful, inviting place to be. The fireplace with its oven provides warmth on these chillier winter days, and I dread moving away from this homey setting come late spring when the temperatures will drive us upstairs. Nonetheless, this arrangement will not be one I confide to Mrs. Telfair and the other fine ladies of Savannah.

"Good morning, Madame Barret," Jessie greets me as usual.

"And good morning to you, Jessie."

The misgivings about Jessie have long been forgotten. The servant's pleasant demeanor and amazing talent in the kitchen have overcome any reservations either my husband or I might have had.

I place my hand on each child's head in turn before sitting down at the end of the long, rough oak table that acts as Jessie's work surface when not in use by the family.

"Gracious, Jessie!" I exclaim as she places the heaping plate before me. "I am already having trouble fastening my dresses. If I keep eating these meals you ply me with, I'm going to pop completely out of them!"

Jessie laughs. "I have told you I'd be happy to alter your dresses or make you some new ones. You needed some weight on you. When I first met you, you could have been blown away by a strong wind."

Mammy grunts from her place beside Fredie who seems to have more breakfast on his face than he does on his plate. I decide to ignore Mammy's displeasure with what the slave considers to be Jessie's over familiarity with her mistress. I have worked too hard to regain this good mood to let Mammy bother me. Besides, Mammy has come a long way. At least she has quit calling Jessie "thet upty wite nigga" loud enough to make sure Jessie hears. The fact that Jessie provides better meals for Mammy, Dovie, and Lewis than most white folks in Savannah enjoy has gone a long way in mitigating Mammy's ire. I don't know if Frederick realizes Jessie feeds the slaves before he goes to work and before the children and I are out of bed, but I am not going to tell him. After all, Jessie saves the best of everything for the family and is great at haggling for the best prices at market, so I see no reason to insist that the house servants eat leftovers for breakfast. I recognize and admire Jessie's ability to salve wounded egos and bring the best out in people, both servants and employers. Jessie has made my own life much easier, and I have more or less turned over the workings of the kitchen, the purchasing of any supplies we need, and the planning of the meals to Jessie who seems able to do it all effortlessly with time left over.

"Mattie, is that a new dress you are wearing?" I address my raven-haired daughter who sits primly on the wooden bench attired in a pink and white gingham I have not seen before.

"Yes, Mama. Tata Jessie made it for me. I hope it is alright that I wore it today. I just wanted to see what I looked like in it. I promise I won't get it dirty."

"You look quite beautiful in it, Mattie, but you should take it off after breakfast so it will be clean for church on Sunday. You will want to show it off to your friends."

I turn to Jessie who is putting a loaf of bread in the rectangular opening above the fireplace. "Jessie, Frederick did not tell me he had asked you to make the children's clothes. I must say, you are a wonderful seamstress. The detail on that dress is amazing."

"Actually, Madame Barret, Monsieur Barret did not ask me to make the dress. I saw the material in the store after closing last week, and I thought what a nice dress for Mattie it would make, so I purchased just enough. I hope you are not displeased that I took the liberty without asking you or your husband."

"No, not at all, Jessie, but I must reimburse you for the purchase and pay you for your time. You could not have made the dress while at work." I ignore the mumblings from Mammy's direction. "I will talk to Frederick about you making the children's spring clothes if you think you have the time apart from your duties here."

"I made Mattie's dress as a gift—it gave me something to do at home at night. But I would be happy to make the children's clothes if you would like, and yours as well, if my sewing is up to your standards. I am sure I can make them for less than Monsieur Barret is paying your current seamstress."

"You amaze me, Jessie!"

My praise is more than Mammy can quietly tolerate.

"She maze me too, fo sho. Mizz Jessie migh be weabin da house carpits, fo it aw ober," she grumbles.

"I do not think I am capable of weaving carpets yet, Mammy, but I did notice the store has some nice, inexpensive yellow gingham from which I could make you and Dovie dresses for church, if Mrs. Barret thinks it appropriate for summer. Would the yellow gingham be suitable for that, Madame Barret?"

I cannot help but smile at the look of surprise on Mammy's face as she sits there in her undyed homespun, the only material that has been used for the servant's clothing for as long as I can remember. But I have noticed that many of the colored women of wealthier homes are wearing ginghams and patterned dresses on Sunday morning as they sit in the balcony of the Independent Presbyterian Church. Frederick is always eager to appear prosperous to his contemporaries, so I know he will not mind the small extravagance of providing the nicer cloth for the servants' dresses, especially since it is something we carry in the store.

"It would be a great help if you made their dresses. Maybe a homespun each for housework and one each of the gingham. Too, if you could make them matching gingham cloths for their heads, they will not have to wear the everyday ones to church. I am sure it will save time on laundering."

Mammy's mouth is clamped tight, now in amazement instead of disapproval, and I imagine she cannot wait to relay the news to Dovie.

"Thet be fine by me, Mizz Abby." Thrilled as she is, she cannot make herself acknowledge Jessie's role in her largesse. Nonetheless, I hear no more grumbling from her side of the table throughout breakfast.

After breakfast, I stay behind to let Jessie measure me for a new dress. I was not jesting when I said my dresses are too tight. As Jessie pulls the string around my middle, she lets the flat of her hand rest so long there that I look up at her. I am sure my face is pink with embarrassment. "I really have been a glutton. I know I could use a little more flesh, but it all seems to be going to my middle. I am afraid I am going to look quite the matron before I am thirty."

Jessie pulls her hand away and jots her findings in a ledger she keeps for sewing. "No, not at all, Madame Barret. It is to be expected. The waistline is always the first place to show, there and in the bosom."

I look blankly at the older woman. "What is to be expected?" Then it dawns on me what Jessie is saying.

"You think I am with child?" I ask incredulously.

"Do you not?" Jessie calmly meets my eyes.

"No, I have not thought that at all!"

"Why have you not?"

"I...I do not know." I stammer, "but now that you mention it, maybe I should have. I guess I might be expecting." My menses have always been irregular, so I never know when they will show up to inconvenience me.

"You need guess no longer, Mrs. Barret," Jessie laughs. "I am telling you—you are officially expecting a child."

"But how can you know that?"

Jessie hesitates so long I think she is not going to answer. Finally she says, "I have seen enough women in your condition to recognize the signs when I see them. Now, it seems we are going to need to make concessions in the dresses we make for you, and we need to make some alterations quickly in the ones you already have."

"Oh My Goodness, Jessie!" It seems the most natural thing in the world for me to take the older woman's hands in mine as I sink to sit on the bench. "Mr. Barret will be home for lunch soon. Do you think I should tell him?"

Jessie laughs at my excitement. "Yes, I think you had better tell him soon. In fact, I am surprised he has not told you. That bulge in your waistline should have let the cat out of the bag, and your bosom is practically coming out of the top of your dress. Surely you have noticed the changes in your body."

"I noticed, but I thought I was just growing plump. I guess I am a little naive about such things. Mother was wonderful, but there were just some things we did not discuss and probably should have." The thought of Mother makes me jump from the bench. "Oh Jessie, I must write my mother the news! If I hurry, I can give it to Frederick at dinner, and he can post it this afternoon on his way back to work."

I leave Jessie holding the measuring tape in her hand. I will come back to her this afternoon so I will have something decent to wear. Suddenly, the idea of losing my slim waistline does not bother me at all. In fact, I look forward to it.

Chapter 17

Frederick Barret sits at his desk trying to focus on the latest bill of laden, but his mind is on other things. Tonight the Stiles are coming for dinner, and it will be his first chance to show off Jessie's skill as a cook, and he knows word of the fine dining to be had at the Barret home will spread like contagion through the Savannah gossip mill and will go far in making an invitation to their home one to covet. He smiles to himself when he thinks of the meals she has put before them and how superior they have been to even the Telfair's. He was thrilled with the invitation to their home, the second from Telfair in just a few months, and the party they had attended last night lived up to his expectations in all ways except for the food that was served. It had clearly been inferior to that which he eats at home on a daily basis.

For years he has longed for a glimpse of the inside of the Telfair Mansion, and now he has enjoyed the opportunity of examining it not once, but twice, and the reality has exceeded his imagination. No wonder William Jay is the most sought after architect in the South. Like the Scarborough and the Richardson homes Jay built, the Telfair mansion combines the English Regency design with the Classical Revival style that seems to be the trend in Savannah right now. Though Frederick knows several years have passed since Jay built these homes, he hopes the man will be available when he gathers the means to build a home. This is not a pipe dream on his part. Frederick knows in his heart, if Providence allows, he will build a mansion for his family, one to rival the showplace he had visited last night. And he will furnish it just as lavishly.

Frederick pushes the bill of laden away and unlocks the top drawer of the desk. He pulls out a piece of drafting paper on which he has been sketching a blueprint, of sorts, for some time. This is one of his favorite pastimes, one on which he probably spends more time than he should. The plan is done in lead and the paper is beginning to wear in places where he has rubbed out lines as he's adapted and added to it.

Now he incorporates some of the details admired in the Telfair layout and makes notes in the margin in his tiny, neat script before returning it to the drawer and relocking it. He looks forward to the day he will share the design with Abby. He hates that it will be some time before he knows what she thinks of it, especially now that Abby is with child. He longs to tell her that he will be building her the home of her dreams soon, that she need not worry about where the new baby, or several babies to come, will sleep.

It has never occurred to Frederick to ask Abby's opinion on the design of her future home. He thinks of the house as a gift he will be giving her and his family—that it is his role as provider to present to her a home created for her maximum comfort and pleasure. Likewise, it doesn't occur to him that her ideas of comfort and pleasure may differ from his. She is a woman, after all, and what woman wouldn't be thrilled with the home he has in mind?

Were Frederick a different man, he might have built a smaller home that would better accommodate his family until he could afford yet a grander one, but Frederick doesn't think that way. Why would he waste resources that can go toward accomplishing his dream? It has occurred to him that he would probably have already bought a well-situated lot if he had not spent the money to establish the store, but without the store, he would not have made the extra money he has been saving for months. Besides, Frederick knows patience to be a virtue, and he will wait until he has the resources to buy a perfect lot, one that he is confident will present itself as a bargain in good time.

Feeling he has daydreamed long enough, Frederick takes the bill of laden and makes his way downstairs to the warehouse. He prefers the action of the warehouse over the quietude of his office. It is a hub of activity today as it usually is. The loading door is open, and he can see the river and feel the breeze off the water. Several darkies are unloading the latest shipment from the Indies. He feels prosperous as he checks off the coffee, sugar, and miscellaneous imports, and he makes note of what to transfer to the store and what to sell wholesale. The store is thriving. Again he prides himself on the wise move of leasing the building and putting it to such good use. He is a little humbled that his family lives above the store, but his frugality outweighs his pride, and he fully believes they will all someday be able to hold their heads high. Besides, there is no shame in enterprise.

"Mr. Barret."

Frederick is not pleased to be interrupted in his inventory, but he has made it his policy to make friends with possible business associates at all costs and by all means, so when he turns and sees a respectably dressed gentleman standing just inside the door, he offers him his hand.

"To whom do I owe the pleasure?"

"Eugene Robinson." The man has a firm, uncalloused handshake. This is not a manual laborer. "I deal mainly in the procurement and distribution of labor."

"As in slaves, you mean?"

"Yes. I'm from down Louisiana way, and your fellow merchant, a Mr. Habersham, gave me your name."

"He did, did he? I cannot think why he would as I neither need help nor am I interested in getting rid of any right now."

"I am sorry, Mr. Barret. I am afraid I have not been very clear. Labor is my business, but what I've been referred to you about is a matter of transport. I have made several purchases in the area, so it is that I am in need of at least one more mule or horse and a conveyance of a nature that will support four or five heavy niggers and a few supplies. Habersham told me you do some bartering and might be able to help me."

Frederick's interest picks up as he is never averse to making money, especially from unexpected sources. "I cannot help you with the conveyance, but I have in the last week acquired a plow horse in way of trade. She is nothing special to look at, but she is strong. The farmer I bought her from used her on his place, so she is accustomed to pulling a wagon. I will have some of the boys load these supplies I need to take to the store, and if you are of a mind, you can ride along and I will show you the mare."

Mr. Robinson strolls casually around the warehouse as the wagon is loaded. Frederick takes the reigns himself, waits for the pair of darkies to seat themselves on the wagon bed, then invites the visitor to join him on the seat. Though Frederick tries to make conversation with the chap, he is unimpressed with the man's discourse. He may be dressed like a gentleman, but Frederick quickly suspects the man from Louisiana lacks breeding.

As if reading Frederick's mind, Robinson asks, "You don't happen to be related to some Barrets down Bayou Teche way do you?"

Frederick's spine stiffens.

"Yes, actually I am. My father and some cousins live down that way." The man waits expectantly. "My father's name is Auguste. He is getting quite elderly now, so he probably does not get out much."

"Well, it's a small world, now, isn't it? That's just the Barret I was thinking of—lives with his cousin Louis, if I recall correctly. How'd you get up this far when so many of your people live down there?"

"I have never lived in Louisiana."

Robinson waits for more, but Frederick remains silent on the seat beside him.

"A finer man you won't find than Auguste Barret, or Louis, for that matter," Robinson finally offers. "That's quite a spread they've got themselves down there. I need to get by and see them cause word is they're looking to purchase some darkies to help run the place. If I remember right, they're from France. I thought I detected an accent when you first spoke to me. How in the world did you stop off in Savannah instead of settling with your people—they've got enough land down there—you'd be set up for life."

Frederick's suspicions are confirmed. The man lacks breeding. He is inquisitive to the point of rudeness, but Frederick controls the impulse to be equally discourteous.

"I never lived in France. My father and I lived in Saint Domingue before coming to America. We came to the States separately. He came several years before I did."

Robinson opens his mouth to question him further, but Frederick speaks first. "But enough about me. Tell me about yourself. Have you lived your whole life in Louisiana? Are you a land holder as well?"

"I own a little piece of land, but nothing to compare with the Barrets. I keep myself one or two niggers. I switch them out depending on how long it takes me to sell them. All in all, I've built a pretty good living for myself."

"Do you have a family of your own, Mr. Robinson?"

"No need to be so formal, Barret. You can call me Eugene. And no, no family to speak of. I've preferred to keep my options open. A wife ties a man down, and in my line of work, I'm on the road more than I'm at home. Fortunately, I don't lack for female companionship. I've established a home-away-from home or two, if you get my meaning."

In case Robinson's oily laugh is not enough to convey his meaning, he attempts to elbow Frederick in the ribs, but Frederick has positioned himself as far as he can get from the man on the wagon seat. He is more than a little relieved when he pulls up to the hitching post in front of the store. "Here we are, Robinson. Let's go out back to look at that horse while these boys unload the wares."

Robinson does not comment if he notices Frederick does not call him by his first name. He has hit upon a subject the man likes, that of himself, and he barely takes a breath as Frederick leads him through the store. Frederick does not waste any time. He cannot wait to get rid of the obnoxious fellow.

Chapter 18

I hum a French tune from my childhood as I work in what I consider to be my kitchen. The house across town is my home, but this, the Barrets' kitchen behind the store, is more mine than the one I actually own. I spend most of my daylight hours here, and I alone decide what happens within these walls. Abby meant it when she said she trusted me to choose and plan their meals, and though I receive help from Mammy and Dovie occasionally, I am the master of this domain. Though the kitchen would be considered rudimentary by many, and though it is certainly less modern than the Maxwell's in Baltimore, this one pleases me more. I was allowed to set it up to my liking because Abby was in Virginia when Mr. Barret rented the home. He purchased for me what I asked of him, and with the help of Lewis, I arranged everything to my liking. Today, I am especially pleased because tonight will be the first time for the Barrets to have guests in to dine and for me to provide a meal for anyone except the immediate household in Savannah. I know Frederick has bragged of my culinary skills to neighbors and friends, so I plan to make it one to remember. I know this is prideful on my part, but there are two things that have made my life endurable throughout adulthood: my skill in the kitchen and my expertise with a needle.

Though I did not realize it at the time, the years I spent in New Orleans proved to be my salvation. After the revolution in my homeland and the last of my family was gone, I was left with few choices. I sold the few family belongings I had managed to salvage, and with the money from those and the little I had secreted away, I had just enough to pay for passage to the States. I ended up in New Orleans by chance—it was the destination of the first ship out on which I could afford passage. It was on that ship that I met Alain Lablanc, a middle-aged businessman who had unsuccessfully returned to the Island in search of surviving family members. He had come at the first opportunity, but it had been too late. His extended family had met the fate of most whites still on the Island, and, at first I thought his interest in me was our similar backgrounds and common loss. It had not taken me long to be disabused of that notion. Alain had turned out to be like most white men I have met—interested in me for my physical attributes—but, now, I no longer resent him for it. After all, had I not used him as much as he had used me? He had unknowingly provided me with a means of supporting myself.

Alain, in an effort to provide female companionship with which I could fill the hours and days he spent with his wife and children, introduced me to two free women of color, sisters, both of whom had white male benefactors. Unlike me, however, they had means of supporting themselves. I spent every free day I had with Claudette helping her make the dresses and hats for which she was known. On the nights Alain was absent, I was with Francine learning to cook French cuisine. Alain realized too late that both cooking and sewing were more than hobbies for me; they were a route to freedom, or as much freedom as one of my station can attain. Now, as I work peacefully in the Barret kitchen, I bear no hard feelings toward Alain. Why should I, really? I was not forced to align myself with him, and to his credit, he accepted my move to Baltimore with more grace than many men in his position would have. We parted amicably, and now, in many ways, I owe Alain for my new start in Baltimore that eventually led here. I have forgiven Alain for taking a part of me I would have preferred not to give, and for the first year or so in Baltimore, I prayed nightly for God to forgive me for what I had taken from Alan's wife and children. After a year of such prayers, I, in my usual practical way, determined that if God had not forgiven me by then, he was not going to, so I might as well stop berating myself and direct my prayers to more useful purposes.

Turning to the pot hanging from the hook above the open fire, I realize I am letting my mind wander from the tasks at hand. I still have much to do though I arrived before dawn to begin the oyster gumbo I will be serving tonight for the first course. Abby agreed to take the children to the park with Mammy for a picnic dinner I prepared last night so I could have the kitchen free from breakfast on. Frederick ate a hearty breakfast and agreed to meet his family on the green if he thought he could not wait until supper. I smile when I think of how excited Frederick is about the meal we are having tonight. It had been he, not Abby, who had gone over the menu with me, and he had supplied extra sugar, flour, and spices from the store. He had made no changes in the menu, so if I can keep my mind on my work, the courses will be timed perfectly for their early evening supper with the Stiles.

I check the boiling mixture of oysters, chicken, and ham that I bought fresh yesterday from the market. The market's fine specimen of shrimp and oysters made me decide on gumbo as opposed to the turtle soup I had originally planned. As an afterthought, I toss the giblets from the roasted duck that is to be the main course into the stewpot along with the other ingredients since I will not be using them in a gravy. Instead I will be making a sauce from peaches I used in the glaze.

I must remember to add the shrimp to the boiling mixture just long enough to pinken it, and I can hear Francine admonish me not to add the sassafras leaves until about a half an hour before serving the gumbo. I put the leaves on the table in the middle of the room so they will catch my eye if I become distracted while preparing the rest of the meal.

I take inventory of the other dishes I have prepared to go along with the gumbo and duck. The sauce for the duck is in a crock on the windowsill along with a fried apple relish and potted calf's head. The coconut cake I have placed as far away from the fire as possible to preserve its moisture. I will remove the mashed potatoes I have mixed with butter, onions, and parsley from the roasted duck's cavity after we have served the gumbo so they will remain moist and warm, and I will heat the duck sauce before pouring it over the duck.

I am so occupied with my preparations that I am startled when the door from the store opens behind me, and Frederick appears followed by a man I have never seen before. I feel Frederick's companion before I actually see him. So oppressive is the man's aura I feel myself pressed against the worktable by the force of it. The sanctuary of my kitchen is violated, and I am angry at Frederick for bringing him into it. I know immediately that this person is someone to fear, so I will myself to closely take inventory of him. I learned early on that a known threat is one easier dealt with than that which takes you by surprise.

The man who trails Frederick looks normal enough if one can overlook his eyes, but knowing that the eyes are a direct portal to the soul, that is the first place I look when meeting someone for the first time. His are an icy blue, so light that his pupils look like two small black pebbles in a clear stream. Though his lips curve upward, the smile has rarely reached his eyes because there are no crow's feet there though the rest of his face is lined from weather and age.

"Well, Barret, what have you here!" The man's large straight teeth remind me of those of a horse. His yellow hair is greased, neatly parted, and combed back behind each ear. His skin is the type that looks constantly burned by the wind or sun, and the extra flesh that rolls over the top of his buttoned white shirt and the creases in his face indicate he is not a young man. The vest, string tie, and tailored pants should lend him respectability; instead, they cause me a greater sense of foreboding. Dangerous is a poor, evil man, but the threat he can pose is nothing compared to an equally evil man with enough money and influence to cover his foul deeds.

I can tell by the look on Frederick's face that he regrets this man's presence in the kitchen. He tries to make up for his error by commenting on the meal I am preparing.

"It smells wonderful in here, Jessie. I do not know if I can wait until our guests arrive to sample what you have come up with." Seeing the look on my face, Frederick moves to get the visitor from the room as quickly as possible. "Right through here, Robinson. Let us not waste any more time so you and I can both get back to our business."

"Let's forget the horseflesh for now. What would it take to buy this little filly?"

Frederick appears shocked and more than a little irritated. "I told you, Robinson, I do not have any niggers for sale. If you want to look at the mule, come on; if not, you can take yourself elsewhere."

I realize that Frederick has not thought before bringing the man through his house. It is unfortunate that I just happened to lie in the most direct path to the carriage house from the store.

"No need to get all riled up on me, Barret. You should be flattered. In my trade, you rarely see a specimen of such quality as you have yourself in this wholesome nigger gal. She may be the highest yella I've ever laid eyes on. It wouldn't take much to pass her for white, if one had a mind to."

The man seems impervious to Frederick's blackening mood or to my attempted disdain. "I'd be willing to give you a price with which you could replace her with two or three. In fact, I've got some back at the hotel stable that I'd let you look at. Maybe we could work out a trade."

"Mr. Robinson, I can only assume you did not hear me when I told you that I had no slaves for sale. Now, you may follow me to the stables or you may return to Louisiana without looking at the mare. Either choice is fine with me."

Robinson finally drags his eyes away from me and focuses on Frederick whose frown can no longer be ignored. "Pardon me, Mr. Barret, I have no wish to offend. I had no idea you were opposed to trafficking in slaves. Your reputation around town misled me."

"Sir, I assure you, I am as willing as the next person to buy or sell a slave occasionally. What I find offensive is your persistence. Now, do you care to follow me to the stables, or would you rather be on your way?"

"By all means, Sir," the man stresses the title, "let's get back to the purpose at hand."

In an effort meant to diminish the tension, Frederick directly addresses me, "Tell Mrs. Barrett I will be back in about an hour. I look forward to tasting what you have prepared."

"Yes, Mr. Barret," I answer, though both of us know I'll do no such thing. Mr. Barret returns home every day at that time.

Frederick jerks the door open with more force than is necessary and escapes into the back yard, leaving me alone with his companion who takes his time as he saunters through the room never taking his eyes off me. I will myself to stand erect, my eyes cold, my nostrils flared. He stops at the back door. I feel my heart stop with him.

"I like a filly with some spit and vinegar, Missy. It makes them that much more fun to break."

He closes the door softly behind him. I slump against the counter, instantly feeling the bile rise in my throat. I heave my breakfast into the dishwater, the contentment I felt moments before forgotten.

Chapter 19

I could not be prouder of the meal if I had cooked it myself. And one might think Dovie herself the chef by the way she, ramrod straight and dignified in her perfectly ironed and starched yellow gingham, bears each course of the meal into our small dining room and places it before our guests as if she is serving royalty instead of Clarence and Bette Stiles, Frederick's longtime friends and business associates. I want to giggle but settle for a smile at the change in Dovie. Dovie is wonderful with the children, but she certainly is not above cutting corners and getting by with as little as possible when it comes to her household duties. Maybe it is the new clothes that make the difference, or maybe it is the fact that the house slaves have a hierarchy among themselves in the community, and no way will Dovie want it to get back to the other darkies she goes to church with that she belongs to a classless owner. I am sure she would especially like for her sister Minda to hear word of how good she looked and what a fine meal she served. Whatever the reason, Dovie is certainly impressive, and she hasn't learned her serving skills from me. I've been completely remiss in teaching the staff. I doubt, too, that Dovie learned her manners from Luella before me because Luella grew up in the same household I did, one in which cleanliness and good manners were mandatory, but the meals were fairly simple offerings comprised of home-grown vegetables and meats harvested from our own livestock or local wild game. When entertaining company at Hickory Grove, the darkies hovered outside the room and awaited summoning by our mother. Dovie now quietly retires to the sideboard and watches until the last person lifts a utensil, then she whisks forth and removes the dishes without comment. She actually brushes crumbs from the white tablecloth before reappearing with the next offering. I have Jessie to thank for the success of this meal, not just the food, but the presentation of it. I can tell the Stiles are duly impressed, and Frederick is beaming. The first entertainment in our home is all he hoped it would be, and I am surprised at how much I am enjoying myself.

Bette Stiles is a petite, pretty woman, dressed tonight in a pale blue dress that flatters her rather plump figure and sets off her best asset, her dark blue, expressive eyes. They are kind, intelligent eyes, and I warmed to her the first time I met her. Clarence Stiles is as tall and thin as Bette is short and round. Though I don't think him a handsome man, certainly not as handsome as Frederick, he has a pleasant enough disposition. Tonight Clarence appears relaxed and at ease in our company, but I have empathized with him in larger groups. There, his laughter appears forced, his gestures and body language revealing a nervousness to which I can certainly relate. I was pleased that Frederick chose them as our first guests, and I know he probably did so because he knows I am comfortable with Bette and unlikely to be intimidated by making conversation with her alone. We have met with the Stiles on several occasions with other people, and they attend the Independent Presbyterian Church with us every Sunday. Now, as Dovie clears away the dessert plates, Frederick catches my eye, and I nod to let him know it is fine for him to proceed.

"My Dear Ladies," Frederick pushes back from the table, takes my hand, and addresses Bette and me, "if you will excuse the two of us, we will find a place to smoke a good cigar and discuss business matters with which we dare not bore you."

"By all means, " I smile. I am pleased to be able to mean what I say. Dovie quietly reappears at her post beside the sideboard. "Dovie, please make sure the men have what they need in the parlor."

"That will not be necessary, Dear," Frederick assures me. "I think Clarence and I can pour ourselves a drink or two on our own. Dovie, why don't you bring the ladies a sherry or another glass of wine to drink?"

"That wine you served with dinner was delicious. I think I will have another glass if it is not too great an inconvenience."

"Not at all." Frederick turns to summon Dovie, but she is already approaching the table with the bottle. Dovie pours Bette a glass and turns to pour one for me, but I decline by shaking my head and placing my hand on my protruding stomach. The baby is already moving about restlessly, and I do not think it wise to indulge in any more food or drink if I hope to get any sleep tonight. Dovie manages not to show her disappointment when I excuse her for the evening to help Jessie clean up in the kitchen.

Alone, Bette and I settle ourselves in the two armchairs that flank the fireplace. The weather this evening is pleasant, and though we can still hear the noise of Broughton through the open window, the cool breeze it provides more than makes up for the distraction.

"Abby, now that we are alone, you must tell me all about this cook of yours. Where in the world did you find a darkie who can cook like that? That soup was unlike anything I have ever eaten, and that cake was as light as a feather. I swear, if I had that kind of food in the house daily, I could not find a corset in Savannah strong enough to get me into a dress I own!"

I laugh. One of the things I like about Bette is her earthiness, a trait I have battled all my life. I am surprised to find myself sharing the sentiment with my new friend. "Bette, I so enjoy your company. I love your unaffected ways."

"Yes, unfortunately, my forthrightness is not my best quality in my husband's eyes. In case you have not noticed, he is a bit nervous by nature, and he often wishes I were a bit more discreet. But then, Clarence cares more about what others think than I do. I think that probably has something to do with him feeling like he has something to prove because he was not born with a silver spoon in his mouth, whereas I have enough blue blood in my veins for both of us. Sometimes I fear my provenance is what attracted him to me."

I realize too late that my face has clearly revealed my surprise.

"Now I have shocked you. I am sorry, Abby, but I get so tired of putting forth my best foot. I love Savannah. I might as well—I have lived here all my life, and I cannot imagine us ever living anywhere else, but Savannah society can be so stifling. It is all about who you are and what you have, do you not agree?"

"Truthfully, I do not yet know enough about Savannah society to answer that question. However, I can certainly say that I sometimes tire of feeling like I have to watch what I say or do for fear of being judged inadequate."

"Exactly," Bette stands, pulls her chair close, and clasps me by the hand. Her blue eyes sparkle with mischief. "Let us make a pact right now! The two of us are free to be ourselves when in each other's company, if nowhere else. Agreed?"

"Agreed!" I grip both of Bette's hands in my own. "You do not know how happy it makes me to find a friend here. I am glad to know Luella had such a friend, too, when she was so far from home."

Bette's face loses a little of its animation, and as usual, her expressive eyes reveal her feelings. "Abby, if we are to be friends, good friends, you must know now that I am terrible at dissembling, so if I do it, I reserve the effort for situations in which I have to. I sense in you a kindred spirit, so I am asking that the two of us be totally honest with each other. May we?"

"Of course, Bette, I would like nothing better." I feel my pulse quicken with dread of what she is about to tell me.

"If I am to be honest with you, I must admit I found your sister to be a lovely and gracious woman, but I cannot claim to really have been Luella's friend, and certainly not a close one. Please do not misunderstand; she was a wonderful person, I am sure. I just never felt a true connection with Luella. Pardon me for saying this, but she always seemed to be right at home in the company of the good ladies of Savannah, a place where I am most often uncomfortable."

I laugh again, but this time in relief. "You do not have to explain that to me. I assumed you and Luella were friends because I knew you socialized with each other, but I agree—Luella never found a social gathering she did not enjoy, and she and I are very different people."

"I am glad you are different, and I think it is in a good way. Of course that is because I am different, and the two of us may be the only ladies in Savannah who think we have the right of it."

"That is fine by me, but I must admit I find it odd you feel as I do when you are native to the city. One would think that you, of all people, with your connections and your heritage would feel right at home here."

"I do not think it is that I feel an outsider," Bette tries to explain. "Instead I think the way I feel is because I am an insider. I have had years to observe the workings of good, old Savannah society. I am an only child, Abby, and from the time I was old enough to know anything, I knew what was expected of me and my kind. I would grow up, marry someone of good standing, give birth to offspring who would carry on the good name and look out for the family's interests, financial and social." Bette's eyes grow wistful as they meet mine. "In marrying Clarence, I thought I was being a little bit of a rebel. Not too rebellious, you understand. Not rebellious enough to get me and my family shunned. Clarence was by no means a catch, though he was respectable enough. I thought by marrying him I could remove myself from the pretense, but instead, it has proved to be quite the opposite. Because Clarence thinks himself of inferior birth, he believes we have to try that much harder to fit in. Apparently money is not enough. He feels he has to earn, in some way, what I was born to."

When Bette sees the wide-eyed look on my face, it is her turn to laugh. "I see I have shocked you again, Abby. I must remember to break you in a little more slowly."

"No, you can always be honest with me, Bette. And I will be with you. But I must say, you are not at all what I expected! In fact, I do not know if I have ever met anyone as open as you. It may take me a while to adjust, but I assure you, I welcome the challenge."

"Good, now that we have established the ground rules, we can talk of something more interesting. Back to your cook. You are going to share some of her receipts with me, are you not, the first one being that coconut cake we had for dinner?"

"If I did not know better, Bette," I laugh, "I would think you were just trying to befriend me in order to get Jessie's secrets. But I am going to have to disappoint you. I do not have access to Jessie's culinary receipts. In fact, I do not even tell her what to cook. However, if you let that be known, I will declare you the worst kind of dissembler."

Bette laughs too, but I can tell she does not believe me. "You sly girl, Abby. Do you mean to tell me you own a slave who will not tell you how she prepares her dishes? Or where she got them to begin with?"

"That is where you are mistaken, Dear Bette. We do not own Jessie. Jessie is a free woman."

"So she is not a darkie?"

"Well, it depends on what you call a darkie. If you look closely, you can tell she is a mulatto, but she is certainly unlike any darkie I have ever known. She is so cultured she makes me feel inadequate at times."

"A free darkie! I have heard of them in town, but I cannot say as I have had much to do with one. Of course I have run across lots of mulattos. They usually are the results of the master putting his pecker where it does not belong."

I cannot help myself—I gasp aloud. Bette laughs so loudly, she brings the men from the parlor across the hall.

"We have decided that it sounds like you ladies are having a better time over here than we are, so we have come to find out what is so entertaining." Frederick's statement sounds like a question.

Now that I know what I do about Clarence, I can detect unease in the look he gives his wife. I hasten to set his mind at ease, already feeling protective of my new friend even though she is older and much more self-assured than I.

"We are just sharing the travails of running a household," I tell the men. "It turns out that Bette and I have so much in common we have realized we are going to be fast friends."

The men seem pleased with our declaration. Bette and I smile at each other. They are both probably thinking the same thing: *I am relieved that my misfit of a wife has found a friend at last!*

Bette rises to leave. After thanking us for the wonderful dinner and praising the cook to high heaven, Bette turns to me. "We really must be getting home, but be assured, Abby, we will continue our conversation later. Shall we meet on the green tomorrow at about one? We can bring the children."

"I look forward to it, Bette." I am delighted to discover she means what she says about wanting to be my friend.

When the doors close behind the Stiles, Frederick takes me in his arms and dances me into the parlor. "What did I tell you, Abby! If Bette Stiles is impressed with our dinners, you can only imagine what the rest of Savannah will think of them! She has traveled about Europe—she has eaten at the Governor's mansion, for Christ's sake, and she could not think of high enough praise for our simple fare!"

"Frederick, do not use the Lord's name in vain!" The admonishment comes out of my mouth before I can clamp my lips around it. He immediately looks contrite, and to make up for being a wet blanket, I plant a kiss on his cheek. "Forgive me, Dear; it appears I am becoming my mother."

"Not hardly, Darling," and my always correct Frederick catches himself to add, "but in this case I deserved your censure. If not for the Good Lord's favor, we would not have prospered as we have."

Maybe it is coming so closely on the heels of the irreverent Bette, but Frederick's words ring insincere, and it brings to mind Bette's observations about her own husband.

"What do you think of Clarence, Frederick?"

"Why, that is a rather odd thing to ask, Abby. Of course I like the chap. He and Bette have been wonderful friends. In fact, they befriended Luella and me when the rest of Savannah did not yet know we existed. I have always admired the way Clarence puts his best foot forward and seems to know what it takes to get ahead in the world." He pulls me up from the chair I have taken and puts his arms around my swollen waistline. "On the other hand, Bette would try the patience of Job. And thank you, Dear, for making a real effort with her. Luella used to have to bite her tongue, and I know Clarence worries sometimes that people find his wife a little odd. Of course, if anyone can get by with it, it's Elizabeth Bullock Stiles!"

I pull away from him. "What do you mean, odd?"

Frederick smoothes the lines from between my brows with his fingertip.

"Maybe odd is too strong a word. Maybe unconventional would better describe Bette."

"I like Bette!" I exclaim, completely removing myself from my husband's arms. "So she is not exactly like every other woman in Savannah. I, for one, am glad. Luella could have stood to be a little more like Bette in some ways!"

Frederick is surprised by my vehemence and more than a little disconcerted. "My Dear, it is not my intention to disparage the dear woman, and I think it is wonderful the two of you are becoming friends. But I feel, too, that it is necessary for me to warn you not to emulate her behavior. After all, you are a newcomer, and I am just now beginning to pull ahead, so what may be tolerable in someone of Bette's lineage could be social suicide for those like us."

I cannot believe what I am hearing. I turn on Frederick.

"I assure you, Husband, there is nothing wrong with my lineage! I will match my family tree to anyone's in Savannah, even to that of Elizabeth Bullock Stiles! But I am quite sure Bette is not nearly as concerned with her lineage as you are, or as her own husband is, for that matter. Let us not end a wonderful evening on a sour note. I am going to thank Jessie and Dovie, and then I am going to bed. Please do not feel like you need to rush to join me."

I pick up my skirts and leave the room as regally as my girth will allow. It pleases me to think that if I could look back without ruining my exit, I would find my husband's eyebrows raised and his mouth agape.

Chapter 20

For the first time since coming to Savannah, I am nervous walking the dark streets alone. That Robinson man has unnerved me. I keep looking back over my shoulder, and I hate it when the lighted streets run out and I am forced to make my way through the dark with only the dim lights coming from the windows of the shacks of Yamacraw. My anxiety turns to anger. I am angry that men like Robinson exist, and I am angry at myself for letting him frighten me. I have let him rob me of the happiness of preparing the first formal meal for the Barrets. I worked hard on that meal, and it was a great success. Both Abby and Frederick came to the kitchen to tell me so. Abby also told Dovie how impressed she was with the way she had tended the table. Mammy and Lewis will surely get an earful about the grand dinner Dovie presided over tonight.

Preparing the meal had taken all of my focus, and afterward, I had cleaned like a dervish to keep my mind off the awful man who had violated the sanctity of my kitchen. Now, his vile essence overwhelms me once again, and I reach beneath the collar of my dress and withdraw the knife I keep in the cleft between my breasts. I actually unsheathe the blade and clutch the short handle in my right hand. My long legs make the trip across town faster than I have ever made it before, but it still seems to take an eternity. When I reach the safety of my house, I look left and right before turning toward the stoop. I pray the man has not followed me for I know nothing good can come of him knowing where I live. I slide the blade back into its leathering before opening the door and am glad I have done so when I find Moses sitting at the table waiting for me. He looks as glad to see me as I am to see him.

Moses rises when I enter, and I am, as always, surprised anew at how large he is. His size comforts me when I go into his arms. He senses my tension and pushes me away to look into my face.

"Hey, Woman, you awrigh?"

"Not really," I admit. I do not intend to tell him about my experience with the hideous man, but I find myself relating the whole episode. Moses does not interrupt, and when my story is told, I realize we are both seated on the bench though I do not remember sitting. I even tell him how weak I feel for being scared all the way home.

"Soun lack you hab cause ta worry," Moses' usually smooth forehead is creased. "Youse da mos level haid bidy I know, so if you tink day a problem, day a problem."

I feel the tension leave my shoulders. No wonder I love Moses Tucker. He is an unusual man. He actually listens to me, and after hearing what I have to say, he does not feel the need to downplay my fears.

"Thank you, Moses." I lean into him and close my eyes.

"Fo wat, Jessie? I ain done nuttin to hep, tho da good Lawd know I wanna. How bou I come wawk home wid you from now on, or lease fo a wile?"

"You are a sweetheart, Moses, but that will not be necessary. I am just spooked. It was all so recent. I am sure I will feel differently tomorrow night."

"Da way you know tings, Jessie, I tink we bes be on gaud in case da cracka ain lef town."

"Let us see how I feel in the morning, Moses. We do not want to let some scoundrel control us or change the way we live our lives."

"No, dass fo sho, bu needer da we wanna be stupit. I lack ta break da cracka wid my own bare hans!"

The ferocious look on Moses face is so uncharacteristic of him I cannot help but laugh. Once I start laughing, I cannot stop. Moses, unoffended, takes me into his arms again, and he does not comment when the laughter turns to tears. He pulls me to the bed and sits with me on the side of it, his huge muscled arms gently draped around my heaving shoulders. "Ebberting goan be awrigh." He holds me until I am at last cried out, then lies beside me, gently caressing my shoulders until I am calm. I stroke his powerful body in return. He makes love to me gently, as if I am fragile. With Moses, I feel cherished in a way I have never felt before. It is all I can do to keep the tears from flowing again, but I know it will upset Moses if I give in to the urge.

Moses has complained that I am not a snuggler, and it is true. I assume it is because I have slept so rarely with another person. It is my usual and natural inclination to seek my own space, not an easy feat with someone as large as Moses in a bed as small as mine, but tonight is different. I cling to him long after he is asleep, but not even Moses Tucker can make me feel safe. Every iota of soul-deep goodness that emanates from his massive frame cannot dispel the sheer evil of the yellow-haired slave trader. Never, not even on the war-ravaged island of Saint Domingue, have I been in the presence of someone who conveyed such malice.

Chapter 21

It takes until noon before my mood returns to normal. I purposely took my time preparing for bed last night. It was childish of me, but I liked knowing that Frederick was waiting downstairs for Dovie to leave me, so I kept her longer than usual. After she helped me undress and placed my clothes in the wardrobe, I asked her to remove my hairpins and brush out my hair. Dovie had to be surprised because I have not asked her to do so since coming to Savannah. These are tasks Frederick usually likes to do. We then talked for a good thirty minutes while I left Frederick cooling his heels downstairs. Unable to think of any way to delay bedtime without creating gossip among the servants, I bade Dovie goodnight and crawled into bed.

Frederick had not spoken as he undressed, but he curled up around me the minute he crawled beneath the sheet. I kept my breathing even and pretended I was asleep when he whispered, "Abby, are you awake?" He sighed loudly when I did not respond. At last he turned away and before long I heard his own even breathing.

I still cannot pinpoint why I was so angry with him. This morning I did not have to fake being asleep, and I was grateful he had not awakened me before he left for the office.

Now I am feeling a little silly about being so petulant, but I will not dwell on it. I need to prepare to meet Bette in the park, so I call Dovie to help me dress. I take extra care to look the best I can under the circumstances. I now have two dresses I can wear around the house and two presentable enough for public. The two housedresses are a pair I owned back when I was tiny, though one would be hard pressed to recognize the garments or the body as those that came before the pregnancy. Jessie had first let out the seams as far as the material allowed, and recently, she had creatively inserted a strip of coordinating material down each side to accommodate my growing middle. If the baby doesn't come soon, we will have to start from scratch as we did with the two dresses I wear in public. Dovie helps me don the dress I did not wear last night, and then she helps me put on my shoes and lace them up as I can no longer reach my feet.

"Laws, Mizz Abby, you goan pop if dat babe doan come soon. An youse goan haf ta hab bigga shoes, too, cause dese gapin open at da top wid yo lags all swole up lack punkins. Yo migh wanna stay in and pu dem up fo a wile."

I am tempted to take Dovie's advice, but it will be more trouble to cancel than to go ahead with our plans. Besides, I feel better if I can get out for a while each day, and I am looking forward to walking on the green. Last night had been the first time in two months that Frederick and I had actually socialized, and though I had had doubts about the appropriateness of entertaining so far into my confinement, I had thoroughly enjoyed the evening. Clarence had tactfully never let his eyes drop below my face. Between his good manners and the cape-like outer garment Jessie had sewn for the occasion, I had not felt uncomfortable with the situation at all. Besides, it is not like he is unfamiliar with what having babies does to a woman's physique. His own wife has had three, and bless her heart, Bette has not lost much of the weight she gained with her youngest Eliza, though the child is now three years old.

Dovie leaves to help Mammy round up the children, and I squeeze into my favorite spot in the armchair by the window, but today I am not interested in what is going on in the street below. Instead, I run my hands over my swollen stomach. I almost tear up with tenderness for our unborn child. I really do not mind the inconvenience of the weight gain and the discomfort as long as the baby arrives healthy. I know the risk that comes with having a child, but I am not afraid. In fact, I find the changes in my body fascinating. The movement of the baby brings to mind a memory from my childhood.

I was seven or eight years old, and Minda and Dovie were sent to a pasture some distance from the house to round up a cow that had not shown up for the evening milking. Luella and I, for nothing better to do, had tagged along even though Mother had told us to go no farther than the field that lies along the back of the pasture behind the outbuildings. The two slave girls got in no hurry to complete the task, and looking back, I can certainly understand why. Who wouldn't rather be running barefoot through the sage grass and playing in a creek as opposed to feeling manure ooze between their toes while sweeping out the chicken houses or gathering eggs?

Unlike Minda and Dovie, Luella and I wore shoes, and we saw this as a disadvantage when we came to the creek—the creek that runs along the back of the front pasture, the same one that Mother had told us time and time again to stay away from. The day was a hot summer one, and the two young darkies shed their thin cotton dresses and were sitting waist deep in the water splashing it up around their thin chests, over their arms, and into their faces before Luella and I could even get our shoes off. We had to be satisfied with lifting our dresses and our summer underskirts and wading in the shallows of the cold water. We knew we would never be able to undress and redress without getting dirty or wet.

Luella and I did not get to enjoy the water nearly long enough before Minda and Dovie pulled their shifts back over their heads, not at all concerned that the material stuck to their wet bodies and rode up around their backsides. By the time we got our shoes back on and caught up with them, they had found the errant cow lying on her side beneath the shade of a big oak tree. The prone cow made for an odd sight. I could not remember ever seeing one lying on her side this way. The cow was breathing heavily, her massive stomach forced to one side, the white hide stretched tight spreading the black patches into patterns that looked like the continents on Uncle William's globe. When we got closer to the cow, she turned her head to look at us, and she mooed the most mournful sound I had ever heard. There was saliva dripping from the corners of her pink mouth.

"What's wrong with her?" Luella demanded, and I was glad I had not been the one to ask when Minda, the oldest of the group, turned on Luella.

"Doan you know nuttin? Dat cow, she habin a caf! She birffin, jus like us goan haf ta do someday!"

Even Luella was at a loss for words, and it was rare that she would let Minda talk to her that way, but she had been just as shocked at the discovery as I was. The four of us stood around the laboring cow for some time before Minda decided we had better get home and tell someone. We left, but not before I noticed the movement of the calf beneath the skin of the mother cow's stomach. The massive mound undulated from one end to the other with the movement broken up by the appearance of a knob here or there as the calf tried to position itself for its journey into the world. I placed my hand on one of the protrusions. Luella grabbed my other hand and jerked me away.

"Do you want to get yourself killed?"

I knew Luella was still smarting from being talked down to by Minda and was trying to reassert her authority in the group. I trailed along beside my sister, marveling at the way the baby calf had felt moving beneath my hand. Now, over fifteen years later, I smile at the memory. I feel weepy, weepier even than I have for the last couple of months. I miss the days of our youth. Most of all, I miss Luella and the simplicity of life on the plantation. I even miss my childhood playmates, Dovie and Minda. I am glad I still have Dovie, and I am reminded that I have been meaning to go see Minda at Bette's. I will ask her about it today when we meet in the park.

I grab a parasol and make my way downstairs as quickly as my cumbersome body allows. Mattie is waiting patiently on a bench by the table while Robart can be heard terrorizing the cat that showed up at our back door not long after we moved into the house. Fredie tags along behind Jessie as she moves about the kitchen with her usual grace and efficiency. Dovie appears to be dozing with her head on the table while Mammy gathers the basket we are to take to the park. Usually Dovie's slacking would irritate me, but my childhood memory is still fresh in my mind, and I feel a tenderness for my old playmate. Being an expectant mother must be making me soft because I do not scold Dovie. I place my hand on her shoulder, and when she jumps straight up as if she has been caught stealing the house silver, I laugh aloud.

"Let's go, Everyone. Bette will wonder what has happened to us."

The walk to Johnson Square is a short one, but by the time our small army approaches Bette sitting among her brood, I am exhausted, and my inner groin muscles feel like they are ripping free from the bones. Bette jumps up to help lower me onto the bench beside her, and I am grateful for the help.

"Are you sure you should be out today, Abby? You look like your time could come any minute." Bette's pretty plump face is lined with concern.

"I am fine, Bette, other than I feel like a beached whale. I'd love to lie on that pallet with your children, but I am afraid we would have to summon the Georgia Hussars to help get me up once I got down there."

By the time Mammy pours us both a lemonade and Dovie has put a folded shawl between my back and the tree and placed both my feet on the upended picnic basket, I feel quite comfortable. "And now I look like that beached whale! But I am a pampered beached whale, thanks to the three of you. One would think a woman never had a baby in this household."

It is a beautiful day even though it is early August. The summer has not been as hot as most, and the day is fall-like. Bette and I fall quickly back into the easy camaraderie of last night, and the children pair up and soon forgot we adults exist. Eight-year-old Mattie and Bette's nine-year-old Thomas are braiding the fronds of palmetto into swords with which Thomas is determined they will dual. Bette and I laugh at what a poor combatant Mattie makes with her gentle spirit and affable disposition. I observe that six-year-old Robart would make a more worthy opponent, but true to his nature, he is happier trying to talk Bette's five-year-old Reggie into taking one of his own inferior marbles for Reggie's best cat eye. I am relieved to see that Reggie is not having any part of that transaction—I would hate to have to give up my comfortable position to intervene. Only Eliza and Fredie play quietly on the pallet. I notice Dovie has chosen the more relaxing task of overseeing the two little ones while her mother keeps sentinel over the other four. I do not worry about that either for I know Mammy well enough to know she will set Dovie straight when she has had enough of it. Looking around, I realize for the first time that Bette has brought no servant with her.

"Bette, are you here by yourself? Do not tell me you have come unescorted with these three children to attend to all by yourself!"

Bette does not seem to hear me. Instead, she is focused on the children in their different pursuits.

"Do you ever wonder what it is like to be them?" Bette asks.

"Are you so old, Bette, that you have forgotten what it is like to be a child? I was just remembering today what it felt like to be young and free and living on the plantation. Unfortunately, it was a birthing cow that brought the memory back."

Bette laughs easily, and I think again how much I like this woman and how at ease she makes me feel.

"Not the children, you silly thing, the darkies! Do you ever wonder what it is like to be a slave?"

I turn to look at her. The question from anyone else would have surprised me, but I am quickly getting used to Bette's unorthodox way of thinking.

"Yes, I have. Oddly enough, that was part of my childhood reminiscing earlier today. I was thinking how lucky Minda and Dovie used to be because they got to run around barefoot in the summer and swim naked in the creek while we had to be booted up, buttoned up, and kept like hothouse flowers most of the time!"

"Thank God there is some advantage to being a Negro! I think it would be the most dreadful thing! It is bad enough to be a woman in the South. Can you imagine what it would be like to be black?"

Bette's vehemence surprises me. "Do you really think about it all that much, Bette? It is just the way things are. That is all they know, and on the good side, they never have to worry about much of anything. They are completely taken care of. They get to remain childlike all their lives."

I turn to find Bette looking intently at me. I smile but Bette doesn't smile in return. "Much like us, Abby, don't you think?"

I feel my face reddening. "What do you mean by us, Bette?"

"Us—women. We are pretty much taken care of all our lives, told what to do and how to do it."

"And that is a bad thing, to be taken care of?"

Bette drops her gaze and lowers her voice.

"Pay me no mind, Abby. I am in one of my moods. Of course I like being taken care of, but I do not care much for being told what to do. But I was not talking about us. I was talking about the darkies. Have you really thought about what it would be like to be one of them? They are owned, for heaven's sake! We do not have a lot of power as women, but we are not completely owned like they are."

"Bette, have you been reading some of those northern tracts or newspaper articles? You sound like an abolitionist! What would Clarence say?" I do not like the reproachful tone of my voice, but I cannot help myself.

"You have not known Clarence very long, but I am sure you know what he would say. But, Abby—and I do not mean to shock you—most of the time I do not care what Clarence would say."

I am uncomfortable. Maybe Frederick is right. Maybe Bette is not going to make the best of companions.

"Bette, what are you thinking?" I am glad that Dovie has roused herself to follow Eliza and Fredie as they toddle around the green. "Surely you know what the Bible has to say about slavery. We are to accept our lot in life, and that is their lot. It is our role to look after the more simple-minded, just as it is our husbands' roles to look after us. What would happen to the darkies without someone to look after them? They would be ill equipped to fend for themselves. Surely you know that."

Bette sits quietly for a moment. "Abby, you do realize that there are many places in the world where blacks are free, and they take care of themselves and their families just fine without having a white person telling them what to do every minute? And tell me, this Jessie who cooked that wonderful meal last night, is she simple-minded? Does she need one of us to look after her?"

Though Bette's tone is gentle, I feel as though I am being reproved. "You know that is different, Bette. She is more white than she is black!"

"And at what point, Abby, does the whiteness supersede the blackness? How white must one be to fend for oneself? Jessie might as well be as black as Mammy or Dovie in the eyes of us noble, white Southerners. She would be owned just like they are if it were not for the fact she was free before she got here. Have you ever thought of that?"

I do not answer. I do not have an answer, and I know it is because I have not allowed myself to think deeply about slavery. I am aware there are people, mainly Northerners, who think we're barbaric for the practice, but it is all I have known, and everyone I care about staunchly supports maintaining our way of life. Why lose sleep worrying about matters beyond our control? I say as much to Bette.

"I do not think it will always be this way, Abby. I think some day, probably long after you and I are dead, things will be different, at least I hope so. If I had my way, I would free every slave we have. Can you imagine the reaction that would cause?" Bette smiles to herself at the thought, but the smile disappears when she sees the concern on my face. "And how do we even know who has black blood and who does not? If you found out some white person you cared about had black blood in his ancestry, would you feel differently?"

"I do not honestly know, Bette. But I do know you must be careful to whom you say these things. Your family has been a part of Savannah society forever, but there are limits to what even you can get by with. Promise me you will not talk this way with anyone else."

I have not known Bette long, but I already care about her, and I do not want her to get hurt. Too, I know if Frederick hears her talk this way, he will forbid me to associate with her.

Bette places her hand on mine. "I am upsetting you, and I certainly should not be, especially in your condition. Of course, I will not talk like this to anyone else. That is why I am so glad I have met you. I get so tired of keeping my thoughts to myself. Just think about what I have said. There are many people elsewhere who feel the way I do, even in our own country—possibly right here in Savannah, though they dare not admit it."

I am relieved when Dovie and our youngest children return to the pallet so the topic has to be changed.

"I told you earlier that I was thinking about Luella and me growing up in Virginia. You do realize that your Minda and our Dovie are sisters, don't you? Mammy is their mother. They were all part of Luella's dowry."

"My Minda? What do you mean by my Minda?" Bette is clearly confused.

"You do still own Minda, do you not? It was my understanding that you and Clarence bought Minda from Luella and Frederick several years ago."

"Oh, *Minda!* I remember now. No, we rented Minda's services for a short time, but we never outright bought her. To tell you the truth, I do not know who owns Minda. I just assumed Frederick still did. I used to see her occasionally in the balcony at church, but I cannot recall the last time I saw her. Wherever she is, I hope she has a good situation. She was a good girl and a blessing at the time. She helped me with Thomas and Reggie before Eliza was born."

Now it is my turn to be confused. "Dovie?" I call. "Where is Minda living now, and who does she belong to?"

Dovie apparently does not hear me the first time, and I have to repeat myself.

"Minda libbin ober in Yamcraw wid er chilrun."

I am really surprised by this information, but more surprised by the closed look on Dovie's face. Yamacraw. I have heard that name before. "Yamacraw? Is that where Jessie lives? I thought that was where poor whites and free coloreds live." I start to ask Dovie who owns her sister, but an unpleasant thought dawns on me. I turn to look at Bette, and Bette's face looks as perplexed as I feel.

Oh no! What have I done! I realize I may have made a horrible blunder! I have heard of arrangements in which the owner keeps a Negro woman as a mistress and the wife knows nothing about it. What if that is the case with Minda and poor Bette thinks they have gotten rid of her? I sneak a sideways look at Bette and she has a look of consternation on her face. I feel myself go pale. Frederick will be furious with me if I have let the cat out of the bag! But it is not my fault if Clarence is a horrible husband and a despicable man! No wonder poor Bette wants to free all her slaves! But then again, apparently Bette knows nothing of the arrangement. I feel so sorry for my friend, tears well in my eyes. I resolve to talk to my husband about this situation at the first opportunity, and heaven help him if he knows of the travesty and has not made his feelings known to Mr. Clarence Stiles!

Chapter 22

Abby does not get the opportunity to speak with Frederick about her suspicions that afternoon, and it will be months before the conversation comes back to her because she is about to give birth to a daughter. When she stands to leave the park, she thinks she is wetting herself, an occurrence that does not surprise her since she has heard this happens due to the pressure the baby applies to the bladder, but she soon realizes this is not the case. The clear liquid puddles in the top of her lace-up boots before building to a stream that evolves into a pale pink lake beneath her feet. Bette immediately realizes what is happening, and instructs Dovie to take all six children to her house. She and Mammy each take an arm and walk Abby home as quickly as they can coax her into going.

"But I am not in any pain," Abby manages to tell them, though at the pace they are walking, she has little breath to speak.

"You do not have to be in pain for your water to break, but I guarantee you, it will not be long now."

Abby is soon miserable, but not from labor pains. The flow has soaked her petticoats through, and though the day is pleasant, the clinging material soon leaves her chilled and chaffing. It is with relief that she finally enters the house through the kitchen. Bette quickly apprises Jessie of the situation, and the three women have Abby stripped, bathed, and in her own bed in no time.

Abby is afraid, but she does not say so. She knows she could not be in better hands. They decide not to send for the doctor because Mammy has delivered several babies, and if everything goes well, there will really be no need for one. Abby lies there waiting for the contractions to start while Mammy hurries around preparing for the delivery. Abby is calmed by the almost festive mood both Jessie and Bette are in. If they are unconcerned, then surely she has nothing to worry about.

"You are going to be just fine, Abby, and you are going to have a beautiful, healthy baby, so you just lie there and rest while you can." Jessie sits on the side of the bed and holds Abby's hand. She would love to tell her that the baby is going to be a girl, but she doesn't dare. Though she knows who Bette has to be, she has never met her and she certainly isn't going to let it be told around town that the Barrets have a witch working for them. She satisfies the urge by adding, "The way you are carrying, I think you are going to have a girl."

Bette, seated on the other side of the bed, is having a hard time focusing on Abby. She can hardly take her eyes off Jessie. So this is the mulatto cook! The woman is striking to say the least. Bette sees what Abby means by feeling inferior. Beside this woman, Bette feels every pound of her short, squat frame, and had the woman not had such a pleasant, calming demeanor, she would have been tempted to put her in her place. Instead, it seems the most natural thing in the world for her to be holding her employer's hand talking to her as an equal. Bette finds her fascinating and hopes for an opportunity to talk with this woman at length. She would stay with Abby under any circumstance, but now she looks forward to a chance to get Jessie alone.

"Abby Dear, I am going to run home and get the children situated, and then I will come back and stay with you until the baby is born."

Abby starts to protest, but Bette assures her there is no place she would rather be.

"Too, you mustn't worry about the children. If it's satisfactory with you, I will have Dovie stay at my house to help, and we will leave them there until their little sister," here she stops to smile at Jessie, "or brother, whichever the case may be, is born. You have a lot of work ahead of you, so I do not want you to worry about a thing."

Bette rises, but before she leaves the room she turns to Jessie. "Between you and Mammy, I know Abby is in good hands, but I want to be here for Baby Barret's debut."

Jessie knows immediately that she is going to like this woman, and it pleases her that Abby has made a friend like her. "She is going to be fine," she assures Bette. Bette believes her though she has no idea why she should.

Bette meets Frederick taking the stairs two at a time. "Is it her time?"

His face is pale, but he, too, is excited. When Bette tells him Abby's water has broken, his face registers surprise, for most women would never speak so frankly to another woman's husband, but then again, most women are not Bette Stiles.

"I knew when I found no one downstairs something had to be happening, but I could not understand why I was not sent for if Abby were in labor."

Knowing how nervous Frederick must be, Bette ignores the censure in his voice. "She is not in labor exactly, but she will be soon, and she certainly must stay in bed. We saw no reason to send for you because Abby has a long way to go before your child arrives, so we thought you better off at work than here where you would just sit and worry. And, according to Jessie, you have nothing to worry about, and I certainly believe she knows what she is talking about. That is some servant you have yourself, Frederick."

The tension leaves Frederick's face and he laughs. "Yes, Jessie is quite something, is she not?"

Bette looks closely at Frederick. She does not think she would want someone who looks like Jessie living under her roof, and Frederick has always seemed to admire a pretty face. However, Bette prides herself on being perceptive, and she does not think anything inappropriate is going on between Frederick and his employee, not because of anything she detects on his part, but because of the way Jessie is with Abby. She acts almost maternal toward the younger woman.

'You best go along and visit with your wife while you can." She tells Frederick the arrangements she has made for the children and makes her way home to take care of things as quickly as possible so she can return. She knows they may have a long night ahead if not a long day or two. She prays as she walks that God will be merciful and the baby will come quickly.

When Bette returns a couple of hours later, Abby is finally having contractions, but they are not intense and they are still spaced far apart. Jessie goes downstairs to heat up leftovers from the night before, and Bette sits at the dining table and eats with Frederick while Jessie returns to the bedchamber. She carries the dishes to the kitchen herself and cannot help but admire the homey atmosphere there due, no doubt, to the wonder woman Jessie. The place smells wonderful; everything is in its place, and a banked fire warms the room. Bette realizes this is a place where she would like to spend time. She also realizes she has never felt that way about her own kitchen. She wonders if Jessie has a sister.

When Bette goes back upstairs, Frederick has pulled the armchair up next to his wife's bed and is conversing with her between contractions. As they start coming closer and closer together, Bette instructs him to carry himself a chair to the hallway from downstairs so he will have a comfortable place to wait. He seems relieved to take the hint, and from that moment on, Bette and Jessie alternate from Abby's bedside to the chair Frederick vacated with Mammy darting in and out to make sure everything is as it should be. In her spare time, she prepares all they will need for the baby once it arrives.

Shortly after dawn, a weak, tearful, pain-weary Abby screams one final time and delivers the healthy little girl Jessie predicted into Mammy's capable hands.

"Tanks be ta Jesus!" exclaims Mammy, and after handing the wailing babe off to Jessie, she returns to make sure Abby passes the afterbirth. She packs the area with clean sheeting before calling out to the other women, "Dare jus a lil bleedin. Mizz Abby goan be jus fine. How dat chile doin?"

Bette and Jessie have cleaned and wrapped the child, and Mammy starts to take it from her, but she can tell Jessie is reluctant to let her go.

"Gul, Mammy see plenny a new chilrun. Day aw look nigh on da same affa day born. Less hab er mama gib er a kiss, den take dat chile ta meet er papa."

Frederick chooses not to wait. He pushes the door open, and seeing the wrapped baby in Jessie's arms, he takes her from her and gazes closely into the little red face. He traces his finger over her small nose and along her full lips. He pulls a wisp of hair gently away from her scalp and asks, "What color do you think her hair will be?"

"Well, I think it will most likely be dark, seeing as both you and Abby have dark hair. Right now it looks almost black, but it is still damp." Looking over Frederick's shoulder, Bette adds, "And as dark blue as her eyes are, I bet they turn brown like yours instead of staying blue like Abby's. Do you have a preference?"

"No, just so the child is healthy."

Frederick seems relieved. Bette knows he is thankful to have both mother and child come through safely. He has experienced a lot of loss in his life, so it is only natural for him to be fearful in this situation. It is a very happy man who walks to the bed and places the baby in her mother's arms.

Frederick has been thinking of names ever since he found out that Abby was pregnant, but neither he nor Abby have mentioned names. Because there are many babies and mothers who do not survive childbirth, most people believe it presumptuous to have a name picked out before God has decided if the child will live or die. Frederick secretly hopes to name a little girl after his cousin Brigitte, and now he feels comfortable in asking, "Abby, have you given any thought as to what we should name her?"

"Yes, I have," she answers as she gazes down into the face of her daughter. "I am going to name her Luella Curtis Middleton Barret after my sister. That is the least I can do. We will call her Ella."

Chapter 23

Frederick is worried and his worry makes him angry. He sits in his office and tries to concentrate on work, but his mind keeps wandering. This is unusual for him. He has several things that need to be taken care of, and he does not like the fact that he cannot concentrate. Frederick Barrett loves a well-ordered life, and he has worked hard to maintain one. He hates it when his life veers out of control. It has been several years since that has happened—the last awful occurrence was the death of Luella, and though he does not realize it, he gives himself credit for wrenching the reins from fate and redirecting his careening life onto the course it has been following smoothly until recently, in fact, until just three months ago.

Frederick considers himself a pious man, one who attends church regularly and gives credit often to God for the abundant blessings enjoyed by him and his. In truth, Frederick sees God as a benefactor who blesses his own ingenuity for coming up with a good plan and having the intelligence and diligence to carry it out. He has noticed things usually go wrong in life due mainly to weakness and inadequacy in others. Though he knows Luella did not intentionally contract yellow fever and die, it was a weakness to which he himself did not succumb; therefore, subconsciously he feels she should have been able to avoid it, and if unable to do that, she should have been able to survive it. Had he ever really acknowledged these sentiments, he would have had the decency to be ashamed and would have immediately asked for God to forgive him for his lack of empathy. Frederick, however, though he prides himself on being a deep thinker, and there certainly is evidence of that quality in the success of his business and social endeavors, spends little time looking inward to evaluate his own frailties or shortcomings.

Today, he feels his hopes for the future are once again at risk though the threat is nothing of the magnitude of Luella's death. In fact, this situation is exceedingly frustrating in that there should not be a situation. This should be a wonderful time of life for both him and Abby, but for some reason known only to God and Abby, his wife has chosen to become someone he does not recognize. Since the birth of Ella, Abby has withdrawn into a world she refuses to let him enter.

Frederick stands to pace back and forth in his office. He decides to go back to what he perceives to be the beginning of the change and work forward hoping he can ascertain where the problem began, address it, and get their lives back on track. The last real night of normalcy was the evening they had shared with the Stiles. That had been a delightful evening, one that had certainly worked to their advantage because the Stiles had so effectively spread the word of Jessie's prowess in the kitchen that three men, influential men, had hinted rather broadly they would like to be invited to dine at the Barret's—that they had heard they served a delicious table. At first, Frederick had been delighted, but now he is worried he may have promised invitations he cannot fulfill.

He remembers now that Abby had seemed unusually displeased with him the night after the Stiles left. He had given it little thought at the time, but he assumes now that it was the influence of Bette Stiles. Though there is much advantage to be had in his wife's association with Bette, there is also risk. Bette has always been odd, a strong-willed woman with rather radical views, but she has always seemed harmless enough. Luella never suffered from the association, but, he has to admit, Abby has a totally different personality from her sister. She is much more meditative and prone to impulse, traits he has enjoyed until recently. Now he needs to reassess the situation. Maybe he should limit Abby's contact with Bette. If so, he will have to do it very tactfully or he runs the risk of offending those of Savannah he cannot afford to alienate. Too, there is the problem of Abby herself. He has discovered she can be quite headstrong, a trait that has taken him by surprise on more than one occasion.

Right now Frederick would enjoy seeing a little spark of rebellion in his wife. Since Ella's birth, she has been as listless as a wet dishrag. Each day he hopes there will be a change when he gets home, but each day he is met with the same lackluster indifference he left that morning. Even the word "met" is a reach. Abby has not been downstairs more than twice since the baby arrived. Jessie has told him to be patient, that many women go through a bout of doldrums after they have babies, but Luella never suffered from any such foolishness. And, it isn't as if Abby is indifferent to everyone. She has chosen to nurse Ella herself, and Jessie tells him she sees the other children each day, if only for a quick kiss and hug. Jessie claims Abby is trying, but now, Frederick determines, she will just have to try a little harder. He knows Bette visits her often, and Jessie tells him they spend an hour or two at a time talking together. Jessie thought the news would encourage him, but now it aggravates him. If Abby has the wherewithal to visit with Bette and Jessie, she can motivate herself to spend some quality time with her husband. Too, it is high time she comes out of her room and starts socializing again. Though he has gone to functions that are appropriate for a man to attend alone, he regrets having to turn down invitations for them as a couple.

Frederick picks up his hat. He will confront Abby this very afternoon, but first, he needs to let off a little steam. He closes his office door, tells his dock foreman he is taking the afternoon off, and leaves the riverfront. He feels much better now that he has a plan. His step is lively as he heads not east toward home, but south toward Yamacraw.

Chapter 29

I am surprised when Frederick appears in our bedroom doorway in mid afternoon. He isn't due home for another hour or two, and I am not happy he has shown up early. I just finished nursing Ella and counted on a nap before having to face Frederick. Bette came around earlier, and I am completely exhausted from the effort to make conversation. Nonetheless, I make myself sit up in bed and meet my husband with what I hope to be a welcoming smile.

"You are home early today, Dear. Is something wrong?"

Frederick does not answer immediately. Instead, he walks to first one bedroom window and then the other jerking the curtains back to let in so much sunlight I have to shield my eyes to look at him. I feel the familiar gripping of panic in my chest.

"Nothing is really wrong, Abby, but things do not seem to be quite right either, do they?" Frederick crosses the room and sits beside me on the bed. This is not something Frederick does. He usually pulls up a chair and sits beside the bed.

"I do not know what you mean, Frederick," I lie, "and please keep your voice down or you will wake Ella."

Frederick walks to the door and yells down the stairs, "Dovie, please come up here." Ella begins wailing from her crib. Neither of us speaks until Dovie appears, though it takes her several minutes to respond.

"I wuz heppin Jessie in da kitchen," Dovie offers in way of explanation.

"I am surprised I did not see you there, Dovie, since I just walked through the kitchen on the way up here."

Frederick is often irritated by Dovie's slacking ways, and I expect him to scold her. Instead he picks Ella up and hands her to Dovie.

139

"I want you to take Ella into Mammy and Mattie's room right now, and by tomorrow I want her crib set up over there. You and Mammy can work out whose responsibility it is to look after her full time. She is plenty old enough to sleep away from her mother."

Dovie takes the child and moves faster than I have seen her move in years.

"Abby, you've been entirely too easy on that girl, and if you don't get her under control, I think we may have to consider selling her."

"We'll do no such thing!" I disagree, though it takes far more energy than I want to exert.

"We'll discuss that later. Right now, we have more important things to talk about."

I do not like the way Frederick is behaving. He looked angry and determined when he first entered; now he is looking at me like he feels sorry for me. I become painfully aware that my hair is an unruly mass around my face, and I have not yet bothered to get dressed.

"Why are you still in your night clothes, Abby?"

I try to straighten my hair and pull myself together, but I am feeling more and more tired by the moment.

"I was about to do so. How was I to know you were coming home early?"

"Do you mean to tell me you stay abed every day until this time?"

I raise my head and start to defend myself, but suddenly it is as if all energy drains from my body. I slump back against the pillows.

"I am sorry, Frederick. I have just been so tired since Ella was born. It is as if it takes all of my energy just to get her fed."

"Do we need to hire a wet nurse?"

"No, please, no. That is the one thing I enjoy, nursing Ella. I…"

"Listen to yourself, Abby!" Frederick interrupts. "You have a wonderful life—a husband who loves you, four children who adore you—four, not one Abby—and all you want to do is lie in bed all day? I'm sending for Dr. Waring. There has got to be something physically wrong with you for you to behave this way."

"No, Frederick, please. You are overreacting. The doctor was here a month ago, and he said I was fine. It just takes time. I am sure I will be better in a month or two."

"A month or two! I cannot allow this behavior to continue for another month or two! If you are not out of that bed by tomorrow, I am writing to your mother. Maybe a visit with her or one of your sisters is what you need. Now, I am going downstairs to check on the store, and when I come back, I expect to find you dressed and ready to eat supper downstairs with me and the children."

He leaves me lying in bed, and I feel I should be angry by his high-handedness, but anger takes energy, and I just do not have any to spare. Besides, I know he is right. I know there is more wrong with me than just having a baby. Though I have never told Frederick, I have experienced spells of these doldrums before. These episodes are what causes Mother to hover and treat me like a child. I know I must garner my strength and do as Frederick asks, or he really will write her. That is the last thing I want. I am sad enough without Mother castigating me for my shortcomings.

Frederick's dressing down comes closely on the heels of Bette's kind admonitions. I realize I have to make a real effort to snap out of it. I know I have responsibilities, and I know it is a sin to wallow in sadness, especially since I have no reason to be sad. What is wrong with me that I have these spells? Maybe the doctor could help me. No, that will not do. I must keep my propensity for despair a secret. Mother is right about that. The fewer people who know of this sinful weakness, the better. My problems are of my own making, and it is up to me to find a way to overcome them. Frederick has every right to be disgusted with me.

I push back the covers, walk to the door and call Dovie who is still next door with Ella. When Frederick returns, he finds me sitting by my window, dressed for supper. As he leads me downstairs, I can tell he is pleased with himself .

"Abby, you alone are not to blame in this. I should have done something sooner. Women are weak by nature, and often they need someone to set them right. Though you are not quite yourself yet, I am pleased you have taken a step in the right direction."

I feel the strongest emotion I have felt since Ella arrived. I fear putting a name to it, for it is evidence of further unnaturalness on my part to feel that way about my husband who is surely only trying to help me.

The children are delighted to see me at the table, and I feel guilty for my previous absences. I vow to do better. I can tell Frederick thinks the evening meal is a huge success. It is a Herculean task, but I get through it. Though I smile and try to make conversation, I long for the evening to pass quickly so I can return to my bed.

Chapter 25

Ilie curled around Moses Tucker. He feels wonderful against me, and I am happy. And why should I not? I have a new life—a home of my own, a good family to work for—and most surprising of all, I have found what appears to be true love at the mature age of forty-four. Moses is an amazing man, and I cannot believe how quickly I have come to trust him. Trust doesn't come easily for me—maybe because I know too much about people. Maybe that is why I have come to love and trust Moses so quickly—I cannot read him beyond general impressions. When he holds me in his arms, my mind is unclouded by the knowing. I am not sensing consequences or forefeeling dire happenings, and I enjoy the simplicity of our coming together. At this, I have to smile. Moses would not appreciate me calling what the two of us experience together as simple. And I will not try to explain it to him—what I mean—because he cannot possibly appreciate the reprieve a relationship lived on the one-dimensional plane of the present means to me. It is like taking a vacation from every day life.

I often wonder why God made me the way I am. Some who have known of my *gift*, as they called it, referred to me as *special*, but I have never felt *gifted* or *special*. The *knowing* is a burden, often an onerous one that causes me sleepless nights, and worse, imposes on me a separateness I have rarely been able to shake. At times I have even been angry with God. Why would he give me the ability to sense what is to come and so little power to do anything about it? My life has been a struggle to prevent harm and sadness to those I care about with few instances of being able to make a difference. I try to console myself with the knowledge that for the few whom I have averted tragedy, my affliction has been a gift from God.

Now, for the first time in my life, I feel truly connected to another human being. My inability to see beyond Moses' surface connects me to him by the uniqueness of the ordinary quality of our relationship. I know what it feels like to be like everyone else. I have grown to love Moses without the benefit, or the curse, depending on how one looks at it, of perceiving things I really feel would best be left unknown.

Even though I cannot read Moses the way I read other people, I can feel him in a way that I am pretty sure other people cannot. He, like all people, gives out sensations, but unlike other people, I don't get glimpses of events to come or reruns of recent experiences.

It seems that women hold on to their essences whether they be goodness, cattiness, self-satisfaction, vindictiveness...I catch shades of those essences, whatever they may be, as they pass by my fingertips. Men are different. Moses, for instance. His goodness flows from his fingertips, his lips, his whole body as he lies with me. It is as if he fills me up with his being. The last time I remember receiving the gift of such goodness by human touch was from my father.

I was but a few years old when he died. I can recall little about the way he looked, but the way he felt is still a part of me. The same consuming goodness filled me when he placed a hand on mine as he taught me my letters. It emanated from his body as he knelt with me beside my bed to hear my prayers, my small self pressed up against his boulder-like strength. I had not understood what death meant when my mother and sister tried to explain it to me, but I understood it all too well when I snuck into the parlor where they had laid him out on the kitchen door after he had succumbed to the violent epidemic that took him and many of our neighbors. I found a moment when no one else was in the room, and I walked up to the door, the absence of which was letting mosquitoes and insects into the kitchen in spite of the netting that temporarily hung there. When I touched him, I jerked my hand back from his arm, not because of what I felt, but because of what I did not feel. The goodness that was his life force was simply gone. So that was what dying meant. The part that makes you who you are, the part that makes you different, just disappears. I wondered where it had gone and what it would take for me to find it again. I wonder still.

My brother had come into the room and found me standing stick straight beside my father's body, tears at last running freely. He took my hand, and I was comforted to feel life again, but his force was not as warm, not as benevolent. Now, as an adult, I wonder if others have my ability to feel or really know a person, and if they do, do they receive the same sensations I do? Does one's being change in connection to others depending on the relationships they share? Would my siblings have received the same impressions of our father if they had been open to receiving, and has Moses filled other women with whom he has lain with the same sweet goodness he gives to me?

I gently extract myself from Moses' powerful arms and take advantage of the rare opportunity to enjoy the beauty of him in the early winter light. His dark ebony skin is amazingly unblemished by scars for a man of his age who has been a slave. The sun has given his upper torso a more russet hue than his pelvis and legs that have been protected always from the sun. His arms and abdominal muscles are well defined, even in repose, by years of heavy lifting. His face is far more formidable in sleep than it is when his eyes are open and reflecting the gentle spirit that lies within. He is such a kind man. I feel a clinching in my chest, a fear. How can someone so good, and more importantly, so good and important to me, survive in a world that has systematically crushed most things valuable, in my experience?

If not for the uncharacteristic queasiness I feel at the base of my sternum, I would awaken Moses to connect with him in the way that always brings me joy and comfort. Instead, I pull my gown from the foot of the bed and just manage to pull it over my own naked form before I feel bile surge in my throat. Dropping to my knees on the floor beside the bed, I manage to pull the chamber pot out in time to catch the vomit that spews from my mouth. Sick as I am, I am immediately thankful the pot is empty. After emptying my stomach, I rise, go to the washstand and rinse my face with tepid water from the basin. Moses, a heavy sleeper, hasn't changed positions on the bed, and I am glad. To see me sick would worry him. I am uneasy myself. I have rarely been sick in my life, and I have been feeling fine. The nausea has taken me completely by surprise. Maybe it is something I ate. I quickly put on shoes and take the evidence of my sickness to the back door and walk to the outhouse that Moses has erected at the farthest edge of my small lot of land. Mine is the only outhouse in sight. My neighbors choose to hurl their refuse in their yards and use the ditch behind a scraggly line of shrubbery for their more private needs.

I dump the pot and return to the house. Moses sleeps on. I let him sleep until I am dressed for work, then I kiss him on his full, wide lips, and finally he stirs. He is up and dressed by the time I have a huge bowl of cornmeal mush ready. I offer to cook him other things, but this is his early morning meal of choice. He says it brings back good memories of when his mama made it for him and Lavinie.

I sit across from him and listen to his plans for repairs on the boarding house, and when he finishes eating, he walks with me as far as his place. As we walk along, I quiz Moses.

"How do you spell "dollar?" I ask.

"D-o-l-a-h."

I correct him. He offers the spelling of "cent" before I can ask. I am pleased he actually includes the "t" this time. I am teaching Moses to read and write. Last night we concentrated on words that will help Moses in his business. Moses is a fast and eager learner. Early on, he was thrilled to learn to write his name. I have found it written on scraps of paper around my house, and I have caught him tracing it with his finger in the film left on his plate after meals and on the moisture that collects on the small mirror that hangs above my washbasin. I often have to correct him because he continues to spell words the way he pronounces them. It amuses me to occasionally hear my own accent and intonations reflected in his pronunciation. He told me that the woman he rents to help him cook the boarding house meals has accused him of being an uppity nigger because of the way he talks. He seems proud she has noticed.

I leave Moses at the boarding house and walk alone to the Barret's. By the time I reach the house on Broughton, all nausea has passed. I am relieved that the early morning spell will not hinder me in accomplishing all I need to do today.

An hour after entering the house through the back door, I have the kitchen warm and breakfast for the servants on the table. Mammy, Dovie, and Lewis sit across from me, and the three of them eat the grits with molasses on bread that I dish out for them. My willingness to serve them and dine with them has at last defused Mammy's resentment. I have grown to enjoy the camaraderie the four of us share each morning before the rest of the household awakes. I have about thirty minutes until Mr. Barret will expect his breakfast upstairs in the family dining room. I have eggs ready to poach and his favorite jam with butter waiting on the tray at the end of the table. My self-indulgence of eating with the others will not get in the way of my house duties.

"Mama," Lewis pauses while spooning grits into his mouth, "Minda say she an da chilrun migh com by fo a wile affa chuch on Sundy if it awrigh."

A frown creases Mammy's usually unlined forehead. "Wat in heben name dat gul be tinkin? She cain be trapsin ober hyur wid dose chilrun. You tell er I come ober dare de furse chance I hab, bu she sho doan need ta be cumin ober hyur."

I am surprised at Mammy's vehemence. I know from earlier conversations that Minda lives in a house over in Yamacraw rented for her and her children by her owner.

"Mama," Dovie joins the conversation, "you know Mizz Abby be wanin ta see Minda sin she got hyur, an puttin it off woan do nobidy no good."

"I naw jectin to Minda cumin roun, bu she sho doan hab no bidness draggin dose haf wite chilrun ub ers wid er." Mammy's frown deepens and her tight mouth brooks no arguments. Neither Lewis nor Dovie argue with Mammy when she sets her mind to something. Both eat the rest of their breakfast in silence.

I now understood Mammy's reluctance to have her daughter visit. Like many slaves, Minda apparently has children by her white master. That explains Minda's rented house in Yamacraw. It is not unusual for a white man to set his black mistress and their children up in a house to remove the offending evidence of his indiscretion from his wife's watchful eye. Mammy must not want to expose Abby to the reality of what some husbands do with their slaves. I think it considerate on Mammy's part and agree it is best that Abby be shielded from the unpleasant reminder of what goes on in some homes, especially right now when Abby is finally coming out of her doldrums.

After Dovie and Lewis leave the room, I place my hand on Mammy's arm meaning to express my support, but I am surprised at the emotion that emanates from contact with the woman. I withdraw my hand, shocked at the intensity of Mammy's disapproval.

"Wat?" Mammy turns on me, her expression fierce.

"I just want to tell you I think you are right to try to protect Abby that way," I try to explain.

"Wat you be knowin bou enna ub dis? You bes stay clare a da whole bidness, bes you kin. I sho wisht I cou." And with that, Mammy throws her dishes in the wash pan and huffs out of the kitchen.

Well, I think, *so much for commiseration.* I have no time to dwell on the problems of Mammy and her family. I take Frederick's meal of poached eggs, grits, bread with jam and butter, and a small pot of coffee up to him. This is another part of my morning ritual I enjoy. It is time I can talk with Frederick without worrying about creating wrong impressions.

Frederick and I have a lot in common, odd as that might seem to some, and it is not unusual for us to discuss the Island we both grew up on, though we steer clear of discussing the personal heartache we endured in our years there. It gives us a chance to speak in our native tongue, and it gives me the chance to catch up on what is happening on the Island. Frederick still does commerce with the Indies, so he often has political tidbits and gossip to pass on. Though observers might find the relationship between employer and servant inappropriate, I indulge myself in the luxury for I know I cause no one harm. I also know that if my early morning conversations with Frederick prove to be a problem for anyone, including Frederick or Abby, I will discontinue them immediately. In no way do I want our relationship to be misconstrued. The earlier hostility I witnessed in Mammy made me determined not to be the cause of any suspicion. I know any misunderstanding on Abby's part could jeopardize my position in the Barret household, and it is one I enjoy immensely. I am already more attached to the Barret children than is probably healthy. In a way, they have become the children I will never have. And there is a sweetness about Abby, a vulnerability, that makes me feel protective. I am relieved she is finally recovering from the malaise that has almost incapacitated her for months since Ella's birth. No, there is no way I will knowingly cause Miss Abby worry.

After my time with Frederick, I return to the kitchen to prepare my fourth breakfast of the day. I enjoy preparing specialties for the children. Today I am preparing a special syrup reduced from sugar and water and flavored with strawberry jam put up in the summer. I will serve it over hotcakes, the children's breakfast of choice. Often I serve them with the unrendered jam, but I have noticed Abby seems to prefer the syrups I serve occasionally. Today, I feel a little melancholy myself, a condition probably brought on by my early bout of sickness and the scene with Mammy and her family. My extra work pays off when I hear the exclamations of excitement from the children and notice the way Abby digs into the hotcakes with relish. The children are done in no time, and Dovie rushes to wash their faces before the older two run out the back door, presumably headed for Wright Square where they spend a large part of their day. Dovie, resigned to the long day ahead of her, hurries after them. I am pleased to see that Mammy has stayed behind with Ella, a far less taxing assignment than keeping up with the older three.

Abby is doing much better, but she still tires easily, so I am not surprised when she excuses herself to go back upstairs to lie down for a while. "I have the meeting with the Women's Benevolence Society this afternoon, so I think it would be wise for me to rest a while longer. Conversing with those women completely wears me out!" She offers, as if she needs to explain herself.

I know Frederick disapproves of Abby's daytime naps, but I know how hard it has been for Abby to fight her way back from the dark place in which she has been. I originally thought it would have been more helpful for Frederick to provide a little more love and understanding, a little less autocracy, but I have to admit his efforts have gotten Abby up and going again whereas Bette's gentle encouragement had not, and besides, who am I to judge such things. Still, I hate that Abby feels the need to explain, even to me, when she chooses to lie down for a few minutes.

"That is probably a good idea, Miss Abby. I cannot imagine having to be in the room with that many woman at one time."

"Oh, you would be better at it than I, I assure you, Jessie. I cannot imagine you lacking poise in any situation."

The two of us have become so comfortable in each other's company that neither find this comment inappropriate. Abby has insisted I drop the title of Madame Barret and call her by her first name, something others may find odd. I take every opportunity to let her know I respect her and her position so she will not think I presume upon our relationship.

"I assure you, Madame, there is no reason for you to feel daunted, either. While you are there, just remember there is not one of them who would not love to look like you. You have not retained an ounce of extra weight you put on with Ella, and you are as beautiful as ever."

Abby blushes from the compliment, the color making her even prettier. Abby's eyes are a dark intense blue, and the paleness of her complexion makes them appear even more vibrant. There is something so innocent, so childlike about her small, heart-shaped face that I often find myself wanting to protect her much as I would one of the Barret children.

"That is kind of you to say, Jessie, but it is not my looks that worry me. I just cannot seem to think of anything to say to some of those women, and when I do manage to come up with something, I feel like many of them think I am simple and inane."

"Remember, Abby, you do not have to impress them. Just be yourself and know that if they do not appreciate you for who you are, they are probably not worth knowing anyway!"

Abby visibly relaxes. "Thank you, Jessie. I wish Frederick saw things the way you do."

Abby rises to leave the room, but she turns back when she reaches the door. "You know, Jessie, you are better than a tonic. I do not think I need a nap, after all. I have a couple of letters to write. I will get those taken care of and walk over to Bette's so we can go to the meeting together."

It makes me feel good to know I have encouraged Abby. Likewise, Abby's appreciation has lifted my spirits. I am humming a tune as I wash the breakfast dishes when suddenly the strangest feeling comes over me. I stop what I am doing and stand perfectly still before the pan of soapy dishwater. What is this feeling, this warmth emanating from my abdomen? It is not a tingling or a burning, certainly not a pain, quite the opposite. It is a pleasant sensation, a kind of radiating force. I dry my hands on the cloth I keep on the nail on the wall beside the kitchen window, and I spread the fingers of my right hand across the affected area. As I do so, I feel a stirring.

Oh, Sweet Mother of God, can this be what I think?

No, I chastise myself. *It cannot be. I am forty four years old—almost forty five!*

A voice, clear as day in my head: *Sarah was ninety years old.*

Like the dubious Sarah of the Bible, I laugh.

There is no doubt as to the origin of the next words I hear. They are from Mammy who has quietly entered the room with Ella in her arms.

"Wat in hebben is you laffin bou? If worshen dose dishes mek you dat happy, I sho wipin Mizz Ella nassy boddum will hab you in stiches! I be jus as happy fo you ta do it."

I whirl to face Mammy, and the older woman's mouth opens and her eyebrows rise in expectation at the joy she sees on my face.

"Mammy, praise God! It is a miracle. I am going to have a baby, and I am pretty sure it is a boy!"

I am shocked at my own audacity. I quickly make the sign of the cross and practically fall to the bench beside the table where I place my propped elbows on the surface and hold my own face in my hands. I can no more stop the tears from flowing than I can stop time.

"Well, days no need ta bawl bou it, Gul! You naw de furse woman ebber be wid chile, bu I mit, you be da furse I know ebber know da chile wuz a boy fo you eben showin a lump in da middle!" Mammy lays the squirming Ella on the table between us and sits facing me.

"I cannot help it, Mammy. I have wanted a child so badly, but I had quit dreaming of such a thing. Here I am middle aged, and I swear, I think I am pregnant. And don't ask me how I know, but I think it is going to be a boy!"

A wide smile breaks across Mammy's thin, tired face, and even in my addled state, I realize how pretty the slave woman still is. I reach across the table and grasp Mammy's left hand with my right. Mammy reaches across the table and takes my free hand with her own. We sit holding hands with baby Ella kicking happily between our connected arms on the table.

"Praise Jesus!" Mammy exclaims, and the two of us rejoice together as Mammy continues to laugh and tears flow down my face to wet the high-necked collar of my gown.

Chapter 26

I finally get the pleasure of meeting the Maxwells: Brigitte, Alexis, their sons Jeffrey and Frederick, the youngest called Fred, and like our own son Fredie, named after my husband Frederick. They have been staying with us since Monday, and with a Frederick, a Fred, and a Fredie, there has been some confusion in communication at times. Too, putting four more people into our already crowded house has placed a strain on my nerves. Apparently, the Maxwells are shorter on funds than they are on charm, so they are unable to afford accommodations elsewhere.

It has taken the combined creative efforts of Frederick, Jessie, and me to come up with a plan to sleep everyone, and though the arrangements seem to be sufficing, they are far from ideal. Mammy has moved Ella's baby bed back into the room with Frederick and me, and Mattie is sleeping in the front parlor on a pallet placed on the floor. This arrangement is made more difficult because the sleeping Mattie has to be moved from our bed each night where she is put to fall asleep. Her makeshift bed cannot be placed in the parlor until the men have vacated it at what appears to be a later time each night. Brigitte and Alexis are sleeping in Mattie and Ella's room, while Robart, Jeffrey, Fred, and Fredie share the boys' room. Dovie sleeps in her customary place in the hallway. All in all, there are simply too many people in too little space. If it were not for the embarrassment it would cause the Maxwells, Frederick and I would have rented a room for them or stayed at a hotel ourselves. Bette has offered to have the Maxwells at their home, but we have declined for the same reason we have not rented the rooms.

Instead, both the Maxwells and ourselves are pretending their visit is a great adventure and all are enjoying the intimacy imposed on us.

By Friday night, I have begun to wonder how I am going to survive another week of such closeness. But now, as we sit around the table with the Stiles, I am on my second glass of the good wine Alexis brought. Alexis is in the Navy, and Frederick has a standing order with him to pick up good wine whenever possible to ship to us. The latest acquisition he brought with him, and the Stiles, the Maxwells themselves, and Frederick all agree it may be Alexis' best purchase yet. Though I know little about what makes wine good or bad, I agree heartily that tonight's choice is to my liking. So it is that Bette, Brigitte, and I are three relaxed, giddy women by the time the men retire to the parlor.

"Can you believe the food their Jessie puts on the table?" Bette asks Brigitte. "Oh, but I guess you can since she used to work for you! However could you stand to part with her?"

"I assure you I would not have, had I any choice, but with Alexis being in the Navy, he goes where he is sent. For the past few years, I have stayed in Baltimore rather than move with two young sons, but now they are older, we have decided it will do them no harm to move. In fact, Alexis thinks it will serve them well to experience as much of the world as possible."

"Well, your loss is certainly Abby's gain, and ours too, for that matter. It is becoming known the Barrets serve the best meal in town."

"I am not surprised," Brigitte agrees. "We had to be choosy about who we invited to dinner when we employed her. We would have had to entertain nightly to feed everyone who wanted to dine at our table."

There is something about Brigitte's laugh and the hand she flips gaily above her head that catches my attention. Maybe it is the wine, the amount consumed by both Brigitte and myself, but it seems that Brigitte is more animated tonight than she has been in the preceding days of her visit. Too, she seems to be louder, her mannerisms more affected, or maybe I have previously been too preoccupied with getting everyone situated to notice. And she had appeared almost flirtatious with the men earlier. Of course, it is not surprising she would be playful with Frederick. He has fallen all over himself to entertain Brigitte over the past week. I have always known, and never really minded, that Frederick appreciates a pretty female, but his behavior has always been only gracious and flattering toward other women. With Brigitte, he is downright fawning, and even I have to admit her looks and figure are enviable. She is small with large, dark eyes that remind me of those of a deer. She has a way of tilting her face forward and peering upward when she speaks, even to me though we are much of the same height. I notice the long lashes actually reach her perfectly arched brows and her hair manages to look soft and natural while staying in place, something my own has never been willing to do. Alexis seems amused by the attention Frederick gives his wife, and they have known each other longer than I, or even my sister Luella, for that matter. If Frederick's behavior does not bother Alexis and it did not bother Luella, I will not allow it to bother me.

"I am afraid if I were you, I would have stayed in Baltimore rather than give up a cook like Jessie!" Bette tells her.

"Oh, what we do for love!" Brigitte says, and again there is the little flip of the hand. "And speaking of love, the move seems to have worked out well for Jessie. I could not believe my eyes when I found her big with child! And married after all these years! I would not have thought her even interested in men. I'm glad she saved that foolishness until after she left my employment. She had all she could do to take care of our household. I would not have been pleased with the distraction her own child is bound to be!"

Bette's lips smile but her eyes do not crinkle at the corners like they usually do when she is amused.

"However did you meet your own charming husband, Mrs. Maxwell?" Bette asks. "Was he a friend of your cousin's? I notice they both speak French."

Though Abby senses Bette is not totally enamored with Brigitte, she certainly seems curious.

"Oh heavens no!" Brigitte assures Bette, "It was quite the opposite! It was I who introduced the two of them. In fact, hard as it may be for you to believe now, they were actually rivals for my affections."

This is news to me as well as to Bette, and I feel my attention sharpen, the pleasant wine-induced lethargy quickly receding as my mind tries to make sense of what my houseguest is saying.

Brigitte seems flattered by Bette's focused attention, no doubt in part because Frederick told the Maxwells before dinner of Bette's lineage and the sway her family has held over Savannah society for the last several decades.

"I speak French, too, you know. I am surprised Abby has not told you Frederick and I are first cousins. Our mothers were sisters—half sisters actually. I do not have the accent Frederick has because I was born in the States, whereas he was born in St. Domingue as my own mother was."

I am shocked. No, I had not told Bette Frederick and Brigitte were first cousins because I had not known they were that closely related. And I certainly did not know that Brigitte was a link to Frederick's life on the Island. There is so much I want to know, but I hate to appear totally ignorant of the details of my own husband's life, so I choose my words carefully.

"Frederick is so reluctant to speak of his life on the Island, Brigitte. Was your mother the same? Did she hate to speak of her past?"

"Oh, not at all! She was quite the opposite." Brigitte pauses to daintily sip the quickly disappearing wine in the glass before her. "She talked of her past *ad nauseum*. But then, her life was so different from your husband's, Abby."

Brigitte turns to Bette and leans in confidingly. "Frederick's life was much more dramatic than my mother's, I am afraid." She turns to Abby. "Abby, this story is really yours to tell. I am sure you do not want to listen to all of this again."

My curiosity outweighs my pride. "No, Brigitte, please go on. Frederick has such terrible memories of his youth that he has told me very little. I would love to know as much as I can—not that I want to intrude upon his privacy, but I am his wife, and surely I can be more supportive if I know what his early life was like."

Brigitte preens under the attention both of us are riveting on her. She prepares to regale us with all she knows by further loosening her tongue with the wine that remains in the glass and fortifies herself for the effort by pouring herself some more.

"My maternal grandmother and Frederick's maternal grandmother were not the same though we shared the same grandfather. My mother was the oldest of their father's children, and her mother, my grandmother, died. Frederick's mother was a child by my grandfather's second wife, and I know practically nothing about her because my mother, as she told it, was sent back to France to live with her father's people before her father ever remarried."

I am fascinated. "So did Frederick come to the States to live with your mother?"

"Oh, no, no, no," Brigitte trills, the hint of her French heritage coming through in her voice. "Neither knew the other existed when he arrived in the States. I do know that, from what eavesdropping I was able to do—well, not really eavesdropping, you understand. We lived in such close quarters it would have been hard not to overhear... Oh, I would not want you to think our home was a hovel, by any means. It was quite a reputable boarding house in a respectable part of town..."

"You were telling us what you knew of Frederick's life before you met—" I rudely interrupt Brigitte's digression to get her back on track. Brigitte does not seem in the least offended, however, and she takes up where she left off.

"My mother did know of Frederick's father because he was older than she. He came to the Island when the French military sent him to map the interior, or something of that nature, if I understood correctly. Too, I know he was married once before he met Frederick's mother to the daughter of a wealthy sugar plantation owner, and they lived on one of her plantations. She inherited all three of the plantations when her own father died, but she and their youngest child died of a fever several years after they married. Though Mr. Barret then married Frederick's mother, the plantations were to be held in trust until Frederick's half sister and brother came of age, but all of that changed, of course, because of the uprising of the local heathen, as you probably realize."

Brigitte's tone turns bitter as she returns to her wine.

Both Bette and I have lost all interest in our own drinks as we lean forward in our chairs to better hear every word. I can tell Bette is every bit as enthralled with the tale as I, and the expression on her face reveals she is equally confused by the meandering telling of the story. There is so much I want to ask, and I am grateful when the ever forthright Bette does some of the asking for me.

"I do not want to appear ignorant, Brigitte, but I know only that there was a slave rebellion in St. Domingue some years ago—one that still makes slave owners here tremble with fear, but I know nothing of the particulars. And what happened to Frederick's father, and why did your mother and Frederick know nothing of each other?"

I feel like an eavesdropper on my own husband's life, but, I think defiantly, if he were not so tight lipped on the subject, I would not have to get my information from strangers.

"My mother was sent back to France to be educated with her people in the same way Frederick's older sister and brother were. That was common practice for the landowners there. My mother's mother died, and her father remarried and had other children, and she knew one of her own younger sisters had married the wealthy widower Barrett. But she knew nothing about Frederick's birth. You see," Brigitte pauses dramatically, not just for effect but also for the opportunity to further imbibe, "little did anyone know life for the aristocratic French and the wealthy Islanders was about to change dramatically. My mother had married in France, but her husband, my father, died fighting for the

Crown as did Frederick's half-brother. In fact," Brigitte pauses again to heighten the effect of what she was about to tell us, "my own father lost his head to the guillotine."

Both Bette and I gasp audibly. "You poor dear, to lose your father like that!" Bette cries in dismay.

"I do not really remember him," Brigitte replies calmly, "but his death certainly changed our lives. Probably not as much as the loss of our holdings in St. Domingue, however. The new black government confiscated my grandfather's lands and left them paupers. With no money from that direction, and with my father dead, my mother was forced to run the boarding house we were in when Frederick ran across us in Baltimore. What a different life I would have lived had we retained control of our holdings in St. Domingue. Just think—Frederick would have been landed gentry with no real need to start over in the States!" Her voice becomes bitter again. "And the ignorant heathens have let the whole country go to ruin. They have neither the means nor the intelligence to even grow the sugar cane that once made the Island one of the wealthiest places on Earth!"

At this point, I have more questions than I have answers. "But Frederick's father lives in Louisiana. How did they become separated?"

"I am afraid I have told you all I know. My mother never really knew Frederick's mother because she never returned to the Island after she was sent to France, and apparently Frederick's mother died young. I do know my mother was quite shocked when Frederick turned up at our boarding house. He came there because his English was poor, and my mother spoke French. You can imagine their surprise when they discovered they were so closely related."

"How did you ascertain the connection?" Bette asks.

"Once again, I do not know the particulars. They stayed cloistered in the guest parlor late into one night not long after he arrived, and after that, neither seemed to doubt the relation. My mother died without really explaining all of it to me, and as you have said yourself, Abby, Frederick does not like to talk about his early years at all. I do know there are some hard feelings between Frederick and his father. In the whole time he lived with us, I do not recall him ever mentioning his father, and I am quite sure he does not communicate with him." She looks coyly at me over the top of her glass. "I would think if anyone would know his inner secrets, it would be you, Abigail."

I feel my face burn as both women turn their attention to me. "I know he has no relationship with his father. I guess I need to be a little more inquisitive," is all I can think to say.

"It might be just as well that you not mention this little conversation. I would hate for Frederick to be angry with me for spilling the family secrets." Brigitte does not seem to be too worried about annoying Frederick, but, by morning, she may be wishing she had not drunk quite so much wine or talked quite so openly. Intoxicated or not, Brigitte seems determined to say no more on that particular subject, so Bette tactfully changes the subject to one we both know she will be unable to resist, that of herself.

"You forgot to tell us how Frederick and Alexis came to be rivals for your affections," Bette prompts. "Surely, Frederick would not object to you telling us about something that is so clearly water under the bridge."

Bette's gentle nudge is all the prompting it takes for Brigitte to launch into her tale of two handsome young gentleman vying for the hand of a young woman who had nothing to commend her but her personal charm and beauty. By the time she finishes and staggers off to bed, I have once again arrived at the conclusion that the week ahead is going to be a long and difficult one. I cannot wait to ask my husband some rather pointed questions.

Chapter 27

I expect Frederick to be asleep by the time I get back to my room after making sure Mattie is bedded down in the parlor with Mammy, but he is wide awake and as amorous as he has been every night this week. I have managed to put him off two of the four nights since our guests' arrival by reminding him of the baby in the crib and the fear of being overheard by the company across the hall. It is not that I object to making love. I usually enjoy it, but Goodness! We have a houseful of people, and I am exhausted from the effort of dealing with all of them. Not only that, Frederick's ardor has an uncommon intensity to it. Now I think I may know why. I am beginning to doubt that he has been making love to me at all. I certainly will not voice a suspicion I do not want to admit to myself, but as I lie impaled by my husband's pumping body, I wonder if it may be the woman across the hall beneath him in his mind instead of his own boring wife. Still smarting both physically from his passion and emotionally from my own errant thoughts, my voice has an edge to it when I address the back he turns to me after rolling off and onto his side of the bed.

"Why did you not tell me that you were more than a little enamored with Brigitte Maxwell, Frederick?"

Frederick is still and quiet for so long, I fear he is going to pretend to be asleep, but at last he rolls over and takes me in his arms.

"I think enamored might be putting it a little strongly," and he laughs to show how unimportant the conversation is to him, but I am not fooled. He is nervous. "I had a crush on her, and what young boy would not?"

My stiffening response tells him he needs to rethink his approach.

161

"Just think of it, Dear—I was a young man in this country. She was the first young lady I met who could converse with me in my native tongue, and she was older and interested in me and the life I had lived. It was heady stuff. It was long before I had been introduced to real beauty, real gentility, like that exhibited by your family, so of course I was impressed and vulnerable."

I am somewhat mollified. "Were you angry when Alexis stole her away?"

He laughs again, less nervously this time. "He did not steal her away because she was not mine in the first place. I could ill afford to court a lady. I was a mere clerk at the time. I did not have two pennies to rub together. But it is true my pride was hurt. This sailor shows up. He not only speaks French, but he is older; he is witty; he has some money to lavish on her; and he is dashing in his uniform. What woman could ever resist a man in uniform? But then I got to know Alexis, and he became my best friend, so I was happy for them. They are much better suited to each other, and if we had married, I would never have met you, my dear, dear wife."

I let the fact that he chose Luella first go by without comment. "But you could have told me about her, Frederick."

"I did tell you about her. You knew all about her. You knew she and Alexis visited Luella and me here in Savannah. You knew she and Luella were friends."

I suspect he is implying I should be fine with his previous relationship with Brigitte if my sister was. I let this pass, too.

"I know very little about the Maxwells, I have discovered. For instance, I certainly didn't know your mothers were sisters!"

Frederick stiffens and goes absolutely still.

"Brigitte told us your mothers were sisters but knew nothing of each other. How could that be, Frederick, and why have you not told me any of this? Did you talk to Luella about your life on the Island?"

"Luella had the graciousness not to talk to others about me behind my back," Frederick's voice is hard, "and she respected the fact that it was too painful for me to talk about my life on the Island. Now, if you do not object, I would like to get some sleep."

He turns his back on me, but I am not ready to let the subject go.

"I do not need to know the details of the hardships you suffered, but surely I should know about your parents, who they were, what they were like. After all, Frederick, they are our children's grandparents."

Again he is quiet for so long I think he is not going to answer me. I place my hand on his shoulder. "You can confide in me. I am your wife."

"My mother was slaughtered by a mob of militant niggers when I was a baby, and my father left me to fend for myself while he fled to save his own skin. Is that enough information for you? Do you think we need to tell our children those facts about their grandparents?"

I feel my eyes fill with tears. I wrap my arms around my husband's rigid back and whisper, "I am so sorry, Frederick."

"I do not need your sympathy, Abigail. I need your trust. You should trust me when I say my past is best left alone. There is nothing good in it, and there is nothing good that can come from talking about it."

There is so much more I want to know, but I dare not persist. Instead, I plant little kisses along my husband's back. "I love you," I whisper.

This time he does not answer. I know I am being punished for meddling. I curl around him hoping my warmth will soften his hardened heart.

Chapter 28

I am glad when the Maxwell's visit is over, and I know Abby is too. I could tell the company was a strain on the household, especially on her. I still fear a relapse on the mistress' part, one that will send her back to her bed and into the darkness that seems to be lurking at the edges of her being. I can feel it there when I touch her, and I am resolute in my determination to help her keep it at bay, even if it means wishing my former employers, the Maxwells, a speedy departure.

I am fond of the Maxwells, especially the boys. Alexis is always a joy to be around. He is affable and kind, though his proclivity for practical jokes can wear thin after a while. It is not hard to see why Brigitte was won over by him. It is harder to understand why he was and still is so taken with his wife.

Brigitte is still a beautiful woman, but she has characteristics that must grow tiresome even to a devoted husband and sons. Though a good conversationalist, Brigitte's favorite topic of conversation is herself. Too, I feel Alexis would be wise not to keep the wine cabinet well stocked when he is away. Brigitte is not physically or emotionally strong by nature, and she does not do well without Alexis by her side. I assume her weakness is the main reason Alexis has decided to move the family from Baltimore. He knows as well as I do that the household suffers when he is away. I found myself attending to Brigitte's personal needs and assuming the role of mother to the boys as well as overseeing the running of the household in Alexis' absences. Though I love the boys and feel myself up to the task, I do not believe the arrangement is good for anyone involved, including Brigitte, so I was glad when Alexis decided to take them with him to his new posting.

It is odd, now that I reflect upon it, that God has placed me a second time in a household with a woman in need of support. Not that Abby is like Brigitte in most ways. She certainly is not as vapid and self-serving. But like Brigitte, there are times Abby needs the aid of a strong woman to help her deal with the complexities of life. In fact, I am beginning to suspect Abby has an ongoing problem with despondency, one I suspect existed before her marriage to Frederick. I have known people before who battle despondency, and Abby exhibits all the signs. Though I often became exasperated with Brigitte's self indulgence, I find myself more and more protective of Abby because I believe Abby does everything in her power to keep her demons in check, and having felt the power of those demons firsthand through my fingertips, I want badly to help my young mistress dispel them forever.

But now that I am drawing close to my time, I know I must focus on my own small family. Not only am I about to be a mother for the first time, I am a newlywed. Moses and I were properly married by Reverend Andrew Bryan at the Second African Baptist Church where we attend. I would have none of that jumping across a broomstick nonsense many of the slaves find sufficient. I would have preferred being married by a Catholic priest, but the one time I attended the Catholic church a few streets over from the Barrets, it was plain to me that in their eyes I am no better than a slave, and if they treat me that way, they will certainly not welcome my much darker husband as a free man. So Moses and I together decided we would attend the Second African Baptist Church where we can sit anywhere we want, and our child will not be relegated to a balcony or back pew. I thought these were the only reasons for our choice, but now I realize Moses had just been waiting for the right time to tell me he must attend the Second African Baptist Church for an altogether different reason.

Moses and I had been married for at least a month before he told me about his "ministry" at the Second African Baptist Church. He admitted that, not long after his arrival in Savannah, he was approached by the pastor himself about a mission to which God was calling him. Upon meeting Moses, a free black man like himself who can come and go as he pleases, Reverend Bryan convinced Moses that God has called them to help free their unfortunate brethren who are being ill-treated by their masters. So it came to be that Moses and many others in the congregation of the Second African Baptist Church have been constructing the new church by torchlight. The structure has to be built by night because the workers are predominantly slaves whose owners have allowed them to go there after their daily duties are done. Little do they know their servants are not only building a church but constructing a hiding place beneath the floor to conceal the more unfortunate among us from masters like themselves. Many of these same slave owners have further supported the cause by contributing funds, as they see it their Godly obligation to bring religion to us heathens. Though I find Moses' actions noble, I fear for his safety.

Today is Sunday, and Moses and I slipped away from church early as we usually do. Though I enjoy the worship services, it has taken me some time to become accustomed to the boisterous way in which the congregation sings, dances, and outright shouts for hours at a time. I do not believe the church is by any means a perfect fit for me, but, there, at least we are free to participate in the service and the administration of the church. I have, however, finally told Moses it wears me out to sit for so long. He suggested I participate more, but this was said with a smile on his face, and both of us laughed aloud at the thought of my reserved self shouting and raising my hands above my head in such an uninhibited way. Now, I especially smile at the thought of such an action with me so close to giving birth. I doubt I would have the energy to last more than a few minutes. So Moses and I went home for a quick dinner, and he has returned to chip away at the underground tunnel he is building from the church to the river. I have made my way to the Barrets' to work on the children's wardrobes Abby has commissioned.

I stop for a moment to relish the quiet of the house. Because it is Sunday afternoon, it is uncharacteristically empty. The store is closed for business, so there is no noise from that quarter either. I cannot remember ever being totally alone in the Barrets' house.

"My, haven't you let your mind wander today!" I say aloud into the quiet.

I take the opportunity to lay my head back against the chair and close my eyes. I place my palm on my stomach and thank God for the life that moves vigorously beneath my hand. I have always wondered what it would be like to carry a child. It had made me sad to think I would never know. I thought I had let that window of opportunity pass. After coming to Savannah, I had reconciled myself to playing the role of Tata Jessie to the Barret children, and I was grateful for even that. Now, at forty-five-years-old, here I am just weeks away from becoming a mother in my own right. I am happier now than I thought I would ever be.

My unborn son seems to relax beneath my hand. He takes the opportunity to rest peacefully for a while. The baby's calm, my fatigue, my contentment, the comfort of the chair and the warmth of the fire combine to lull me into a much-needed sleep, and I do not know how long I dose when a noise from the back of the house awakens me. I reluctantly push my swollen body out of the comfort of the armchair and make my way to the kitchen to see who has returned.

I know immediately who the visitor is when I open the kitchen door, though his name does not come to mind. Instead, I feel him before I see him as was the case of our first meeting. In fact, I cannot see him at all when I enter the kitchen because he has positioned himself behind the door, and he pushes it closed behind me as I enter the room. I whirl to face what I know instinctively to be a grave threat to me and my child.

"Well, well, well, if the arrogant high yeller niggress ain't with child! Can't say I'm surprised. A master'd be a fool not to tap the likes of you."

Robinson. That is what Frederick called the man. I fight the urge to back away from him as fast as possible, but I dare not show weakness for I know men like him are empowered by it.

"Mr. Barret is not here right now. You will need to come back later, or better yet, you need to look for him at his office. He does not conduct business here."

"You think I don't know that, Missy! You think I'd come calling through the back door without so much as a knock if I didn't know you was alone here? I may be many things, little woman, but stupid ain't one of them."

The man's cruel smile and lifeless eyes chill me to the bone. Though I know I need to stand my ground, I find myself backing toward the counter against the wall where I hope I can find a butcher knife. When at work I place the knife I carry with me behind a crock in the far corner on the pie safe.

"Do I detect some fear on your part, Mizz Yella?. That's what I'm gonna call you as you ain't seen fit to tell me your real name, high and mighty as you are. Well, we'll see how uppity you are after ole Gene gets through with you. I'm gonna show you what it's like to be taken by a real man, not some nigger lover who don't know how to teach you to treat your betters."

The man's talk is coarser than it was when Frederick was present. He sounds less educated and far less civil. I assume his current speech reflects his true character as there is no one in the room to impress.

"For the love of God, Sir, surely you can tell I am with child. I beg you to think about what you are doing. Mr. Barret will not let you get away with this. Surely you know that."

"Looks to me like it's gonna be your word against mine, Mizz Yella. And, pretty and pale as you are, it's still gonna be the word of a nigger against the word of a respected businessman like myself." He stops his approach to smile even more broadly. "And one no one has seen in these parts for weeks. So now who do you think they're gonna believe, Mizz Yella?"

I am backed against the counter and grasping around behind me for anything to use as a weapon. I try to keep the fear out of my voice, but I know I sound as frightened as I am. My hand comes in contact with something. I am disappointed to realize it is just a wooden handle. I bring it around in front of me and thrust it between myself and the advancing man.

"Do you actually think you're going to stop me with a wooden spoon? You disappoint me, Yella. I'd hoped for a little more fight outta you. I like some resistance. It makes me want it that much more. You'll like that too, won't you, me wantin you that much more?"

I strike out at him with the spoon, but he merely laughs and grabs me by the hair, wrenching the spoon from my grasp and striking me across the face with it. I do not feel the blow, but I am immediately weakened when he grabs me around the middle and thrusts himself against me. The physical contact is overwhelming. The evil I sensed the first time we met is nothing to that which jolts my entire being when I actually make physical contact with the man. I am so weakened by his essence that, if not for the child stirring within me, I would give up and let him do with me what he wants. But I cannot just give up, not with my son moving beneath my ribcage as if he too knows the threat of the man who holds me. I know I must do what I can to protect my child.

I let my body go completely limp. I am not a small woman, and Robinson has to let go of my hair to hold on to me. He manages to clasp both of my arms to my sides, so all I have to fight him with are my encumbered legs and my teeth. As he turns me to lay me across the kitchen table, I let my face fall forward onto his neck, and as repulsive as it is to be skin against skin with him, I bite down with all the strength I can muster.

"You cunt!" Robinson screams as he throws me from him. I feel the skin of his neck come loose in my teeth and I taste blood before pain courses through my body. He has thrown me against the table, and I feel the sharp edge tear through material and skin before my body hits the brick floor. I spit his flesh from my mouth and try to roll away from him, but he reaches down and grabs my hair and pulls me upright. He thrusts his face into mine. "You're going to pay for that, Bitch."

He bites into my neck and I scream. He mocks me, "How do you like being bitten. Don't feel so good, does it?"

He is enraged. He lets go of me with his right hand long enough to deliver a blow to my face that snaps my head backward so hard I am amazed I am still conscious.

"Please," I manage to beg, "think about the baby. Please. If you are going to do this, do not hurt my baby."

I can no longer see my attacker due to the pain and the swelling of the eye that took the impact of his blow, but I can hear the malice in his voice, and I know we are doomed.

"Like I give scat about some half-nigger whelp! Here's what I think of your nigger child, Yella!" Robinson draws back his fist and hits me as hard as he can, this time in the stomach.

"No!" I scream. I try to wrap myself around the baby. Instead of being deterred by my efforts, the man seems to be aroused. After the third blow to my abdomen, I try hard not to scream, but the pain is so bad, I cannot keep from crying out. The man is so strong, so incensed I can do nothing more to stop him. On top of his strength is the havoc the sheer vileness of the man reeks on my senses. I am helpless against the assault.

He finds the knife I had been looking for on the table, and I think he is going to put me out of my misery. Instead, he takes the tip of it and spreads the blood from my bite wound over my face, then uses it to slice the top of my dress open to the waist. Throwing the knife on the floor, he rips the dress completely off my body. He pulls me by the hair until I am lying lengthwise on top of the table. I drift toward unconsciousness, but I am painfully revived as he thrusts himself between my legs. The bile rises in my throat, and I instinctively turn my head to the side so I will not choke when I throw up the contents of my stomach. Robinson doesn't seem to notice the vomit at all as he pumps between my legs. I feel the flesh tear, but I soon become numb to the pain. I try again to wrap my arms around the mound of my stomach to protect my son, but Robinson grabs both wrists and thrusts my arms above my head. The position puts him face down in my breasts, and he bites and sucks like the wild animal he is until at last he falls forward on top of me, his weight pressing the baby into my backbone. I try to push him off, but he is too heavy. He reaches beneath himself and grabs my breast in one hand. He squeezes hard, and I at last lose consciousness.

I do not know how long I am out before a blow to the back of my head revives me. I am on the floor again. I know my head has struck the brick beneath me, but I feel nothing, not even the last kick to my stomach that Robinson puts his full weight behind. I sink back toward oblivion, but I do not get there before I hear his promise.

"I'll be back, Mizz Yella. We'll have more fun when you don't have that bastard whelp taking up all that space between us."

Chapter 29

"**O**h My God!" I say at least three times before I collect my wits. "Dovie, take the kids upstairs. Mammy, get the washtub." I do not have to repeat myself to either of them. They seem to grasp the situation before I do. Dovie, with Ella on her hip, is already dragging Rob from the room before the words have left my mouth. Mattie stands rooted to the floor, staring at the heap she understands to be her Tata Jessie. Her face is blank; her arms hang loosely by her sides. She looks like I feel.

"Gul, git on odda hyur." Mammy, with Fredie in tow, grabs Mattie's arm and pulls her toward the door. As soon as she has pushed her up the stairs and handed Fredie off to Dovie, she hurries back downstairs and out the back door.

I sink to the floor beside Jessie who is curled in a fetal position around her massive stomach. She shivers as though it is freezing instead of the ninety-odd degrees it actually is. I pick up the torn remains of Jessie's dress and try to drape it around her.

"My God, Jessie, what happened?" Jessie's one open, dry left eye stays fixed on something above my shoulder while liquid oozes from the slit between the two red, swollen mounds of flesh of the right. I wrap my arms around her and gently begin to rock her back and forth. I am so relieved when Mammy returns with the tub I almost cry. Neither Mammy nor I speak as she takes the pail of boiling water from the hook in the fireplace and pours it into the tub. She rushes to the barrel by the back door and drops the bucket into it. I register the hiss as the hot bucket is thrust beneath the cold water. Mammy adds two buckets of cold water to the tub, then kneels beside Jessie and me and starts to gently lift Jessie up off the floor.

"What in God's name happened to you?" I ask again. I really do not expect an answer, but it is all that will come out of my mouth.

"Wy you keep axin dat? Some man gaw ta er," Mammy spits angrily. "Sho ta Gawd you kin tell dat much!"

I stare blankly at Mammy's set, angry face. "But how…why…right here in our own house?"

"Jessie be jus nuff nigga dat day doan haf ta be no reason! Jus hep me git er in da tub."

"We have got to send for Dr. Waring," I finally realize.

"I awread do dat. Lew on da way."

The two of us start to lift Jessie from the floor, but Mammy stops suddenly, and I am forced to stop with her.

"What are you doing, Mammy? I cannot do this by myself!"

"We migh bedder naw put er in da tub, Mizz Abby. Da wadda broke, and dare blood ebberwhar down dare!"

The two of us manage to get the much taller Jessie off the floor and onto the bench by the table. We have had a hard time finding a place to grasp Jessie's body because so much of her coffee-colored skin is marred by angry welts and forming bruises.

"Get some quilts and we will put her on the floor and clean her up the best we can," I decide.

I have never known Mammy to move so fast. She is back in no time and the two of us lower Jessie onto the pallet Mammy makes for her.

The water in the tub becomes a streaky rust-colored broth as we rinse our cloths time and time again. Finally, I wet a cloth in a clean bucket of water and gently smoothe the hair back from her face. Jessie does not wince as I lightly pat her swollen eye with the cloth. "Mammy, there's a nasty bump on her forehead, and I can feel a huge one on the back of her head."

"Das da las ting we need ta warry bou. She aw tore up down hyur, an wid da wadda gone an aw dis blood, she gonna need some hep. Aw dis blood ain comin from da beatin."

"Oh My God," I say again.

"I done tol you, dis ain nuffin ta do wid Gawd! Dis haf ta do wid sum wite baster dat kin hab wat he wanse!" Mammy shouts at me.

I am not shocked by Mammy's anger, but I am surprised by the tears running down her cheeks. I have not realized until now that I am crying, too.

"Whoever did this will pay for it, Mammy! No one can come into our home and do this to one of our servants! Let's get her to the couch in the parlor—it is the closest place—then you see if you can find someone to send for Mr. Barret. Jessie, do you think you can help us get you to the couch, or do we need to wait for the doctor?"

"I doan tink we shou moob er," Mammy reminds me. "case da bleedin git wurse."

I know Mammy is right, but I want to do something to help Jessie. I hate leaving her here on the floor. We wrap a muslin sheet around her, and I fold another one to put beneath her head.

"We sen Lew fer Mose wen he git back," Mammy says when we have done all we can think of to do.

"No." It is the first word Jessie has spoken since we found her.

"But, Jessie, he has a right to…" I begin.

"I said no. Please…"

"Jessie, we have to think of the baby. Moses needs to be here…"

"It is too late." Jessie's voice is barely audible. "He's gone."

"Who is gone?" I ask, but Jessie has slipped back into unconsciousness.

Jessie still has not awakened by the time the doctor comes. Frederick is not far behind him, and he stops just inside the door to stare at Jessie's still body. When Dr. Waring kneels to start his examination, Frederick crosses the room and disappears into the hallway beyond. Even Dr. Waring who must see awful things is shocked by Jessie's condition. Mammy and I stay on the floor beside Jessie while the doctor examines her. She has been beaten terribly, but the wounds that horrify me most are the bites. I can actually see the individual teeth prints in the deep gash on her neck, and her breasts look like they have been attacked by a dog.

Dr. Waring's mouth is set in a hard line, but he says nothing until he is finished, then he gestures for us to follow him to the hallway where Frederick waits.

"This is some bad business," he tells us, as if we have not realized it. "The good news is the bleeding seems to have stopped." Dr. Waring's eyebrows pull together in concern as he lowers himself wearily to the bench beside Frederick. "The bad news is I can feel no movement from the baby."

I try to suppress the sob, but I cannot, and Frederick rises to comfort me. I turn my face into his shoulder. Though no one asked Mammy to join us, it seems only natural she is beside me, and though her face registers no emotion, the tears of earlier have returned to course silently down her face.

"Hopefully, the trauma has just put the baby into some kind of shock. If this woman survives, the baby may be fine, but I would not count on either. I have never seen anything like this."

"The baby will have to come soon, with or without my help, and then we will know more. It is imperative she does not lose much more blood. We need to get her to a bed where we can get her situated before the labor begins. Where shall we put her?"

Frederick appears to be in shock, and for once he is at a loss for words. "Take her to our room," I decide. Then, in case there is opposition, I add, "It is the only place that will not be needed for the children."

"Mammy," Frederick gathers his wits and turns to Mammy who has been hovering close to my side, "send Lew to get Moses. We need to know what he wants to do—whether he wants to keep her here or take her home."

"She cannot be moved, Frederick!" I insist, shocked my husband would even think of such a thing.

"That is not our decision to make, Abby. Moses is her husband. It is for him to decide."

Moses arrives quicker than any of us think possible. He rushes into the room, falls to his knees beside Jessie, takes both her hands in his, and begins to weep, his massive frame shaking all over.

"Is she gonna be awrigh?" he looks to the doctor for encouragement, apparently unworried about what we think about his unmanly display of emotion. The doctor looks down to avoid the misery in Moses' eyes.

"Only God knows that, Boy. We will just have to wait and see."

The sound of Moses' voice must have registered with Jessie. She opens her eyes, and though they still show no sign of life, she lifts her hand to her husband's face before closing them again.

"What do you want to do, Moses?" Frederick asks. I think he is glad to pass the responsibility off to someone else.

"I doan know, Missa Barret. Wat you tink bes?"

"We think it would be better to keep her here, Moses," I interject. I have no idea if Frederick thinks this is the best plan, but at the moment, my only concern is Jessie.

"Den dat wat we do," Moses agrees immediately.

Though Frederick offers to help him carry Jessie upstairs, Moses mumbles, "I kin do it," and he lifts his wife as easily as if she were a child. He carries her up the stairs and places her gently on the bed Mammy has rushed ahead to prepare for the birth.

"I am going to dose her with some cod liver oil, and that should get things moving. I think we have the best chance of both of them surviving if we get the baby out as soon as possible."

In the hallway outside, I instruct Frederick, "Get Moses a chair and wait with him. I'm going to send the children to Bette's with Dovie. Mammy, please help Dr. Waring any way possible."

I know the last instructions are unnecessary, but I am keeping myself from thinking by taking action. Mammy meekly answers "Yessum, Mizz Abby," and Frederick hurries downstairs to get a chair for Moses as if it were the most natural thing in the world for a black man to be sitting outside his bedroom door awaiting the birth of his child.

Chapter 30

I am going to kill the bastard who did this! Frederick promises himself as he sits beside Moses in the small hallway.

How dare some man violate the sanctity of his home! The violence of the crime against Jessie brings back memories Frederick has tried hard to forget. Beneath his anger, there is fear. A dormant panic has been awakened, one he had hoped to never feel again. He thought he had left such uncivilized behavior behind with his old life, and though he knows things like this go on in his adopted country, he had assumed they happened to the poor, uneducated masses in America. True, Jessie could be considered a Negro, but she certainly is not uneducated, and she is his hired servant, for Christ's sake! *Whoever did this foul deed will pay for it, no matter who he is,* Frederick vows.

Moses sits with his elbows propped on his knees, his head in his hands, his eyes closed, his mouth moving in what Frederick assumes is prayer. Frederick is not surprised, for he knows it will take an act of God for both mother and child to survive the beating Jessie has taken.

Who could have done such a thing? No white man among his society would dare enter another man's home in broad daylight and commit such a crime, no matter the level of lust. It must have been someone's slave or some poor, white trash from Yamacraw. It is a known fact that the Negroes and the Irish get drunk every Sunday at those tippling houses down on River Street. *Something has to be done about that, and I will be just the man to see it happens.* He has made some name for himself in Savannah, and he will use the clout he has to pass laws to keep the riffraff of this town off the streets.

Frederick's plans are interrupted by Dr. Waring who opens the bedroom door and steps out into the hallway. Frederick has been listening for the cry of a baby, and he knows the news is not good because they have not heard one. As Moses gets slowly to his feet, Frederick knows he, too, anticipates the worst.

"I am sorry to say the baby was dead when we delivered him."

Dr. Waring speaks more to Frederick than to Moses, but when the former turns to the big man whose arms hang limply by his side, he addresses him instead. "Your woman may very well make it. There has been no more bleeding, and she seems to have endured the birth as well as can be expected."

Tears again roll down Moses cheeks, and there is no hint of anger in his voice as he addresses the doctor. "It be a boy den?"

When the doctor tells him it was, Moses nods his head. "Jessie say it be." He wipes a tear away, then looks directly into the doctor's eyes. "Our chile be gone, bu lease da Lawd spare Jessie. Fo dat I be grateful, ta Him and ta you. Tank you, Docta."

Frederick marvels at the man's composure. If he had just lost his only chance at a son, he would be railing against God, something he is not proud he had done when Luella died. This man, on the other hand, is thanking God.

"Well, I have done all I can do here, Frederick. The woman seems to be in good hands with your servant. Send for me if you think I am needed."

As Moses moves to enter the room, Frederick reaches up to put his hand on his shoulder. "Moses, find out the name of the bastard who did this to her."

I ten to, Missa Barret. You kin coun on dat." The iron determination on the big man's face makes Frederick resolve never to cross him. "I fully ten to."

With that, Moses leaves Frederick in the hallway. Within a moment, Mammy exits the way he came, quietly closing the door behind him.

Chapter 31

Frederick sits at his office desk ruminating about the bad luck that has befallen his family. The attack on Jessie in his home on Broughton Street has cast a pall over his whole household, and in an effort to make things better, Frederick is determined to move up his plans to build the mansion of his dreams. It has been a year since the travesty, and though Abby took Jessie to Hickory Grove with her for the summer, neither woman came back to Savannah as recovered from the incident as Frederick had hoped. Jessie is back at work and there is no physical evidence of what happened, but one need only look into her eyes to know she is far from normal.

As for Abby, she has become downright paranoid. She demands that Lewis or one of the dock workers be at the carriage house at all times, even when the store is open for business. If Frederick is not at home, she wants a male there to keep an eye on the back entry of the house. *God help that bastard Robinson if he ever shows his face in this town again!* He has brought the violence of the Island to his own doorstep. Frederick is determined the man will pay for disrupting his life and causing those he cares for pain and heartache.

Frederick has been trying to come up with a plan as to how he can legally deal with the criminal if he ever runs across him, but so far, he has thought of no way to prove the man guilty of anything. Though Frederick has asked everyone he knows who might have come in contact with the slave trader, no one admits seeing the man in the vicinity within weeks of the intrusion. If he had not known Jessie as well as he does, he might have thought she was mistaken as to the identity of the man. After all, she had seen him only once before, and then only for a moment. But Jessie has told both Moses and Frederick who her attacker was, describing him exactly as the man Frederick remembers from their one-time business transaction. She had even remembered his name: Robinson.

Frederick Barret keeps meticulous records of all his business deals, even those some might consider inconsequential, so he had had no trouble verifying the accused's name. He had written the name Gene Robinson in his ledger as the purchaser of a horse he had received as payment for some wares from a small-time farmer outside of town. Frederick was not surprised Jessie remembered the man from her brief encounter because he too had remembered him, and not favorably. He had thought the man an oily character, but he would never have suspected him capable of what he had done. The beating and rape of Jessie rivaled anything he had seen done by the darkest heathens on the Island.

Just thinking about how awful Jessie had looked and how devastated she and Moses had been over the loss of their child, Frederick is infuriated all over again. Killing would be too good for the bastard, and at the moment, he is not opposed to dealing with the man covertly if he cannot come up with a plan the law will condone. Without evidence other than the word of his colored servant, he knows there will be no way to bring the man to justice. Frederick is a man of action, and he does not like the helpless feeling this whole unsavory incident leaves him with.

Frederick decides this line of thinking is getting him nowhere. He might as well dwell on something that gives him pleasure. He unlocks the drawer of his desk where he keeps his house plans, and lying on top is the letter he received from his father over a month ago. It seems his morning is to be consumed with unpleasant thoughts.

After looking up the business transaction he had had with the Robinson man, Frederick had remembered him claiming to know his relatives in Louisiana, so he had written them in Bayou Teche to ask what they knew of the man. He had been careful to address the letter to his cousin, so he had been surprised to receive a reply from the great man himself. This was only the second letter he had received from Emile Barret in his life, so it was no surprise that the real purpose of his letter was to ask a favor of his all but forgotten son rather than to supply the information Frederick had sought. Now, Frederick spreads the letter in front of him to read again.

My Dear Son, his father writes in French. Apparently the old man has never learned to write in English. The endearment itself is a mockery.

Your cousin Solange was kind enough to read me the letter he received from you, and it was with delight I learned you and your small family are well.

Frederick is curious as to the source of the old man's information about his *small family* since he himself has communicated nothing of his personal life to him. While Frederick was still in Saint Domingue, he had remembered the names of the cousins his father was reported to be staying with, and after much effort on his part, had come up with an address at which to write the man he could barely remember. He had been quite excited to get a quick reply from his father until he realized it was to let him know he could not, in his current position as a guest in the home of his cousins, find his way clear to help Frederick upon his arrival in the States. The letter had been brief, but it left no doubt as to its purpose. It was a politely worded message that more or less said his son would be on his own as far as his father was concerned, just as he had been on his own since his father had escaped the Island. He had sailed on the last transport out to Cuba arranged for the few French officers who managed to survive the slave insurrection that had finally and completely unseated the French government in St. Domingue. Upon receiving that first letter, Frederick had vowed to be done with the man, but in spite of himself, his father's rejection still hurts.

Though we have met the slave trader of whom you inquire, we have had no personal dealings with him, so Solange passes on the message that he cannot in good conscious recommend him to you. Frederick had not told Solange why he was asking about the man, and he had even asked him to keep the inquiry to himself, so it is no surprise his cousin would assume he was thinking of using his services. *He may very well be a reputable trader, but as Solange and his brother have not yet dealt in slaves, they know little about his reputation.*

That out of the way, Emile's letter gets interesting. *Both Solange and his brother Baptiste were surprised last year when visiting your area to find they had a close relation living there, and they tell me you are a man of some social standing. I told them I was not surprised as we Barrets have always been good businessmen who traditionally land on our feet when met with adversity. I have told them I am sure you will be glad to make their acquaintance when they next visit your city, a place they tell me is quite beautiful. It would greatly please me if you would offer them assistance in locating and purchasing some Negroes to help run their considerable holdings here in Louisiana. They feel, as do I, it would be much better to trust a member of one's own family in such matters. Though Mr. Robinson may be a fine man and we have no cause to suspect otherwise, Solange and Baptiste would much rather get your advice in so important an undertaking.*

This part of the letter had made Frederick furious. It still does. It tells him much about his father. First of all, it makes him aware that his cousins had known nothing of his letter to his father telling him he was coming to the States—indeed, they may have known nothing of his existence—and they were more than willing to claim him as a family member. Now that his father knows he is doing well for himself in Savannah, he, too, is willing to acknowledge his existence. In fact, he actually had the audacity to request a favor of him! How little effort or thought his father had put into aiding him is now obvious. He had not even told the relatives he had a son coming to the States. Frederick wonders if he had even told his cousins he had left a son behind on the Island. Frederick would be willing to bet every cent he has that he had not told them of his existence.

Frederick can stand to read no more. He had vowed to burn the letter when he'd read it before. Now he crosses to the fireplace where a small fire burns. He tosses the letter on the coals and returns to his desk to pull out the house plans he has been distracted from in the first place. It is time to put his plan in motion.

Frederick has been over and over his finances, and he has decided it is time to move on the tract of land, two prime lots on the corner of Bull and Harris right across from the army barracks. He will go today and talk with his friend, John Andrews, the president of Planter's Bank. Maybe something good can come from this tragedy that has befallen his household. It has spurred him on, and the family will benefit from the expediency with which he is now willing to act. The fact that Abby is expecting again makes the move that much more imperative. It is his goal to break ground on the mansion by Christmas. Development has just begun on Bull Street, and he trusts his good business instincts that this is going to be an address to commend him and his family to Savannah society, one that will say, "The Barrets are not just accepted into our midst; they are a family to know." Frederick had hoped to enlist the services of William Jay, but rumors indicate he is in poor health, and he cannot risk hiring someone who may not be able to complete the task. He has heard of an architect, a Cluskey, who was commissioned to build a fine home or two in Savannah, and he will have John contact him as soon as possible.

Now that the decision is made, Frederick is eager to tell Abby about it. Maybe the good news will help her put behind them the whole unfortunate affair with Jessie. Maybe it will help Jessie, too. In a year or two, she will have one of the best kitchens in Savannah to call her own, in a manner of speaking.

If Frederick's father thinks he is successful now, he can only imagine what the old man will think when he finds out his son is building one of the biggest mansions in Savannah. Frederick determines to make sure the news travels that way, and he will make sure he does it soon. He knows his father had a family before him, so he has to be getting along in years. He would hate for the old man to die without knowing how misguided his refusal to acknowledge his own son has been.

Chapter 32

I walk to Potters Field on my way home from the Barrets. I take a small bouquet of roses I picked in the garden behind the house and follow the trail I myself have made to the small grave in the corner of the section set aside for Negroes. There is a cross roughly a foot wide by a foot and a half long lying on top of the grave. Moses made it by piecing together three long, slender rocks he found by the river. The rectangular stone at the base of the grave is set inches from the end of the three-foot casket lying beneath the ground. Moses made that too. Now the end stone reminds me how small is the resident beneath the cross. There is no name because we did not give our son a name, but in my mind and in my heart he is Joshua for that is what he would have been called had he lived. Moses handed the reins of responsibility to Joshua when Moses himself had become too old to carry on. It was Joshua who led Moses' people to the Promise Land. It was for that reason I named my son Joshua. Our son could have done no better than to carry on where his father leaves off, to be the good man his father is.

I do not cry. I have never cried. If crying could give us our son back, I would shed tears enough to flood this desolate tract of land, but that is not the way things work. Joshua is gone, and all I have left of him lies beneath these four rocks that Moses picked up and hauled back from the river.

I do not know why I continue to come here. Moses does not. He says it just makes him sadder. I do not think anything can make me sadder than I already am, so what can it hurt? Maybe I want to pay respect to the little boy who fought so hard to live under the blows of a madman.

Maybe I want to show him, if he is capable of knowing, that I still think of him and will always.

I place my little offering at the base of the stone cross and pull the few straggly weeds that have dared to rear their heads since I was last here. Though visitors may not know the name of the child who lies here, they will be able to tell he is loved by the care given to his grave.

The days are long this time of year, and when our house comes into sight, I notice how good it looks. Moses has worked feverishly since my attack, and both our house and the boarding house have taken the brunt of his energy. Once I would have glowed with pride to own such a home. Now it means little other than I am glad Moses has a way to release the frustration he feels for not being able to punish the man who took so much from us.

When I enter the house, I look around with fresh eyes. There is plenty of room in the living room because Moses has moved our bed to the back room he completed. He started it right after we were married in preparation for the child we were to have. Now the front room simply looks empty and neglected. For Moses sake, I need to make more of an effort. He deserves more than I am giving though he would never say so. He treats me with kid gloves, as if he still sees my battered body when he looks at me unclothed. It took him months to make love to me again, and that was only after I led him to it. His love and the comfort of his body are about the only things that make me know I am still alive.

I notice a piece of paper on the table, and when I cross the room I see it is written by Moses in precise, oversized letters. *Jes, come to da boaden house. Big Sprize!*

I am tired. I do not want to go to the boarding house, but I will not disappoint Moses. He asks little of me. I put the bonnet I have just taken off back on and close the door behind me.

The sun is finally setting and the air is cooling some by the time I get to Moses' house of business. Lamplight in all the windows indicates he has no vacancies. It is amazing how well it is doing. Moses even has some white renters these days, and I am not surprised. There are few places for people of little means to lodge in Savannah, and Moses' house offers clean rooms and good food to anyone who can afford the low price, and on occasion, those who cannot.

I speak to a couple of full-time lodgers who are sitting in the rockers Moses made on the front porch. I nod at a man I have not met. I open the door and enter the large, rectangular room that serves both as a place for the tenants to congregate and a dining room. Moses is standing beside the table closest to the kitchen holding an infant in his arms. My heart quickens at the sight, and I am gripped by sadness. This is what Moses holding our child would have looked like. It does not make me happy to be reminded, so I am not smiling when I approach him. I am distracted by the child in his arms, and I do not notice the woman sitting on the bench beside the table until I am within a few feet of them. I cannot believe I missed her, for she is not a small woman. When she stands, she is taller than I, and that is rare for a man, let alone a woman.

I look at Moses. His face is open and smiling—happier than I have seen in a long time. I am confused and a little angry. How can he possibly be happy holding this woman's child when mine lies dead in the ground?

"Jessie, dis Lavinie, da sistah I tole you bout!"

I am shocked. I look the woman square in the face and I see Moses reflected there. My smile is genuine, and she seems relieved to see it. I am instantly ashamed because I know my previous displeasure must have shown on my face.

"Lavinie!" I exclaim. "It is wonderful to finally meet you!"

I hug the woman, a fact that surprises us both. She returns my hug before stepping back to look at me. She takes inventory of me as I do her.

"Good ta know you, Mizz Jessie," she says, and she dips her head in deference.

"Please, just call me Jessie. We are sisters now."

The woman's smile grows broader, and I realize she is younger than I first thought. We both stand smiling, taking each other in until Moses interrupts the silence.

"Jessie, look wat I hab hyur. Dis baby Dinah."

He holds the wrapped baby out to me, and I hesitate. Sensing my reluctance, Moses places one arm around my shoulder and turns me to face him. He holds the baby against me and acts as if he is about to release her, so I have no choice but to take the child in my arms. A little dark face with bright eyes and a pink rosebud mouth looks up at me. She wiggles, and the cover falls back to reveal a plump, squirming baby.

"How old is she?" I whisper.

"She be nigh on eight munts now," Lavinie tells me. "An er name be *Di-an-a*." Lavinie stresses each syllable slowly and clearly.

"Dat wat I say—*Dinah*," Moses insists. "Less set down." Lavinie and I sit on the bench he pulls out, and he sits across the table from us.

"Lavinie," I manage, "I had no idea you were coming. Moses never said."

"Moses nebber say cause Moses dint know," Moses laughs, but he sobers when he continues. "Lavinie cide ta come ta fine me wen Rube sole off ta a rice fawma ow on Tybee."

"But I thought you were sending money for Lavinie to buy him!"

"I was, bu da massa's wife die an he up and sole aw ub em an move wes fo Rube know wat happen. Lavinie tuck da money I sen er an come lookin fo me affa she hyur Tybee be jus a piece from hyur. She hope Rube new massa low em ta come see er, or mabe we kin come up wid da money ta buy em."

"You poor thing!" I drag my attention away from the baby and really look at her. Her clothes are poorly made and dusty from travel, and her face shows her fatigue. I can only imagine what it took for her to get here on her own with this small child.

"I dint hab no way ta tell Mose I be comin cause I cain write an da missus dat write fo me wen nawth fo da summer. So I jus haid ow on ma own. Wuden da smartus ting I ebber do, bu now I hyur, I glad I do it."

If any woman should be able to make it on her own, I think, it should be Lavinie if physical appearances mean anything. She is a large woman, a kind of female version of Moses, but whereas their looks are good for a man, they render poor Lavinie somewhat homely. I am immediately ashamed of this thought, especially when I see the warmth in her troubled brown eyes. They remind me so much of Moses', I know I am going to love her. Looking down at the child in my arms, I am immediately smitten. Just as I know I will love her mother, I know I will move heaven and earth to protect this beautiful child.

"The two of you must come to the house! Have you eaten yet? I know you must be exhausted—we need to get you home so you can clean up from your trip and get some rest." In my head I am already thinking about how we can arrange things so Moses' sister and baby can move in with us.

"We awready tawk bou dat, Jessie," Moses tells me, "an we cide it bes if day stay hyur fo now til we know zackly wat we wanna do."

"But don't they need to be with family? We can make room..."

"Dey mo room ober hyur, Jessie, and dey someone ta cook fo dem and hep durin da day til Vinie be back on er feet. You be gone ta wuk mos days. Once day res up, dey kin come ta da house fo dey meals if dey wanna, an mabe we kin add annuda room on da back ub da house fo dem latta."

I know he is right, but I want them to come to the house with us. I realize it is not my decision. After talking a while longer, I feel the baby restless in my arms, and Lavinie looks like she is about to fall asleep at the table.

"Do you need to go to bed, Lavinie?" I ask.

"If yaw doan mine. I nuss da chile, an den I tink she sleep. She probly plum tucker ow."

I hate to give up the baby. I watch as Moses leads them upstairs to a room. I wait for him, and the two of us walk home together. Moses is full of plans to help them get settled. My mind keeps going back to Diana's sweet little face. I ask Moses, "Do you think Lavinie will need help with the baby?"

"I doan know bou needin hep, bu I tink she wan it. Vinie hab a rough time. Da mo help we kin gib er, da bedda. I jus hope I kin fine Rube an do sumpin bou dem gettin ta see em."

I hope so, too, and if Lavinie needs to travel to see him, we will be glad to keep Diana. But, of course, Diana's father will want to see her as well. Maybe we can buy him and they can all come to live close by in Savannah. There are plenty of jobs a free man of color can hire out for—maybe Moses can even use him around the boarding house, or maybe I can ask Frederick if he needs help down at the wharf. I try to reign in my racing thoughts. I know I am getting ahead of myself. Lavinie and the baby may not even stay in Savannah. We have no idea what she will eventually decide to do.

Later, lying in bed, I remind myself that I must not get too attached to our little niece. Still, this is the closest thing to a child either Moses or I will ever have. I cannot help but hope we will get to be a part of her life. I felt such a connection when I held Diana in my arms. It was as if she belonged there. I know this is dangerous thinking, but I feel the stirrings of hope, the first I have felt since Joshua died. I feel something akin to contentment when I tuck myself against my husband and fall asleep.

I actually sleep all night without waking, and in the morning, I remember nothing of the nightmare that often wakes me in the night, the one in which Robinson returns to finish what he started, the one from which I awake determined to be ready for him when he comes.

Chapter 33

The women in this household are quickly outnumbering the men. The birth of little Brigitte Maxwell Barret who now sleeps in my arms brings our small family to two boys and three girls, but when we tally in Frederick, Jessie, Mammy, Dovie, and me, this house is harboring a total of seven females to three males. Frederick doesn't seem to mind being surrounded by women, but both he and I hope the building of the house moves along quickly now that Mr. Cluskey has completed the blueprint and the builders have been employed. There are only so many people one can put under one small roof.

Frederick was very proud when he presented me with his version of the house plans—his surprise for me, he called them. It is true they were a surprise. I knew he was planning to build us a new home—we had discussed that. What surprised me was he had a complete set of plans that I had never seen before. In retrospect, I should not have been surprised at all. Frederick is a very take-charge man, and I know he thinks constantly about what is best for his family. I hope I did not let him know his surprise was somewhat of a disappointment to me—not the plans themselves; they, once I looked closely at them, are far grander than I would have imagined or hoped for. But, I had assumed I would be asked for input into what the house—our home, supposedly for the rest of our lives—would eventually be, and the surprise I was presented with was quite complete, right down to the details. Too, it came as an even bigger shock when I discovered Frederick had purchased a lot without first taking me to see it. The site for our new home turned out to be a good decision, as well, I must admit, because I can think of no place I had rather be if we plan to remain in Savannah proper, but I had hoped

Frederick might consider living out in the countryside, close perhaps to the Andrews who have a plantation out in Effington. Though I have not previously mentioned it to Frederick, I miss plantation life and would like to rear our children in a manner similar to my own upbringing, for I think there is much to be said for country life. When I suggested as much to Frederick, I was sorry to see he was quite disappointed in my response to the news that he had purchased not one prime lot, but two connecting and situated on a corner in what he tells me is going to be a very sought after location on Madison Square. He went on to inform me that he intends to purchase some land in Effington close to his friend, but it is to be used for outings, hunting for the boys, some plantings perhaps, but that he has no desire to own a plantation and the number of slaves it would require to run one as John Andrews does. He says slaves in those numbers are not to be trusted, and he feels it unsafe for his family to live far out in the midst of their numbers. Though he does not tell me so, I know his fears stem from the slave uprising in his homeland, a topic that has been discussed much among our peers.

Regardless, we are to have a home designed by him on Bull Street whether I like it or not, and I have decided to like it, for I really have no other choice. Sometimes I find my husband high-handed. I assume most men are, and I am just unaccustomed to their ways as I was reared solely by a woman, if one does not take into account the influence of my uncle. Though I am not and will never be as forthright about it as my friend Bette, I am beginning to think we women have little say in our own lives. But I must not complain. Life is good for me right now, and I thank God for that, for I have seen up close how awful things can happen when one least expects it. I got word just a month ago that my sister Anne's husband has died. It was quite unexpected; he simply fell asleep in his chair, apparently of some heart ailment no one knew he had. I didn't know Edward well, but my heart breaks for Anne. She has taken Luella and Caroline and moved home to live with Mother.

I think how devastated I would be if something happened to Frederick. The attack on Jessie was horrible enough, but at least her life was spared. And Jessie finally seems to be doing better. I will never forget how broken she was at the loss of her child, and I so empathize with her. I cannot imagine losing one of mine. True, her infant never really drew a breath this side of the womb, but I know I would have been crushed if either Ella or baby Maxie had not come breathing into this world after I had carried her for nine, long months.

But I must think happier thoughts, or I will be cast down, and I must not let that happen. I feared I would succumb to a bout of despondency after Maxie's birth much as I did with Ella, but I miraculously escaped a repeat of those awful months. I have no idea how that came to be, though I know Frederick thinks he is responsible in part for my lifted spirits. He thinks he has distracted me with the promise of a new home. If anyone should be given credit, it should probably be Bette, for I have found her to be a wonderful confidante, one with whom I can share my anxieties without fear of censure. She and my sister Sophie were wonderful companions during my confinement. Sophie showed up unexpectedly a few days after Maxie was born and stayed until a week ago when she returned to Baltimore and her own husband. I think she may have come as much to get used to dealing with a newborn as to comfort me, for she is expecting her second in the spring. Her Jimmy hasn't been a baby for some time. Regardless of her reasons, I was thankful for her company, and I will return the favor and be with her at Hickory Grove where she plans to give birth. I myself would have done likewise if Maxie had been born in the unhealthy season, but she had graciously appeared in winter, so I stayed in Savannah.

Maxie is a beautiful child. Like Ella, she has her father's dark, curly hair, brown eyes, and almond skin. I know it is more fashionable for women to have fair skin like I do, but I think all three of our girls are going to be beautiful women, the promise of which Mattie is already fulfilling at the age of ten. Too, I only hope the two I have given birth to will be as loving and compassionate as she is. She is quite the little mother herself doing her best to steer her willful sister Ella into ladylike deportment. I heard her gently correcting her just yesterday.

"Ella, you mustn't smack Fredie with your doll! He's your big brother, and it's not good for your dolly, either."

It is good that Mattie tries to mold her. I am busy with Maxie, both the boys are smitten, and Frederick seems to think everything she does is delightful. Ella, unlike the other children, seems unfazed by Mammy's scoldings. I must make more of an effort to help Mattie influence my strong-willed daughter, even though it will be hard for me to give her the attention she needs when Maxie is such a joy to me right now. I regret letting my sinful nature rob me of the months I might have enjoyed with Ella, but I cannot get that time back. Maybe my lack of attention is the reason for Ella's willfulness. I was too bogged down in my own gloom to connect with her the way I have Maxie.

"Hey, little Maxie," I coo to my daughter, "you are Mama's little bit of sunshine."

I have chosen to nurse her as I did Ella. I like nursing my babies. It makes me feel bound to them in a way I don't think possible if someone else is allowed to nurse them. I now thank God I fed Ella, for I know I would be even less connected to her than I am if I had not done so.

Maxie. I know it is an odd name for a girl, but I can't bring myself to call her Brigitte. Secretly, I fear calling her by her namesake's name may make her more like her. I was weak to let my husband name our child after a woman for whom I don't have the utmost respect, but I gave in. He started his campaign the minute she was born, so I guess I just wore down with time. I began to feel petty about my reluctance, and knowing she is the only relation my husband claims, I thought it was only fair I name a child after her. After all, I did not consult him about naming Ella after my sister.

I call Mammy who is across the hallway with Ella in the room she shares with Mattie. "Mammy, please take the baby, and I'll spend some time with Ella."

"Goo luck wid dat," Mammy mumbles. "Dat gul be a hanful!"

I cross the hallway and find Ella on the floor playing with some blocks I recognize as belonging to Fredie.

"How's my big girl?" I ask her as I pick her up from the floor.

"Down, Mama." Ella scowls her displeasure at being taken from her play.

I tuck my skirts and sit on the floor with her. "Can Mama play, too?"

She acquiesces by passing me two of her blocks. I place these one on top of the other, and I reach for her pile to add to my own. "No, Mama. Mine," she says.

I take her tiny hand that can barely hold the block she has reclaimed. "You must share, Ella. That is what good girls do."

Ella merely stares at me for a few seconds, her eyebrows drawn down in thought.

She quietly reaches over and takes the block back. "Mine."

I can't help but smile, but I am determined to prevail. Our battle goes back and forth for some time, but finally Ella relents. Not only does she let me take that block, but she offers me another of her own, and I build a small tower with her help.

Well, this will not be as difficult as I first anticipated. My daughter just needs some focused instruction.

"Will you hand Mama one more block, Ella? We'll put it on the top, and our tower will be finished."

Ella picks up another block and holds out her hand as if to give it to me, but at the last minute, she pulls it back and kicks out with her small shod foot to topple the tower. She then bends at the waist and scatters the whole pile of blocks. She looks up at me with a delighted smile, and though it is hard for me not to smile back at her, I reprimand her instead.

"Ella, that is not nice. You destroyed Mama's nice tower."

My unrepentant daughter hurls her small body at me and hugs me tightly around the neck. I cannot resist. I hug her in return and plant kisses across her laughing face.

It is true: we are going to have our hands full with this one.

Chapter 34

I am growing entirely too fond of another woman's child. She is adorable, and when I hold her, I feel like she is my own. I would not worry about these emotions so much, but I know Lavinie and Rube are trying to find a way to be together, and if they do, they may move away and take Diana with them.

Lavinie allowed me to take Diana to church today and home afterward. She may even spend the night with us, for Lavinie is taking her second trip to Tybee Island to see Rube. She has discovered a fellow boarder willing to take her across by boat for a small fee. The fellow is Soloman, a slave who is hired out by his owner, John Andrews. Andrews pays his board at Moses' house because he lives too far out for Solomon to make it back to his plantation each night after the late hours he works in Savannah. Solomon is eager to make extra money however he can because his owner allows him to keep most of what he makes in his free time, and he has crafted himself a small boat he uses to collect shrimp that he sells at the city market. Sunday being his only day off, he decided it would be profitable for him to row Lavinie to the island, spend the day shrimping, then row her home after dark in the evening. This is the second time they have left at dawn, and we all agreed it would be best to leave Diana with us in case she gets back as late as she anticipates.

Diana is worn out from the day's activities, and she falls asleep in my arms as I rock her. I place her in the crib Moses made for her. I have it beside the window because the open front door pulls a breeze across the room. I place a mosquito netting across the top and over the sides of the crib even though the pests do not seem to be as attracted to the dark skin of Moses and Diana as they do to my lighter shade. Still, I do not want to risk the child being bitten.

Diana Tucker. That is what they have decided to call her because Rube has no desire to give her the name of his previous or current owner. Though his previous owner was kind enough, Rube is angry with him for selling him with no notice, for not giving him time to make arrangements with Lavinie. His current owner he hates.

I have met Rube only one time, and then the meeting was brief. He had snuck away from the plantation on Tybee Island late one evening and found his way to the boarding house just before dawn. I had stopped by before going to work, so I happened to be there when he arrived. Lavinie had been horrified to see him. The consequences for Rube being away without permission are grave, and she could not believe he took such a risk. Rube assured her his master was away on business, but Lavinie knew the overseer would report him if he noticed Rube's absence, as she was sure he would, so Rube did not stay long.

Rube does not look anything like I imagined. He is lighter in color and smaller in stature than I pictured him in my mind. He is shorter than I by at least two inches. Though his arms are muscled from hard work, he is slightly built. If one saw him and Lavinie from behind, one might mistake them for mother and son. His face has a boyish charm, and I think Diana looks much more like him than she does her mother. I think this will prove advantageous to Diana, for Rube's features and size lend themselves more to feminine good looks than do Lavinie's. I would never have pictured Rube and Lavinie together, but there is no mistaking the genuine affection they have for each other. They go to great lengths and take considerable risks to be together. I understand because I know Moses and I would do the same.

Sadly, Rube has seen his daughter only the one time, that morning, since he was sold away. Lavinie thinks, and I wholeheartedly agree, that it would be too hard on her and the baby to take her to the island in the boat. Their loss is my gain, and I intend to enjoy every minute God gives me with this beautiful child. Though nothing can take away the pain of losing Joshua, Diana has managed to make the loss bearable. She has not yet said Tata, but neither has she said anything that anyone can actually credit as a word.

Moses comes home from his work at the church for supper. He plans to go back later, but we both cherish this time we have with Diana. I hold her on my lap and feed her from my plate. Moses puts some mashed potatoes on the end of his forefinger and offers it to Diana.

"Hyur ya go, Swea Pea, le Unck Mose gib you some taytas. Dey pu some meat on dat lil bidy."

"Ow!" he cries dramatically when she bites down on his finger. He yanks it back and acts as if she has done real damage. He is rewarded with a giggle.

"Moses," I scold, "you do not want to teach her that biting people is funny!"

"Aw, day time fo er ta figga dat ow layta. I goan do it one mo time an see if she laugh ow loud agin. She doan do dat offen."

I allow a repeat performance, though I know I should not. I want to hear her laugh again as much as Moses does. After three more bites and three more laughs, I make them stop. Moses takes his niece out back for some fresh air while I clean up after dinner, then he returns to the church for what I know will be several more hours of work on the tunnel he says is coming along quickly since he has recruited some help. I try not to think about his clandestine mission.

I put Diana to bed early and sit to sew on a dress I am making for her thinking I will work on it until Lavinie comes home. After several hours, I decide to go to bed. After I don my nightgown, I walk over to take one last look at Diana. She looks like a little angel with arms flung out to the side and legs splayed as if they are wings. Her delicate face is completely relaxed in sleep, and I bend to place a kiss on one of her plump cheeks.

What would it hurt for her to sleep with me tonight?

I pick her up as gently as possible and take her to the bed with me. I put a pillow on Moses' side so she will have a hard time rolling off, and I lie as close to her as I can without touching her. Her face is turned toward me, and I bring my own within a half inch of hers. I can feel her sweet breath on my face, but after a few moments, my neck aches from holding the position. I settle for a few inches away, and I am still asleep there when Moses wakes me.

"I din spec to fine da chile still hyur," he tells me, and I can see concern on his face.

"You know Lavinie planned to leave her if she came in too late. I will bring her by the boarding house on my way to the Barrets; that way Lavinie can sleep in a little later. You know she is bound to be exhausted."

"Wat a bidy do fo lub," Moses laughs.

He crawls in on the other side of Diana to catch a couple hours sleep before he has to rise. He takes some of that precious time to prop his face on his elbow and look down into the child's face.

"Eeder I bline wen come ta dis gul, or she be bou da purtiess lil ting you ebber lay eyes on."

"I think it may be some of both," I tell him.

I allow myself to lie with the two of them for the next half hour before I drag myself up to prepare breakfast. We enjoy the meal together before we see Uncle Moses off with numerous kisses. I enjoy getting Diana dressed and am about to leave for the boarding house myself when Moses surprises me by walking back through the door.

"Vinie ain come home." His face reveals his worry. "An Solmon ain back neeber."

I feel a catch in my chest.

"That's odd, but let's not jump to conclusions. Something may have come up and they may have had to spend the night."

"Like wat?"

"Well, I cannot think of anything right now, but there has to be a simple explanation."

"Wat we gonna do wid da babe. You gonna haf ta go ta wuk."

I have not thought of this problem. "I guess I will just have to take her with me."

"Mizz Barret be awrigh wid dat?"

"Well, all I can do is ask. What choice do we have? I am sure she would rather have me there with a baby and cooking rather than the whole family going without meals. Of course, if she minds, Mammy can cook. She used to cook for them all the time."

"I kin take er wid me, bu I doan tink thet be good, do you?"

"I certainly do not!" I say this more firmly than I intend, but Moses is preoccupied and he does not seem to notice.

"Awrigh, you take er wid you, an if da Missus doan like it, jus bring er back hyur an wait fo me. I be back soon I know sumpin."

I assure him we are worrying for nothing, but when he leaves, I allow myself to dwell on the possibilities. I regret not touching Lavinie before she left yesterday. In fact, I cannot remember the last time I touched Moses' sister. If I had hugged her before she left, I might have felt it if something were going to go wrong. But Lavinie is not outwardly demonstrative, nor am I, and if I am honest, I was so eager to get my hands on the baby, I paid little attention to the child's mother. Now I badly wish I had at least grasped the hand of my sister-in-law.

I create a sling of sorts out of some muslin I wrap under Diana's bottom, around each of my shoulders, around my middle a couple of times, then tie at my waist. I try to replicate what I have seen island women do, but never having the need for one myself, I produce a rather awkward contraption. Diana likes her new conveyance and wiggles about the whole time, kicking her legs and clutching parts of my dress within reach until she discovers the ribbon of my bonnet. These she treats much like one would the reins of a horse. By the time I get to the Barrets', my bonnet is askew, my hair is a mess, and my back is aching from her weight. It is with relief I untie my burden and use the muslin for a thin pallet on the floor. Unfortunately, she is not content to stay on it. I prepare breakfast with one eye on her and one on the task at hand. My biggest fear is that she will get into the fire. I have never been so relieved to see Dovie and Mammy when they show up for their morning meal.

"Wat da cat done drag in hyur?" Mammy asks when she almost trips over Diana. The child clutches at Mammy's skirts and tries to pull herself upright. Mammy picks Diana up and places her on her hip. I notice how natural a pose it is, one she has undoubtedly perfected over time. No telling how many babies Mammy has carried there.

Diana seems quite taken with Mammy and greets her and Dovie by giving them her widest smile, one that shows to advantage the four front teeth she has acquired in the last month.

"She is Moses' sister's child—Diana. The one I told you about. Her mother did not make it back from Tybee Island last night, so Moses has gone looking for her. I had to bring her with me or stay at home. I hope Miss Abby does not mind me bringing her. I hoped one of you might hold on to her while I serve Mr. Barret. I do not see any reason to bother him with the problem."

"Wat one mo chile gonna be ta dem? We kin jus hab er wid da brood upstair long as need be."

I want to hug Mammy I am so relieved, but I know she will not appreciate it if I do, so I thank her instead. Lewis joins us, and I treat them to some peach preserves though they are usually reserved for the family. Dovie takes Diana so Mammy can eat, and I get breakfast to Frederick without him having to know I have brought my problems to work with me. I know he probably would not object, but I prefer not to find out.

Dovie takes Diana with her to get the boys up while Mammy attends the girls. I know it is her practice to take Maxie to Abby for feeding before getting Mattie and Ella dressed.

"Mammy, will you please tell Abby my situation and let her know I am willing to take her back home and let you do the cooking, or we can make out best we can here together."

"I tell er, but I know dey ain gonna wan Mammy ta do da cookin. You done spile dem rotten."

I smile warmly at Mammy. This is the first time she has acknowledged me as a good cook other than to tell me something I have given them at breakfast is good.

"Thank you, Mammy. I will not forget you helping me like this."

Mammy turns at the door. "I sho you do da same fo me, if need be."

She doesn't wait for a reply. My eyes fill with tears. How silly I am, I think. I did not cry when my son was beaten from my body, yet I cry over a few words from a slave who is kind when I need her to be.

I have everything prepared and on the table when the whole remaining family files in, for I know I will need my hands free for Diana. I cannot have her crawling under Abby's feet, and both Dovie and Mammy will be occupied with their own charges. Dovie hands the still happy Diana to me, and I notice one of them has changed the child's wrappings. I had not even thought to bring extra with me I had left the house in such a rush. It was a miracle she had not soiled herself and my dress on the way over.

"Miss Abby," I immediately begin, "I hope you are not displeased with me for bringing the baby to work. I had no time to do anything else. I hope Mammy told you I am willing to take her home if you prefer."

Abby smiles and again I am relieved. "It is no problem whatsoever, and though I am sure Mammy would do a wonderful job cooking again, she says she prefers her current responsibilities, so if you can manage, it will be fine that you have the baby at work today."

"We hep er wid da chile," Dovie puts in, and I hope Abby does not think Diana will take away from her own children's care.

"After all," Abby reassures me, "what is one more in this house full of children?"

Mattie rushes through her breakfast and stands up. "Tata Jessie, may I hold her?"

"If it is alright with your mama, you can."

With a nod from Abby, I hand Diana over to Mattie who is used to toting around younger brothers and sisters. "Mattie, you are going to make a wonderful mother some day," I tell her.

She beams. I realize that the Barret children have had little contact with Negro children since no one in our household has young ones.

"What is her name, Tata?"

"Diana," Abby repeats. "What a pretty name. I wonder how her mother chose it."

"I actually know the answer to that," I tell her. "Lavinie is a free woman, but she had a sponsor whose name was Diana. She lived not far from her, and she helped Lavinie learn to do all kinds of things after she was freed. I know she took her back and forth to see her husband and wrote letters to Moses for her. Apparently Lavinie was quite devoted to her, and she wanted to show her appreciation, so she named her child after her."

Abby is interested in Lavinie's story. "So Lavinie was freed by her owners. Do you know why?"

This is a conversation I have not imagined myself having with Abby, and had I a choice, I would not be having it on a day when my wits are addled by the circumstances of the morning. I know I need to tread lightly with this subject, no matter how gracious my mistress is.

"She was owned by the same...man"—here I catch myself before saying benevolent man, because I do not want to imply that one who does not free his slaves is otherwise—"as Moses. He inherited them from his father, and he chose not to own slaves, so he freed all of his, including Moses and Lavinie."

My tale has the attention of Dovie and Mammy as well as Abby. Abby seems to forget the company she is in when she says, "Bette thinks we should all free our slaves."

The minute the words are out of her mouth, she seems as shocked as the rest of us adults.

Young Robart has apparently been paying attention to the conversation, as well.

"Everybody knows that's stupid talk!" the nine year old declares. "Only *radcal* northerners think like that, and you know what Papa thinks of them!"

"Do not use the word stupid, Robart, and the word is radical," Abby corrects him, but I can tell she is uneasy about her slip up. "I misspoke. What I meant to say is that Mrs. Stiles mentioned that there are those who think all slaves should be freed, but you are right, Robart, the concept is radical. Whatever would we do without ours! And this certainly is not a conversation for the breakfast table."

The atmosphere in the room is uneasy, and I am glad the kitchen is filled with rowdy children who keep it from becoming downright awkward. Neither Mammy nor Dovie opens her mouth, and I remove dishes from the table as if nothing is amiss. I hope Robart or Mattie do not repeat what Abby has quoted Bette as saying. Frederick would not like it.

Abby excuses herself, and Mammy and Dovie take the kids, including
Diana, upstairs to prepare for a few hours outside. For a while I am
troubled by the conversation and the possible consequences of it, but
soon my mind is drawn back to the graver worry of Lavinie. By noon I
have still not heard from Moses, and I decide to slip away to the boarding
house if I have not heard something soon. I am about to go upstairs
where Dovie has laid Diana down for an afternoon nap when I hear
a light tapping on the door. I open it to Moses and know immediately
by the solemn look he is wearing that he has not come to tell me that
Lavinie is home.

"What has happened?" I ask before he is through the door.

"Nuttin fo sho," he tells me, "but tings doan look good."

"What do you mean? Is there word from Tybee?"

"No wud ub en kine, bu Solmon boat worsh up on da bank dis side
ub da ribber wid nuttin in it."

I gasp, and I feel the blood drain from my face. "What are we going
to do?"

Moses sighs and sits wearily on a bench by the table. "I doan righly
know," he admits. "Da only ting I know ta do is go ober ta Tybee an tawk
wid Rube. Dat da only ting I know ta do."

"Oh, Moses, I am so sorry." I sit beside him and place an arm around
his shoulders. "Maybe our fears will come to nothing. We do not know
anything for sure yet."

I really do not believe what I am saying. Maybe at one point in my life
I would have, but no longer. Too many bad things have happened, and I
know in my heart this is another.

"Vinie cain swim," Moses says sadly, "an eben if she cou, wat chance
she hab in aw dem clothes?"

I do not try to console him with any more empty words. "Just go
to Tybee. See what you can find out. But, oh Moses, poor Rube will be
crushed. I am afraid of what he will do."

"Wat kin he do? He a slave."

"He can do something stupid. Talk to him, Moses. Tell him the
importance of staying calm, for Diana's sake. Tell him we will continue
to work on getting him free. His daughter will need him now more than
ever."

"We still doan know nuttin fo sho, Jes. Vinie cou still be alibe." Moses
looks at me with pleading eyes, but I cannot bring myself to give him
false hope. If Lavinie were alive and able, she would have returned to
her child.

"You are right, Moses. We do not know anything yet. I just want you to prepare yourself, in case."

This is the best I can offer.

Moses leaves to go to Tybee, and I spend the rest of the afternoon praying for something I know in my heart isn't going to happen. I make my way home late that evening with an exhausted Diana strapped to my aching body. Moses arrives even later to tell me that Solomon's body has washed up on shore and Rube is inconsolable. I sleep not at all as I try to work out in my head what we are going to do about Diana. I know our lives will never be the same, but it isn't like they were all that good to begin with. I continue to pray that Lavinie will be found alive against all odds, and that Rube will keep his wits about him. Neither happens.

Chapter 35

I have been thinking a lot about Minda lately. Maybe it was seeing little Diana with my girls that reminded me again of my childhood playmates. I have said nothing to Frederick about my suspicions about Clarence Stiles. There has never seemed to be a good time. When I think of it, Frederick is either at the office or we are with company or the mood doesn't seem to be right for so sensitive a topic. I think I will go see Minda. I will get Dovie or Mammy to go with me. I cannot believe I have been in Savannah all these years and still not laid eyes on the girl. Some of our friends' slaves go to church with us and sit in the balcony, just as ours used to do. But ours asked some time back to attend the Second African Baptist Church, and Frederick allowed it. I am sure Minda goes there since the rest of her family does. Even Jessie attends the Negro church now.

Seeing Jessie with Diana is odd. It reminds me that she is actually a colored woman. It is easy to forget when you are in her company alone. Though I would never say so to her, it is also odd she has married a man as dark as Moses. I know from listening to the slaves here and in Virginia that many of them take pride in lighter skin. I wonder that Jessie doesn't feel like she is stepping backward or beneath herself with Moses. I have not seen them together enough to know how she acts around him. I know he was the most attentive of husbands after the attack, and on the occasions I went there with Dovie or Mammy to take her food while she was convalescing, I could tell both she and he take pride in their home. That, too, was an eye opener. No matter how refined and dignified Jessie is, she still is a resident of Yamacraw, and the walk to her house was intimidating. Rarely have I seen such destitution and filth.

I guess the Scavengers do not bother with clearing the debris in that part of town. And the homes many of those people live in are inferior to the outbuildings we had at Hickory Grove, and certainly inferior to our slave quarters there. Jessie's is an exception. Though small, their house appears to be well-built and clean, yet the furnishings are still rudimentary and sparse. I can't help but think what it would be like to be Jessie. Frederick would say this is Bette's influence, and maybe it is, but I cannot help but think it is wrong that someone of Jessie's intellect, beauty, and talent cannot rise above a life lived out in Yamacraw.

I go to the kitchen to find the subject of my ruminations hard at work as usual. In the corner sits Diana in the pen Moses built for her. It is a square enclosure large enough for her to move around some and sleep in, but most importantly, it keeps her from being underfoot and getting into the fireplace. She is often with the other children, but Jessie says it is placing too great a burden on the already overtaxed Dovie and Mammy to expect them to help out with her child as well as ours. She is right about that as she is most things. I have already talked with Frederick about getting more help for the household, and he promises we will do so as soon as we move into the new house. He thinks we may be able to move within the year, but I am not so sure. We walked by the site after church just last Sunday, and there is not much more than a footprint there. I was amazed at what a large foundation they have dug, and Frederick says it appears small in comparison to how large our home will be when we build three stories up—four actually, counting the basement. I cannot believe this mansion is actually going to be ours, and I certainly cannot see how it is going to be completed within the year. As I watch Diana trying to climb over the top of the railing on her chicken wire covered prison, I do not know how this arrangement will continue to work until we move.

"Jessie," I say, "That girl is getting too big to contain that way. She is trying to climb that wire, and I am afraid she is going to cut her feet on it."

"I know," Jessie sighs. "We are going to have to make other arrangements. Have you given any further consideration to my suggestion that you find another cook, one that can fill in for just a year or two until Diana is old enough to come with me and stay out of trouble?"

I am immediately sorry I have mentioned the problem. Right after the child's mother died, Jessie came to me with this same suggestion. I did not like it then and I do not like it now. I have not even mentioned the possibility to Frederick because I know he will throw a fit. We have been entertaining more and more, and he loves the attention Jessie's cooking has garnered. There is no way he will want to put our entertaining on hold while Diana grows up. I know for a fact he is planning to extend even more invitations to dine once the house on Bull is completed. Though I would be happy to entertain less, I am becoming more comfortable with my position as hostess, and there is no doubt that our invitations and the table we set have definitely helped elevate us in the circle of Savannah society. Women who barely acknowledged me when I first came to this town now actually seek me out for conversation. I am not foolish enough to think it is my charming intercourse that draws them.

I speak honestly with Jessie. "You know Frederick is not going to agree to that plan. We will have to think of something else. He will simply have to get some more help around here before we move. How hard can that be? I will talk to him about it tonight."

Jessie does not endorse my plan but neither does she dissuade me. I take this as a good sign. I change the subject before she has time to think about it.

"Do you know when Dovie will be back with the older children—I want to visit Minda, and I would like for her to go with me."

"Minda?" Jessie's face is blank as she turns to look at me.

"Yes, Lewis and Dovie's sister, Mammy's oldest daughter. You haven't met her. She belonged to us in Virginia. Frederick and Luella sold her, and I have not seen her since I moved to Savannah."

"Actually, I have met Minda—at church. She sits with her family."

"That is right—you go to church with her. I hoped she would drop by to see Mammy, but if she has, no one has told me, so I have decided to seek her out."

"Dovie did not say when they would be back from the green. You know how the children love to be outdoors. They may not come home until supper time."

"I guess I could walk to the green and they could proceed with me."

"It is not my place to say so, Abby, but I do not think Mr. Barret will want the children walking about in Yamacraw."

I know she is right. "Will you come with me? I am sure it would do Diana good to get outside for a while."

Jessie appears distracted. "I do not know exactly where Minda lives, and I still have a lot to do before supper is ready."

I am disappointed. Now that I have decided to go, I do not want to wait. "I know—I will just get Lewis to walk with me. I am sure he is out back."

Jessie's eyebrows draw together, and I realize I have probably reminded her of the reason Lewis is near, always. I have insisted that Frederick keep a male at or near the back entrances since our home was invaded by that evil man. It has been almost two years since the attack, but I am still not comfortable being without help nearby, even if the store is open.

"I will leave the door open into the hallway so they can hear you in the store if you should need something. I will be back shortly."

I find Lewis tending the small patch of vegetables in the back yard. He seems surprised at my request, but he washes himself off in water he draws out of the barrel by the kitchen door, and we begin our trek across town.

We travel much the same route I did when visiting Jessie, but we turn left a street or two before coming to Jessie's house, and I am pleased to be taken to the door of a house very comparable to Jessie's in size and condition. At least Minda is not living in abject poverty like many around her. Lewis hangs back, and I am left to approach the door by myself. It is of solid wood construction, so there is no way for the occupant to see who is calling without looking out a front window. I assume the young girl who opens the door has done just that, and seeing Lewis, she probably expects to be greeted by her aunt or her grandmother instead of a strange white woman.

She is a pretty little girl of about seven, light-skinned as I suspected Minda's children would be. Her large brown eyes register surprise and maybe a little fear. I assume I may be the first white woman to knock upon her door.

"Mama, day a wite woman hyur!" she calls back into the room behind her.

Minda comes to the door, and had I not known whom to expect, I probably would not have recognized her. I wonder if I have seen her on the street and not known who she was. Gone is the gawky adolescent I remember. In her place is a pretty woman with a child on her hip. This youngster appears to be a year or so older than my own Maxie. I guess I have changed too because Minda looks at me like I am a stranger.

"Minda, it is me, Abby!"

Minda's face finally shows some emotion, but it is not what I expect. She looks startled, as if she has been caught doing something she shouldn't. I immediately want to put her at ease. I know she is likely embarrassed for me to know she is being kept by a man, a white man at that, but in this I agree with Bette. If a slave is taken by a white master, it is rarely any fault of her own, even though the wives of those men rarely want to think so. Poor Bette. I am glad she does not know.

Minda still has not spoken, so I say, "May I come in? I will not stay long. It is just that I have not seen you since coming to Savannah, and I wanted to, so I just decided to come uninvited."

Her silence is making me uncomfortable, and I find myself chattering. She steps aside. I take that as an invitation and step into the room. It is neat and clean, and like Jessie's, it is furnished adequately, but there are certainly no luxuries here. I walk into the room, remove my bonnet, and sit on a straight back chair Minda pulls forward for me.

"How have you been, Minda?" I ask.

"I be fine, Mizz Abby." Minda finally finds her voice and I am relieved. I was beginning to think she wasn't going to speak.

"I had hoped you would stop by and see me, but since you haven't, I decided to come to you. If Mohammed will not come to the mountain…" I trail off.

"Kin I git you some watta or sumpin, Mizz Abby?" she asks.

"No, Minda. I can just stay a minute."

Minda has pulled up another straight back chair and sits in it. She puts the child, a little boy, on the floor and turns to the girl who opened the door.

"Daisy, take Jude ta da back room." The little girl takes her brother by the hand and the two of them disappear through a door across which hang a couple of brightly colored curtains on what appears to be baling wire. The curtains are bright yellow with a profusion of multicolored flowers on them, a pattern that looks familiar to me.

"Daisy—that is a pretty name," I say for lack of anything else when Minda does not seem inclined to talk. Gone is the chattering young girl I knew.

"It be Mama name," she says simply.

"Daisy is Mammy's name?" I ask. I am sure she hears the surprise in my voice, for I do not remember ever hearing Mammy called by anything other than Mammy. That has been stupid of me, I realize, and I am sure Minda does too. Of course Mammy would have a name, and one would think I would know what it is. I wonder absently if Luella knew Mammy's name is Daisy.

"Wy you hyur?" Minda asks. I am more than a little embarrassed by her abruptness.

"I just wanted to see you, Minda. We were girls together. I see Dovie and Mammy all the time, but I have not seen you in years. You have turned into a beautiful woman. Last time I saw you, you were a knappy headed young thing with a smart mouth. Now look at you, all grown up with children of your own."

Finally Minda smiles, and with relief I see the girl I used to know.

"You waren much mo dan a chile da las time I see you, needer. Dubie tell me you hab a whole passel ub chilrun yosef.

"Yes, we have so many Dovie and Mammy cannot take care of them all. I am about to talk to Frederick about getting some more help. We are moving soon, and he wants to wait, but with Jessie with Diana…"

I trail off. I cannot believe I am talking of these things with a slave, one we used to own at that, but I am nervous and eager to make conversation. I do not know what I expected. I am seriously doubting the wisdom in coming here. I think I have not been honest with myself about my motives.

"Mama tole me bou dat. Dat sad fo da lil gul mama ta die lack dat. She lucky to hab somebidy lack Jessie ta take er in."

I am relieved that Minda has decided to talk to me.

"Yes, and Jessie is making a wonderful mother. It is just that she's trying to take care of her and cook and sew, and so far that is not working out too well. Jessie is a free woman, so we have to find some more help, or I am afraid we may lose her."

A thought comes to me. "I do not suppose you would be able to work for us again, since you apparently are not working for anyone else."

Minda laughs aloud, but it is not the laugh I remember of her.

"I doan tink I be lowed ta do dat, Mizz Abby. Sides, I haf ta hab bof da chilrun wid me. We sho hab a houseful den."

"You are right," I concede. "Maybe when we get the new house built. We will have room enough for everyone and more by then."

"Mabe den," Minda concedes.

"It is just that my family has always tried to keep our people together. I do not know what happened with you and Luella, but I would like to try to buy you back if Mr. Stiles is agreeable. I could talk to him if you would like."

Minda stares at me blankly for a while, and I recognize the look as one she used to wear when she did not want to commit one way or the other on a subject. She, her sister, and her mother have this way about them of letting their features go completely slack making it impossible to read what they are thinking.

"I tink we bedda jus le tings be da way day be. I ain wuk fo Mizz Lella fo a long time, an I doan tink day en goin back."

I see sadness in Minda's eyes, and I wonder what her life is like. I think of talking to her about it, but her expression is closed.

"If you change your mind, Minda, or if things get hard for you or your children, promise me you will send word to me by Lewis or Dovie."

"I promise, Mizz Abby." Minda rises to let me know it is time for me to leave. I am being dismissed by my former slave. I should be offended, but I am not. I sense no anger on the woman's part, just sadness. I wish there was something I could do to help her. It crosses my mind to talk to Bette, but I know I cannot do that. I will not intentionally hurt my friend.

I place a hand on my old playmate's arm at the door. "At least tell me you will come by to see me occasionally."

"I try, Mizz Abby." I think she means it.

Lewis and I walk home in silence. He walks with his eyes lowered as black men are trained to do, and I know he will not initiate conversation unless I do. I do not feel like talking. In fact, I feel like crying. Though I cannot talk to Bette about the specifics of Minda, I can talk to her about the treatment of slaves in general. I am interested in hearing what she has to say.

When we get home, Mammy is in the kitchen with Ella by the hand and Maxie on her hip. She does not seem happy with me.

"Wat you doin traipsin aw da way cross town b'yosef?" she demands.

"Why, Mammy, I was not by myself; I was with Lewis."

"You know dat ain propa, waukin roun wid jus a nigga man fo cumpney. Massa naw gonna like dat one bit!"

"Then I guess we should not worry the master with it," I tell her. I am getting a little tired of being talked down to by servants. She is probably right. Frederick probably would not approve, but what harm is there in me going to see Minda? I may not tell him. I do not feel like explaining myself. In fact, I feel like lying down. I feel oppression setting in. The meeting with Minda has bothered me on some level I cannot yet identify. I find I want to be alone.

"Not that you asked, Mammy, but Minda looks well. I have invited her to drop in to see me. I hope you encourage her likewise. Now, I am going to go lie down for a while before supper."

I kiss Maxie and extract myself from Ella with promises that I will hold her after Papa comes home. I leave Jessie in the kitchen doing a balancing act between cooking and entertaining Diana while Mammy scowls at me while trying to console a crying Maxie and a restless Ella. I should take one of them off her hands, but I am just too tired. I go upstairs to lie down. I sleep until Frederick gets home from work.

I do not bring up the subject of extra help at supper because I do not want to talk about it in front of Mattie, Rob, and Fredie. Afterwards, we take the children for a pleasant walk along the riverfront, and by the time they are all put to bed, I simply do not want to have a serious conversation. I tell myself I will talk with Frederick tomorrow at dinner, or if not then, supper at the latest. Though I have had a nap, I am eager to go to bed and do so as soon as Frederick pulls out his dog-eared house plans and starts pouring over them by lamplight.

Chapter 36

Iknow that dozens of little darkies around here are raised in the
sand and dust outside their shacks by children not much older than
themselves, but I don't want Diana to be one of them. I may have Negro
blood coursing through my veins, but my early childhood was not so
different from that of the Barret children. Though we didn't live in
town, we, too, had slaves who did most of the manual labor. Though our
situation changed drastically before I was in my teens, I would be lying
to say I do not cherish the memories of life before deprivation. I comfort
myself by believing I surely would not have owned slaves myself had I
grown to adulthood with the option to do so, but I will never know that
for sure. No doubt my current life from this side of the racial divide has
influenced my way of thinking. Slavery is an abomination to me just as it
is to Moses, and I will be damned if Diana will live the life of a slave child
if it is within my power to prevent it. I want to give her all the advantages
this country will allow. Moses feels the same.

We have just put Diana down for the night, and we sit at the kitchen
table discussing what we are to do about our situation. Should we try to
find someone at the boarding house to look after Diana during the day,
or should I simply put my foot down with the Barrets and take a year or
two off to raise the child myself? I am torn. I have been miraculously
given a child of my own to rear. I hate the circumstances that gave her
to me, but I love the child as my own already. Considering my age and
the amount of abuse my body suffered at the hands of Robinson, Moses
and I both know it is highly unlikely I will conceive again. It is a miracle
I conceived in the first place, one I am still wondering why God allowed
if it were going to end so disastrously. Regardless, I have a child now,

and it is not a blessing I receive lightly. I know how often children die before adulthood, and I want to be present to safeguard this gift. On the other hand, I love the Barrets, all of them, and I am grateful for the security they give my family. Though I am sure I will be able to find another position later, I am equally sure it will not be with a family as accommodating as the Barrets. Abigail treats me almost as an equal, and I know that is almost unheard of in southern society. It will hurt me to have to leave them, but neither can I cage Diana up like livestock every day of her life. Then again, Moses and I need the money my jobs bring in. I can still sew, of course, but we are trying to save money to buy Rube, and after that, we want to build another room on to the house so Diana will not have to sleep in the living room. Moses has already approached Rube's owner, a guy named Jarveson, but the man assures Moses his slaves are not for sale. We have not given up despite the claim. Moses believes he is holding out for more money, so we are trying to save as much as possible as quickly as possible. It is bad enough that Diana has lost her mother. We do not want her to grow up never knowing her father as Moses, Lavinie, and many of the slaves we know have.

Moses and I talk for some time, but we have come no closer to a resolution when we hear a light tap on the door. Diana is asleep in the crib in the corner, so I am glad the visitor does not knock loudly. Moses goes to the door and I stand behind him as he opens it. Our visitor is a black man I have never seen before. The man quickly makes it obvious that he does not know Moses either.

"You Mose Tucka?" he asks.

When Moses tells him he is, he asks if he may come in. Moses moves aside, and the man enters the room. I would never have invited him in had I been alone, but men do not have as much to fear as we women do, especially men the size of Moses. In spite of my husband's presence, I am immediately wary. That is something else for which I have Robinson to thank. I am much more anxious by nature than I was before I realized men like him exist.

"I hab a message fo you."

At least the man makes no move to sit, so I am hopeful he does not plan to stay long. "Day a man down by da ribber say he da husbun ob yo sistah. He wan you ta come down dare and tawk ta em."

My chest tightens. There is only one reason Rube would be down by the river this time of night and unwilling to come to our door himself. Moses understands this immediately, and he does not hesitate to leave with the visitor. I have just enough time to beg him to be careful before the door closes behind them.

I wait for what seems to be hours. I can find nothing to occupy my time, so I finally give in to the urge to pace, though I do it quietly so as not to wake Diana. I am not startled when the door opens and Moses helps a battered Rube into the room. Moses is practically carrying the much smaller man. His clothes are dirty and blood stained.

"Jes, we need ta clean em up. He whipt bad."

We take Rube to our bedroom and I light a lantern after pulling the curtains together. We, especially Rube, could use the fresh air from the windows, but we dare not risk someone seeing what we are doing, even though most of our neighbors in Yamacraw would sympathize.

"Is it safe to have him here? Won't this be the first place they look?"

"Day woan know I gone til monin, Mizz Jessie."

I am surprised to hear Rube speak. I had thought him unconscious.

"How can you be sure, Rube?"

"Cuz day whipt me an lock me in da smoke house. I kikt ow some boads an crawl back ta da quawta. Day row me ober an lef me on dis side."

I can tell the effort to talk is hurting Rube, so I tell him to lie as still as possible while I clean the bloody stripes on his back. His entire back is a mess, and I find myself growing angrier by the minute. What kind of human being could do this to a person? Then I remember that by many, we are not considered people, just as in Haiti, the ruling blacks treated whites no better than Rube has been treated. I cannot imagine abusing an animal this badly! I have not met Mr. Jarveson, but in my mind he looks a lot like Robinson. Death would be too good for either of them.

"Rube say da Massa git fed up wid em mopin roun an axin ta come see da chile. Rube say he doan much care if he lib or die."

"It looks like whoever did this stopped just short of killing him. What are we going to do with him, Moses?"

"You know wat I hab ta do, Jes. We git em fixt up, git some food in em, den we do wat we do wid da ubbers." Moses is whispering. It would not be hard for someone outside to overhear our conversation.

I finish cleaning up Rube's back, coat it liberally with salve Mammy gave me for Diana's bottom, and wrap his whole torso in clean muslin. Moses gets him into one of his own work shirts, and he looks like a child in a nightdress. He manages to sit at the table and eat the cornmeal mush I put before him. Our efforts have much revived him, and I know this beating will not kill him if infection does not set in. If we can keep him from being caught, he has a chance. Though I want to help Rube all I can, I know the danger he has put us in by being in our house. If our part in harboring a runaway slave is discovered, our lives are as at risk as his, even if we are free. I shudder to think of what will happen to Diana if neither Moses nor I are around to take care of her.

With all of this in mind, I wrap some biscuits, some bacon I fried for supper, and a crock of milk in a dishtowel and give it to Moses. I send enough for the other man who is already secluded beneath the church that is Rube's destination. I only wish the tunnel to the river were complete, because I know Moses will run another huge risk in getting them both to transport at the riverfront when that leg of their journey is set up. We allow Rube only a few minutes to gaze down upon his sleeping daughter, then I practically push both men out the door. I wish I could bring them back as soon as they are gone. They have a long walk to get to the church. It is a consolation that the town sentries rarely come to this part of town.

I go to bed, but I am still awake when Moses crawls back into bed beside me. I am so thankful that I wrap both of my arms around him even though he smells of perspiration and fear.

"Eberting fine," he assures me. "Now, if we kin jus git em ta da ribber Tues nigh."

This is just Thursday. I know Moses will have to get more food to the men before then. He goes to the church to work on Sunday anyway, so at least he will have an excuse to be there.

While Moses has been away, I have allowed myself to think about what this development means for Diana and for us. Her father is a runaway slave. If he survives and makes it to his destination in the North, it is highly unlikely any of us will see him again. That being the case, Diana is, for all practical purposes, an orphan. Moses and I will be the only parents she will ever know. God forgive me, but for this I am grateful. We have a child. Maybe this is God's way of making up for the one stolen from us.

My responsibility for Diana is heavy on my mind when I reach the Barret's. I prepare a quick breakfast for Mammy, Dovie, and Lewis. I get Frederick's ready for him and wait impatiently until I hear him come down the stairs. He is not surprised when I sit down across from him when I serve him his meal—I often sit and talk to him while he eats his breakfast. Though I have already brought up the subject of Diana with Abigail, I know who will ultimately have to be told, and I want to be the one to do it. Abigail has a kind heart, but she is no match for Frederick's strong resolve, and I know he is not going to be receptive to me leaving for a year or two. I want to do all I can to make sure I have a place to come back to when Diana is older.

"Frederick, I need to talk to you about Diana. I do not know if Abigail has spoken with you about me taking a year or two off to tend to Diana..."

"No, she certainly has not," Frederick interrupts. I can tell by the way he sets his fork down and gives me his undivided attention that this conversation is not going to go well. His eyebrows are pulled downward and his upper lip disappears in the straight set of his mouth.

"Surely we are not going to let one small black child, a child that isn't even your own, disrupt the favorable arrangement we have here!"

"Diana may not be my biological child, Frederick, but she is mine, nonetheless, be she black, white, or somewhere in between."

I manage to speak in the same quiet voice I used to introduce the topic, but I feel the blood rush to my face. I put my clinched hands in my lap. "Regardless, she is my responsibility, and I have found it almost impossible to look after her while meeting my obligations here. I had hoped you would want me to return as soon as Diana is old enough to be in the kitchen with me without endangering herself around the fire.

"And I had hoped you would realize your first obligation is to us, your family, for all practical purposes. Have we not treated you as one of us? Have I not personally gone out of my way to insure your happiness here in Savannah? Surely you realize the advantages you have enjoyed would not have been possible without my sponsorship."

"I am well aware of that fact, Frederick, and you know me well enough for it to go without saying how appreciative I am for all you have done for me. I hope my service is proof of that gratitude. But surely, Frederick, you understand that I must take care of Moses' motherless niece. She has only us!"

"I am sorry to sound callous, Jessalyn, but I cannot help but believe that the problem is one that Moses needs to address. I would think that he, too, would appreciate all I have done for him because of his association with you. This is just something he will have to deal with. I am sorry to deny you this request, but it is just simply out of the question."

I can no longer hide my irritation, but I fancy my tone is conciliatory. "Frederick, this is my decision to make. I am a free woman, and as much as I love you and your family, I must do what I think is best for Moses, Diana, and me. Rest assured, I will return, if you will have me, at the very earliest possible date—as soon as Diana is able to control herself. Too, I will be more than happy to sew for you. Maybe I can also do an occasional special dinner for you and guests if you can find someone to look after Diana while I prepare."

Frederick rises and turns his back to the table. His silence makes me nervous, but I am determined not to give in to his high handedness.

"Perhaps you have forgotten, Jessalyn, that it is I who have made it possible for you to own your own house, for you and Moses to go and do freely where and what you want. If you are not in my employ, I, of course, will no longer be able to sponsor you. Unfortunately, you are a person of color—a fact that is easy for those of us who care for you to forget. Not everyone in Savannah is as unmindful of that fact as we are. I think it is best you think twice before you sever your relationship with us."

I cannot believe what I am hearing. I rise slowly, and I, in turn, am silent so long that Frederick turns to face me. I no longer make any attempt to hide my anger.

"Frederick, are you actually saying you will cut all ties with me if I take time off to tend my daughter? Does our relationship mean so little to you?"

Frederick has the decency to be embarrassed. He will not meet my eyes.

"No, Jessie, I do not wish to sever ties with you. I think I have made it quite clear that I will go to great lengths to avoid that. You are a part of this family, and a part of this family you must remain."

I turn to leave the room, but he reaches out to place a hand on my arm. I stop but I do not turn to face him again.

"Jessie, I am not a heartless man. You know that. I care about your welfare, and if you care about this orphan you have taken in, I will get you the help you need for her. There is no need to disrupt our whole household for the sake of one child! Leave it to me. She will have the care she needs and you will stay here where you belong. Now please, let me finish my breakfast in peace."

This last he says to save face, for he knows I have no desire to stay in his presence. I leave the room without responding. I am furious he has forbidden me to do what I have the right to do, but I know that thwarting him in this could be a big mistake. Though I do not think he will really cause problems for Moses and me, I cannot be sure. I would never have thought he would threaten me the way he just has. There is no doubt about it, Frederick Barret could certainly cause problems for my small family, but then again, I could cause problems for him and his. But I know I will never willingly cause him, Abby, or his children grief. I have no choice. I will have to trust Frederick to provide the help he has promised. This conversation would never have taken place had he already done so. Too bad he has not, for words spoken cannot be unsaid.

Chapter 37

Jessie has just left the room when Abby enters it. Frederick stifles a sigh. *Am I to have no peace this morning?*

"Good morning, Dear. You are up and about much earlier than usual. To what do I owe your pleasant company at the breakfast table?"

Abby's warm smile is like a balm to the hurt feelings Jessie's unreasonable request has produced in him.

"I know you need to be off to work, but I wanted to speak with you without the children present. I meant to last night, but one thing led to another, and I was in bed and asleep before the opportunity presented itself." Abby takes a breath and plunges right in. "We really must obtain more household help, Frederick, or I fear we are going to lose Jessie. She is concerned with the little darkie that is Moses' niece, and I fear she will actually quit us to take care of her if we do not provide someone to look after the child."

"Perhaps you are right, My Dear."

Frederick enjoys Abby's surprise. He smiles congenially at her over the top of his coffee cup.

"Why the sudden change of heart? A week ago, you told me we would have to wait until the new house is finished before I could have more help."

"The household is your concern, Dear, and after giving your request some thought, I agree that there is no need to wait. It is not as if we cannot afford it. I am just concerned about where we will house a new slave, but I am sure we can work something out. I will address the issue today. We must not risk losing Jessie. She is too great an asset."

Abby is thrilled by her husband's easy acquiescence. She quickly decides this is the opportunity she has been waiting for to discuss the more sensitive subject of Minda.

"There is another issue I have been wanting to bring to your attention, Husband, and if you are not in too great a hurry, I will share with you a concern I have had for some time."

Frederick is immediately alert. *Has this day not already contained enough upheaval? What now?*

Abby laughs. "You mustn't look so concerned, Dear. The topic is not grave enough to warrant such a frown. I simply want to discuss Minda."

Seeing the blank expression on Frederick's face, Abby thinks he does not remember who Minda is.

"Minda—Mammy's daughter…the slave you and Luella sold to the Stiles…"

"What of her?" Frederick is wary.

"I do not know why the two of you sold her, but I cannot help but want to reunite her with the rest of her family. It has never been my family's practice to separate family members, so unless she did something terribly grievous, I would like for you to approach Clarence with an offer. She could be the answer to our problem. She could return to help with Diana."

Abby is so caught up in her appeal, she does not notice the hard set of Frederick's face.

"In fact, I mentioned the matter to Bette not long after we married, but it is obvious she does not know they still own the woman."

Abby reaches across the table and takes her husband's hand. "Oh Frederick, poor Bette has no idea what has been going on right under her nose! It is awful what Clarence has done!"

Frederick cannot believe what he is hearing, and he is horrified to see his wife's eyes fill with tears.

"Just what is it you think Clarence has done, Abby?"

"It is not what I think Clarence has done. It is what I know he has done!" Abby's tone goes from compassionate to angry. "I have seen the result with my own eyes! I went to see Minda yesterday, and Clarence's little half-white bastards are proof of his disgraceful behavior! He has actually set Minda up in a house in Yamacraw so Bette will not find out what a horrible man she has married!"

Abby pauses long enough to notice the dumbfounded look on Frederick's face.

"I know this is probably as shocking to you as it is to me, and I hate to even talk of such a matter, but it's true! But you must not blame yourself. You and Luella would never have sold Minda to the Stiles if you had known what Clarence was capable of! Oh, Frederick, I've been so torn. Should I tell Bette? I feel like I should, but I am afraid such news will destroy her! I know it would me. What should I do?"

"Nothing, Abby! You should do absolutely nothing!"

Abby is surprised by his vehemence.

"Why? Should Clarence be allowed to continue in such behavior, with no thought as to the vows he made or the sins he is committing? And am I not being disloyal to Bette by keeping this secret?"

Instead of answering her questions, Frederick asks her a couple of his own.

"What in the world were you doing in Yamacraw? You did not go there alone, did you?"

"Of course not." Abby sees no reason to mention she went with Lewis only. "I wanted to see Minda. I have not seen her since I came to Savannah. And you did not answer my question. Why should I not tell Bette?"

"Do you want to cause your friend grief when you do not even know for sure that Clarence still owns Minda? What if he has sold her? What if those children belong to someone else? Just think of the problems you could stir up with misinformation. I think the best thing you could do is put the subject of Minda from your mind."

"I can tell you are upset with me, but I refuse to regret caring about what has happened to Minda, and I think you should care, as well. It is our responsibility to look out for the darkies in our care, and though it is not your fault—what has happened to Minda—she still belonged to you at one point, and her fate is the consequence of her not remaining in our family." Abby is tired of beating around the bush. "Frederick, I want you to tell me exactly what Minda did that was so bad she had to be sold."

"For goodness sakes, Abigail, do you think I can remember exactly what happened that many years ago? I vaguely recall Luella being dissatisfied with her—something about her not taking proper care of the children. What difference does it make now? We sold her. She does not belong to us and her fate is none of our business. I will ask you again—no, I will tell you as your husband has the right to do, drop the subject and stay out of Minda's affairs."

For the second time this morning, before he can even finish his breakfast, a woman is furious with him. He cannot wait to get out of this house, but Abby is not ready to let him go.

"Where do you think you are going? We are not through with this conversation."

Abby's voice rises. He is afraid the whole household will hear, and he certainly does not want Jessie who is already angry with him or Mammy and Dovie who have an interest in the subject to be privy to their discussion. Frederick sits down again but not before sighing heavily to let Abby know that he is much put upon by her behavior.

"Are you telling me you refuse to find out who owns Minda and what it would take to buy her back?"

Frederick sighs again. "No, Dear, if it will set your mind at rest, I will look into it, but you mustn't get your hopes up because if a white man has set her up in Yamacraw, and if she really does have children by him, there is probably no way he will sell her. And if he would sell her, she will surely not want to leave her children."

"Of course you will try to buy the children, too! In fact, the little girl is almost old enough to be a nurse for Diana. If he will not sell Minda, maybe he will sell the girl. Her name is Daisy. She is named after Mammy, Frederick! Surely you understand the importance of us doing the right thing by reuniting Mammy with her grandchildren."

"It is not like they live in another state, Abigail. Mammy probably sees them every Sunday."

"She does now, but what is to keep the owner from moving away with them, or if he gets tired of Minda, even selling her away?"

Abby walks around the table and wraps her arms around Frederick. She places her face against his chest. "I am more than a little upset with you, but I know you to be a good man, and I know you will want to do the right thing. Tell me you will do your best to find out who owns Minda."

She pulls back and looks beseechingly up into his face. When he refuses to meet her eyes, she places her hand behind his neck and pulls so he has to look down. "Tell me you will try to buy Minda and her two children."

Frederick pushes her from him. "I have got to get to work."

Abby follows him to the door. He cannot bring himself to close it in her face. He turns, hat in hand before leaving for the day.

"I will look into it. That is all I can promise. But you must promise me something. You must not take matters into your own hands, and you must not spread rumors you do not know to be true. Will you promise me that?"

Abby smiles, and feeling the battle is half won, she concedes, "I promise to mind my business if you will do all you can to bring Minda back where she belongs."

Frederick shakes his head in frustration and closes the door.

Chapter 38

By late afternoon, Frederick is in no better mood than he was when he left home. In fact, it has been a dismal day. Frederick likes harmony in his personal life, and the two family altercations of the morning have set the tone for the rest of his day. Determined to make some progress toward restoring peace within his household, Frederick decides to first take care of the problem of acquiring help for Jessie and the child she is determined to call her own.

Damn the woman! Damn women in general!

Though Frederick has been irritable all day, his mind has not been idle. He has come up with a plan to add another slave to the household without having to provide more space for housing. It is to this end that Frederick walks around to the back of the house to see Lewis before going in for his mid-afternoon meal. He finds him hoeing in the small vegetable patch located at the end of the carriage house. Lewis is not surprised to look up from the row to see his master coming his way. Frederick often hunts him down to give him odd jobs or send him on errands.

"Lewis, stop what you are doing for now and come sit with me in the shade. I have something I want to talk to you about."

This is unusual. It is rare that the master wants him to sit for any reason, and usually there is little two-way conversing. The master usually talks and Lewis usually listens and does what he is told to do. He is more than a little nervous when he sits down on the bench beneath the live oak tree.

"Lewis, have you given any thought to taking a wife?"

If Lewis had had time to speculate, he would never have guessed this to be the topic of conversation.

"Naw much, Massa, seein as niggas ain really lowed ta mare."

"Though it is true it is not legally binding, you know as well as I do that many slaves, in fact, I would say most slaves, marry among themselves as long as their masters approve their mates. I'm thinking it might be a good thing for you to marry, Lewis. What do you think of taking a wife?"

"I cain say I posed ta it, Massa, but I doan see no use takin a wife if I cain lib wid er. You ain tinkin on sellin me, is you?"

"No, Lewis, I am told I need more help, not less. And you have been a good servant. I do not have any complaints. But I need another house girl, and I thought to myself, why not kill two birds with one stone? If you have some woman you are pining for, maybe I can buy her from her owner, and then you will be happy and the missus will be happy—everybody will be happy. If you do not have some woman you have your eye on, I will find you one. It would just be easier and you would probably be happier if you had some say in the matter."

What Frederick does not say is that he knows Abby will be unhappy with him if he tries to force some woman on Lewis that he might or might not come to care for.

"Day dis gul in chuch I fancy some, bu I ain sho she willin ta mare me or naw. Doan know dat er Massa sell er, eeder."

"You leave the master to me. If you want to ask her first, go ahead, then I will ask her master. I do not want to waste time asking her owner to sell her if she is not going to say yes to you, unless you want me to try to buy her regardless of how she feels about you."

"No, Massa, I doan wan dat. I ax er furse, den I tell you wat she say. I sho doan wan no woman dat doan wan me!"

"That is fine with me, Lewis, as long as you get with it. In fact, you can have the rest of the day off to go find out if she is willing to marry you. If she is agreeable, I will have to meet her and talk with her owner. We will be using her as a house nigger, so the missus will have to approve her."

And Jessie, too, he thinks to himself.

"Who owns the girl, Lewis?"

"She blongs ta Massa Greene, I tink."

"James Greene who owns the stable down by the river?"

"Yessa, I tink dat be em. Cressa wuk in da house. She doan wuk in da stable."

"That is good to know. Do you think you can see her this afternoon if you go on down there by yourself, or do you want me to go with you?"

"I tink I kin see er. I go mysef an if I cain, I come back an tell ya."

"That sounds like a good plan. I will be here long enough to eat; then I will be at the office for the rest of the day. If you get a chance to talk to her, come by the dock and let me know what you find out. I will not mention this to anyone in the house until I talk with you."

"Den I bes be goin. I jus worsh up a bit furse. No gul wuth nuttin gonna wan a man dat look lack I do righ now."

Frederick laughs and slaps Lewis on the back. "Just do not take too long freshening up. I want to get this thing settled as soon as possible. I hope you are persuasive because I do not know how good I will be at matchmaking."

Frederick laughs again when he turns to see Lewis frantically splashing himself down at the horse trough.

Chapter 39

Frederick may not be my favorite person right now, but I must admit he gets things done when he sets his mind to it. It has been less than a week since our conversation in the dining room, and tomorrow there is to be a wedding, and day after tomorrow, I will have help with Diana. Of course, Cressa will have duties other than tending Diana, but I know Frederick has put this whole plan in motion to appease me.

I am pleased with Cressa—she seems like a warm-hearted girl and quite level-headed though she looks to be no more than sixteen or seventeen years old. Abby and I met with her and she seems pleased with the arrangements. Lewis, too, has a pleasant disposition, so they should be compatible in that area though Lewis looks to be solidly on the uphill side of thirty. I am glad the girl had some say in marrying Lewis. That's another mark in Frederick's favor. High-handed as he seems to be all of a sudden, at least he did not pick Lewis' wife for him and force them upon each other.

The house has taken on a festive mood. I am making a cake for the couple. It seems they are to have a proper wedding on Sunday afternoon. The Reverend Bryan will marry them just as he married Moses and me, but Lewis and Cressa are getting married out back here instead of at the church. Abby brought me one of her old dresses, and I have reworked it for Cressa. She also gave Lewis a pair of Frederick's pants and a coat he no longer wears. They fit him well enough without me having to do anything to them. After the wedding, Cressa will move into the rooms above the carriage house with Mammy and Lewis. Apparently, there are two rooms there, so they will have a little space to themselves. They have the advantage of eating all their meals here, so really the rooms only act as sleeping quarters and a place to spend what little time they have off from their duties.

Mammy has not had much to say on the subject of her son's wedding, but she appears to be happy enough about it, and I think we would know if she were not. Dovie may be the person most pleased about the upcoming nuptials for several reasons. Apparently she is well acquainted with Cressa from church and thinks highly of the girl, but more importantly to Dovie is the fact that she will be getting help with her duties. The two women will share the responsibility of looking after the children, including Diana, and cleaning the house. With the older children capable of looking after themselves more and more, Dovie has assumed more of the household chores. With Mattie and Rob going to the academy during the day, Dovie is free to do more around the house. I hope Cressa can stand up to Dovie or she may end up doing more than her share of the work. Abby is wonderful in many ways, but she is not always aware of who is doing what. Mammy has always kept Dovie pretty much in line, but the young Cressa may not be up to that challenge. It will not be long until we move into the big house, and when that happens, all three women will have more to do than they can imagine.

As I work around the kitchen, I keep glancing to the corner to check on Diana. I keep forgetting she isn't there. Though I am glad she does not have to be cooped up all day, I miss her. I have grown used to picking her up throughout the day, kissing her, feeding her from my lap. The room seems quiet with her gone. I hated it when she cried, but I loved it when she chattered and giggled and played contentedly.

I am not sure how I feel about Diana growing up with the Barret children. Their lives will take very different paths with the Barret children going off to the local academy and then to boarding schools while Diana will be tutored by me at home, but still, she cannot help but be in their shadow throughout every minute they are together. I have no delusions as to whose needs will come first, but it is an arrangement I plan to watch closely. I know many people will think us lucky to have an employer who will raise our child with theirs, and I do know there are many advantages to the association. It will, however, be hard for me to see my child treated as inferior though I know she will be perceived as such for the rest of her life. It is one thing for others to treat me poorly, but it will be much harder for me to see Diana treated as all black children are treated by whites here. I wanted a child so badly, and now that I have one, I would move heaven and earth to do right by her, yet I now question that desire.

It is a horrible thing to see one I love more than myself, one totally dependent on me for protection from the cruelties of life, exposed to the prejudices that come from having black skin. The most horrible thing about it is that I am in most ways powerless to prevent much of what Diana will be subjected to. What had I been thinking when I was so joyous while carrying Joshua? It was like pregnancy clouded my mind, temporarily causing me to forget what it would have been like for him, what it is like for any Negro child—or any Negro, for that matter. True, Diana may never know any difference, but I have, and I want more than anything to spare my child what I know is inevitable here.

My Goodness! These are dark thoughts for what is to be a time of celebration. Diana is with Mammy and the younger girls. If she were not, I would stop what I am doing to hold her, not so much as to reassure her, but to reassure myself. When I am with her, especially when it is just the three of us, I can block out the fear for her future. I must learn to do that when we are apart. Fear does no one any good and robs one of joy. I must remember to live each day as it comes whenever possible.

I place the first layer of the wedding cake on to bake, and turn to preparations for the cold supper I will serve for the evening meal. We had ham for dinner, so I will serve that again along with some of the bread I cooked earlier today, applesauce, cheese, boiled eggs, sliced tomatoes and pickles. Our evening meals usually consist of leftovers, served cold, from the earlier mid-afternoon meal that I serve warm. Occasionally I will cook something special for the evening meal, but I usually occupy my late afternoons preparing for the next day, sewing for the family, or preserving whatever is in season that lends itself to being put up for future use. My routine is drastically different for days before we are to entertain socially. Abby tells me we will not be having company for dinner until the week after next, and for this I am grateful. That will give Diana time to become acquainted with Cressa, and I will be free to give my undivided attention to the meal. The few times I have had to prepare for company with Diana underfoot have been a trial for both of us.

I hear a knock at the back door, and I know it is someone other than family or the family servants, for they never knock. I am quite accustomed to their comings and goings, but it is rare that someone knocks on the back door. I am wary, for obvious reasons, but I remind myself that Robinson would not knock and he would not come when there are people here other than me.

I wipe my hands on my apron and open the door to Moses. I am immediately on guard for he rarely comes to the Barret house.

"Moses! Is everything alright?"

"I hopin you kin tell me."

He stands outside with his hat in hand. He makes no attempt to enter.

"Missa Barret sen wud fo me ta come down ta da dock da furse chance I git. I tink you migh know wat he wan wid me."

"I have no idea, Moses. I told you about the arrangements he has made for Diana, but I cannot imagine why he would want to talk to you about that."

"I guess I bes go on down dare. I jus tink he migh say sumpin ta you bou wat he wan wid me. Sides, you righ on da way, an I nebber miss da chance ta lay eyes on da bes lookin gul in Svanna."

I ignore Moses' attempt at flattery. Now I will be dying to know what it is Frederick is up to. Before my argument with him, I would not have worried at all, but now, I am not sure of anything.

"Will you come back by here and let me know what it is about—so I will not dwell on it all evening long?"

"Sho will, Babe." Moses smiles his most carefree, jaunty smile, and I immediately feel myself relaxing. I smile in return.

"Can I get you a glass of water before you go, Husband?"

"No, Dawlin, I bes be on da way. Doan wanna keep da big man waitin. Bu I migh jus gib Mizz Dinah haid a kiss she be close by."

"Sorry, Darlin," I mimic, "but she is upstairs with Dovie. You will just have to wait until you come back by on your way home. If you do not have anything else you have to do until I get off, you can pick her up and take her with you."

With a smile and a tip of his hat, Moses is gone and I am left to try to think of a hundred different reasons Frederick may want to talk with Moses. The most likely I can come up with is sinister, and if I am honest, probably fueled by my recent aggravation with my employer. Surely he will not try to threaten Moses as he did me. But why would he do that? He got what he wanted. I am going nowhere, and he has done what he said he would do, so why would he feel it necessary to confront Moses?

After about an hour of fretting, I decide the best thing I can do is to be as busy as possible so time will go faster. It isn't long until I hear another tentative knock on the door. I fly across the room and jerk the door open, and this time I pull Moses into the kitchen and close the door behind him. I think it best that Lewis or anyone else hanging around out back not hear if Frederick has indeed done something we are not happy about.

"Cam yosef, Woman." Moses laughs, but his chuckle sounds forced to me.

"What is going on, Moses?"

"Nuttin ta wore bou. He jus wan me an a cuppla niggas ta hep em down a da dock tanigh. He hab a job too big fo is crew ta hannel."

"What kind of job?" I am skeptical. Frederick has never asked Moses to help out with anything, not at the docks, not here.

"Jus some heavy liffin. I tole em I see wat I kin do. If I cain fine nobidy else, a lease I hep em ow."

"Are you sure you are telling me everything?" I ask. There is something in Moses' manner that does not feel right to me. I put my hand on his arm, but, as usual, I can read nothing. At times like this I wish I could.

"You wore on tings too much, Jessie. Eberting fine. Bu I bes naw take Dinah home cause I haf ta roun up a crew an I probly be down dare a wile," Moses tells me. He looks around before kissing me quickly on the lips. "I git on outta hyur fo somebidy come in an ax wat you doin messin roun wid yo man in da kitchen wen you spose ta be cookin."

He kisses me one more time, and I have no choice but to let him leave. As the door closes, I dread the hours ahead of me before we meet again. Maybe then I can get him to tell me what is really going on.

Chapter 40

Frederick sits alone in the parlor, the sole lit lamp chasing the shadows from the circle of amber light he is endeavoring to read by. The household is quiet but Frederick doesn't especially enjoy the solitude. When at home, he likes to be in the midst of his family. He has had enough separateness to last a lifetime. Rare is it that he does not go to bed when Abby goes to bed. She was surprised that he did not do so tonight. He had told her truthfully that his day at work had been arduous. He then lied and told her he needed time to unwind from the day. Abby had not bothered to ask him to share the events of his day, for she had learned early in their marriage that he thinks wives and daughters should not be bothered by business matters—that it is his job as the head of household to shield her from the unpleasant aspects of making a living. Abby, for a while, had tried to get him to confide in her, but eventually she had given up, just as she had finally quit asking him abut his life before he came to the States.

He listens for Moses who is to tap on the front door when the job is done. Some time between midnight and one in the morning, it comes. Frederick opens the door and steps out onto the small stoop. Though there is little light by which to see Moses' face, he has no doubt it is he for he knows of no other man who casts such a large shadow. Moses has returned to the foot of the steps. Frederick descends and leads the big man away from the house because the evening is mild and the windows are open. He wants no one, family member or slave, to hear the conversation he is about to have. Neither speak until they reach Wright Square. The green appears deserted, but Frederick takes no chances.

He settles for the complete darkness beneath a live oak, the branches of which are so laden with moss they produce the effect of an airy room. If anyone is about, it will be impossible for them to testify with certainty the identity of the two who converse there.

"Is the deed done?" Frederick asks into the darkness.

"Da deed done," comes the answer.

"Did you kill the bastard?"

"No, bu I sho wudda like ta. We lef em wishen he dead."

"Did he recognize you?"

"Doan know how he cou. Nebber see me fo. Bu if he ebber do come back, woan be har ta figer ow. Naw many mens roun da size ub me."

"The other men, will they keep their mouths shut? We will not have to worry about them bragging about this to any of their buddies, will we?"

"No, dey hol der tongue. Dey naw egga ta swing fo awmos killin a wite man. An I know dem. Dey ain gonna say nuttin."

"Good. Where did you leave the bastard?"

"We waitin wen he come oudda da tippin house you tole us he be. We stuck a rag in is mouff an drag em down ta da en ub dat alley were dat clump a palmetta be wid de unddagrow righ up nex ta em. We lef em dare. He ain goin no place tanigh. Dey be lookin fo who done dis wen day fine em. Dey be no cause fo nobidy be lookin dis way."

"You did well. I knew I could count on you."

"I do it fo Jessie," Moses states simply. "I wanna kill em, bu you say it bes naw ta, bu I wanna kill em. Be bes fo ebberbidy he be dead."

"I agree with you totally, but if we had killed him, the hunt for who did it would have been relentless. If he lives, they will think he was robbed by some greedy niggers out breaking curfew. You remembered to rob him, didn't you?"

"Dint hab nuttin lef in da way ub money. We take is timepiece, bu I trow it in da ribber. Doan wan nuttin ta come back on us."

"Good thinking. As I said, you did well."

"I do it fo Jessie," Moses repeats.

Frederick gets the man's point, but he is not offended. If someone left his wife in that shape, he would kill the son of a bitch, but he would have had the law on his side. Moses is as good as dead if he is even suspected.

"Well, do not go telling her what you have done. The fewer people who know about this, the better. Besides, it would just worry her. She would never stop looking over her shoulder for someone to show up to drag you off."

"Doan wore bou dat none. I naw gonna tell er. No need fo er ta be tinkin on dis."

The matter settled, the two go opposite directions.

Frederick goes home to lie beside his wife, satisfied that justice has at last been done. It is some time before he sleeps so worked up is he at the events of the day. What good fortune it had been for him to see Robinson leaving the tippling house late yesterday evening when he was walking home from Yamacraw. The bastard had probably thought himself safe from being spotted by him or anyone respectable. Robinson has underestimated him. No man, white or not, is going to enter his home and attack one under his protection. He would have been enraged had it been a common slave, but to attack Jessie was unconscionable. Robinson will think twice before crossing Frederick Barret again. He hopes the man will connect tonight's beating with him, and he will unless he has carried out similar atrocities around Savannah. He hopes he has not, not just because his behavior offends his Christian sensibilities. He wants Robinson to know he is the one to mete out justice. Maybe now Frederick can at last put this whole unfortunate episode from his mind.

Moses keeps to the shadows as he makes his way home. He feels none of Frederick's elation. The big man is experiencing a strange mix of emotions. Though it had felt good to pummel the man who had violated Jessie and taken his son's life, he knows frustration. He would have liked to completely remove the menace from the world, for as long as the man draws breath, Moses knows in his heart he will do harm. Too, he would have liked to at least whisper into Robinson's ear that this was being done because of what he had subjected Jessie to, but he could not. He was not even sure Robinson would recognize Jessie's name.

As Moses creeps along he feels fear—not of being out late after curfew—he does this habitually to carry out his work with the underground. Not even of getting caught. His real fear is for Jessie. What if the man does know the cause for the beating? Will he try to exact his revenge on the innocent Jessie? Moses will never be able to forgive himself if Jessie endures further suffering because of his actions.

Moses reaches his house without mishap. He reluctantly opens the door and enters. He is dismayed that Jessie greets him from the bed as he tries to quietly climb in beside her. He tells her the lies he knows he must, but the dishonesty grieves him. He knows she does not believe him by the way she draws herself as far away from him as possible. He wants to hold her but knows it is best he does not. He is afraid she can smell the violence on him and hates he has brought it into their home. He lies awake until sunlight lightens the room. He rises, fills a wash pan with water and takes it out back where he tries to scrub the evidence of last night's deeds from his body.

Chapter 41

The hot Savannah sun sends rivulets of sweat down poor Lewis'
face as he stands beside his young bride before Reverend Bryan.
He shifts from foot to foot while she stands perfectly still, eyes forward.
Cressa looks like a Black Eyed Susan in her hand-me-down yellow gown,
her dark face solemn beneath the matching yellow scarf that adorns
her head. She holds a small Bible between her hands. The threesome
form a decorative centerpiece for the rest of us. There are Mammy and
Dovie dressed in their Sunday best. Dovie's face reveals her excitement;
Mammy's reveals nothing. The child Daisy stands between them, a hand
in each of theirs. On the other side of Mammy is Minda with her son Jude
pressed up against her knees. The dress she is wearing is a simple one,
made I am sure by Minda herself from a blue calico print I recognize as
one stocked in the Barret Mercantile.

Looking to my right, I see the Barrets clad in their everyday wear so
as not to outshine the bride and groom. Mattie has Maxie by the hand
while Frederick holds Ella in his arms. She is too large to be carried,
but she is her daddy's girl, and I am sure it is easier for him to keep her
in check this way. Abby stands with hands clasped beneath her chin, a
tender look upon her face. She is still young, I reflect. Young enough
to believe in romance and happy endings—even for slaves. The boys
surreptitiously slap at each other behind their parents' backs, eager, no
doubt, for the wedding to be over so they can have some of the cake they
saw resting on the kitchen table.

I stand between the two families with Diana in my arms. This is my
household, be what it may—white, black, and somewhere in between.

Diana is the only one present besides the minister who doesn't actually belong to this family in one way or another. She is here because I am here, and at this point in her life, if something happens to me, I know the association will come to an end and Moses will be left to take care of her on his own. He will do a fine job as long as he is able, but I cannot help but worry about Diana's fate if something should happen to both of us. She would become an oddity in the South—a free black child without the protection of a parent. I have given this subject much thought. There is nothing I can think of to do but pray that Diana grows to adulthood with at least one parent, Moses or myself, for I will be surprised if we ever hear from Rube again.

Diana looks up at me as if she knows I am thinking of her. Maybe she can feel my concern. She is being cooperative today. It is unusual for her to be still for more than a few minutes at a time. I smile at her and squeeze her little form to me, but she is having none of that. Her pudgy hands push away from the heat of my body, and I think she may demand to be put down, but instead, her attention returns to the ceremony. She looks on as if she can understand the words of the minister, the purpose for the gathering. I note proudly that she is dressed as well as the other children. Even Minda's children wear shoes. I realize my child is the darkest in the group. Her little face is as ebony as the darkest adult present. Minda's children are almost as light as I. My glance moves directly from the lovely caramel-faced Daisy across the circle to the paler Mattie. I am not listening to the words of Reverand Bryan, so my thoughts are free to wonder. I find my eyes going back and forth between the two girls and my mind registers discomfort. I try to focus in on my unease, but before my thoughts can coalesce, the gathering erupts in cheers. Apparently, the affair is over. Lewis and Cressa are now husband and wife until death do they part—or until one of them is sold away to another owner.

I chide myself. This is no way to be, and it is unlike me to be of a negative bent. I do not think Frederick will ever sell one without the other, not unless one of them does something awful, and I cannot imagine either Lewis or Cressa doing anything that bad. I know my sour mood has nothing to do with the wedding of Lewis and Cressa and everything to do with Moses coming home late last night smelling of something other than sweat and hard work. Though I cannot read my husband as I do others, I deem my powers of instinct elevated in comparison to those I consider *normal*. The atmosphere around him felt different last night, and my suspicions were further aroused when he rose before me to bathe in the back yard. At breakfast, I noticed lesions on his right hand, and when he saw me looking at them, he looked away with no explanation as to how they got there. I refused to ask because I feared he would lie to me. I guess they came from all the *heavy lifting* he was doing for Frederick.

"Tata, are you going to bring the cake out here and put it on that table over there, or are we going to have to go into that hot kitchen and get ourselves a piece?"

Rob's tugging on my skirt snaps me out of my reverie.

"Of course you are not going to have to go get it yourself, Master Rob! Tata will have it out here before you can round everyone up."

I look to Dovie for help, but she is busy congratulating the newlyweds, so I set Diana on the ground and make my way alone back into the kitchen to get the cake. When I return with it, Mammy has already gotten the gallon jug of lemonade from the tub under the shade tree and is pouring it out into the cups waiting on the table. There are oohs and ahs at the sight of the cake. I dish it out on saucers as Frederick leads the new couple in the broom jumping ceremony. I am sure it brings back memories of the Island for him as it does for me.

I cannot help but respond to the gaiety around me. I cast my heavy spirits aside and eat cake and drink lemonade with the rest of them. I am pleased that the cake is delicious and everyone is enjoying it, especially Diana and Maxie who soon have more on their faces than they do in their mouths. Mattie takes both girls under her wing, so I do not have to worry about keeping up with Diana. I think again what a loving little girl Mattie is. God willing, she will make a wonderful wife and mother.

The ebullient mood is no match for the heat, and soon the party breaks up. The newlyweds leave with a pass from Frederick to do I have no idea what, and the Barrets take themselves with their children off for a carriage ride in the countryside. It is Sunday afternoon, so Mammy, Dovie, and I are free to do whatever we want after we clean up the dishes and the back yard. Dovie immediately disappears with Minda and her children leaving Mammy and me to do the work by ourselves. Mammy does not bother to comment on her absence. Diana plays alone in the yard until we finish.

I wrap a piece of cake in a cloth from home. I take Diana by the hand, and the two of us set out. She toddles along beside me for some time before becoming tired, then she raises her pudgy arms. "Up, Mama!"

she commands and I carry her on my hip for the rest of the way. By the time we reach home, I have decided to trust Moses with his secret. If he believes it is something I should not know, I will accept that I do not need to know it. Trust is hard for me, but I know if it is to be had on this earth, it can be had in Moses.

Chapter 42

My Goodness, I am as fertile as the bottomland that runs along the creek at Mama's Grove. If I were a darkie, I would bring high dollar on the block. I am expecting again and Maxie not yet two years old. Frederick is delighted. I know he is hoping for a boy though he spoils the girls far more than he does Rob or Fredie. The boys are hoping for one to even their numbers. I am just hoping to survive another confinement with a healthy child to show for it.

It is a good thing the move to the house on Bull Street has begun because this little place on Broughton is bursting at the seams. Not only am I with child, but Lewis' Cressa just told me she thinks she is as well, and from the looks of her swelling middle, there is little doubt. We will have a new slave before my own child is born.

Because of my condition, I am to spend the day with Bette instead of helping with the move. This is fine with me since Jessie and Mammy will be there to make sure nothing is damaged and everything is put where it belongs in the new house. In truth, there is not all that much to move. We rented the furnishings with this house, and much of what we do own has grown quite shabby with use. We are setting up enough household so the children may remain in Savannah while Frederick and I sail to New York to purchase new furnishings. We are stopping in Baltimore to visit Sophia and James. We will return just in time for the children and me to pack up and return to the Grove for the summer. I do not know which I am the most excited about, moving into the new house or traveling to New York with just Frederick for company! I think it may actually be the latter. I cannot remember the last time Frederick and I spent more than a day alone together. I love my children, but I am looking forward to a break from them. It has all worked out beautifully for Maxie is weaned and old enough to be left behind.

Dovie walks with me the short distance to Bette's house. Bette is expecting me and she answers the door herself.

"Dovie, you can go on home. I will send Pearl back with Abby when she is ready to leave."

Dovie turns and flees, not even bothering to ask for permission. She is not about to look a gift horse in the mouth, and I almost feel bad when I call her back.

"Go find Cressa and see if she needs help with the little ones." I am wise enough to know that Dovie can get around Cressa easily so I add, "and if she does not need you, ask Mammy or Jessie to give you something to do."

"Yes, Missus."

I can tell by Dovie's still chipper demeanor she has no plans to do as she is told, so I call after her retreating figure, "And, Dovie, I will ask all three what you did to help."

Dovie doesn't reply, but I can tell by the droop of her shoulders she has gotten my message. I am sure she is disappointed to see her hopes for a full afternoon of idle gossip with Minda dashed.

"That girl," I laugh to Bette. "She spends more effort trying to come up with ways to get out of work than she does working!"

"Cannot say as I blame her! Come on in here, Friend, and let's catch up. It seems I have not seen you in forever!"

"I know! And I have much to tell!"

"Really! I am dying to hear all, but let us get settled before you start."

"Pearl," Bette calls, "will you please bring Mrs. Barret and me tea in my sitting room?"

"Yes, Mam, I be glad to."

Bette leads me up the stairway to her private bedroom off of which she has a small sitting room we have become accustomed to using for our chats. Bette has a wonderful, elegant old home she inherited from her father, and though she has always seemed to be equally at home in our small rented rooms above the store, I am glad I will soon have a more fitting place to entertain my friend.

We settle in matching chairs before a lit fire. I comment on how good it feels. It is January, and the walk over was chilly. Without acknowledging it, we both know we will wait until Pearl has come and gone before we discuss anything of importance. Over the years, Bette and I have become so comfortable with each other's company, we think nothing of sitting in silence until Pearl arrives with the tea.

"Pearl, do we have any of those coconut cookies Cook made or have the children eaten them all?"

Pearl smiles. "I put some to the side jus fo you, Mizz Bette. I know they be yo favrit."

"You are a sweetheart, Pearl."

The servant waves the compliment off, and I notice today as I have noticed before what an easy camaraderie there is between Bette and her Pearl.

"Pearl has such a pleasant disposition, Bette. You are lucky to have her. Has she been with your family a long time?"

"A very long time, Abby. She belonged to this family before I did. In truth, Abby, Pearl is my half sister."

I gasp so loudly I suck the tea I have just taken into my mouth down my windpipe. Bette is forced to leave her seat to take my cup and my napkin from my hand. She stands silently by until I manage to stop coughing, and then she returns calmly to her seat as if she has said nothing in the least bit provoking.

"You cannot mean that, Bette Stiles. You are trying to shock me, as usual."

Bette laughs. "It is true I love nothing more, but I have discovered it is entirely too easy an accomplishment. For someone who has grown up in the South surrounded by darkies—and on a farm at that—you are the most innocent, naïve women of your age I have ever known!"

"I am not!" I object. "I am quite as worldly as the next woman, but surely you would be shocked if I had just declared to you that a darkie is my sister! Admit it, you made it up!"

Now Bette is laughing outright. She is laughing so hard, she has to put her own cup down, and she is practically bent over in her chair. She actually points at me, and when she can get the words out she exclaims, "You should see your face, Abby! You are as pink as Eliza when she is forced to meet strangers!"

Seeing that I am not as amused as she is, Bette manages to get herself under control while I sit and try to appear composed and disdainful of her mockery. This is not the first time Bette has laughed at me, and now, as I have on previous occasions, I wonder why I put up with it. The next moment, however, she reminds me of why I suffer her teasing.

"Oh, Abby, I am sorry. You know I do not mean to hurt your feelings, and you are my dearest friend. Please do not be cross with me. But you are simply too naïve for a woman who has borne two children and is the mother to five! And though it is true that I love to tease you, I must tell you I am not jesting about Pearl. She really is my half sister."

"But how can that be?" I say, and I regret it the moment it is out of my mouth because it looks as if my comment is about to put Bette back into stitches. I hold my hand up to ward off what I know is to come. "I know how it could be—I am not stupid—but you know what I mean. How has it come to pass that you are living with a Negro woman you claim to be your sister?"

"Abby, Abby, My Sweet Abby," Bette begins as if she is explaining to her daughter Eliza instead of to me, "surely you know this kind of thing happens all the time. There are dozens, maybe even hundreds of girls and women living in households in the South with either their own Negro siblings or the Negro offspring of their husbands. I know life is not so different in Virginia. How can you not know of these things?"

Though I am still embarrassed, I know Bette loves me almost as much as my own sisters love me. I can talk to her in a way I can talk with no one else including my mother, my sisters, and in matters such as these, Frederick. I make the choice not to be offended.

"I know I am somewhat naïve, Bette, but in my defense, you must remember that my mother insisted on a very pious home, and there were no men in residence at Hickory Grove unless you count George and the male darkies. George was younger than I, and mother kept us girls completely ignorant as to what went on in the slave quarters, so how would I know of these things? I admit I have heard of such decadence, but I certainly would not have thought...It just seems to go entirely against all decency...It is surprising to me that you can be so cavalier about the fact that adultery went on in your own household!"

Bette has quit laughing, and now she dabs solemnly at her eyes with her napkin. Pearl returns with the cookies, and I wonder by the way she puts them down quietly and leaves without a word if she has overheard our conversation.

"In some ways, Abby, I envy your naiveté. I am sure you were a happier child due to your mother's sheltering. It was hard growing up in a household in which everyone refused to acknowledge the elephant in the room."

Bette's face has lost amusement. I can now read sadness in her eyes as she leans forward in the way she does when she is about to impart something personal and heartfelt.

"I will never forget the day I asked my own mother about Pearl. I was probably not quite as old as your Mattie, and the day before, I had been out back when Cook's son Arthur—Arthur who is now our driver—told me that Pearl was my daddy's child. I told him he was a liar and I hit him. He, of course, couldn't hit back, and he made himself scarce because I am sure he regretted telling me. If I had told on him, he would probably have been beaten. But the seed was planted, and I could think of nothing else. I could not sleep that night.

"How horrible for you!" I exclaim and pull my chair closer to her.

"That was a long time ago, Abby, and I assure you I have since been subjected to many more and probably worse shocks, but at the time, it was devastating."

"How did your mother explain it to you?"

"She didn't," Bette states simply. "We were in the downstairs parlor, just the two of us. She was teaching me some fine point of embroidery, I am sure. In the midst of whatever it was we were doing, she asked me if something was troubling me. She said I seemed quieter than usual. I will never forget the courage it took for me to get it out. I said, 'Mama, is Pearl really my sister?' She slapped me before she had time to think, and she immediately regretted it. My mother was a gentle spirit, much gentler than I. I was so shocked and hurt when she struck me, I jumped up to run away, but she grabbed me by the shoulders and there were tears in her eyes. 'I am so sorry,' she told me, 'but you must never say such things! You must never, ever say such things!' Then she put her sewing down, left the room, and the subject was never discussed between us again."

"Then maybe it is not true."

"Oh, it is true. I knew it was true the moment my mother left the room in tears. Why else would she get so upset? When my father died, he freed Pearl. He would have manumitted Pearl's mother, but she had died in childbirth, probably trying to give birth to another of my father's bastards."

"I am so sorry, Bette. How absolutely horrible for you." I want to say more, but I can think of nothing else.

"Not nearly as horrible for me as it was for my mother. Or for Pearl. Or for Pearl's mother."

"Still..."

"The saddest part of the whole story for me is that I never felt the same about my father after that—or men, in general, I think. I cannot say

I hold the whole sex in very high regard. I think most men are capable of the same behavior if they think they can get by with it."

"But surely you do not blame Clarence and other men for the indiscretions of your father. One ignoble man—and please forgive me for speaking badly of your father—does not make the whole lot bad."

"There is no explaining the psyche, Abby, and maybe my cynicism toward men stems entirely from that one traumatic episode, and maybe men such as my father are in the minority. And do not get me wrong, my father in many respects was a good man. He was quite loving to me, and at least he did not do as many men would have done and sold off his own daughter to cover his sin."

I do not know what to say. Poor Bette! I realize that Frederick is right. I can never tell her of my suspicions about Minda and Clarence. I do not know what she would do if she knew she had married a man of the same weak nature as her father.

Bette stands and turns her back to me and holds her hands out to the fire as if the conversation has chilled her.

"Maybe Pearl's existence and our connection is what has sparked such a dislike of slavery in me, Abby. If something happens to Clarence before me, I intend to free all our slaves. I would do it now if the law would allow it. I have already talked with my sons. If I should die before their father, I want them to honor my wishes by freeing the slaves. Reggie is of a kind nature. I think he may actually do so, but I am afraid Thomas is too much his father's son."

"Quit talking that way, Bette. You talk as if you are about to die! You are not exactly in your dotage."

This seems to lighten the mood, and Bette smiles, "Yes, since I am unable to have more children, I may actually make it to fifty!"

"Speaking of which, Bette. That is part of my news. I am with child again."

"Oh, Abby!" Bette, contrite now, crosses to take my hands and pull me from my chair. "Let me look at you. One cannot tell yet! And here I am prattling on about things that happened forty years ago!"

The rest of our afternoon together is spent talking about the children, our move to the house, my upcoming trip to New York. I can tell Bette is trying to keep things light, and I wonder if she regrets her earlier confidences. Though we talk of many things, our visit is more subdued than usual. Before leaving Bette asks me if I mind shipping some things to her from New York, and I tell her I will be delighted. She moves to a small desk in the corner and jots down a list. When she returns, she also has a copy of a small volume. She hands it to me along with the list.

"I know you do not agree with me on many things, and I love you the more for loving me in spite of our different viewpoints. I have no one else I can speak forthrightly with, and though I do not ask you to agree with me, I want you to understand me. It is important to me that I know at least one person in Savannah actually knows me for who I am."

I start to open the small book, but she puts her hands around each of mine and closes it. "Look at it later. Alone. It is not a book Frederick will want you to read."

"Bette, I do not know that I am comfortable…"

"For me," Bette says. There is an intensity, a need in her eyes that makes it impossible for me to refuse her offering. I tuck it in the pocket of my cloak.

The knowledge of who Pearl is makes the walk home with her uncomfortable. When I arrive at the house on Broughton, I walk through and find it completely empty of our belongings. Tonight will be the first night in our new home. I return to the room that has been Frederick's and mine, the room in which three children have been conceived. I pull the book out. It is not much more than a tract. It is entitled *An Appeal to the Christian Women of the South*. Beneath the title is written the name Angelina Grimké. The last name seems foreign to me, but the title itself sounds safe enough. If the woman is a Christian, how perverse can her message be?

For wont of a chair, I half sit, half lean upon the sill of the window. I thumb through the little book. Words jump from the page—words common enough in our own drawing room as well as those of our friends and acquaintances—words mostly bandied about by the men, but occasionally by us women as well. *Slavery, abolition, North, South.* I read a paragraph. I feel my pulse quicken. The words are familiar, but the putting together of them is not. This woman is combining them with words like *sinful, polluted, ruin, conscience, duty, obligation.* I hastily close the volume and cram it back into my pocket.

As I turn to leave, I hate that the last act I commit in here is one intentionally deceptive. I do not intend to tell Frederick of the book, and I do intend to read it though I know Frederick will not be happy if he finds out. I am not sure why I make this choice. Maybe it is because Pearl is Bette's sister. Maybe it is because Bette's father hurt her deeply. Maybe it is simply the memory of Bette's eyes as she pressed the book into my hand, or maybe it has nothing to do with Bette at all.

Chapter 43

James Howe has done well enough for himself and his family, Frederick determines, but how hard can that have been, all things considered. Alone in the Howe's informal dining room, Frederick looks around with a critical eye. He is free to do so because James is at his office and Abby and Sophia are out shopping. The Howes have moved since their last visit, and their new home, though elegant enough, cannot hold a candle to the house on Madison Square to which he and Abby will be returning next week. He wonders if Abby is proud that she has married better than her sister, for surely she realizes she has. Too, he wonders if the sisters compare the two men. Though women, they must realize how much more wherewithal it has taken on his part to make what is becoming a small fortune when compared to James who has his father, an established Baltimore lawyer himself, to thank for his modicum of success. Then again, maybe they do not, for how could they know? The Middleton girls grew up much like James Howe. Though neither family had been particularly wealthy, their children had never wanted for anything nor had they had cause for any pecuniary concern. It is a point of pride for Frederick that he has now accrued much more than both of his wives together brought to him in the form of dowries. Though Abby often tells him how proud she is of all he has accomplished, he inwardly believes she has no clue as to what it has taken to elevate himself, her, and their children in Savannah society.

Now Brigitte Maxwell is another story! The memory of the time spent with the Maxwells brings a smile to Frederick's face. Meeting up with them had been an unexpected pleasure, one they had no idea they would be enjoying until the day before they left Savannah. Abby had not seemed nearly as enthusiastic as he to learn that Alexis was to furlough in Boston during the time they would be in New York. He had convinced her to swing through Boston before going to Baltimore, but that effort proved unnecessary. A telegram to the Maxwell's hotel had apprised them of the accommodations the Barrets had arranged for themselves in New York, and the Barrets had been there just two days when they returned to the hotel from a bout of shopping to find the charming couple waiting in the lobby for them.

Though Frederick had thoroughly enjoyed the time alone with his wife before their arrival, Abby's condition necessitated more rest than usual, and being a man of much energy, he was delighted to have the companionship of the Maxwells during Abby's daily rests. Though Brigitte was herself a constitutionally frail woman, Frederick was reminded anew of her almost limitless capacity for gaiety. That is one of the things Frederick always enjoys about her. To his knowledge, the woman has never encountered a social gathering she does not love, and she has a way of turning a simple outing among friends into an adventure. Too, if he is honest, Frederick has missed the admiration his cousin has always lavished on him. She alone among his acquaintances in America knows how quickly he overcame the adversity of his youth and how far he has come from his humble beginnings here. And to make the whole acquaintance even more perfect, she is married to a man who does not appear to have a jealous bone in his body—a delightful fellow whom Frederick considers one of his longest and closest friends. He did not seem to mind at all when Frederick purchased a couple of trinkets for Brigitte or treated the two of them to a lunch they probably could not have afforded on their own.

Frederick rises from his chair. Enough reflection, he decides. He is restless. He walks around the room and wonders how much longer it will be before the women return. He considers going upstairs to look in on the Howe children, both sweet youngsters, but he decides against it for he knows they will only make him miss his own more. In truth, he longs to go home, as does Abby, but they made the arrangements to stay with the Howes before leaving Savannah, and it would be rude to leave precipitously. Frederick has actually given some thought to claiming expediencies at work as an excuse to go on before Abby, but considering her condition and the trouble it would take to arrange an escort, he has decided to tough it out. Frederick is never really comfortable when both he and Abby are away from the children though he knows he has no actual cause for worry. After all, Jessie is there as well as Mammy, Dovie, and Cressa. They have Lewis to do for them, and if anything arises that a person of color cannot handle, they have the assurance of Bette and Clarence that they are just a messenger away. Still, Frederick has seen enough of life to know how unexpectedly it can mete out a blow that can change everything, and he would like nothing better than to be back where he can keep a finger on the pulse of his household and his business.

Too, there is the draw of the new house. Though there had been meager furnishings there before they left and they had offered little in way of comfort, he had thoroughly enjoyed walking from room to room just to admire the architecture, the moldings, and even the vast amount of space itself. He and Abby had spent hours while in New York choosing the furnishings for the house. Though most of them were new, they had come across a few fine pieces at an auction house. Now, he is impatient to get back to oversee—along with Abby, of course—the laying of the rugs, the placement of the furniture, the hanging of the gilded mirrors, the putting together of the mansion itself. For a mansion it is, a fact that still amazes him. That he owns it, that he actually had the place built from the money he acquired entirely on his own, is almost more than he can take in. His chest swells with pride.

Frederick has to have something to do. He walks to the corner desk and finds a piece of paper. He sits, dips the nib of the pen in the ink well and begins a list of all the people they must invite to their housewarming. After he has made a list of one hundred people or so, he pulls out another piece of paper and begins a list of libations, victuals, and other necessities he thinks they may need. He writes this in French without thinking, but when he realizes he has done so, he leaves it. It will be best in this form to show Jessie for she is the one with the real understanding as to what will be needed, and she will be the one to make the purchases at the local market, those he cannot procure through his shipping contacts. It dawns on him that Abby will not be able to read it, but he dismisses the problem by assuring himself he will simply read it to her before going over it with Jessie. Alexis has promised him a large shipment of the best wines he can manage in time for the big event, and Brigitte has promised they will do all they can to be there.

He and Abby have decided on January for the gala. Their number will be one more by then, and Abby will surely have recovered completely from his appearance upon the scene. Frederick scolds himself for calling the baby a he, but he so wants another son. He crosses himself without thinking—old habits die hard—but he reminds himself and God that he will be thrilled with another little girl, if that is what Abby is carrying. His three daughters are a delight to him, but he knows he will someday be forking out dowries for his little ladies, and though he will begrudge them nothing, it cannot hurt to balance the ledger with sons who will hopefully bring money into the family coffers.

Frederick returns to the matter at hand. The housewarming. Not only will Abby be fully recovered, but January will be the ideal time for the event because Christmas will be behind them, the plantation owners will have returned to the city for the season, and Charleston's horseracing season will not yet have begun. Everyone who is anyone will be in town, and Frederick cannot wait to reveal their new home to those who a few short years ago barely acknowledged him when they passed him on the street. Oh, the sweet, sweet taste of success!

Engrossed as he is in the plans for what he considers the Barrets' true social debut, Frederick finds himself a little disappointed to be interrupted by the sound of the front door opening. He blows on the paper one last time, then folds the sheets and places them neatly in his jacket pocket. He greets his wife with a kiss. He is pleased to see color in her cheeks and a smile on her face. The time away has done her a world of good. She looks younger and happier than he has seen her in a while.

"May I have the honor of escorting you two beautiful women to dinner at the place of your choosing, Miss Sophia?"

Sophia giggles like a schoolgirl though she too is growing big with child.

"You may, Dear Sir, as soon as the two of us can stash these parcels and freshen up a bit."

As the two women start to make their way up the stairs, Sophia turns back. "Do you think we may walk by James' office to see if he cares to join us? We can dine at the Baltimore House across the street from there if that suits the two of you."

"We have a plan! But please make it quick ladies, for I am famished, both for food and for your most desirable company."

"Quick I will be!" Sophia promises, and making good on her word, she scurries upward.

Abby surprises him by turning back. She returns to him and tiptoes to plant a kiss on his lips.

"I love you, Husband," she states gently. She turns and heads back up the stairs without waiting for a response.

"I love you, Wife," he calls quietly after her.

Ah, life is good, Frederick thinks. May it always be so.

Chapter 44

I am so bone-tired and soul-weary it is all I can do to lift Diana into her bed though it is but a foot off the floor. I feel every day of my fifty years upon this earth. Though I will not admit this to anyone, even Moses, working for the Barrets and taking care of Diana for the past few months has almost done me in. I thought once the Barrets returned to Savannah and I no longer had to worry about the children's safety and well-being, I would be able to regain some energy and peace of mind. Though my chores did not really increase while the Barrets were away, the daily responsibility of making sure nothing happened to the five children took its toll. I knew both Abby and Frederick were trusting me to be the one to make sure all went well in their absence. As usual, Mattie was a tremendous help with the younger children, but the boys were a different story. The two of them have more energy than all the girls put together. Thank Goodness Dovie proved she could be relied on when necessary. She became quite the sleuth. When the boys weren't in school, she spent most of her time trailing around behind them, but on two occasions they gave her the slip, and it took Lewis to track them down. The first time they were located down on the docks talking to sailors, and the second time they were discovered in the company of the Green boys coming out of the entrance of the tunnel that runs from beneath the Tavern House to God only knows where. The Barrets have their work cut out for them with Rob, and if he is not watched closely, he will drag Fredie along the road to perdition with him!

I got my first good night's sleep in two months the night we took the children down to meet Frederick and Abby as they sailed into Savannah

Harbor. Since then, I have unpacked crates, helped shove furniture from one room to another, mended the children's clothing in preparation for their summer away, and performed what seems like a million other tasks totally unrelated to my role as cook and seamstress. I did all of this while putting together my kitchen in the basement of the house on Bull.

As tired as I am, the thought of the new kitchen brings a smile to my face. In actuality, it is more like two kitchens. The whole basement beneath the new Barret mansion is comprised of service rooms. There are two gigantic work areas both with fireplaces that any cook would salivate over, and Frederick has stocked it with the latest in utensils and bake ovens. Anything I suggested, he bought. We have decided to use the other large fireplace and the space around it for a laundry area, but the fact that the fireplace is separated from my kitchen only by the through corridor opens up all kinds of possibilities for me as a cook. I can pop back and forth between the two in no time at all, and on hot summer days, I can heat up that section without creating a stifling work area for myself. We call the floor the basement, but it is actually above ground, so there's ventilation running throughout. I would be the envy of cooks everywhere if I had occasion to show it off, but as most of the families we know own their cooks, I can think of no one to invite. I am sure there will be plenty of people parading through for months to come, for Frederick loves nothing more than to show his peers throughout the house. Sometimes I feel like he presents me on tour much as he does the other accoutrements. I can hear him now.

Notice the double adobe bread oven that can be taken directly from the heated enclave above the firebox. I acquired that from Mexico from a dear friend who did me the service of having it commissioned. And at the block work table built from white oak logs felled and hewn on site at John Andrews' Oakwood Plantation is our cook Jessie. She comes to us from St. Domingue by way of New Orleans where she learned the art of French Cuisine. Can you imagine the delight in one of her station to be presiding over a culinary heaven of this quality...

I feel guilty for making fun of Frederick, if only to myself. I do not fault him for being proud of his accomplishments; in fact, I am proud for him for I know the obstacles he has overcome to be where he is today. And he is right to think me fortunate. There is no one of color of my acquaintance who has the freedom and the privileges I have. Maybe my understanding of this is, in part, why I am so devoted to the Barrets and determined to make them never regret their association with me. But it is hard for one to be grateful when one is bone-tired and soul-weary.

"Will you please quit squirming and crawl beneath that sheet, you little wiggle worm!"

Getting Abby and the Barret children off to Virginia today has invigorated Diana as much as it has exhausted me.

"I not a wiggle worm. I Diana!" my daughter giggles.

I laugh with her, and I take the opportunity to lie beside and cuddle her to me. As I pull her stocky little frame to my chest, I feel a jolt—I sense something.

I lie as still as the child will permit while I try to evaluate what it is I am sensing. This is the first time I have felt anything of a negative nature upon contact with her. Though the sharp sensation subsides somewhat, it is still present. I am reading something in my daughter, and it bodes ill.

"I hot, Mama!" Diana scolds and pushes herself from me. "I need to pee."

I do not want to walk her to the privy at the back of our lot because I know it will take little to stir her up again, and I badly want her to sleep so I can rest. There is much I need to do, but now that Abby and the children are gone, I have a whole summer ahead of me to catch up on things at the Barret House and here. I long to catch a nap of an hour or so before Moses gets home.

I pull the chamber pot from beneath Diana's bed, and I refuse to respond to her efforts at conversation. Not only do I not want to stimulate her, I am preoccupied with the ill-boding I sense from her. I have lived too long and experienced too many of these sensations not to take this one seriously. I must be on guard, for if my intuition is correct, something bad is about to happen concerning Diana. I cannot afford to dismiss this warning as foolishness on my part. I cross to the door and turn the wooden bar that serves as an inside lock.

Once Diana is on the pot, it becomes evident that she needs to do more than pee. When she is finished, I cover the pot with the lid, and I place Diana back in bed, and just as I hoped, she is asleep in no time. I take my knife from behind the bean crock in the kitchen, and I place it in the cleavage between my breasts. It gives me comfort even though the heat of it against my skin makes me sweat. I curl up next to Diana and comfort myself that Moses will be home soon.

Maybe it is my heightened sense of awareness, but the smell of the chamber pot beneath the bed becomes a stench. I know it will not get better as the night goes on, and ordinarily I would not hesitate to take it to the privy and dump it, but I do not want to leave Diana alone, and I certainly do not want to wake her to take her with me. I decide to wait until Moses gets home. I lie, unable to doze, for another thirty minutes, and the smell becomes more and more annoying. I think I can move it to our room, but I really do not want the odor there, and in truth, I do not want the smell to be the first thing that greets Moses when he walks through the door. I am sure he would laugh at me for thinking this way, but I try to make our home as pleasant as humanly possible for my husband and child. It is one of the few gifts I can give them.

The windows are open as they must be this time of year, and I remind myself that if someone wants in, they can simply crawl through the window. *But I am here if they do,* I tell myself, *and if I go out back, Diana will be alone. But how long can it take me to run out back, dump the pot, and run back?*

Finally, I rise from the bed, dip several dippers of water into a pitcher, pull the offensive vessel from beneath the bed, and do what I know I need to do if I am going to be able to rest at all. I put the pot down long enough to unbar the door and look around outside before I pick the pot up, pull the door closed with my foot, and rush to the privy where I perform the task as quickly as possible and rush back. I am relieved when I reach the porch, and I decide to leave the pot there until morning. Though I rinsed it out at the privy with the water from the pitcher, it probably needs a more thorough cleaning. If Diana needs it during the night, which is unlikely, she can use the one beneath our bed.

The minute I open the door I know I have made a grave mistake, one that may cost me my life or the life of my child. I feel the man before I completely enter the room. *Why could I not have felt him before? He must have been close.*

The sole candle burning beside the bed confirms my fears, and my heart leaps into my chest to see the subject of my worst nightmares perched casually on the bed beside Diana. He lies with his head propped on his hand, his elbow resting beside Diana's face on her pillow. The curve of his body toward her suggests an intimacy I know to be intentional.

"Hello, Yella. Remember me?"

"What do you want?" I ask, more to stall for time than anything else, because I know what he wants. I think of running for help, but I know I cannot leave Diana alone with this man for a second.

"You know what I want, Yella, what I've wanted since the first time I laid eyes on you."

I cannot see the man clearly, but there is something different about his face. Apparently he is thinking the same thing about me because the next words out of his mouth are, "But I can't say you look quite as enticing as you did the first time I saw you. You're looking a little longer in the tooth than you did then. But then," Robinson rises to a sitting position on the bed, "neither am I the fine specimen of a man I was the last time you had the pleasure of my company, am I?"

He walks around the bed making sure he keeps himself between Diana and me. He picks up the candle from the night table and walks—with a limp, I notice—to within a foot or two of me. He holds the candle before his face.

"Look what that big buck of yours did to me, Miss Yella," he snarls, and the hatred fills the room with a stench more putrid than that the chamber pot had produced. The light on his face reveals a marred version of the visage that has haunted my dreams for years. His right eye pulls downward, the edge of it disappearing into a crease that connects to the edge of the sneer from which he speaks. "He took the use of my eye, and I've got a few other souvenirs I am going to give you a closer look at here in a minute. He and those nigger friends of his almost did me in, but they underestimated old Eugene. It will take more than a few niggers and a nigger-loving white man to best a Robinson. We been taking care of the likes of you since way back."

"I don't know what you are talking about," I say clearly. I speak the truth, and I am surprised that my voice sounds so strong. I realize I am not afraid of this man. Instead, I am determined. He will not hurt my daughter, and I realize that if I am to have a chance, I must act before he gets a good hold on me, for I have not forgotten the havoc his vile touch played upon my senses last time.

"You may do what you want with me, but leave the child alone. She has nothing to do with this."

"Oh, but she does, you all do. I must admit I was a little surprised the whelp survived, but niggers are a prolific and resilient lot. Now I'm kinda glad she made it. She'll provide some entertainment when I am through with you. Won't that big buck of yours have a nice surprise waiting for him when he gets through taking care of that little diversion I created for him over at his nigger boardinghouse." He pauses to see what reaction this little bit of news causes. "I couldn't have him coming home before I was ready for him, could I?"

I have been easing to my right as he talks, and my resolve grows stronger when I hear what he plans for my family. I know it is important for him to think me incapacitated with fear, so I try to put a quaver in my voice.

"Please, please, don't hurt my child. You can do with me what you want, but please, please don't hurt my child!"

"You can beg and cry all you want, Missy, but you're going to pay for what you and yours did to me. And the good thing about it is, I am going to enjoy every minute of it. You may not be the specimen you once were, but you're still nothing to scoff at. I cannot wait to see what you feel like beneath me without that big ole belly you had last time."

I have maneuvered until my back is toward the kitchen and the man is no longer directly between me and Diana. I drop the meek demeanor and push toward him with all my strength. I catch him off guard. His bum leg gives beneath him and he stumbles backward toward the cabin door. It is the chance I am waiting for. I turn and run for the bedroom as if I am trying to escape him. He follows, bellowing like a bull, and I have accomplished my first two goals. I have him out of the room with Diana, and I have time to pull the knife from between my breasts. He thinks I have backed up to the open window to try to escape, but instead, I use the opening and the two hands I have behind my back to unsheathe the blade.

Robinson lunges across the room, grabs me by the shoulders and flings me toward the bed. It is all I can do to keep the blade away from my own body as I fall. I land on my back, my arms flung wide. I am relieved that the man is so fueled by the evil that drives him, he does not see the weapon clutched in my hand. He leans forward at the last minute to push my skirts upward and out of his way, and the clothing provides a perfect shield as I clasp my hands together around the hilt of the knife to point the blade upward.

"This is what you get for messing with Gene Robinson," he snarls, and he throws himself up and on top of me. I hear him grunt, feel and smell the release of his rancid breath directly into my face as he lands. It is all I can do to hold the knife steady against the impact, and once he is impaled there, it takes even more effort not to squirm from beneath him. I must make sure the deed is done.

I look up into his eyes. At first they register confusion, then surprise. I am curiously detached. It is as if I have gone somewhere else, and this being lying here in my place has been left behind to do a job she knows needs to be done. This other person notices the jaundice-yellow white of his good eye, the puckering of the scar around the other. She notes the chapped, thin lips and the spittle seeping out at the corner. The skin on his face is rough and deep pink. It reminds me of cow tongue before it is cooked. I lie stiff and unyielding as the skin turns redder and redder. He tries to say something and the spit drips from the corner of his mouth onto my face. It jars me from the place I have gone, and I pull upward with both hands with all the strength I can muster. I feel the blade sever the sternum. The rest of his breath leaves his body and I turn my face just in time to keep his from landing on top of mine. Still, I do not move. I do not know how long I lie there before I feel the heavy stickiness of his blood upon my torso. I push the animal off of me onto the floor. I rise on shaky legs and look down on him. I feel absolutely no remorse for taking a life—the life of Eugene Robinson. I know there is much to do, but before I do it, I lean over and whisper, "And that is what *you* get for killing my son and threatening my family."

Chapter 45

Where in the hell is Jessie?

The curtains of the family parlor are drawn and the house has a deserted feel to it. Frederick walks to the small hallway between the parlor and the family dining room. There is plenty of light here because there has been no need to cover the floor-length windows that act as a passageway to the back verandah that runs horseshoe-like around the house as does the one above it. Through the windows he can see evidence of a beautiful day dawning, and he is tempted to take a walk along the porch, but he knows he has much to do today and he needs no distraction. There will be plenty of time for that later. Glancing around the dining room he admires the curve of the back wall. Cluskey had suggested this feature and Frederick, knowing of no other like it in town, is thrilled with the effect it and the egg and dart molding that calls attention to it create. More than one person has already commented on the extravagance of the room meant only for family use, and that has pleased Frederick to no end. He loves the idea that he may be thought of as a man who has the ability to spare no expense for his family. He hopes they picture him, his wife, and his children seated around the mahogany table being served up the best food to be had in Savannah.

Thinking of food reminds Frederick that there is none awaiting him at his place at the table. *Where in the hell is Jessie?* In the hallway again, he descends the circular stairs that spiral from the basement to the attic. The windows below are still shuttered, and there is little light to see by. Had the sheet of parchment lying on the wood surface of the worktable not been the only thing there, he might have overlooked it.

Walking closer he sees his name scrawled across it in what he recognizes as Jessie's small, neat penmanship. Educated in the same West Indian school, Jessie's handwriting is similar to his own. He picks it up, opens it, and is not surprised that it is written in French.

Frederick,
Please come to our house when you find this. It is urgent.
Deckie

Frederick has to lean against the counter to support himself. This message can bode nothing good. He calms himself. *What can be so awful that Jessie would write me this cryptic summons? Abby and the children are all on their way to Virginia, and Jessie could not possibly have received a summons regarding them. If there were bad news relating to his family, he would have been notified.*

Still, Jessie is not one for theatrics and she does not overreact. He does not take the time to run back upstairs for his hat. Instead, he hurries out the service entry door onto Harris Street and makes his way as quickly as possible through Yamacraw. Frederick knows the area well, but he has only been to Jessie's house a couple of times, once when he went with her before she purchased it, and the second time after the unfortunate attack that almost killed her.

Arriving at the door, he bangs loudly and tries the door intending to walk right in. Surely they will be expecting him. He tries the knob a couple of times before he realizes the door is barred. He has little time to think about this before the door swings inward and the mountain of a man that is Moses looms above him. Moses steps aside, and neither man speaks as Frederick enters the room.

Jessie looks up from her preparations of what smells like breakfast at the fireplace. *At least I may get something to eat before I go to work.*

Frederick's eye is caught by the little darkie playing with a rag doll in the middle of a small bed in the corner.

"What the hell is going on, Jessie?" Frederick does not try to keep the irritation out of his voice. He automatically sits down at the kitchen table where there are two places set.

"I am in trouble, Frederick." Jessie's tone does not match the message. She seems detached, her face lifeless, her movements marionette-like.

"You better be, ordering me across town like a lackey when I have a hundred and one things to do today."

"I killed Robinson," Jessie states flatly.

Frederick's mouth opens, but nothing comes out. Jessie puts a plate before him, and he looks down to observe the meal that looks much like what he eats every morning at home but served up on rudimentary dishes. In spite of what he has just heard, Frederick is surprised that someone of Jessie's poise and abilities eats her meals on this dull gray ironstone.

Moses finally speaks. "Do you hyur wat she say, Missa Barret?"

"I heard her. Sit down, both of you, and tell me what you are talking about."

"I killed Robinson."

"I've got that part. Tell me what happened. When did you kill Robinson? Where did you kill Robinson? And where is he, for God's sake—the body?"

Both Jessie and Moses sit. Frederick is surprised the small chair Moses pulls from the corner bears his weight.

"He came here to rape me again and hurt Diana. He planned to wait for Moses when he was through. He insinuated that Moses had beaten him almost to death and he was here to get even. Moses tells me he did beat him and you had a hand in bringing that about."

Frederick squirms a bit that Jessie is privy to these details, and she must notice.

"Do not misunderstand me, Frederick. I am glad Moses beat him. I only wish to God he had killed him at the time."

"Start from the beginning. Tell me everything that happened; then I will know best what can be done."

Jessie retells the story much as she might tell of the events of a day in the kitchen with no more emotion attached to killing the man than she would expend in the wringing of a chicken's neck and preparing the carcass for dumplings.

"Where is he now, for God's sake?"

"He roll up in a ole quilt unda da bed," Moses offers.

"Is there no mess?" Frederick asks.

"There was," Jessie starts.

"He pur much bleed ow," Moses finishes for her.

"Moses burned my clothing, the mattress, and the covering out back late last night."

"I care anudda mattress obber from da boadin house," Moses includes, as if this is important to the story. Frederick is amazed by their behavior. Looking more closely at Moses, he notices the fear in the big man's eyes. Glancing at Jessie, he guesses she is in shock. What woman can kill a man, even one who needs to be killed as badly as Robinson, and appear so unaffected by it? Frederick recalls what Robinson had done to Jessie. Too, he remembers some of the atrocities of Saint Domingue. Besides those two things, Jessie is not your typical woman. He smiles at her in spite of the predicament they are in.

"Sounds like you did the world a favor, Jessie."

"No doubt," she agrees, "but how do I keep the world from knowing?"

"You tink da sherf bleve us if we tell da truf?" Moses asks the question but Frederick can tell from the look in his eyes that he already knows the answer.

"He may well believe you, but bottom line, he is going to know one of you killed Robinson, a white man, and I don't have to tell you how that is going to play out."

"So wadda we do?" Moses asks then answers his own question. "I tink I haw da carcuss down ta da ribber an dump it wen it turn dawk."

Frederick starts to ask whom he is going to get to help him carry the body, but then he remembers to whom he is talking. Moses could probably carry three men if necessary. Thank God they will not have to bring anyone else into this.

"We need to get Jessie out of town," Frederick tells them. "There are a few people who know the man, and there are a few more who know what he did to Jessie. We need to make sure there can be no connection."

"I can take Diana and leave for a while. I have some friends in New Orleans who would take us in."

A plan is taking shape in Frederick's mind. "I have a better idea. Let's send Lewis with you tonight to Charleston in the trap. There you can catch a steamer to Virginia where you can join Abby. If Robinson washes up," here he turns to Moses, "and I suggest you weight him down well enough so he will not float up until they will have no idea who he is and how long he has been dead," then back to Jessie. "Everyone is going to remember that Abby and the servants went to Virginia. No one is going to remember you were not one of them. If the body is discovered in time for them to ascertain an approximate time of death, and if they are smart enough to check the steamer records, there will be no records of you leaving the Savannah Harbor on your own. "

The room is silent except for the sound of Diana talking to her doll on the bed.

"What about Moses?" Jessie asks. What is going to keep people from suspecting him? Especially since he had help in beating the man? I am sure Robinson has talked to someone about the attack and his opinion as to who committed it. I am surprised there wasn't more of an investigation into that at the time."

"Robinson was in no shape to tell anybody anything for a good long time." Again, Frederick cannot keep the smile off his face, "and he was a prideful bastard. I am sure he wanted to take care of matters in his own way in his own time. He just didn't know who he was messing with, did he, Jessie?"

If Jessie sees anything humorous about the situation, she doesn't reveal it, and she is not going to be distracted from her earlier concern. "What about Moses? I am not going to leave him to deal with this on his own."

"I be fine, Jessie." Moses takes her hand in one of his and turns her face to make her look at him with the other. "You godda git outta hyur. You godda tink bou Dinah. If I lebe now, day sho nough gonna be spicious. I nebber lef da boadin house fo mo dan a day. I lebe town an dat bidy float up, day gonna hab da dogs ow lookin fo me fo da sun come up."

For the first time Jessie shows concern. "Oh Moses, what have I done? I'll never forgive myself if this comes back on you!"

"You do wat you hab ta, Jes. An you ain by yosef in dis. I da one dat beat em. He migh nebber botha us agin if I lef it be."

Frederick clears his throat. He knows Moses would never have acted in the first place if he had not instructed him to do so, but he chooses not to remind them of this fact.

"Then it is settled. Jessie, you lie low today. Do not let anyone see you or the child. You sneak out as soon as it is dark—wear dark clothing—and come to the house. Lewis will have the trap ready. Moses, you wait until about midnight, then get rid of that body. Put as many rocks in his pockets and pants as you can."

Frederick takes the lack of response as agreement to the plan.

"No use letting this breakfast go to waste."

Frederick picks up his fork and begins to eat the cold meal.

Jessie pushes the other plate toward Moses. "Eat, Moses. I ate with Diana."

The three sit at the table and finish their breakfast while the corpse of Eugene Robinson lies mere feet from them beneath the bed.

Chapter 46

A letter from Frederick is awaiting me when I reach Mother's. *How sweet of him,* is my first thought, then, *I hope nothing is wrong!* I am exhausted from the trip, as are the children, and I decide to wait to read the letter until I can get the children settled and find a moment to myself. If something is wrong, there will be nothing I can do about it right now, so it can wait. Besides, knowing Frederick, he probably is missing the children, alone for the first time as he is in that huge house, and he just wants me to send word that we have arrived safely.

"Are you going to read it, My Dear?" My mother is at my elbow. I can tell by her eagerness to hear the contents that she fears, as I do, that a letter this early may not be a good thing.

"No, Mother, I am going to wait until I get the children settled. I have decided there is nothing I can do about it tonight, even if it is bad news, so I will deal with it later. I will let you know what it says as soon as I read it."

"I was not meaning to pry, Daughter. Of course, you should read it when you are ready."

I look at my mother. She looks well though I know she suffered a prolonged cold last winter. I have missed her terribly, and I certainly do not want to start this stay out on a negative note.

"You have every right to be concerned." I hug her to me. She hugs me back and I feel my muscles relax in spite of the unknown of the letter in my hand. "I have missed you, Mother!"

"I have missed you, too! Let's get the children and the servants settled, your letter read, then I will bring a cup of tea to your old room and we will catch up."

We have a cold meal served up in the dining room, and the children are easier to settle than I expect. Mother has set up enough cots for all of my children, Anne's two daughters, and Sophia's daughter and son who will not arrive for another day or two. Luella and Caroline—Anne's two girls—do not seem overly pleased to be on the sleeping porch with their younger cousins, and who can blame them? At sixteen and fourteen respectively they are young women, not children. It is selfish of me, but I am pleased they are out here, for Luella is more like her mother Anne in temperament than she is her departed namesake, and I know she will mother the rest of them. I notice Maxie chooses the cot between her older sister Mattie and Luella, whereas my bolder Ella has left the cot on the other side of Luella vacant and is settling in the one on the outer side of Caroline who has chosen to sleep next to Mattie. Mattie and Caroline, only a year apart in age, get along well. Caroline looks more like the elder Luella looked at her age than does my niece who is named for her, and I feel a moment of sadness when I notice the resemblance. I am glad there will be room for little Gail, Sophia's daughter and my namesake, beside Luella, for I think it best the two youngest girls be closest to the oldest and most responsible out here.

My mother has had three cots for the boys placed at the other end of the long narrow screen porch. Rob and Fredie choose the two closest to the girls leaving the one in the corner empty for the youngest of the male cousins, five-year-old Jimmy Howe. I notice Rob has chosen the bed closest to the screen door. I frown a little at this. None of the servants will be on the porch with the children, so I put in a word of caution before I leave for the evening.

"Rob, you are to leave this porch under no circumstances without first telling Luella, Caroline, or Mattie, and then only to use the privy and come right back. Luella, I hope you are a light sleeper because I would not put it past Rob to try to lead his brother astray."

"Do you want me to sleep by the back door, Aunt Abby, to make sure the boys stay put?"

"Will that be necessary?" I ask Rob, and he assures me it is not. "I will just ask Justice to bunk down on the back lawn."

I have no intention of asking Justice to sleep in the yard, but it cannot hurt for Rob to think I might. Justice has a formidable appearance—he is not much smaller than Jessie's Moses, and I know the children are all a little afraid of him. Maybe Rob will think twice before risking an encounter with Justice.

I squeeze between the cots to kiss the children, nieces included, good night. Though Rob indicates as he has every night for the last year or so that he is too old to be kissed by his mother, I know he still likes that I tuck him and his brother in. Their father usually makes the rounds at night, as well, so I give each child an extra kiss and say, "This one is for Papa."

The younger girls giggle at this, the boys roll their eyes, but Mattie says, "I wish Papa could be here. Then everything would be perfect!"

I remind Mattie that she is going to be so occupied with her cousins that her father would feel neglected—that it is best he is not here. He might get his feelings hurt. It dawns on me too late that our banter may be hard on Anne's two girls who no longer have a father to tuck them in or make them feel special.

With everyone settled for the night, I am free to climb the stairs to my old bedroom. It looks much as it always has even though I know it has become Luella's and Caroline's since Edward's death. Anne told me during my first visit home after she returned with the girls to live at Hickory Grove that Mother had told her the girls would have to move in with her when Sophia and I returned for the summer. Anne had hinted it was not for Sophia that Mother was so accommodating. I feel guilty now as I look around the room in which I spent twenty odd years worth of nights. I hate that Luella and Caroline are displaced and Anne, and probably Sophia if the truth be known, think I receive preferential treatment from our mother. Nonetheless, I am relieved to know the room is always here waiting for me, much like my mother, to offer comfort no matter what else is going on in my life. I realize Frederick would not be pleased if he could know my thoughts right now.

The thought of Frederick reminds me of the letter in the pocket among the folds of my skirt. I take it out and place it on the bed long enough to unlace my boots and remove my petticoats. I climb into the middle of the bed and prop the two feather-filled pillows behind my back to pad the iron bedstead. Though Frederick has not written a return address on the front of the envelope, I know by his neat, miniscule script that it is from him. Mother, too, easily recognizes the distinct handwriting for she told me when I arrived the letter was from my husband. I tear it open and find a single sheet of parchment I recognize as one we keep on hand at the house. It is the same stationery I use to write Mother, my sisters, and those few friends with whom I still correspond. The message is short and confusing.

My Dearest Abigail,

I write in haste. Jessie and the child will arrive at Hickory Grove a day or so after you. Tell your mother that I have decided I want you and my children to be fed by the best throughout the summer. Though that sentiment is true, it is not the real reason for the visit. She will explain all, but it is best you tell your mother nothing more. I cannot commit more to paper. Know that I miss you and the children already and impatiently await the passing of the months between now and the end of your confinement. I will come when you tell me your time is near. My love for you is strong, as always,

Your devoted husband Frederick.

Why ever can Jessie and Diana be coming to Hickory Grove? Though we have discussed her coming before, I have always been reluctant to leave Frederick behind without anyone to cook or care for him. Mammy has even come along on this trip because we knew she might be invaluable in the delivery of the baby I am carrying.

There is a knock on my door, and I know it is the promised visit from Mother. I quickly slip the note from Frederick behind the pillows on which I rest and call for her to come in. Direct as usual, Mother comes to the point.

"Have you read the letter from Frederick? Is all well in Savannah?"

"Yes, Mother, more than fine. Frederick is sending us a gift, of sorts. He is sending Jessie to cook for us this summer. You remember Jessie, don't you?"

"One is not likely to forget Jessie," Mother says. "It will be nice to see what this woman can do. If you remember, she was recovering from that unfortunate incident the last time she was here."

"That is right; she was, so you have never gotten to experience the meals she prepares. Frederick says since you have not agreed to come to Savannah to enjoy our hospitality, he is sending it to Hickory Grove."

I amaze myself with the improvisation. I know there has to be something amiss for Frederick to send Jessie, and I instinctively know I need to talk with Jessie before I tell Mother anything, not that I really know anything to tell.

Mother's eyebrows pull down in thought. "That surprises me, Abigail. I wrote to Frederick myself just last month that I will visit as soon as you all get settled in the new house."

"You know how Frederick is about the children, Mother. He probably just wants them to have Jessie here to cook for them." Another idea comes to me, so I quickly add, "Besides, Jessie has been with me for the birth of both girls, and I am sure Frederick will feel better knowing she is here should the baby come early."

Mother sits on my bed. "Do you think he finds the food here inferior? Does he think we cannot make sure the baby is delivered as safely as it could be in Savannah?"

Now I must deal with my mother's hurt feelings. "Of course he thinks the food is good enough here, Mother. You know he has always loved dining with you." I struggle to come up with something plausible. "You know what a family man Frederick is. I am sure he just wants to provide what he thinks is the best for us even when we are here."

I can tell by the stormy look on Mother's face I am making things worse.

"I am not saying this right. Let it suffice to say you have never eaten meals like the ones Jessie prepares. Neither had I or anyone else I am acquainted with, so they tell me. I do not know—maybe Frederick wants to offer Jessie's services so she may train Cook in some meals she prepares. I really think Frederick is just trying to be nice."

Though obviously not completely mollified, Mother seems to realize I can offer nothing more in way of explanation as to why my cook is spending the summer with us. "Very well, but where will we put this woman? It is my understanding she is a free darkie, so will she be comfortable in the quarters out back? Do you want to put her on the porch with the children?"

I have not thought of where we will put Jessie. The last time we were here, we put a cot in the upstairs hallway because of her injuries. The arrangement had not been very practical, so it is understandable Mother does not want to repeat it.

"Do you have an empty cabin? She will be bringing her daughter—her adoptive daughter of sorts—Diana. She is a black child, but she too is free."

I can tell my mother is finding all of this last minute jockeying irritating. She is a woman who prides herself on running a tight, smooth household, and bringing a stranger—one of an odd position, at that—into her household with so little notice has thrown her for a loop.

"I will have Cook moved into the kitchen, and we will put her in her cabin."

"Oh, we mustn't do that, Mother!" I tell her. I can still remember how Mammy reacted to Jessie. "Cook will never accept Jessie in her kitchen if we give her her cabin. How about the spinning hut? Could we use it?"

"Well, I guess I could have it cleaned well and a bed put in. We will not need it for the cloth for a while, and I guess we can do that in the laundry hut, if necessary." Here my mother stands up as if she is eager to get started on making the changes. "Regardless, it is not for you to worry about. Though inconvenient, we will do what we must. The woman is coming no matter how long we discuss it."

Mother sounds thoroughly put out, and she must realize it, for in the next instance she placates, "Frederick is a wise man and a courteous one. If he thinks it best to send this woman to us, we will just have to trust he is right. Things happen for a reason, and who am I to turn away free help?"

Mother bends to place a kiss on my forehead. She is preoccupied and she leaves the room without the promised catching up session. I am so tired, this omission is, in itself, a blessing. Though I plan to think more on the whole Jessie coming to Virginia surprise, I am exhausted. The last thing I remember before waking to the rooster crowing is pulling my pillows down under my head and beginning my prayers.

Chapter 47

What now! Frederick has just donned his clothes and has been contemplating whether he should go to the City Hotel or make his way over to Moses' boarding house for breakfast. He is none too happy about having to do either. He knows he must come up with a plan for what to do in Jessie's absence, but he has barely had time to think, and now this infernal knocking on the door just after dawn—it cannot bode well, and it is with reluctance he makes himself descend the stairs. He is surprised when he opens the door, for John Andrews, his friend and financial advisor, is the last person he expects to see.

"John Andrews! What brings you out at this time of the morning?" Realizing he is leaving the man standing on the front porch, he invites him in, and he notes with pride the way the wealthy bank manager and plantation owner looks around his foyer with open admiration.

"I say, Barret, you have done well by yourself. This place is impressive. Why haven't I been invited over sooner to have a look at it? Have you forgotten who your friends are?"

Frederick laughs, his sour mood of earlier forgotten. "You will, My Friend; you will. We have barely moved in. I had hoped to have you over for a gentlemen's only meal, but the help is all in Virginia with Abby. All I have to offer you is a breakfast at the City Hotel, if you would care to join me."

"I would love to, Barret, but I am in a hurry. I have to get to the bank, and I only have a moment."

"You must at least come into the parlor. I am sure you have something to say or you would not be here, and I would prefer to discuss my business in comfort, no matter what the nature of it."

Andrews laughs and follows Frederick under the archway and left into the formal parlor. Andrews agrees to sit down, but does so only after admiring the finer points of the room. Finally he says, "But I have not come to discuss architecture; I have come to impart a bit of information I have just come across that you may not be aware of. As you know, I sit on the City Council..."

"Yes, that and about half a dozen other boards around town," Frederick interjects, and he feels his pulse quicken. He has long hoped to become a City Council member himself, and maybe his good friend has come to tell him of an opening.

"We had an early morning meeting, and the sheriff was there as usual, and he tells us of a disturbing development last night. His men were making their rounds and they came across a nigger transporting an unwieldy burden through the back streets."

Frederick feels the blood drain from his face. He forces himself to sit still. He hopes his expression is bland.

"There was much that did not look right to them, so they kept a distance and followed the boy to the river to see what he was up to. They say they could tell he was making every effort not to be observed, so they acted likewise and refrained from approaching him to demand his pass. Their efforts paid off, and when they finally stopped him, he was about to chuck his bundle into the river. As you may well have guessed, the package turned out to be a body—a dead one. What you probably would never have guessed is..." here Andrews pauses for effect, "the body was that of a white man!"

Frederick makes himself gasp because he knows what is expected. "You cannot mean it!" he manages to get out, and he must be somewhat convincing for his friend continues.

"That is all bad enough, but not consequential enough for me to make a special trip over here. The most shocking aspect of this whole sordid tale is who the black man is. The sheriff tells me they have arrested that big buck, the free one who owns that boarding house over in Yamacraw. When he told me that, I remembered you had some business dealings with the man, and then I recalled why. Isn't he the husband of your cook? The high yella with the good body and the pretty accent?"

"Are you referring to Moses—Moses Tucker?" Frederick asks. "Surely not!" He is impressed with his own acting ability. "Moses is a gentle man. There must be some misunderstanding. What does he say for himself?"

"What can he say for himself? He was caught red-handed—or rather black-handed, as this case may be!" Andrews laughs at his own joke until he realizes Barret is not laughing with him.

"I know this has to be hard for you, Man. The husband of your cook. Is she here? Does she know?"

Would I be sitting here feigning surprise if she knew! Thank God I had the forethought to get Jessie out of town.

"She is in Virginia with my family." Apparently Andrews wasn't paying attention the first time he told him the help had gone north. "They left three days ago."

Frederick stands and walks to the closest of the floor length windows. Looking out, his back to Andrews, he says calmly, "She will be devastated to hear this. Surely the sheriff will listen to what the man has to say."

"Barret, the man is a nigger and he was caught carrying a dead white man across town to dump in the river! He is as good as dead, and rightly so! We cannot allow such a heinous crime to go unpunished!"

"Certainly not," Frederick agrees. He remains at the window. "But you know as well as I do that all white men are not law-abiding and all darkies are not vicious killers. Maybe Tucker was provoked beyond endurance."

Andrews, clearly agitated, rises and walks over to stand behind Frederick. Frederick is forced to face him, but before he does, he makes sure his face is set in what he hopes is an appropriate expression. He thinks concern is understandable, but he is careful not to appear too indignant about what will probably be the loss of a black life.

"Yes, Dammit, that is true. But regardless of what this white man did—and if it was bad, it has cost him—he is dead—we cannot allow a black man who kills a white man, regardless of the reason, to live! Think of the implications. Have you forgotten Saint Domingue?"

Frederick is insulted, but he tries hard not to show it. "Still, I feel like I must speak for the man. I am the sponsor to his wife. She is in my employee. The sheriff needs to at least hear what he has to say. Nigger that Moses Tucker is, he has the reputation for being a good man—an honest one—and the sheriff needs to at least hear him out before he strings him up."

Andrew's eyebrows pull together in what Frederick interprets as irritation. "Go on down there, then. See what you can do, but you know as well as I do you will be pissing in the wind."

The man turns to leave, but when he gets to the door, he turns to Frederick who has followed him. "Just take a word of advice, My Friend. People are going to be real stirred up about this, and you do not want to come down on the wrong side of this thing. It is fine for you to share your concerns with me, but you sure do not want to come across as a nigger lover. You have done well for yourself. Do not jeopardize your standing in the community for one nigger."

With that, John Andrews is down the steps and striding up the street with his hat still in his hands. He does not look back.

Oh My God! What am I to do?

Frederick feels sick to his stomach, and though it is long past the time he usually eats his breakfast, he is not hungry. He absently chooses a hat from the three that hang on pegs on the foyer wall. He locks the door behind him and walks to the jail. On the way there, he prays that no one noticed Lewis driving Jessie away last night. It may certainly be to their advantage that their home is the only one on the block, yet the barracks face them right across Bull Street, so anyone coming or going from there could have noticed the departing buggy.

Frederick wonders what Moses has told the sheriff, and he dares to hope that his name has not been brought into this. He knows he is taking a huge risk going to the jail, but he feels he has no choice. He must find out what Moses is saying, and he knows he will eventually have to answer to Jessie. Jessie knows enough to implicate Frederick, though he cannot imagine that she would. Still, he wants to be able to tell Jessie he has done all he can do.

When Frederick is in sight of the jail, he has hope. It is in such disrepair, it looks as if someone of Moses' strength can escape by simply pushing the rickety boards apart and walking away. He is not surprised that the jail is unattended, for there is no room for an office there. It is an old square box of a building, probably no more than twelve feet by twelve feet with a roof made out of palings that cannot possibly keep out the rain. Frederick can actually make out Moses slumped on the floor against the far wall by peering through a crack in the building. The stench from inside the room makes looking through the boards distasteful, but Frederick does his best to see around the room before he calls out to Moses.

"Moses, are you alone in there?"

"Yes, Missa Barret."

By the time Frederick walks around to the wall closest to the chained Moses, the big man has risen and is pressing his face to a crack in the wall.

"What have you told them, Moses?"

"I ain tole dem nuttin. Wat kin I tell em? I cain say nuttin bou wat he do or dey be tinkin on Jessie. I cain say nuttin an needer kin you."

A wave of relief passes over Frederick. "They're going to hang you, Moses, then Jessie is going to hang me. Do you think you can get out of there? The building looks like it is about to fall down."

"The billin ain da problem. Dese sheckle an dis stone da problem."

Frederick stands on tiptoe to look downward. So the security lies not in the building itself, but in the shackles and chains attached to ballast taken from the riverfront.

"I migh be able ta take one ub em outta hyur wid me, bu dey got me chain up ta two ub em. An I tink dey broke my shoulda. Dey beat me hawd haulin me back hyur. I din come easy."

"Do you think you could pry the shackle apart?"

"I migh hab I sumpin to do it wid."

"I will bring you a bar tonight. I think I can find one we can get between these cracks. If not, I will use it to pry some boards apart."

"I doan tink I be hyur ba nighfall. Dey tawk lack dey string me up soon as day git roun ta it."

Frederick goes quiet for a moment.

"I will do what I can, Moses. You are entitled to a trial, even if you are a nigger. I will talk to the sheriff and remind him of that."

"Tank you, Missa Barret. Bu jus in case I doan make it ta sunup, will ya tell Jessie sumpin fo me. Tell er naw ta come back hyur ta Svanna. Tell er ta head on up Nawth. She need ta git her an da chile outta hyur. I hyur it bedda for cullud foke up dare. Da futha she go, da bedda."

Frederick agrees to give her the message, but he has no intention of fulfilling that promise. "You need not give up yet, Moses. I will do what I can to buy you some time. Listen for me tonight. I will bring the claw as soon I think it's safe."

As Frederick walks away, he hears Moses call out to him, "An tell er dat I lub er an da chile. She know it, bu tell er enway."

Frederick does not reply, but he is even more determined to talk the sheriff into giving Moses a trial. When he arrives at City Hall, the sheriff is indeed ready to swing Moses from a tree today. He tells Frederick they are going to hang Moses as soon as they can round up a crew to get it done, but Frederick forces him to admit the man is entitled to a trial.

"The nigger almost killed two of my best men! And he won't say a word about what happened so what good is a trial going to do if he has nothing to say for himself?"

"Another night to think on it may bring about a change of mind. After all, what has he got to lose. He might as well tell us what happened if he is going to swing anyway. I for one would like my curiosity satisfied. I have been good to the man. I want to hear an explanation as to why he did what he did. Maybe he will come clean with me there in the courtroom looking at him."

The sheriff doesn't give in easily, but after listening to Frederick talk for a full thirty minutes, much of the conversation pertaining to whom Frederick knows and what he has done for the community, the sheriff agrees to the trial.

"Ten o'clock tomorrow morning. We'll hang him at noon so those who want can be there to watch before going home for dinner."

Frederick leaves the government building and finally makes his way to the City Hotel. He realizes he is starving. He is pleased he will be able to tell Jessie what he has done to try to save her husband's life. Who knows, maybe the poor bastard will be lucky and actually get away tonight. He hopes so, but he also hopes he will steer clear of Virginia if he does. Jessie might take the notion to go with him, and he certainly will not stand idly by while that happens.

The food comes and he decides not to borrow trouble. Frederick Barret eats a late breakfast while he thinks about how he is going to find a crowbar and get it to the jail without being seen.

Chapter 48

I can tell Mrs. Middleton does not know what to think of me. I can also tell she is not thrilled by our arrival. Neither of these things surprises me. Abby, on the other hand, seems to be excited to see me, mainly, I am sure, so she can find out what has happened that Frederick would send me to her so shortly on the heels of her own departure. Abby's efforts to get me alone are thwarted when her mother goes with us to show me the cabin in which I will be staying.

The cabin Diana and I will occupy is more than satisfactory, but I can tell Mrs. Middleton is second-guessing herself in putting me here. She makes the mistake many do of assuming I expect more because of my light skin. Light as my skin may be and free as I am called, I am still considered a Negro in America, so my living arrangements could be far worse than what Mrs. Middleton has arranged for us. I tell her I will be more than comfortable, and though Abby tries to stay behind to talk with me, her mother insists she accompany her to the main house to *discuss the noonday meal.* I am sure the topic of discussion will be my unusual self and maybe the black child I bring with me. Regardless, I appreciate the reprieve I have been given to collect my thoughts and settle Diana who is losing her battle with exhaustion. She has been trying hard to remain awake so she can explore her new surroundings. I take the opportunity to rest by insisting she take a nap.

"Diana, there will be plenty of time to play with the other children when we are rested."

I am concerned that Mrs. Middleton will not want Diana to play with her grandchildren, but I do not share this fear with Diana. I will deal with that problem when I must. Right now, I simply want to close my eyes and sleep so the worries that have plagued me since leaving Savannah can be kept at bay.

Diana drops off quickly, but I cannot do likewise. My fear for Moses keeps me staring at the ceiling. Though he put in an appearance at the boardinghouse, he returned home as soon as possible to spend the majority of the day we were to leave with Diana and me. I would have liked to lie with him, but it was impossible with Diana underfoot and Robinson decaying under the bed. We had to satisfy ourselves with being together. We embraced so often that Diana picked up on our mood and insisted on being held between us. For the first time ever, I resented Diana's presence.

Moses walked with us to the Barrets as soon as it was dark, and I had clung to him in spite of Diana pulling on my skirt and demanding to be included. Though I could read no more than usual from contact with my husband, the magnitude of what had happened finally caught up with me, and I experienced an overpowering sense of foreboding that made me want to refuse to leave. Lewis had gone to the house to tell Frederick of our arrival, and he had returned with him to insist we be on our way. My last glimpse of Moses was of him framed in the wide doorway of the carriage house. I strained to see him as long as possible, but I lost sight of him quickly for the dark clothes and his dark skin were sucked into the equally dark night. I should have been glad of the protection the night gave him, but I could not shake the fear that I might never see him again. Though I reasoned with myself all the way to Virginia, I still fear I will not see him again.

Moses has been a part of many clandestine forays into the night, but this one feels different, probably because I am so far from him. We have not been apart for more than a few hours since we were married, so I know our separation is probably the cause for my anxiety, that and knowing I left him to dispose of the body of a man I murdered less than three days ago. One would think this would be what is worrying me, but it is not. Though I am no longer in shock, I still do not regret killing the animal that took so much from me. What I regret is leaving Moses behind to clean up the mess of my making, but I am rational enough to know that I had no real choice in what I did. No matter which way I look at it, Eugene Robinson had to die, and though I have created many scenarios in my mind, none of them could have resulted in a cleaner, less problematic way of going about it. I console myself now with the realization that if Moses has gotten across town and dumped the body without being seen, we are in the clear, and I will never have to worry about Robinson again.

Though I want to sleep, I am relieved to be distracted from the effort when I hear a series of short raps. Abby stands in the open doorway. I start to rise.

"No, please, stay where you are." She whispers to avoid waking Diana. "Are you comfortable? Would you like for me to have a cot brought in? I know you are not used to sleeping with the child nor she with you."

"This is fine the way it is," I assure her. "It is a comfort to have her close to me right now."

I cannot lie flat on my back while holding a conversation with my employer. I sit up, swing my legs over the side of the bed, and try to gather the unruly strands of hair back into their place among the others in the loose bun at the nape of my head.

"I know you must wonder why I am here..." I begin, and I see a look of relief cross Abby's face. She spans the short distance from the door to the bedside and sits a couple of feet from me on the side of the bed.

"I can think of no easy way to relate what has happened, so I will tell you as straightforwardly as possible. I stabbed Eugene Robinson and Frederick has sent me here in case there is some fallout."

For a second Abby's face registers nothing. "Eugene Robinson..." she repeats. A light dawns in her eyes and they widen in disbelief. "You stabbed the man who attacked you? Did you hurt him badly?"

"I killed him," I state flatly.

"Oh Jessie! How horrible for you! Can you tell me exactly what happened, or is it too painful for you to talk about?"

"Oddly, I feel no remorse whatsoever for killing the man. I merely worry about the consequences."

I spend the next half hour giving Abby a point-by-point explanation as to what happened. She interrupts only a couple of times with questions, and she doesn't comment at all on what I tell her. She appears as calm as I feel about killing Robinson. After I have told her all I can think of on the matter, we both sit in silence for a bit while Abby takes it all in.

"The way I look at it, Jessie, you didn't really kill the man. He killed himself. He threw himself on the knife. And you had no choice. I shudder to think," and here she actually does shudder, "what he would have done to you and Diana had you not had the knife."

I am surprised when Abby reaches across and lays her hand on mine, not only by what she says, but by the sensation I get from the contact with her. Her words, "I am proud of you, Jessie. I do not think I would have been strong enough to do what you have done, necessary as it was!" should be a comfort to me, but the message I get from contact with her overrides the encouragement.

"Abby," clasping her hand in both of mine, I ask, "are you feeling well?"

Abby's face reveals her confusion at the sudden change of topic, but over the years, Abby has picked up on my heightened awareness of things *unknowable,* and she searches my eyes.

"Why, do you feel there may be something wrong with the baby?"

The question itself is telling.

"I have no way of knowing if it is the baby or you. The two of you are too closely connected. I simply sense you are not well," I lie. I do sense something different about the child she is carrying. I had purposely placed both hands on her before she left the house just days ago, and I had felt the vibrancy of the separate life running like an undercurrent beside her own. Now, though I still feel a separate life force, it is dimmer, less dynamic.

"In truth, Jessie, I have not felt well since the night on the steamer. I was nauseated then, and I thought that was to be expected due to the movement, but it has not gone away. Too, I feel listless, and the baby seems to be feeling the same way. The child was so active the night before we left, Frederick could feel it moving beneath his hand." Abby turns pink and looks away when she realizes she has cast an intimate image of the relationship with her husband. "Now, I cannot feel any movement at all."

"You must rest, Abby. The last few months have been chaotic for the whole family, and you, in your condition, have probably had more physical and emotional stimulation than is wise for one carrying a child. But you are strong and healthy, and I am sure you will be fine if you just take care of yourself. And I say this after I have just told you the most shocking of news. Please, try not to dwell on any of this."

"I will try, sincerely try. And your news has certainly not caused me any harm. In fact, maybe it has jolted me out of my selfish doldrums. It has taken all I can muster to keep Mother from knowing I am on the precipice of one of my moods."

Abby rises from the bed and pulls me up with her. She continues to hold the hand she grasped while sitting on the bed, and she takes the right one as well as she faces me. "I am so glad you have come, Jessie. Not just for me, but for yourself. We must help each other. You will be here for me as you have always been when I need you, but this time, I will be here for you, as well."

Abby hugs me to her, and I find tears running down my cheeks as I feel the inevitable flowing between us. When we separate, she notices the tears and thinks they are the result of all I have been through.

"You have done only what you had to, and I know the Good Lord will not judge you for protecting yourself and your own."

"It is not the Lord's condemnation I fear, Abby."

"I know what you mean," she says, and she thinks she does, and though the white establishment in Savannah is certainly to be feared if they learn of what I have done, it is not the cause of my greatest current fear. I see no benefit in setting Abby straight. Instead, I try to express my gratitude for her understanding.

"Thank you, Miss Abby. Remember what you said about admiring me? Well, I admire you every bit as much. You are stronger than you know. You must remember that."

Abby leaves, and I find no pleasure in the fact that I have buoyed her spirits, for I know what she cannot. It is simply the calm before the storm. I lie back down and curl myself around my daughter, careless of the fact that I may wake her. I selfishly draw comfort from the only source available to me.

Chapter 99

Moses tries not to get his hopes up, but Mr. Barret seemed to mean it when he said he would come back with a bar. He knows he needs to be as rested as possible in case he makes good on his promise.

He eases himself off the back wall and stretches his full length on the floor and gets as comfortable as possible. He was exhausted from lack of sleep and stress before last night, and he cannot understand how he keeps from falling asleep in spite of the pain from the shoulder and the beating. The big man has been wide awake since he saw Jessie off at the Barrets. In order for his body to rest, his mind will have to slow down, and so far all he can think about is Jessie, the child, and what is bound to happen if he is still here come morning. Moses has been trying to pray all day, but as his shoulder throbs and his head rests awkwardly on the right arm he has drawn up to support it, he prays again.

"Lawd, please be wid me. I know I ain da bes man, but neeber hab I be da worse, an I axin you wid aw da stringt I hab lef in dis broke bidy ub mine fo hep oudda dis mess I in. I ax naw so much fo me, Lawd, ba fo Jessie an lil Dinah. Dey need me, Lawd, awmos as much as I need dem. Day loss much in dis worl, Lawd, an I hate ta be tinkin on dem losin mo. Please le da man do wat he say he do, an gib me da stringt ub Samson. I goan need it wid dis shoulder painin me lack it be. An if I ain a goan lib true dis mess, I ax dat Jessie be strong nuff fo da two ub us. Take care ub dem, Lawd. Dis is wat I pray."

Moses is able to relax enough after praying to get drowsy, and he must fall asleep because he is startled by a tapping next to his head.

"Wake up, Moses. I cannot believe you can sleep at a time like this," comes a whisper. The voice is followed by a creaking sound of a board being pried loose and the thud of something dropping next to him. "Can you reach the claw, Moses?"

"I kin, Massa, I kin."

"You're on your own now, Boy. Stay low and in the shadows. There's a moon out and no clouds so you're going to have to make yourself invisible. And lose that claw somewhere where it can't be found. There are hundreds like it, but still…"

"I git rid a it, Massa, an tanks. You din haf ta take da risk. I blijin ta you."

If Frederick is still there, he doesn't answer. Moses grasps the metal tool in his right hand and puts it in his lap. He would like to use his left to find the metal ring that anchors the chain to his ankle, but the injured left shoulder renders it almost useless. He manages to position his knee in a way to lever the claw. Frederick has found one with a head small enough to fit through the metal ring, but it is short, so Moses cannot find a way to get his full strength behind it. It does not help that he is made weak by hunger, pain, and exhaustion. After several attempts, he rises, grimaces against the pain while he uses the left hand to steady the claw, and places his right foot on the handle. He lets go of the claw at the same time he steps down on it with all his weight. The ring lets go, but the claw rolls and Moses is thrown sideways onto his broken shoulder. He must black out from the pain, but the same pain revives him. He finds himself sprawled on the floor with a dangling chain on his right foot while his left is still bolted to the stone.

Moses lies still in the dark. His efforts have had to be loud, but now he can hear nothing but the distant barking of a dog. He gives himself a few moments to rest, then tackles his left ankle chain. He knows what will work now, but still it takes him two attempts. He is ready for the rolling of the claw so he manages to stay upright when the ring gives way. He wishes he could get the shackles from around his ankles, but he can think of no way without causing further injury to himself and wasting valuable time.

He is dismayed by the clatter the chains make with each move. He shuffles his feet as quietly as possible across the wooden floor and tackles three weak-looking boards he had chosen while it was still daylight.

The moon had been a blessing when it seeped through the cracks to help with the chains, but here, on the outside, he feels exposed. He knows anyone passing can see him. He huddles against the wall just long enough to get his bearings, then pushes off and sprints across the clearing toward an oak that provides some coverage. The rattling of the chains sounds like an alarm to him, and he has to concentrate to keep from tripping himself up. When he gets to the tree, he takes precious minutes to wind them around his ankles and tie them with strands of Spanish moss. He knows his ankles will be itching in no time from the parasites the moss contains, but it is the best he can do.

Seeing no one at all, Moses sets out on the course he has laid out in his mind. He knows he cannot go home or to the boarding house, so he has determined to go to the only place he thinks might be safe—the secret hiding place under the Second African Baptist Church. If he can reach that refuge, he knows he can hide there until he can make it to the river for transport when the time is right. He darts from one darkened spot to another, looking ahead for any structure, tree, or bush that might offer seclusion. He is about half way to his destination when he pauses beside the well on Percival Square. He slides the covering away from the lip and squeezes the claw through the opening he has created. He hears the plunk as it hits the water, and he is about to leave the shadows when he hears first one dog, then several, begin to bark. He has known the dogs kept by white folks could pose a threat, but that was yet another problem for which he had no solution. He pushes away from the well and moves as swiftly as the chains and his body will allow toward the church. He knows he is in trouble when he hears a deep voice from a couple of houses ahead of him yell, "Rosco, stop that racket!"

He fears the dogs will alert one of the watchmen who patrol the city after dark. Sure enough, voices travel on the night air and he hears more than one man talking. Moses determines to put as much distance between himself and the voices as he can. He knows he is another twenty minutes or so from the church, so he runs. He ignores the pain in his shoulder, the chains around his ankles, and he runs. The farther he runs, the more dogs he hears. He stops behind a tree to catch his breath, and he is terrified to hear the voices of several men and dogs not far behind him. They must know he has escaped, or if not that, they are determined to discover what the dogs are worked up about. Moses believes he can get to the church, but he knows the dogs will be right behind him. His heart sinks. The church is no longer an option. He cannot lead anyone there, for there is at least one man hidden beneath the floorboards. There is no way he can get through the secret opening without leaving a scent for the dogs. Not only would two lives be lost, but he would also be responsible for undoing all the hard work he and many others have done to save people in the kind of trouble he is in now.

Not knowing where else to go, Moses turns and heads for the river. Maybe he can get far enough into the river for the dogs to lose his scent without drowning himself. Moses is not a good swimmer, and the chains around his ankles will make treading water for very long almost impossible. An image of Lavinie enters his head, but soon he can think of nothing but the pack he hears behind him. Moses runs blindly. He no longer feels pain or fear. He has no real plan for what to do when he reaches the river, but that is his focus. The river becomes the goal.

He is almost to Bay Street when he feels the moss restraining the right ankle chain give way. He barely has time to register what has happened before he feels it wrap around his left ankle. It is as if he has been grabbed by both feet, and he can do nothing to keep himself from pitching headlong into the street. Though the landing is buffered by the sand, he cannot stop himself from screaming in pain. The noise makes no difference. The dogs then the men are on him. The dogs do not attack; instead, they form a circle around him and howl their victory. The men are less merciful. Their kicks can cause no more pain than his shoulder already does, yet he wishes himself a weaker man. He would love to pass out or simply die now to deprive the mob of the satisfaction his capture is apparently bringing them.

Moses lies on his side in the sand with his eyes closed; his right arm tries to protect his left shoulder. He draws his knees as close to his chest as he can. Still, he makes a large target, and the men, as frenzied as the dogs, use their boots, sticks, whatever they have to make sure he does not put up the fight his captors encountered last night. Soon he is numb to their blows.

Four men, satisfied their prey is no longer capable of resistance, grab his legs and start dragging him back the way they have come. The thumping of the back of his head on the ground accomplishes what their blows could not. At last he sleeps. He is disoriented when he awakes with one noose around his neck, another beneath his arms. He feels himself being pulled upward, feels something solid beneath his feet. Their voices surround him, but his mind no longer seems connected to the body they are working hard to keep upright. Instead, it takes him home to the house he shares with Jessie and

Diana. The two of them are waiting there. He is glad to see no fear on their faces, no sadness; just love and tenderness. The rope no longer holds him; he is in Jessie's arms. He feels her hand on his face; he smells her fresh scent. He relaxes into her, and the contentment he has only with Jessie comes to him. He closes his eyes.

The sheriff gives the order, but he does not hear it. The platform jerks backward and Moses Tucker swings free.

Chapter 50

Frederick actually makes it out the front door onto Bull Street before he realizes that today is going to be another bad day. He thinks little of it when he sees the first man hurry past him, but he knows something is up when next a man and a woman, then two women and their black servants rush past as if going to a fire. That is what he hopes it is—simply a fire—one far from his business on the bay will be fine—but there has been no fire bell, and in his heart, he knows this is somehow connected with Moses. If he is lucky, there is just a gathering to discuss the escape of the nigger who killed the white man, but as he falls in with the growing crowd moving east, his hope fades. Frederick Barret has not gotten where he is today by sticking his head in the sand, so, characteristically, he admits to himself that this development has to be big. Still, he cannot bring himself to simply ask one of the many hurrying forth to tell him what all the commotion is about.

By the time Frederick gets to Percival Square, the crowd is so thick he cannot get close to the large live oak tree situated in the center of the pressing mass of human flesh. But the tree grows upon a slight knoll, and the many gawking people cannot hide the massive body of the black man who hangs from a strong branch probably ten feet off the ground. Had he been a smaller man, he would swing in the slight summer breeze, but the great weight of the man holds him there, immobile, the broken neck casting the face downward so Frederick does not have to see the lifeless eyes of the man he helped free from the city jail just a few hours ago. Spanish moss has settled upon his shoulders and in his hair, a rustic veil of sorts, a buffer from the prying eyes of the giddy crowd.

Frederick must sit down. The park benches have filled long before he arrives, so he finds a tree and leans up against it. He doesn't feel the rough bark beneath his clothes as he slides down the side, his backside abruptly coming to rest upon the sand beneath. He is thankful he can no longer see above the crowd. Though he is no stranger to death—though he has seen many bodies dispatched to their makers, and some in a more bloody fashion than hanging—he has never before felt he was responsible for their demise. He knows he is as guilty of hanging Moses Tucker as the men who drew the noose around his neck.

Moses would never have beaten Eugene Robinson had Frederick not instructed him to do so. Moses and Jessie would have gone to the sheriff if Frederick had told them that was the thing to do. The sheriff might have listened to him if Frederick himself had told him that Robinson had beaten and raped his servant. Hell, he could have told the sheriff he killed the bastard himself. But even as dismayed by all of this as he is, he knows he would never have done that. Maybe he would do something that sacrificial for Abby or his children, maybe even William Robart or John Andrews, but never for a black man. It isn't that he didn't like Moses well enough. He did. He was a good man, and Jessie loved him. But he was still a nigger and there is no way Frederick would jeopardize all he has accomplished to save the life of a nigger.

Frederick stands, wipes the sand from his slacks. He starts to walk. He is somewhat surprised to find himself at his office. Though he did not really decide to come on to work, he is now glad he did. Work will keep him from dwelling on what he can do nothing about. But first, there is something that must be taken care of.

Frederick pulls out a piece of stationery, opens his ink well, and begins a letter.

Dear Abby,

I have the saddest of news to impart, news that will no doubt be almost more than Jessie can bear.

Frederick lets his pen fall idle between his fingers. He must think this through. If he sends this letter, what shape will Jessie be in for the rest of the summer? Will she even stay in Virginia? And if she leaves, how will he ever find her again?

Too, what about Abby if Jessie leaves or is in no shape to be of any use to any of them? Thinking of Abby, Frederick recalls his wife's sensitive nature. No telling how she will react to Moses' death and Jessie's heartache. Though Abby has tried to hide it from him, he knows she has been battling that cursed despondency ever since they returned from visiting her sister, though for the life of him, he cannot understand why. She has everything to be happy about. Still, Frederick knows his wife's nature, and he knows Jessie's. He must think about their welfare and that of his children, not to mention that of what he is convinced is his unborn son.

Frederick picks up the paper on which the ink has had time to dry. He balls it into his fist, then tosses it in the trash can beside his desk.

I am doing the right thing. I will wait until the baby is born, then I will travel to Virginia and break the news to Jessie while I am there. What good can come of telling her now? Isn't it humane to postpone the unhappiness this news will cause her?

Frederick sits for some time thinking upon the matter until at last he turns to pull out a bill of laden from the tray that rests on the corner of his desk. He gives little thought to the dead man who hangs from the live oak in Percival Square. When his mind finally returns to the troublesome matter as he prepares to leave for the day, he still refuses to dwell on what Moses' death will mean to Jessie or acknowledge his own cowardice in not telling her that her husband is dead.

Frederick does not feel like being alone tonight, but neither does he want to be with any of his friends. He finds himself moving along the riverfront. He walks for several blocks, then he cuts inward toward town. He stops at a tippling house. He throws back four shots of inferior liquor as fast as they are served to him. As he prepares to down the fifth, he becomes aware of a group of three men, Irish riffraff from the looks of them, huddled together around a rough-hewn table in the corner, seemingly more interested in him than in the dice they are taking turns throwing. Drunk as he is becoming, he recognizes the threat they pose. He turns reluctantly from the bar and lurches toward the doorway. He is halfway down the block when he hears one of the men yell, "Snake Eyes!"

He thinks of trying to find another house to finish numbing his brain, but decides there are better and safer ways to take his mind off of the image that keeps trying to plague him.

Chapter 51

I am in a room much like our parlor in Saint Domingue. I am a child again. The room is filled with everyone I love, even my father who still looks as young as the last time I saw him. My mother is there, as well as my brother and sister. There is food out on the sideboard, and I can hear the servants singing a mournful tune out back. I have heard them do this before. It means someone has died.

I turn quickly to look up into my father's face. He is smiling. He picks me up and walks with me into the adjoining room. The room is empty except for a chair that stands alone in one corner. He walks to it and sits down, forming a lap for me. Again, I look up into his face. I am reassured by his smile. Someone has died, but it cannot be him, for he is here with me. I reach up to touch his face, just to make sure.

"You must not be afraid, Diana," my father says. "Everybody has to die sooner or later. It is the natural way of things."

I want to remind him that I am not Diana, that I am Jessie, but when I open my mouth to tell him, I hear myself saying, "Even Mama? Will Mama die, too?"

"Yes, Baby, even Mama. But that will not be for a long time now. You will be a grown woman yourself before that happens."

"But what about Daddy? Why did Daddy have to die?"

"Makes no difference, Baby, why a person has to die. They are still just as dead, no matter the cause that got them there?"

I am distracted by movement at the door. I am surprised to see Lavinie there. She is holding a handkerchief and I can tell she has been crying. She walks to the center of the room, and she looks down at a body lying on a door. The door was not there before, but now it is, and upon it lies a body. Quickly I look up again, relieved to see my father still smiling down at me. At least the body on the door is not his.

"You can go look. There is nothing there to hurt you."

"No," I say. "I do not want to look. I want to sit here with you."

"You must look, Baby."

With that, my father gently sets me down on the floor beside his chair. I try to crawl back into his lap, but he pushes me away.

"It is what you have to do."

I feel tears spring into my eyes, but I fist them aside and walk toward Lavinie who is standing beside the door. She turns, stoops to pick me up, and I feel the wetness of her garment seep through my own. Lavinie is soaking wet and she has a musty smell. I feel chilled and I want her to put me down, but when I ask her, she does not seem to hear me. Instead, she turns me toward the door and says, "Mose be a good brudda—a good man. He doan zerve dis."

At last I look down and I see Moses laid out upon the door. I cry out and try to turn my head away. I turn my head into Lavinie's shoulder, but it is the warm one of my father's that meets my cheek. Instead of Lavinie, it is my father holding me again. Again he says, "It is what you have to do."

I look back, and I feel a pain unlike any I have ever felt. It is so intense, I think the bones of my frail chest will be severed by it. I force myself to look, in spite of the pain. Moses lies on the board much as I have seen him lie in bed, flat on his back, one arm resting across his chest, one lying along his side. His legs are bent at the knee because the door is not nearly long enough to accommodate his frame. His feet are bare; they are covered with red blisters, and there are angry red welts around his ankles. My eyes cannot linger there. They dart back to his face. His eyes open and his lips part in a smile. I struggle to get out of my father's arms. I want to put my arms around Moses, to lie close to him.

"You be a good gul fo yo Mama, Swea Pea. An you tell er ta take you nawth. Dey ain nuttin fo da two ub you in Svanna no mo. You tell yo Mama dat, you hyur me?"

"I hear you, Papa," I say, but I want to cry, "You are not my Papa! Moses, you are not my Papa! You know you are not my Papa!"

Moses closes his eyes and, though I am young and I do not recall seeing a dead person, I know he is dead. His head falls to one side and I see a vicious red ring around his neck.

"No," I scream, and once I scream, I cannot stop.

I am awakened by Diana who is shaking me and crying, "Mama!" over and over.

Tears are running down my cheeks, and I realize Diana is sobbing. I take my frightened child in my arms. She asks me, "What is wrong with you, Mama?"

I rock back and forth with her. "Nothing's wrong, Baby. Mama just had a bad dream. Go back to sleep."

I sit upright in the bed, and I rock Diana long after she falls asleep again. Finally, a piercing pain in my back forces me to lay her down. I crawl from the bed, walk outside of the cabin, and close the door behind me. I stick my fist in my mouth and bite down as hard as possible to keep from waking the whole plantation with my screams.

Moses is dead, and I want nothing more than to join him. If not for the child in the bed I have just left, I would find a way to make that happen.

Chapter 52

Today has been a long, tiring day and it has taken every ounce of energy I possess to get through it. It has not helped that Mother has trailed so closely upon my heels that I am in danger of being run over should I stop too quickly. Her hovering presence behind me is pushing me closer and closer to a yawning abyss. I feel even worse, both physically and mentally, than I did yesterday. I have not felt the child move at all today, and I have been unable to eat because of the nausea. Mother, of course, has noticed and asked me at least ten times what is wrong with me. *Is it the baby? Is it something to do with that Jessie woman? Is it despondency? If so, what do you have to be despondent about?* If I had the energy, I would scream. Both Anne and Sophia have tried to divert her, but she is like a dog with a bone. She is convinced there is something wrong with me, and, because she is right, I have been unable to muster the wherewithal to convince her otherwise. I long for the comfort of my old room in the old house on Broughton where I could have slept the day away once Frederick went to work. No one would have bothered me. I long for the comfort of the familiar. The thought of my old room, small, shabby, and pedestrian as it might have been, makes me even sadder because there is someone else using it now. There is no going back there. Waiting for me is the large, lavishly decorated suite in the large, lavishly decorated house on Bull Street built and furnished to meet my husband's exact and meticulous specifications. My mother is right. I am an ungrateful and undeserving woman. Though this is not exactly what she says, I know this is what she thinks.

Before I crawl into bed, I force myself to kneel beside it in the hope that my appeal may save this baby I am carrying. Though I do not have Jessie's gift of premonition, I have carried two other children, and at no time did I feel as I am feeling now in the months before they arrived. Maybe God is testing me. As I pray, I pledge to overcome my tendencies toward despair if he will only allow this child to live. I promise I will drag myself out of bed every day after he or she is born if I am only allowed to carry the child to term. I am not convinced I can fulfill these promises, so I am sure my request falls upon deaf ears. I sigh deeply. I start to rise, but I remember Jessie and all she is going though. When I went to see her this morning, I was alarmed by her demeanor. I was shocked when she told me that Moses was dead. When I asked if she had received a message, she told me she had, but not of the kind I was speaking. She told me she had dreamed Moses was dead. I protested that we all have dreams of loved ones dying and that her dream is just a manifestation of her fears.

"Maybe you are right, and I will continue to pray that Moses is fine, but in my heart, I believe he is dead. Will you please write Frederick and ask if he has seen Moses, and if not, will he please check on him? I would write him myself, but I know your urging will carry more weight."

I promised I would and did so the minute I returned to the house. I got Justice to post the letter, and I hope Frederick heeds my bidding to respond as quickly as possible. If it were Mammy, Dovie, or Cressa asking me to act upon a dream of theirs, I would scoff and tell them not to be silly. But it is Jessie who has asked, Jessie who has always seemed to know things before anyone else. I fear with her.

Too, I asked Frederick to talk with Clarence Stiles and see if he can hire Minda to come in and cook for him and do what must be done around the house until we can make other arrangements. He has still not admitted knowing anything about the arrangement between Clarence and Minda, but I think he may consider my suggestion because he cannot possibly maintain that house even if he manages to feed himself for the next four months.

I realize I am no longer praying; I am worrying about matters instead of turning them over to God. I hastily try to do so and am relieved to push myself up off the floor, to climb into the bed. I am about to doze off when Sophia opens the door. I can tell by her efforts to be quiet that she thinks I am asleep.

"I am awake, Sophia. Has everyone gone to bed?"

"Yes, I looked in on the children. They all appear to be out cold, all lined up in their little cots like chickens on a roost."

I smile. "That is what they look like with their homespun sheets tucked up under their chins. It pleases me to have them all together like this."

"Me too. I think Rob and Fredie are good for Jimmy. It seems most of our friends have girls, so he rarely gets to play with other boys. I am afraid he has a bad case of hero worship—especially of Rob."

"That bears watching, Sister. Rob will lead him around by the nose if we do not keep an eye on him."

"I know," Sophia laughs. I move over and make room for her so she can crawl in beside me. "I think Rob actually has him believing he is a captain in the Georgia Hussars."

"I think Rob actually believes it himself sometimes. I do not think we have to worry too much, though. Fredie will set Jimmy straight. Though he secretly admires his older brother, he will not let him get too big for his britches."

"Speaking of being too big for one's britches—Good Gracious!" Sophia says as she tries to get comfortable beside me. "What was Mother thinking putting us both in the same bed? I am big as a barn, and you are not much smaller."

"Maybe she thinks we are contagious. She is quarantining us."

Sophia laughs again, and under normal conditions, we would probably laugh and talk to the wee hours of the morning. I think about telling her my fears, but exposing them may validate them, and besides, the effort would be too great and accomplish nothing. Maybe by morning I will see things differently. Maybe the child will wake with me in the morning, and my fears will be allayed.

"If you are contagious, Mother will certainly catch whatever you have. She has practically had her nose up your derriere since I arrived. I do not know how you stand it."

"She means well." I hear the exhaustion in my own voice. I hope my sister does as well. She gives up after another attempt or two at chit chat. She takes the hint at my mumbled replies, and I do not know which of us falls asleep first.

I awake with a start and realize Sophia is sitting up in bed beside me. "What is it?" I hear her say.

When I sit up, I see Luella holding a candle with Mattie standing close behind her.

"The boys,' Luella says, "they are not on the porch."

Sophia is out of bed and getting dressed before I can swing my legs over my side.

"Do not be overly alarmed, Sister. We will find them. I am sure Rob has led them on some kind of night maneuver."

"You are probably right. Should we wake Mother and Anne?"

"No, let us look around the yard first. We will wake Justice."

"I am sorry, Aunt Abby, Aunt Sophia! Mattie is the one who noticed they were gone. I should have heard them leave. I guess I was just so tired…"

"It is not your fault, Luella. Rob is known for this kind of thing. Frederick has had to be quite stern with him for sneaking around the house at home during the night."

Sophia and I light a kerosene lamp, and I am thinking about what I am going to do to Rob when I get a hold of him. I am much too tired to be dealing with his shenanigans.

"You two go back to bed, and do not worry," Sophia tells Luella and Mattie. "We will wake the servants if we need help looking for them."

There is a full moon, and though the night is somewhat overcast, we can see fairly well, especially when the moon slips from behind a cloud. The two of us walk around the yard, and not seeing the boys, we make our way to Justice's cabin. His is the second nearest the house with only Cook's closer. As Sophia is knocking, I turn back toward the house, and I catch a glimpse of white as the moon shows its face. Justice opens the door as I tell Sophia I see them, and he follows the two of us across the lawn to intercept the boys. The moon has once again slid behind a cloud, and we are almost on top of them before it reappears.

I feel as if my heart stops when I realize there are only two boys ahead of us. "Rob," I call, "where is Jimmy?"

Both Rob and Fredie whirl at the sound of my voice. Neither answer me. I am sure Rob is trying to come up with an acceptable reason for the two of them to be about at night.

"Fredie needed to go to the privy. I took him," Rob finally tells us.

By this time, we have reached them, and I can fully see both boys' faces in the lantern light. "Do not lie to me, Rob. You are coming from the wrong direction."

Sophia pushes past me. She takes Rob by both shoulders, and looks into his face. "Rob, where is Jimmy?" I can hear the fear in her voice.

"I don't know where Jimmy is. He was asleep in his bed when we left."

"Oh my God!" Sophia whispers, and I put my arm around her.

"Rob, Fredie, where have you been? You must tell us the truth. We have to find Jimmy."

"We went to the creek," Fredie confesses. "We were pretending to be night scouts."

I whirl around and face Justice. "Justice get the servants up. Get some lanterns and go to the creek." Justice is sprinting toward the slave quarters before I finish speaking."

"Oh My God!" Sophia whispers again. This time I hear panic.

I kneel for the second time tonight, this time upon the grass before Fredie. I put my left hand on his shoulder and hold the lantern high and to the side of his face. "Fredie, you must tell us everything. What did you do at the creek?"

"We wanted to wade across, but the water was too high," Fredie begins. "We found an old log and crawled across it. Jimmy didn't follow us. I would have seen him." I feel his frail shoulder shudder beneath my hand.

I can see a candle at the screen door on the porch. "Fredie, you go tell Luella to wake Grandmother and Anne, then you stay on the porch with the girls. Do you understand me?"

"Can't I help look for Jimmy?" Fredie whimpers.

"No, you cannot. Do as I say. Do you hear me?"

I push him toward the house after he answers me, and I take Rob by the hand and we follow Sophia who is running as fast as her girth will allow. I want to call out to her to go back in the house—this cannot be good for her in her condition, but I know it will do no good. Instead, I call, "Wait up, Sophia. Rob can show us exactly where they went."

We catch up with Sophia and Rob leads us as a group across the pasture. I think of the time our sister Luella and I went with Minda and Dovie looking for the cow across this same field. The creek had not been threatening at all then. Surely Jimmy will be alright.

As we cross the field, I pray. It is all I can think to do. I take Sophia's hand. "Sophia, it is just a creek. It is not a river. Jimmy will be fine."

"He cannot swim at all, Abby. He is just four. He cannot even dog paddle."

"He will know not to get in the water, Sophia."

"The log..."

She does not finish her sentence. She does not have to. She has the same fear I do. Jimmy may have seen the older boys crawl across the log, and he may have followed. *Please, Lord. Let us find Jimmy soon. Let us find him safe, standing on the bank or sleeping beneath a tree. Please, Lord...*

The servants fan out along the creek that looks more swollen than I recall seeing it, the only evidence of them the lights they hold in their hands. Mammy carries no light, so I do not know she is next to me until she touches my shoulder.

"Mizz Abby, you need ta go on up ta da house. You ain well. Jessie tole me you ain well. Git on up ta da house. We fine da boy. Massa be madder dan a hornet he know you ow hyur lack dis."

"I cannot leave Sophia, Mammy."

"Den git er ta go wid you!" Mammy orders. "Aw dis ain no good fo er eeder."

I find Sophia, and I try to coax her back to the house. She refuses, so I resort to the only thing I can think of to make her come with me.

"Sophia, I am hurting."

I am surprised to find I am telling the truth. The muscles in my groin area feel as if they are giving way, and there is a dull ache down low in my abdomen. "I will not go to the house unless you do. We both need to be inside. There is not a thing we can do here that is not being done."

Sophia holds her light up to my face. She apparently does not like what she sees, for she turns and walks with me back to the house. By the time we get there, I am glad I have her support. I am fighting hard to keep from crying. It is not intermittent pain that makes me want to weep; the ache is no longer dull and it has moved to the center of my back. Mother is waiting for us at the door, and when she sees me she asks, "Where is Mammy?"

"She's out searching," Sophia answers. Her hand leaves my arm to swipe across her nose. "I've got to go back."

Mother does not try to stop her. "Try to find Mammy and Cook, and send them to me."

"Get Jessie," I manage to get out. "She will know what to do."

"Fine. Get Jessie then."

I turn when Sophia releases me. "Please, Sophia, stay in. You are in the same condition I am."

Sophia hugs me briefly before turning to leave. "I am well, Abby. I feel physically strong. You worry about yourself. I have to help find Jimmy."

Mother leads me through the sleeping porch, and the frightened children gather around us.

"Go on back to bed, Girls," my mother commands them. "There is nothing you can do but wait and pray, for Jimmy and for Abby."

Mother alarms the children more than she comforts them. I open my mouth to soften her words. I hear a deep groan and realize it comes from me. All but Ella do as Mother tells them. Ella wraps her arms around my legs and begins to cry. Her crying brings Maxie running to join her. Little Gail begins to cry from her bed. Luella and Mattie drag my two off of me while Caroline picks up Gail. The scene I leave to straighten itself out is minor pandemonium. I do not dwell on it long, for the pain takes my whole attention. By the time Jessie gets to me, I know I am in labor. She does all she can, but within the hour she holds my tiny stillborn son in her hands. Mother asks if I want to hold him before he is taken away. I can barely hold my eyes open—it would be impossible to raise my arms. Jessie leaves the room with the small wrapped bundle that I will never lay eyes on again. I fall asleep. I am conscious of trying to drag myself up from a far depth, but again the effort is too great. Finally, I surface to find Mammy thrusting a spoon between my lips. Jessie is sitting beside the bed sewing. I have the sense she has been sitting there for some time.

I swallow what tastes like thin oatmeal, and I try to speak. My tongue seems to have forgotten how to work. Finally I squeak out, "Jimmy. Did they find Jimmy?"

Neither woman answers immediately. Mammy looks at Jessie. Jessie turns back to her sewing.

"Day foun da chile bou haf a mile down da ribber."

It is not a river! It is a creek!

I slip back beneath the comforting cover of sleep.

Chapter 53

"Abigail, there has been quite enough of this."

Frederick has called her Abigail. She knows he is more than a little bit angry. He is furious with her. Her mother, on the other hand, is frightened. Abby herself is numb.

"You have been lying up here for a month! It is high time you got out of that bed and got on with life. You are not the only woman who has lost a baby in childbirth! You must think of your living children—your mother—me even. If you cannot think of us, think of the Howes. If they can manage to go on in light of what has befallen them, surely you can pull yourself together!"

"That is enough, Frederick! You are only making matters worse."

Abby feels the strongest emotion she has felt in days: surprise. She, nor anyone else in the room, has remembered Jessie even being there, so they are all taken aback, not only by her presence, but by the fact that she speaks to Frederick this way. Mrs. Middleton cannot let it go unaddressed.

"Jessie! How dare you speak to Mr. Barret that way! You may find something else to do. Your presence has done absolutely no good so far, so I am sure your services can be better utilized in the kitchen. That was why you came, was it not? To help in the kitchen?"

"It is fine, Mrs. Middleton. I am quite used to Jessie's high-handedness." Frederick's tone is meant to lighten the mood, but neither Jessie nor Mrs. Middleton follows his lead.

"Very well, Mrs. Middleton. I will leave the room. I will leave your home all together. I will leave as soon as Abby is up out of that bed and functioning on her own again."

Mrs. Middleton is more than a little intimidated by the regal woman who rises from the chair and faces Frederick.

"But you, Frederick, are making matters worse instead of better. Why must the both of you heap coals on her head? Do you think she wants to be in this state? I have told you before these moods are not something she can control. If I may be so bold as to say so," Jessie stops and looks from Frederick to Mrs. Middleton, "Abby's health would be better served if the two of you left the room and I stayed."

Though Mrs. Middleton is afraid much of what Jessie is saying may be true, she cannot get beyond the fact that a darkie, for all practical purposes, has the audacity to speak to them like this.

"You dare tell me what I need to be doing in my own house?" Mrs. Middleton is practically sputtering she is so indignant. "You dare tell me how to handle my own daughter? You dare instruct a husband on how to relate to his wife?"

"The two of you do not seem to be handling matters too well. I would think you both would be wise enough to consider a course of action other than your own."

"You will leave this room this minute!" Mrs. Middleton's huge bosom is heaving as she points in the direction of the door.

Jessie looks to Frederick. He shakes his head in disgust as if this whole affair has tested him sorely. Jessie assumes she has no choice, so she picks up her skirts prepared to make as dignified an exit as possible under the circumstances, but she is stopped by Abby herself.

"No, Jessie, please do not go."

Every person in the room turns to stare at Abby, who in the midst of their arguing has sat up in bed. She looks as pale as death, but she is actually sitting up, and Frederick immediately sits beside her and takes her hand.

"This is more like it, Darling." He turns to Jessie. "You see, sometimes a good, strong talking-to is in order!"

"I need a bath," Abby declares. "Mother, will you tell Dovie to bring up the tub and some bath water? Frederick, is not there something you need to be doing?"

Mrs. Middleton rushes to the bed and props the pillows Abby has been lying on for days behind her back. She leans forward and kisses her daughter on the forehead.

Frederick waits until the woman quits fluttering around the bed before he answers. "There is nothing more important than you, My Dear. But yes, there are plenty of things I need to be doing. Unfortunately, they need to be done in Savannah."

"Then go there. Please."

Mrs. Middleton chooses this time to deliver the summons to Dovie. Jessie takes one look at Frederick's scowling face and decides it is time for her to leave the room also. She tries to ease her way to the door, but Abby calls her back.

"Jessie!" The older woman takes Abby's outstretched hand. "Thank you for trying to understand. And, please, do not pay any attention to Mother. She can be hard to take at times, but her frustration with me is understandable. She has been dealing with these moods of mine all my life."

"Your mood is justified, Abby. You have just lost a child and a nephew. And many women suffer from depression of the spirits immediately after childbirth, even if it is one that ends in a healthy birth. I have lost a child myself. I know what it feels like. You mustn't be so hard on yourself, and neither should anyone else be hard on you."

The look Jessie throws Frederick's way is just short of a glare. Frederick opens his mouth to say something but thinks better of it under Jessie's direct, unblinking gaze. When he does speak, the frown is gone from his face and his tone is cordial.

"Jessie, may I have a word or two with my wife—alone."

"Of course, Frederick. Please excuse my thoughtlessness. Mrs. Middleton is right. Sometimes I do forget my place. Abby, I will check in on you later."

"Before you go, Jessie, have you heard anything more about Moses?"

The look on Jessie's face answers Abby's question. "We have all had so much sadness, Abby. Let us not talk of Moses today. There is time for that when you are stronger."

Jessie leaves the room, and Abby turns to her husband. "Oh, Frederick. It is true then? Moses is dead?"

"I am afraid so, My Dear. But Jessie is right. We do not need to dwell on that right now. We must think of getting you better and getting you home where you belong."

Abby's small frame seems to sink into the pillows propped behind her. "It is as if the world has gone crazy, Frederick. Just a month ago we were traveling, buying things for the house...It all seems so trivial now."

"What do you mean, trivial, My Dear?"

"All of it. All of it except the children, our family, our close friends—have you thought of it, Frederick? Here we are putting all this time and energy into a house—into furnishings—into entertaining—and for what? We could all be dead tomorrow."

"Abigail! This is your sickness talking! I do not want to hear you speak that way!"

"This is the first time I have heard you call my problem a sickness, Frederick. Is that the way you think of me? Sick?"

Frederick's face turns pink. "Do not put words into my mouth. I never said you were sick, for Christ's sake!"

Abby lets the blasphemy go. "You know, Frederick, I think I may be sick. I think there is something genuinely wrong with me. I will be completely happy, then all of a sudden, I feel like this state we call living is highly overrated."

"Stop it, Abby! You heard Jessie. She said what you are going through is perfectly normal."

"You certainly didn't seem to think she was right a few minutes ago. Neither did Mother." Abby takes Frederick's hand. Tears come into her eyes. "I am so sorry, Frederick, that I agreed to marry you. You and the children would have been so much better off with a stronger woman, a normal woman. I should have told you..."

Frederick is stunned. "Abby, what you are saying is crazy!" The look on Abby's face makes him realize what he has said. "Not crazy," he quickly corrects himself, "just misguided. You are a wonderful wife and mother! It is true there have been a few occasions when you seem to lose your purpose, your resolve, but they pass, just as this..." Frederick pauses to think of a word to best describe what it is Abby has been going through.

"Lunacy?" Abby supplies.

"That was not what I was thinking. Again, quit putting words into my mouth."

"I am sure that is what others think. That I suffer from lunacy. Sometimes I think it myself."

"Abby, you are truly frightening me. I will not listen to this."

"Take Sophia for instance. Her son drowns, and where is she?"

Frederick answers the question as if she actually wants to know her sister's location. "James took her and little Gail back to Baltimore."

"That is exactly what I mean. She is not lying flat on her back contemplating the futility of life. She is functioning under the worst of circumstances. I lose myself sometimes when there is no cause at all. And look at Jessie. Her husband is dead, a man she loved dearly, and she is consoling me. What is wrong with me, Frederick? Why do I have this darkness inside of me that hangs there waiting for the smallest of openings to ooze its way in and surround me like a black, woolen blanket I cannot see through, even breathe through? I feel smothered—I actually have difficulty breathing sometimes."

"Everyone is different, Abby." Frederick tries to think of something to say to comfort his wife, but it is hard for him because, in truth, she is voicing his own concerns. Why can't his wife be like other women, strong women? It is almost expected for a woman to lose a child or two along the way. True, it is devastating, but shouldn't she be dwelling on how fortunate she is to have survived a failed childbirth? Frederick has made the exact comparisons Abby is voicing. He chooses to see this as a good sign.

"I think it is good you realize your shortcomings, Abby. Now, you can avoid giving in to them. When we get back to Savannah, you will be so busy getting the house going smoothly, dealing with the children, getting ready for the house warming event in January..."

"Surely you do not intend to entertain—to have something that elaborate—when we are in mourning?"

"I do not think people will find fault with us for not observing mourning when the child was born so prematurely..."

"And what of Jimmy Howe? Was he too young when he died to deserve a proper mourning?"

Frederick is ashamed to admit he has not even thought about the role the child's death should play in their lives.

"You may be right, Dear." He sighs heavily.

"How are Rob and Fredie? Do they feel terribly guilty over Jimmy's death?"

Once again, Frederick has not even thought of that possibility. Now, he thinks they may indeed be feeling responsibility for what happened to the child.

"They both have been very reserved. I have attributed it to worry for you, but you may be right. Now that you are better, I will try to spend some time with them before I leave. I will reassure them—tell them none of this is their fault—that it is no one's fault."

"You are leaving then?"

"I must, Abby. You couldn't know this, but *The Pulaski* exploded just outside Savannah Harbor right after you came to Virginia. The losses have hit Savannah hard, and that along with quite a few cases of Yellow Fever..." Frederick sees the dismay in his wife's eyes and tries to change the subject. "I have shipments arriving and there is still some work to be finished at the house..."

"Were many people lost? In the explosion and to the fever?"

"I am tiring you, My Dear. I am sure Dovie is waiting outside to bathe you. Why don't you get that behind you, then rest awhile, and we will talk again?"

"When will you leave?"

"I will stay another day or two—a week at the most. The sooner I get things done there, the sooner I will return. Maybe I can stay the later part of October with you here, then we will all travel home together."

Frederick remembers something else he needs to discuss with his wife.

"Will it be satisfactory with you if I take Cressa home with me? If she gets home now, she can have that child and be of some use to me before you get home. It appears you have more than enough help around here. That, or I could ask Jessie to return with me. However, I do not think she will want to leave you yet."

"It is fine with me if you take Cressa unless Mammy and Jessie think her too close to birthing. I know you need help there. Did you get my message about Minda?"

"Yes, I did, but I did nothing about it so little time did I have before I was summoned here. I will probably try to engage her as well. There is plenty of work for both her and Cressa to do. I want the house to be clean and ready and waiting for you and the children when you come home."

Abby is glad when he leaves the room. Likewise, she is glad when Dovie finishes bathing her. The whole time she has been worrying about the loss of life in Savannah. How many people died in the explosion? And of the fever? What of Bette and her family? Are they all well? She knows it will do no good to ask Frederick, because if something has happened to them, he will not tell her right now.

Abby sits up long enough for Dovie to change the bed linens, then she lies back and waits for blessed sleep to overtake her. She turns her back to the door in case her mother or Frederick returns. She does not want either to see her tears.

Chapter 54

The sun feels good against my face this morning. I have fallen into the habit of walking every morning with the children, and the fresh air and sunlight have done much to improve my state of mind. I have chosen never to walk in the direction of the creek. Yesterday, Rob chose our path and it took us by the family cemetery. The boys ran ahead and were standing by the small mound of dirt that scars the otherwise green lawn. "Is Jimmy still down there?" Ella asked.

Before I could answer, Rob yelled at her, "Of course not, Stupid! He is in Heaven."

"Don't call your sister stupid," I admonished him. "Tell her you are sorry."

Rob apologized. I put my hand on his head, but he did not want it there. He raced ahead again. I know he is struggling with what happened, all the children are. I will talk to them when we get back to Savannah. An in depth conversation about death and the afterlife is more than I am up to right now. Too, I think it best to give us all a little time, a little distance. Maybe Frederick and I will talk with them together. About Jimmy and the baby. This is our first loss together as a family—we need to face it as a family.

Mattie walks closest to me and when I glance at her I am reminded that she may remember her mother's death. I put my arm around her shoulders. She is almost as tall as I am, and when she looks up into my face, I am reminded of Luella. I have been thinking a lot of her. It is hard not to here at Hickory Grove among so many memories. I hear her name spoken daily even if it is in reference to our niece. At least I do not startle anymore when I hear someone call out *Luella*. Maybe we make a mistake in naming our children after their forbearers. Maybe it would be best to let their memories rest in peace with them. Sometimes I think Luella, my sister Luella, that is, is better off than I. I would often trade places with her.

I realize what I am doing, and I stop myself. I must not allow my thoughts to travel such a negative path. I must stay focused on what is important—being a good wife and mother. My children need me. My husband needs me. At least that is what I am told.

Frederick arrived yesterday afternoon. We will stay out the week here and then head back to Savannah. I have mixed feelings about going home. I will be glad to be out from under Mother's constant vigilance, but I will miss her, Anne, and the other children. Too, the thought of the new house overwhelms me. There is still so much to be done, and I know Frederick will want to have people in often. He still has not given up on a housewarming. I think having it will be disrespectful to Sophia and James, but Frederick says it is to be a local event and they need not even be aware of it. I do not understand why it is so important to him.

Mother is waving at us from the front porch. When we get closer, I realize she has a letter in her hand. I can tell by the smile on her face it is good news. Heaven knows we are due.

"Sophia has delivered a healthy, baby boy!" she cries, as we all clamor up the steps. "And she has survived the ordeal. Thank God for that!"

Tears spring to my eyes. I know Mother, Anne and I have all feared the Howe family might face more loss when it came time for Sophia to give birth. We did not know if she had the strength to endure the rigors of bringing a child into this world so soon after having one taken from her.

"Will she name him Jimmy?" Fredie asks innocently, and much of the joy goes out of Mother's face.

"Probably not, Fredie," I tell my son. "Why don't you take Ella and Maxie and go look for eggs in the chicken yard?" This has been one of the younger children's favorite pastimes this summer. "And remember to watch where you step!"

Mattie goes in search of her older cousins and Rob wanders off in the direction of the chicken yard to join the younger children, I assume. Anne joins mother and me on the front porch. Mother leads us in a prayer of thanksgiving for the safe delivery of Sophia's baby.

"Does Frederick know the good news?" I ask.

"Probably not," Mother tells me. "Justice has just now brought the mail."

"He told me a few minutes ago he was going to go speak with the servants. He is probably back at the Quarters," Anne offers.

I trail around the side of the house. I see the children in the chicken yard. Ella has commandeered the basket. It is half as big as she is. I smile to see Rob with them. He wants to be a young man so badly, but there is still a lot of little boy there. This thing with Jimmy has sobered him. I notice he hangs with the girls more, less eager to be off with Fredie on one of their excursions.

I am about to round the corner of Jessie's cabin when I hear Frederick's raised voice. I stop between the corner of the hut and the window that has nothing but mosquito netting over it.

"You are not thinking straight! You are far too level-headed to do such a thing!"

I stop.

"Look where my level-headedness has gotten me so far." Jessie's voice is as calm as Frederick's is agitated. "I have made my decision, and I hope you accept it graciously."

"You will do no such thing! I will not allow it."

I do not intend to eavesdrop, but it never enters my head to call out.

I hear a laugh, or something like one. It is a hard, bitter sound, and I assume it is from Jessie.

"You cannot stop me from leaving, Frederick. I am a free woman. Have you forgotten that?"

"You need my sponsorship. I will not give you a pass if you insist on this foolhardiness!"

I am stunned by the discovery that Jessie wants to leave us, but I am not surprised that Frederick will try to stop her. Maybe I should join them—tell him he has no right to be so highhanded—try to find out why Jessie wants to leave. Before I can decide, Jessie's voice rises.

"If you will not provide me with a pass, I am sure I can find a new sponsor—one who will think more about what is best for me and not what is best for himself!"

"Jessie, be rational. You have no one to help you in the North. We are family. Have you forgotten that?"

"I have not, but I think you may have, Frederick. Would you want the kind of life I have for any of your other family members?"

This conversation is taking a strange direction. I do not blame Jessie for being put out with Frederick for trying to keep her from doing what she wants to do, but her tone of voice surprises me. She is talking to Frederick as if she is an equal. The only time I have ever heard her come close to talking to a white person in this tone was the day in my room when she chastised Frederick and Mother for the way they were talking to me.

"I have to make a life for myself and Diana. If I had only myself to think of, I might remain in Savannah. But I must think about my child. You know what life will be like for her in the South."

"Do you mean to tell me you are willing to put the needs of a nigger child, one that isn't even your own, before me and my children, your blood relatives?"

I must misunderstand. It sounded as if Frederick has just referred to Jessie as a *blood relative*.

"Nigger child, Frederick!" I can hear real anger in Jessie's voice. "Nigger child! Have you forgotten who you are?"

"Stop it, Jessie." Frederick's voice has gone quiet. He sounds almost afraid. "Do not talk like that. Someone might overhear."

"Then you need to think twice about refusing to help me get away from Savannah. My devotion to you has proven to be far stronger than yours to me. But regardless, I will do what I have to do. You have a family. I have only Diana now."

"Have I not made sure you have been taken care of? Did I not arrange for your position with Brigitte? I know things were rough for you in New Orleans, but you know as well as I do I was not yet in any position to help. Have you not had everything you needed since then?"

"You have been good to me, Frederick. Very good if I were merely who we pretend I am. But you and I both know I am not. I know you did not know your mother, but I did, and I assure you, she would not be pleased to know what my life has become—what we have become to each other—master and servant." There is a few moments of silence. I can picture the two of them, faced off eye to eye in the small cabin. "Yes, you have been good to me, but have you forgotten that you are alive today because of me—because of the sacrifices I made for you on the Island after Mere died."

"That is not fair, Jessie. I was just a boy, *a white boy*. I could barely show my face let alone provide for the both of us."

I feel sick to my stomach. It is as if Frederick's desperation is seeping from his pores, through the cabin wall, and into my chest.

"I have never regretted the sacrifice, and I have always known how things have to be. But do not, Frederick, try to act like a martyr and my

CHAPTER 54

savior. I do not begrudge you your life. I am happy for you. I would do it all again, if not for you, for Josie."

I want to scream, *Who is Josie? What are you two talking about?*

"I know you did not have much choice, considering what the consequences would be if you acknowledged me here. That would have been societal suicide for you and your whole family. I never expected more where I was concerned, but—" Jessie's voice changes—I think she may be crying, "but the least you could have done was to try to protect Moses! He was a good man—the best man I have ever known! They would have listened to you!"

"What—and implicate me, or you? Surely you know I did all I could to save Moses! What more was I to do?"

Frederick is yelling now.

"You could have talked to the Sheriff. You could have told him it was me. I could have run away! There were many things you could have done had you not been so intent on pretending you had no part in any of it!"

I can feel my heart pounding in my chest. There is complete quiet. I fear one of them will walk out and find me here, listening, but I cannot move. I have to hear it if there is more to be heard. Finally Frederick speaks. His voice is flat, determined. This is a voice I have heard before.

"As you wish, Jessie. I will help. But there are some conditions."

"I do not think you are in a position to give me conditions."

Frederick continues as if he hasn't heard.

"You must come back to Savannah long enough to make sure Abby is over this latest bout of whatever it is that comes over her. And, surely you can stay long enough to help us with the housewarming."

Here it is—the crux of the matter. Frederick is devastated by the loss of his cook. Jessie has given him clout among his friends. He will do everything he can to keep her. I know it. Jessie's next words indicate she knows it, too.

"I will go back for Abby. I think she needs me right now, and I will stay long enough to make sure your party is suitably impressive, but hear me on this, Frederick. I will not stay beyond that, no matter what guilt you lay at my feet. And I have some conditions of my own. You will help me sell my house and Moses' boardinghouse and give me passes to sail north. If you fail to do any of these, I will not be responsible for the outcome—son of my sister or not!

Oh My God! I do not realize I have gasped these words aloud until Frederick is standing in front of me.

"Abby! What are you doing? How long have you been standing there? You are as pale as death!"

No paler than you, My Husband. I cannot draw my eyes away from his face. He looks down, and I put my hand on his sleeve.

"Frederick," I say, but he will not meet my eyes. "What does she mean? How can that be?"

Frederick's anger shocks me. He pulls away from me and marches toward the house. I lean weakly against the side of the cabin. Jessie comes and leads me inside. She pours me some lukewarm water from a pitcher she has sitting on a windowsill.

I flop down on the bed, fall back upon the uncovered pillow ticking, too weak to stand. As I do this, Mother enters my mind. She would be horrified to see me sprawled on the bed in a darkie's cabin—she has already scolded me for sitting on the side of the bed with Jessie.

Jessie says nothing. She busies herself around the room while I lie with my eyes closed. I do not know how much time passes before I find the strength to talk.

"Jessie, what did you mean when you referred to Frederick as your sister's son? How can that be possible?"

"I think this is something you had better discuss with Frederick. It is not my place..."

"Please, Jessie. I have tried to talk to him about his family. He gets angry, walks away..."

"Now, I guess you know why." Jessie's face is hard. I think she is trying to keep it that way, but then she softens. "Abby, there are some things best left alone. I have very little left to lose..." she pauses. I know she is thinking of Diana.

"Jessie, haven't we been close—almost like friends? If you will not tell me, no one will. My imagination will probably conjure up scenarios worse than the truth."

"I do not know as that is possible." Jessie slumps tiredly on the bed. "You know Frederick and I both came to the States from Saint Domingue?"

I nod. I know much more than that since listening outside the door, but I need for her to tell me—to make sense of it.

"Frederick's mother was my sister."

"Your half sister? You shared a father. That is the way of Bette and Pearl."

Jessie looks into my eyes. I can tell she is making a decision.

"The truth, Jessie, please..."

"No, Abby. Josie and I shared both a father and mother."

"But you are part Negro…"

"Yes, I am." Jessie's eyes look steadily into my own. "And so is Frederick. He just arrived a generation later."

"Frederick is a mulatto?" I clutch my chest, my face must reflect my disbelief.

"To those who matter in America, he is, if they know. His mother's skin was about the same shade as mine. Our brother was slightly darker."

The implications of what she is saying is more than I can take in. My face is tingling—I feel numb around the mouth.

"Breathe, Abby. Take some deep breaths. You need to get some air to your brain."

I obey.

"You do realize you can tell no one this." She is talking to me as I would to Mattie or one of the boys. "This would destroy Frederick. It would destroy you and the children if this becomes known."

"What do you mean?" I whisper.

"If people find out Frederick or your children have Negro blood, diluted as it is…" She hesitates. "Just as one drop of ink taints a glass of water, so does a single drop of Negro blood defile a person in the minds of most people with whom you associate, Abby."

My hands move to my mouth. I feel a sob catch in my throat. "My mother," I whisper.

Jessie doesn't speak for a moment, then she says, "Your mother will love your children regardless of who their father is." Her face tells me she is no more convinced of that than I am. "It is not her you need to worry about. The ladies and gentlemen of Savannah are the people who can cause you and the children the most harm."

I remember something. "I thought Brigitte and Frederick were cousins. Does Brigitte have Negro blood, too?"

"Brigitte's mother was my half sister, though I never met the woman. Her mother, a white woman, was married to my father, but she died and Brigitte's mother was sent to France to live with relatives there. I knew of her existence, but I did not know she had moved to the States until Frederick contacted me. He ran across her in Baltimore. That is how I came to be in Brigitte's employ."

"Does Brigitte know of your relationship to Frederick?" I ask.

"Maybe, but I doubt it. I do not know how much Brigitte's mother knew about our mother. She may not have known that Frederick's mother was of mixed blood. If Brigitte did not hear it from her mother,

I assure you, it is not something Frederick would have told her. I know I certainly never have."

"So Brigitte is your niece just as Frederick is your nephew?"

"Half-niece, I guess you would say. I am sure she would be quick to point out which half if she were told of any connection at all. I doubt that Brigitte knows any of this."

There is no bitterness in Jessie's voice.

"Tell me. Tell me everything."

"Frederick's mother was killed at the beginning of the slave revolts in St. Domingue. I was young, but I remember the night she died. She had braved the dark and the woods to get Frederick to safety—he was just a few months old at the time; we called him Emile then. She and our brother went back in case her husband—Frederick's father—was looking for her. They left Frederick with us. That is why he lived."

Once Jessie starts talking, it is like a dam has burst. She opens her mouth and the words come out like they have been waiting for the opportunity to get free. I think how hard it must have been for her, not just on the Island after her mother died, but since. It is bad enough to think about what she has lived through, but to have to live among us and keep these words locked in her head, her soul...I think of Frederick—the fear he must have felt all these years lest he be discovered. I think of him now. What must he be thinking now that he knows I know? What does he think I will do? What will I do?

God help us! What will I do?

The question rings in my head, but there really is only one answer. I will do nothing, of course. I am married to a man who is part Negro; therefore, my children are part Negro. It is knowledge I must take with me to my grave. Right now, I pray, God willing, I can arrive there soon, for I can think of no safe place for me and mine ever again upon this earth.

Chapter 55

I leave Bette's by way of the front door. I know she sensed things are not well with me, but how is that unusual? She probably thinks nothing of it, for she has been jostled up and down on the currents of my emotions for years now. The despondency she sees on my face today is nothing new to her. I wonder if she sees beneath it the panic that keeps trying to claw its way to the surface to overwhelm me completely.

I have gone to Bette's today seeking solace. Maybe I thought, because of Pearl, I would experience some peace in her presence— some solidarity. I come away instead more anxious than when I arrived. It is one thing to have a mulatto sister waiting upon you in the house— it is entirely different to have at home children you hope upon hope will never display enough of their heritage to be found out. Knowing what I know now, I am surprised Frederick risked having children at all. This new knowledge of mine does explain a lot. I now understand Frederick's obsession with keeping the children covered from the sun. I am sure he is concerned that a darker tint to their skins combined with their dark curly hair might cause speculation. Too, I understand now his intense concentration on their small faces after they were born. I remember the way he outlined both the girls rosebud mouths and tiny noses with his fingertip. I am sure he did the same with the first three. What would he have done if their noses had proven flat and wide—their lips pronounced like the servants? Would he have drowned them in the washtub like a couple of unwanted kittens from a stray cat?

I shudder at the image. I cannot believe I am having these thoughts about my own husband. Frederick. Poor Frederick. I do not know if he is relieved that I have shown no more inclination to bring up the elephant in the room than he, or does it make him as fearful as I am? I know he thinks me unstable. Does he fear what I will do? Does he worry that I will tell Mother? If I could find humor in anything right now, the thought of Mother's face upon receiving the news would cause me to laugh aloud. But I find nothing funny right now—nothing enjoyable whatsoever. The only comfort I can find is in the knowledge that no one, not Luella, not Mother, none of our friends, no one—has ever suspected such a thing.

This thought gives me pause. Maybe there is speculation and I just do not know it. I am the most naive of people. Bette tells me so often. Would I pick up on it if people were talking?

Probably not, but still I think there is little chance that they are. We would not have been accepted in Savannah if there were even an inkling in anyone's mind.

I realize I am walking at a snail's pace. Poor Lewis has to be chomping at the bit. I quicken my step, but I feel like I am walking uphill through ten inches of soft sand.

It is Sunday afternoon. Frederick has taken the children down to the river to watch boat races. Though it would be nice to go home and go to bed, I know Frederick will be very displeased to come home and find me there in the middle of the day. True, Frederick would probably say nothing right now. He has been treating me with kid gloves ever since we came back from Virginia. His attentiveness reminds me of the early days of our marriage other than his preoccupation with this damnable housewarming he is determined to carry off, come hell or high water!

I decide I will walk to Jessie's. She is the one person I can talk openly with on the subject that is haunting me, even though I have chosen not to. There is a reserve between us that did not exist before our talk in Virginia. Still, I feel like I must talk with someone or risk throwing myself into the Savannah River.

"Lewis, I have decided to visit Jessie."

Lewis merely nods, and I remember I am taking him from Cressa and the baby on his free Sunday afternoon. "You can leave me there, and we will ask her to walk back with me. You can go on home and spend some time with your family."

"Thank you, Mizz Abby. Thet be nice."

We turn down the street toward Yamacraw, and we encounter many darkies out for Sunday walks. They cast looks my way, and I think this may not be a good idea. I do not belong here, and Lewis should be with his family. But we have come this far; it will be as much trouble for him to turn back as it will be to drop me off and go about his business. I hope Jessie is home and available to walk back with me later.

I see a small group of women and children walking toward us down the sandy pathway that suffices for a sidewalk in Yamacraw.

"Thet be Mammy, da guls, an da chilrun," Lewis informs me, and his face breaks into a smile when he sees Cressa among them, young Deke in a sling across her chest.

We stop and talk with them. Minda stands behind Mammy and Dovie, and I do not realize until we are about to part that she is pregnant. My eyes fall to her stomach, and when I look up into her eyes, she looks away.

"You are expecting again, Minda!" I say without thinking.

"Yes, Mizz Abby, I be." There is no emotion in her voice, and I understand why. She knows I know her situation, and she is uncomfortable with me seeing the physical evidence of her unholy alliance. I look more closely at her, then at Daisy and Jude. I feel something that I did not feel before knowing what I now know about my own children. When I glance at Daisy, something in me goes still. My glance returns to her face, hangs there.

Mattie. Daisy looks like Mattie.

I can feel my eyebrows pull together in confusion. I shake my head to cast off the thought, but it clings there, refusing to be discarded.

Mammy clears her throat. I realize I am staring at the girl. "You bes be gittin on obber ta Jessie if you goin. Massa be back in a bit an speckin you home."

I look into Mammy's eyes. What I see there stops my breath. She sees I see it, and she looks down. "Lez go, Chilrun," she says, and they walk on, the group of them moving around me like a dark current around a captive twig in a stream.. I cannot move. I look after them.

"Mizz Abby, you awrigh?" Lewis asks.

I need to steady myself, but I know I cannot touch Lewis. "No, Lewis. I am not alright. I need to go home."

"Can you wauk wid ow hep?"

"I guess I will have to."

My voice does not sound like my own. We turn and walk behind the group. I am relieved when they turn before we are upon them. I do not think I can make conversation, pretend I do not know what I know. As I walk behind them, I notice Minda's narrow hips, her regal carriage. Daisy is built like her. Jude is shorter, stockier, much like Fredie.

These children do not belong to Clarence Stiles. And Minda is expecting again. Probably four or five months along. I have been in Virginia for that long— in Virginia where I was losing my own child, watching Sophia lose hers.

A wave of emotion washes over me. It is new to me, but I embrace it. It gives me the strength to get home, to get to my room. Once there, I am no longer exhausted. I am no longer sad. I pace back and forth across the large room. I go to my chifferobe, kneel before the bottom drawer, find the box I am looking for and pull it out. In it are the many letters I have received from Frederick over the years. I untie the bundle and start with those oldest and move forward. Finally I find it—the letter Frederick wrote telling me about Jessie's arrival. I read *Brigitte assures me this woman has been with them for years...Jessie (that is what Brigitte calls her)."*

My husband is such an accomplished liar! I turn, and though I do not know I am going to do it, I pick up the water pitcher and fling it, water and all, at the clothes press. I am disappointed it falls short of its mark to land dully on the thick rug Frederick and I purchased second hand from a broker in New York. I catch my reflection to my left in the mirror above the fireplace. I move closer, as though I am attracted to my own visage. I draw near, fascinated by the hate I see there in my own blue eyes. I hear Frederick and the children arrive downstairs. I turn to meet them, but I know this will not do. I cannot see Frederick in the presence of the children. I hear him call from the bottom of the stairs, but I do not answer. He must assume I am resting, for he does not call again. I pace. I wait.

Finally I hear him mounting the stairs. The door knob turns, and he sticks his head around the door.

"Oh," he is surprised. "I thought you were resting."

The smile leaves his face when he gets a good look at me. He enters the room, warily, reluctantly.

"Is something the matter, Dear? You look . . ." His eyes scan my face; he settles finally on "different."

"I feel different, Frederick. I just ran into Mammy's family while I was walking. I was quite surprised to notice that Minda is expecting a child."

Frederick turns pale, but he holds my gaze. "We have talked about this, Abby. You know we cannot interfere in that situation."

I see the deceit in his face. I wonder why I have not noticed it before. I see the weakness in the set of his mouth, a slight jerking at the corner of his eye.

"Oh, but I think I can," I say, and I see real fear in his eyes; the jerk has become a full-blown twitch in the right. I move closer.

"I have been the worst kind of fool, haven't I Frederick?"

"I don't know what you mean," he stammers. I walk within a foot of him.

"You are a liar and a cheat!" I spit the words into his shocked face, "and I hate the mere sight of you!"

Frederick slaps me. It is not a hard slap. I don't feel it. He immediately grabs me by both shoulders and shakes me. "This is lunacy! I do not know what you are talking about!"

"You do, Frederick. Those children are not the bastards of Clarence Stiles—they are yours! No wonder Luella sent Minda away! She knew, didn't she?"

Frederick pushes me away. He turns his back on me. His shoulders sag. He walks to the window, parts the drapes and looks down at the street. He stands there for a minute as if he is interested in something going on below.

"Who told you this rubbish?" His voice is calm now.

"No one told me, Frederick. No one probably ever would have. No one is going to tell a woman that her husband has a Negro mistress."

Frederick seems to make a decision. He turns to face me. "Grow up, Abigail. You are not twenty years old living on a farm any more. These things happen. What can you expect? Luella, then you—you pack up your things every summer; you take my children and off you go for months at a time to your mother. You leave me here alone to do for myself. A man has needs. He takes care of them." His voice rises. " I took care of them!"

"So you siring bastards is my fault—was Luella's fault—because we left you alone for a few months?"

"If fault must be placed, then yes, I guess that is true."

Here he walks across the room as if he is going to touch me. When he reaches out a hand, I do not back away.

"Do not touch me, Frederick. You are to never touch me again!"

His hand falls. "For Christ's sake, Abigail! Do not be so dramatic. You act like I have run away with another woman. I have simply relieved myself upon occasion with a slave. It is more common than it is not."

There is no longer any hint of anger in his voice. I look into the face of the man I have lived with for almost ten years. The man I have slept with, had children by. The man I would have trusted with my life. I realize I do not know him.

"Abby, we have a good life. Do not make more of this than it is. You are my wife. I love you and only you. That girl means nothing to me. "

"And those children? Do they mean nothing to you?"

"I don't know!" He waves his hand like he can wave away the existence of two children, soon to be three, by another woman. "For Christ's sake," he repeats, "they are slaves! What difference does it make who fathered them?"

"Does the presence of Negro blood in their veins make them devoid of feelings?" I ask. "Do you have none about your own father? Will you deny them the way your father has denied you?"

"That is not the same thing at all, Abby, and you know it." The words are ground out between Frederick's clinched teeth. "My father was married to my mother. She was a free woman."

"Yes, Frederick, she may have actually had a choice in lying with your father. I guess you are going to tell me this was all initiated by Minda?" Frederick starts to say something, then clamps his mouth shut around it. He has the decency to turn red. "You are as despicable as Eugene Robinson. You take your pleasure where you please and when you please because you can."

I feel like I have slapped him as surely as he slapped me.

"I do not know how I can continue to live with you, Frederick. I do not know what I am going to do, but I know things will never be the same. I do not know you."

"We will discuss this later if you think it a worthy topic for discussion— when you are more rational." He turns toward the door. "And if you are thinking of doing something foolish like returning to Virginia, you must realize your mother will not let you come home, not for any length of time. She knows your place is here with me no matter what you claim I have done. And she knows you, Abby," he says softly. "Your family worries about your tendencies. They know, as I do, that you need to be here with me, where you can be looked after—taken care of. You are far too unstable to look after the children. Think about that."

Frederick is calm, determined now. He turns the doorknob, looks back at me. "This all will pass, Abby. We will be as we were before." He leaves, taking my energy, my determination with him.

I move to the bureau. I take the small vial of laudanum I use to treat the children from the top drawer. I tip it to my lips and lie down on the bed to wait for sweet oblivion.

Chapter 56

Frederick stands to the side of the room and surveys the crowd. Though he is carrying on a conversation with a small group of men around him, his mind is elsewhere. Tonight is the realization of years of dreams—a validation of his hard work and perseverance. The milling crowd is larger than even he has dared hope, and more important than the number of guests is the caliber. He has been checking off a mental list of the most important invitees, and every last one of them has now made an appearance. There are at least a hundred guests in this room alone, and he knows there are twenty or more wandering around the rest of the house. The sliding double doors are wide open, the furniture is pushed back against the walls, and still the room is a tad too crowded. Though the Barrets have opened all the floor length windows, no one has chosen to step out onto the side porches even though Mother Nature has certainly done all she can to lure them there. Frederick hopes the desirability of the company and the magnificence of the room are keeping them from leaving the room. There is a wonderfully cool breeze causing the flames of the gas chandeliers to dance festively over the heads of the crowd. The light from twenty globes reflects off the large gilt-framed mirrors over each fireplace. The mildness of the evening and the pressing of the crowd have made fires unnecessary, and for this Frederick is glad. He knows coal fires can create an odor and a dust, and he wants nothing to mar the beauty that he—and Abby, of course—have worked so hard to create.

The servants have risen to the occasion. One would never guess they were the same country slaves Luella had brought to their marriage.

Lewis, acting as butler, stands straight in the new suit of clothes Jessie made for him and ushers guests into the double parlor as if he has been doing it his whole life. Dovie, Cressa, Mammy, and two hired slaves are vivid spots of white in their starched dresses and matching head covers as they move about serving wine and Jessie's finger foods from silver trays Frederick picked up for just this purpose while in New York.

"Have you heard a word I have spoken?" Alexis resorts to nudging Frederick with his elbow.

Frederick laughs, and turning so the other men cannot hear him, he whispers, "No, Sir, I must admit I have not. Please forgive me. I am quite caught up in the moment."

"As well you should be, My Good Friend, as well you should. You have indeed come a long way since I first met you." Alexis raises his glass toward his wife who is holding court halfway across the room. "If Brigitte had had a crystal ball, I am afraid I would have lost out to you. I wonder if she is regretting her choice tonight."

Frederick knows Alexis doesn't believe a word of what he is saying, but he likes hearing it nonetheless. He looks at the laughing face of his cousin who is the center of attention, as she always is in a crowd, and he cannot help but contrast it to that of his own wife standing across from her. Frederick's mood has been like a ship at full sail all evening. Now it sinks as if someone has lowered him to half-mast. He cannot help but feel a pang of guilt that his own wife's face, though composed and attentive, reflects the sadness for which he is responsible, or at least, partly responsible. *Hell, Abby would find something to be sad about if he were the best husband on Earth!*

Frederick knows he is not being fair. He knows how hard Abby has tried to overcome her problems, up until now. He looks at her from across the room, and a wave of tenderness passes over him. She looks so small and frail—vulnerable, he realizes. He longs to make things right with her, and it isn't as if he hasn't tried. She has been cordial enough. Thank God there has been no repeat of that disastrous display of temper in their bedroom. But then again, maybe it would be preferable to the cold indifference she has subjected him to ever since. He is beginning to fear she was speaking the truth when she said nothing would ever be the same between them.

Why did all that mess have to come to light! And what can I do about it now? If I offer to sell Minda, what of the children? And if I should offer to sell the children with Minda, what will Abby think of me? Since hanging out with Bette Stiles, Abby has gotten some radical ideas about darkies.

The thought of darkies reminds Frederick of Abby's comments implying that he himself is a darkie, and the memory brings on a clutching around his chest.

How dare she! And how dare Jessie! After all I have done for her.

Frederick realizes he cannot allow his thoughts to travel this path, for he knows he will not like where they lead. Just the thought of Jessie now depresses him. She is still determined to leave, and he is still determined to keep her. Besides the fact that he cares for her personally—after all, she is family though no one else must ever know it—there is the problem of what he is going to do if she leaves. Frederick knows that much of tonight's success is due to Jessie's talent. Her cooking and the reputation of her expertise in the kitchen has opened doors that Frederick admits to himself would have been a lot slower in admitting him had it not been for the lure of an invitation to sample what others had raved about. Too, she has garnered quite the clientele as a seamstress. No doubt about it, Jessie is an asset. For the life of him, he cannot understand why she has gotten such a bee in her bonnet to leave town. She has it made here. There is probably not another woman—possibly even a white woman—who makes as much money or has as much freedom as Jessalyn Devereux Tucker.

"You are doing it again, you insolent bastard! I might as well be talking to myself!"

"Far too much talking of any kind, My Friend, if you ask me. Let's wave down some more of that good wine you found for me and fill our mouths with it! This is a celebration. Let us act like it!"

"Now that is more like the Frederick Barret whose good company I enjoy!"

Alexis lifts his voice, one worthy of the Naval officer he is.

"Friends and family! Gather around! Let us drink to the Barrets' health and happiness! May their future be bright, their happiness constant, and this house—and what a house, I might add—may it be warm!"

Glasses rise in response and good wishes reverberate off the high ceilings. Frederick moves his own glass to his lips. He scans the happy faces surrounding him before they come to rest on the sober, lifeless eyes of his own wife.

Chapter 57

I have done what I set out to do. I have made it through this evening. I see the last guest off. I go to basement where the servants are in a festive mood. I do not linger there. I thank them for the wonderful job they have done. I tell them to feel free to eat to their hearts' content. They expect this. They do not expect me to tell them they can drink a bottle of wine, and when I do, Lewis actually whoops, either from surprise or joy, I am not sure which. I tell them to clean up only what they have to—the rest can wait until morning which is a mere three or four hours away. Dovie is out the back door before I can finish getting the words out of my mouth. I am sure she has Clell, her beau from church, waiting out back to share in the bounty she was sure to think forthcoming. It does not bother me. They can invite all of Yamacraw for all I care.

I turn to Jessie. "Do you need someone to escort you to the Stiles to pick up Diana? I can get Lewis to go with you."

"No, I will be fine by myself. There is no one out there to hurt me anymore."

Or to help you either, I think, but I do not share that with her. My mood and Jessie's mood have been similar lately. I do not know which of us is the unhappiest. I do know which of us is the strongest.

"Well, Goodnight, all of you," I say. I turn back before I start up the stairs. "You are all wonderful servants—have always been," I add.

They all look blankly at me. I can tell they do not know what to make of this declaration.

"I just wanted you to know," I add lamely. "I do not know what I would have done without you—what my children would do without you."

"Thet jus wat us niggas do, Mizz Abby. We know our fambly cain take care ub deysef." Mammy's voice is gruff. "Now git on up ta bed. We know how wore ow you be."

Jessie walks toward me. She has a look of concern on her face. "Are you feeling well, Abby?" she asks. She reaches out to touch me. I take two of the steps upward to keep that from happening. I do not want Jessie reading me.

"I am fine," I tell her.

Jessie looks behind her. Mammy, Lewis, and Cressa are making their way out the back. "You do not act fine. You have not acted fine for some time now."

"I am as fine as you are, Jessie."

Jessie just looks up at me. We each hold a candle, and the light from hers illuminates her face. She does not bother to contradict me. Jessie has been different since we came back from Virginia. She has continued to work every day but Sunday and she has not complained, but there is a difference in her demeanor. She is respectful, but she is not subservient. She is also more direct, stating her opinion and speaking her mind in a way she never did before Moses died. Frederick may think she has decided to stay with us, but I think she is simply waiting for me to pull myself together. I hope she is strong enough to stand up to him.

"Jessie, when are you moving north?"

"As soon as I think you will be fine without me," she states bluntly.

I pull my mouth up at the corners and hope the effort passes for a smile. "Then you can go tomorrow."

I turn and mount the stairs. I sense she is still standing below looking after me when I reach the main floor.

"Abby," I hear Frederick call out to me from the family parlor. I walk to the doorway but I do not enter the room. "Will you join me for a while?"

"No," I say. I do not mean for the answer to sound so curt, but the evening behind us has taken all the small talk I have in me.

"It was a wonderful evening, don't you think? I am sure we will make the paper this week."

That I can answer. "Yes, I definitely think we will make the paper this week."

He waits for me to say more. I do not and after a few moments of silence, he asks, "Are you ever going to forgive me, Abby?"

"I have forgiven you, Frederick. You can no more help who you are than I can help who I am. I guess we will both just have to forgive each other."

"Abby?" I hear him call out, but I am already halfway up the stairs to the second floor. I do not answer him.

I stop in the hallway outside our bedroom door. I think about going to the children's rooms, but I decide not to. They are not there. They have spent the night at Bette's. I asked some time ago if they might. I did not want them here.

The children—they are all such good children. I fear for them, but I know there is nothing I can do to protect them. I wonder if Luella ever regretted having her three. I wish they had not been born just as I regret bringing Ella and Maxie into this world. I hate the many years ahead for them. I cannot bear to think of them suffering as I have suffered.

I manage to get out of my dress and the corset I wear beneath it without the help of anyone else. It is a good thing, because I would sleep in it before I would allow Frederick to touch me. I think about putting on my everyday petticoats, but I decide against it. I pick up the gray dress I wore before I got dressed for the evening, and I climb back into it. It buttons up the front, so it is easy for me to fasten myself into it. I think about combing out my hair, but I decide to leave it as it is. I sit before the fireplace where coal is set for a fire that will not be lit tonight, and I lace up my everyday shoes.

Fully dressed, I walk to the window. I slide it upward and step out upon the porch. The breeze that felt so refreshing earlier in the evening when it was spread among the crowd is nippy now, I suppose, though I register no discomfort. It is dark out here except for the moon that lights my way to the railing. I stand where I have stood many times since moving to this house on Bull Street. Though it is dark, I am well aware of how far it is from here to the ground. I have stood below and looked up as well. I have estimated the distance from where I am standing to the ground at right at twenty feet. The basement is above ground, so the downstairs porch is roughly ten feet off the ground, so allowing for ten more feet for the main floor, that should put this porch at twenty feet.

I purposely call to mind the things that have bothered me most in this life. Nothing bothers me much at this moment, but I know it is important not to forget them. I stand in the cool breeze on the porch twenty feet from the courtyard and I concentrate hard for I do not want to leave anything out.

I think of Father who died too young and before I could etch an image of him on my brain, one that would survive him.

I think about George—the little brother I loved so much but haven't seen since he married—I see Mother's grief when he told her he was moving to be close to his wife's people.

I think about Luella. I imagine her lying hot and sweating and yellow. I imagine me in her place—me dying instead of her. It would have saved us all so much trouble. But then, if Luella had lived, she would have had to deal with what I am dealing with now, so maybe the fever was a blessing.

I think of Anne and her girls living with Mother at Hickory Grove instead of with Edward. I picture Luella and Caroline moving their stuff from my old room to make room for me. I picture Anne on the front porch with Mother, rocking, rocking.

I think of my own tiny son—I should have held him at least one time before he was taken away—after all, he had lived within me all those months and I should have at least said goodbye to him.

I remember my niece Luella offering to sleep by the back door in case the boys tried to sneak out. I think of a limp, blue lifeless Jimmy being clutched to the breast of a hysterical Sophia while I lie unknowing in a room above.

I remember the way Jessie looked when the Robinson man got through with her—the huge Moses crying like a baby when they handed him his dead son.

And Moses. Moses being dragged to a hanging tree while people gather to watch, Frederick mute in the shadows.

I think of Bette, of her sister Pearl.

I imagine Jessie as a little girl, Frederick as a baby, sister and mother murdered. I think of the two of them together as children, young adults, hiding in fear and struggling to stay alive.

I am ready now. I think of Minda. Quick, hot anger toward her gives way to pity. I see her—young, pretty, happy in her slave kind of way. I imagine Frederick coming upon her in one of Luella's rooms. I imagine him holding her from behind. I can imagine her trying to push him away, but not too hard. He is the master. I can imagine her fear. I see Frederick lying on top of her, moving up and down and in, her naked and hurt and frightened, him powerful and oblivious. I imagine the scene again, only here, in this house, then again in the little house in Yamacraw, the house with the curtains made from fabric from the store above which I live, the house where Daisy and Jude cower in the bedroom without a door.

I picture Mother opening the door to me, all five children lined up behind me on the porch. I see the shock upon her face. I hear her telling me to go home to my husband—to grow up.

I see the years stretching out in front of me. I feel the strain of months upon months of mornings, the onerous task of getting up to face those days that follow those mornings.

I see the pitiful looks cast my way. I hear the neighbors' mutterings, my children's excuses, my husband's admonishments.

I am ready. I turn from the railing. I stoop to climb back through the bedroom window. I walk out into the hallway and turn left. I climb the stairs to the attic. I walk through the large unfinished space that is meant for the children we will never have. I walk to the small double windows that are directly above the side porch. I open one of them, pull my skirt between my legs and worm my way backward until I am in a sitting position on the seal. I once again appreciate its width and depth because it provides ample room for me to first sit, then push my way up into a standing position. I look down. Another ten feet for the attic—I guess thirty feet, thirty-five at the most. I hold the sash long enough to balance myself. I turn loose of the window, bend my knees, and push as far away from the wall as possible. I feel the cool air biting my face, and I am relieved to know I have cleared both balcony railings.

Chapter 58

Diana squats in the sand beside Moses' grave. I have been teaching her to write her name, and now she uses her forefinger to trace the letters into the clean surface we created by clearing the debris with our hands and a piece of board. Moses did that, I remember—scratched newly learned letters on every makeshift tablet he could devise. Six months worth of elements have leveled the mound on which Diana writes. If it were not for the stones on top of Joshua's grave, I would no longer be able to tell where Joshua's ends and Moses' begins. I am glad. It is easier to leave this blended site. I know it is silly—that neither of them is really down there—but it is a comfort to me that even their remains will not be totally alone. They will have each other.

"Who will look after their graves with us not here?" Diana squints up at me, her dirty hand shielding her eyes from the midday sun.

"No one, probably, but that really does not matter. Remember, they are not actually down there."

"I know. They are in Heaven." She returns to her scribbling. "Is Miss Abby in Heaven with Daddy and baby Joshua?"

"I hope so, Diana. I like to think of the three of them in Heaven together."

"Will they let Daddy and Joshua use the same Heaven as Miss Abby?"

I wonder who Diana's heavenly *they* are. "Yes, I think they will. It is different in Heaven." I tell my daughter what I want to hear. "They will not have any choice. God is the boss of Heaven, and He will not let any other masters tell him what to do. So, yes, I think they will be together in the same Heaven."

Diana trots along beside me as we turn for home. I am careful to walk slowly because her short legs have to work double time to keep up. She gets distracted by first one thing then another, and I would like to take her hand to hurry her along, but I would have to bend down to do so, and my back would be killing me by the time we cover the distance to home. I think of carrying her, but there is still a long day and night ahead of us, and I know I need to save my strength.

"There's Uncle Lewis!" Diana shouts and runs toward the buckboard that waits in the sandy street before what used to be my home, the one I bought with my own money and lived in with my own husband. Now the house belongs to a white tradesman by the name of Gibbens who plans to rent it out, probably to someone needing quarters for slaves they rent out in the city. I would have preferred to sell it to a family, but Frederick reminded me it would be almost impossible to find someone with enough money to buy the place willing to live in this part of town. Though there are more free blacks in Savannah than there are in the whole rest of the state of Georgia, few of them can afford to own their own homes. Most rent from white men like the one who bought my house.

Lewis loads our trunk on the wagon. That is all we are taking with us. I sold the contents of the cabin and the boardinghouse with the buildings. We are taking only our clothes and a few personal items. We are truly starting over.

We arrive at the harbor, and Lewis unloads my trunk. He hugs Diana, tips his hat to me, climbs back on the seat and heads for Bull Street. Diana and I wait alone for them to let us board. We said our goodbyes to Frederick, his children, and his servants yesterday. I look around. I had hoped Frederick might come to see us off, but I am not surprised he does not.

I keep a close eye on Diana as she dances along the wharf. The child is beside herself with excitement, so maybe all her busyness will burn off some of that energy. The steamship is all she has been able to talk about since I told her a week ago we were leaving, that and what it is going to be like *Up North*. I hope reality lives up to my promises. I hope her first voyage is all she thinks it will be. Her excitement is evidence that I have been able to keep my fears to myself.

A Negro boy takes our trunk, so I have nothing to sit on while we wait. About twenty feet away are four backless benches. A lone man sits on a bench while two others are occupied by what appears to be a family of a mother, two girls, and a servant. The fourth is vacant, but I know we cannot sit there. My eyes are drawn back to the family. The young mother reminds me of Abby, and a chill runs along my spine.

Oh Abby, why did you do it?

It is still hard for me to believe Abby is dead. Her death has been harder for me to accept in some ways than that of Moses. I long for Moses—I have thought how different this adventure would be if he were with us, and I have cried knowing the three of us could have done what Diana and I are doing now. We could have sold out and moved north. If we had, Moses would probably be alive—we would still be together.

Yes, the loss of Moses has been the hardest thing I have ever experienced, but the death of Abby has been the most confusing. Though I knew she suffered, I would never have thought she would take her own life—not and leave her children to live with knowing she had. I guess I underestimated her misery, her despair. I have spent hours trying to recall every conversation between us, every action I observed, every interaction I witnessed leading up to that final night. It is true I knew something was different about her, and I traced the beginning of the difference back to Hickory Grove at her mother's place. I can only imagine how unsettling it must have been for her to find out Frederick was not at all who she had supposed him to be. However, if finding out her husband had a single drop of Negro blood flowing through his veins drove her to such madness, I have misjudged her.

In truth, I think a combination of things drove Abby to do what she did, and it was Dovie who finally shed some light on what might have been the straw that broke the camel's back.

On the night that Abby died, I thought Dovie had run off somewhere with Clell, but she must have been close by because she was in the back yard by the time I got there. I had just been finishing up when I heard Mammy scream. I took my candle and rushed out. Mammy's white dress was huddled beside what appeared to be a pile of clothing. With the aid of the moon and my candle, I saw that it was Abby. Mammy continued to scream, and I guess Frederick heard her through the raised windows, for suddenly he was there as were Dovie, Lewis, and Cressa. Frederick immediately told Mammy to shut up and sent Lewis for help, but the rest of us just knelt around her, afraid to move her in any way so contorted was her body. It seemed like forever that we were there watching her struggle to take in air. Though her body looked broken, her chest came off the ground with each intake. It was horrible to watch but we were powerless to do anything else. The only one of us who said anything was Frederick, and he kept repeating over and over, "Oh, Abby, my precious,

precious Abby." He was crying. We were all crying quietly until Abby's body lifted one last time then lay still. Mammy started wailing again, but I was glad when Abby stopped breathing for I already knew she would not live. I knew the moment I gingerly held the hand that Frederick did not. Worse to me than the sight of her twisted body was the labored gasping for breath. I was glad when it stopped. I knew she was too.

After Dr. Waring came and we laid Abby out in the front parlor, I returned to the kitchen to get my stuff. I had to go tell Bette Stiles what had happened and make arrangements for the children and Diana. Mammy and Dovie were there. When I came in, Mammy drug herself up off the stool she had been sitting on and walked toward the door. She looked like she had aged ten years in the past few hours.

"I cannot believe she did this," I thought to myself. When Dovie replies, I know I have spoken the words.

"Sho peers she trow ersef ow dat winda."

"I knew she was disconsolate, but had I known she was so bad…"

"I tink I know wy she do it," Dovie blurted out.

I have never seen Dovie so upset. I wondered if she could know about Frederick and me.

"It wuz cause a da massa an Minda. Minda say she know. I doan know how she fine ow, bu Minda say she know."

"What are you talking about Dovie?" I asked, but I feared I already knew.

"Minda chilrun, dey be da massa's. We ow wawkin on a Sundy some time back, an we come cross Mizz Abby. She look real strange lack a Daisy, den Lewis say she make em wawk er home righ den. Say she wite as a haint."

"Does Mammy know this?" I ask.

"She dare wid us, bu she ain say nuttin."

"I mean does your mother know Minda's children are Mr. Barret's?"

"Ub course she do. She know way back wen Massa furse be messin wid Minda—fo Mizz Lella hab da feeber. Dat wy Massa tole Mizz Lella he sole Minda."

"So Frederick still owns Minda, has all this time?"

"Aw dis time. Dat wy Mama nebber wan da chilrun roun hyur—case Mizz Abby know."

I have never said anything to Frederick about any of this. I was tempted when he went on and on about how Abby would want me to stay, about how much the children need me. I told him the children had Mammy and Dovie and Cressa and Lewis to look after them—that

I, as a servant, could do no more than they. Frederick had not given up easily and at times I considered staying. In the end, the thought of dealing with Frederick's complicated household was more than I could stomach. He has told the children and everyone else in Savannah who will listen that Abby went out on the balcony to enjoy the breeze, that she leaned into a railing not properly secured by the builders and fell to her death. I know Bette does not buy this story, and the children will someday wonder, I am sure. But Frederick is becoming a powerful man, and I think people will pretend to believe the story whether they do or not. He will move heaven and earth to keep his children and him from suffering the consequences of Abby's actions. I like to think that Abby knew Frederick well enough to know what he would do, that he would cover for her. It breaks my heart to think she may actually have thought the children better off without her. She probably knew Frederick as I do, knew that he will marry again as soon as he thinks it will be socially acceptable. I hope he finds someone who will be good to the children. Too, I hope the new wife never discovers Frederick's secrets. I, for one, no longer want to be a party to keeping them.

Finally, the white passengers are boarded and Diana and I are allowed on the ship that is already building up steam. I lead Diana by the hand to the railing, and we look back at River Street. There is a slat on the railing at Diana's eye level, so I pick her up and let her sit on the top rail. I hold her tightly. She is all I have left. I remind myself that she is more than I came here with.

"Look, Mama!"

I follow her pointing finger and I see Mammy, Dovie, Cressa, and the children climbing off the back of the buckboard. Lewis has returned with them to see us off. I wonder if Frederick knows they are here. Tears come to my eyes. They are all waving frantically, and I wave back.

The children are yelling, but I cannot make out what they are saying. Mattie cups her hands around her mouth and yells at the top of her lungs, "You promised to write, Tata—you mustn't forget!"

"I will not forget," I yell back. I feel the ship move beneath us. I pull Diana off the railing and wrap both arms around her middle. She uses both of hers to wave madly at the people who have been her family for as long as she can remember. I let go of Diana with one arm so I can wipe the tears away in order to see them there, waving. When they are out of sight, Diana wants down, but I tell her I must hold her a while longer. I rest my chin on my daughter's head and let the tears flow unchecked. "I will not forget," I whisper.

I move to the other side of the ship, Diana still in my arms. I put her down at the railing as close as I can get to the front of the ship without crowding the white family we saw earlier on the dock. Diana and I stand side-by-side, face forward into the wind as we move northward.

Study Guide

1. At what point in the story did you become aware of the connection between Frederick and the baby Emile of the prologue. Did it cause you to question Frederick's relationship to Jessie?

2. It was an accepted practice for men of that time to marry fairly close relatives. It was also common in the South for widowers to marry the sister of a deceased wife. Abby conforms to this practice, but she is bothered by it. How did Abby's feelings contribute to her insecurities and depression?

3. The author lets the reader know from the beginning of the story the identity of Minda's benefactor. How did knowing the truth make you feel when reading of her concern for her friend Bette? How did knowing the truth make you feel about Frederick's response to Abby's concern for her friend Bette?

4. The author uses first person present tense when the chapter is from the female perspective of Abby or Jessie. She uses third person present tense in those chapters from Frederick's perspective and when observing them all in general. Why do you think she chose to switch person? Was her method effective, in your opinion?

5. Was Jessie's "gift" believable? Would you want such a gift?

6. Jessie could not *read* Moses as she could other people. Why do you think she was unable to do so and how did this inability affect their relationship?

7. In fiction, a foil is a character who contrasts with another character in order to emphasize or highlight particular qualities of the other character. For which characters do you think Bette and Brigitte act as foils, and what qualities do you think they emphasize in them?

8. What purpose did the character Pearl play in the story? What insight did she give the reader into Bette? Into Abby?

9. Discuss Abby's relationship with her mother and what effect, if any, it had on her condition?

10. In many ways Abby had less freedom and choice than Jessie. Why was that?

11. Abby suffered from severe depression at a time when it was misunderstood and considered shameful. Knowing that and her situation, what could she or others have done differently to offset the tragic culmination of her life? In her circumstances, what do you think you would have done?

12. Did you consider Frederick a villain or a sympathetic character? What impact do his upbringing and the conventions of the South have on his poor choices and does either make his mistakes more forgivable?

13. How were Frederick and Moses alike and how were they different?

14. Who, if anyone, is to blame for the tragic events in this story, especially the fates of Abby and Moses? What, if anything, could the other characters have done to alter these tragic outcomes?

15. Do you think Jessie was wise in taking Diana north? What obstacles can you foresee for them as they carve out new lives for themselves?

Acknowledgments

Though *A Single Drop of Ink* is fictional, I was inspired to write the novel by the Francis Sorrel family who lived before and after the Civil War in Savannah, Georgia, in what is now known as The Sorrel-Weed House. I first wrote the history *The Sorrels of Savannah* to document what I could validate as truth about each member of the historical family and the interesting and tragic lives they led, but the research left me with more questions than answers. One will certainly recognize plot parallels and character similarities, and I would have loved to write a true account of their lives, but research provided too few certainties for me to undertake that endeavor. Instead, I created a unique family named the Barrets about whom I could conjecture at will. Nonetheless, I am grateful to the Sorrels for launching me on this journey in the first place and to some of their descendents who have done everything possible to help me in my research. I want to thank them and the many people of the beautiful and fascinating city of Savannah who steered me along the way, provided me with personal documents, and encouraged me to write this story. Their contributions, I hope, lend authenticity to this fictional tale.

On a personal level, I thank Pauline Ramsey, my dear mother and personal motivator, for continuing to push me to do what she knows I have always wanted to do. For reading and rereading and being brutally honest but always encouraging, I thank my sisters Jan, Pat, Judy, Kathy, and Lisa; my brother Mike; my friends Pam Andrews, Gina Becker, Lee Hartz, and Jeff Freymann. I so appreciate my sweet daughters Carlee and Tory for cheering me on. Last, I thank my dear husband Ron who has been, as always, a sounding board, an encouragement, and a friend.

CPSIA information can be obtained
at www.ICGtesting.com
Printed in the USA
LVOW13s2309290317
528993LV00006B/158/P